The Best American Mystery Stories 2007

GUEST EDITORS OF
THE BEST AMERICAN MYSTERY STORIES

1997 ROBERT B. PARKER

1998 SUE GRAFTON

1999 ED MCBAIN

2000 DONALD E. WESTLAKE

2001 LAWRENCE BLOCK

2002 JAMES ELLROY

2003 MICHAEL CONNELLY

2004 NELSON DEMILLE

2005 JOYCE CAROL OATES

2006 SCOTT TUROW

2007 CARL HIAASEN

The Best American Mystery Stories™ 2007

Edited and with an Introduction
by **Carl Hiaasen**

Otto Penzler, *Series Editor*

HOUGHTON MIFFLIN COMPANY

BOSTON · NEW YORK 2007

www.houghtonmifflinbooks.com

ISSN 1094–8384
ISBN-13: 978-0-618-81263-9   ISBN-10: 0-618-81263-6
ISBN-13: 978-0-618-81265-3 (pbk.)   ISBN-10: 0-618-81265-2 (pbk.)

Printed in the United States of America

VB 10 9 8 7 6 5 4 3 2 1

Contents

Foreword

A QUESTION FREQUENTLY ASKED of me by mystery writers is where to submit their short stories. *Ellery Queen's Mystery Magazine,* celebrating more than sixty-five years of continuous publication, with no plans to retire, is always the immediate first thought, followed by its sister publication, *Alfred Hitchcock's Mystery Magazine,* which is nearly as geriatric. Unhappily, I have then used up my entire store of knowledge and advice. Fewer and fewer short fiction works appear in general magazines. Such women's magazines as *Redbook* (which first published Dashiell Hammett's *The Thin Man,* among much else), *Good Housekeeping,* and *Ladies' Home Journal* proudly ran stories in every issue, as did such men's magazines as *Argosy, Esquire, Stag, Gentlemen's Quarterly,* and *Playboy* (and some men actually *did* read the stories, contrary to commonly held belief). Now, if they still exist, publication of fiction in magazines like these is as rare as a conservative defense lawyer.

There were other mystery magazines, too, in the 1950s, '60s, and even into the '70s: *Manhunt* (in which stories by Ross Macdonald, Mickey Spillane, and Ed McBain first appeared), *The Saint Mystery Magazine, The Man from U.N.C.L.E.,* and eponymous digest-sized magazines by Rex Stout, Ed McBain, Mike Shayne, Edgar Wallace, and John Creasey (the latter two published in England).

A little earlier, there were such high-paying and prestigious general interest magazines as the *Saturday Evening Post, Collier's, Scribner's,* and *Cosmopolitan* (before it changed its target readership to primarily women). There were, too, the famous pulp magazines, filled almost exclusively with fiction, which had a life from around

1915 until the early 1950s. At one time, as many as 500 different titles were published per month. While television frequently is blamed for the demise of the pulps, indeed of most magazine fiction, it was mostly the creation and proliferation of mass market paperback books that killed their more cumbersome relations.

The New Yorker still publishes quality fiction, and several others still throw a small bone to fiction writers by offering a single story per month. Beyond that, I am at a loss as to what to say to writers who want or need to earn a living with short stories. Thank heaven for the literary journals that publish thousands of stories a year, but they only provide nourishment for the soul, unable to pay more than a few dollars and a few copies of the magazine for a work on which a serious writer may have labored for a month or more. And this is princely compared with electronic magazines, which pay for work with a hearty "Thank you." The last remaining option for a short story writer is one of the many anthologies published each year, though most of the contributors tend to be established authors who are commissioned to write for the book.

For mystery writers specifically, obstacles to getting published are more numerous than for those who work in a less genre-specific form. *The New Yorker* frowns on genre fiction, *Playboy* in recent years has eschewed it altogether, and many literary journals are reluctant to admit that they publish it at all, though they have been the source for some of the best crime fiction in the history of this series.

A high percentage of the stories in recent entries in *The Best American Mystery Stories* have been, not surprisingly, from literary journals and other anthologies, with a generous sprinkling most years from *EQMM* and *AHMM*. I hear the hopeful and happy rumor that *Black Mask Magazine* may be revived, which would provide a new market mainly for hard-boiled writers, but knowing what a difficult battle a pure fiction magazine would face, I'll believe it when I see it.

Having pointed out how hard it is to find a venue for short mystery stories, I will confess that, as in prior years, more than fifteen hundred mystery stories published in the 2006 calendar year were examined in order to identify the fifty that seemed most worthy of being considered for inclusion in this series by this year's guest editor, Carl Hiaasen, whose job it was to select the top twenty.

As is true every year, I could not have perused those fifteen hundred stories on my own, much of the heavy lifting being done by my invaluable colleague Michele Slung, who is able to read, evaluate, and commit to seemingly lifelong memory a staggering percentage of these stories, culling those that clearly do not belong on a short list — or a long one either, for that matter. She also examines twice as many stories as that to determine if they have mystery or criminal content, frequently impossible to know merely by reading the title. The same standards pertain to every one of the volumes in this prestigious series. The best writing makes it into the book. Fame, friendship, original venue, reputation, subject — none of it matters. It isn't only the qualification of being the best writer that will earn a spot in the table of contents; it also must be the best story.

While it is redundant for me to say it again, since I have already done so in each of the previous ten volumes of this series, it falls into the category of fair warning to state that many people regard a mystery as a detective story. I regard the detective story as one subgenre of a much bigger category, which I define as any short work of fiction in which a crime, or the threat of a crime, is central to the theme or the plot. While I love good puzzles and tales of pure ratiocination, few of these are written today, as the mystery genre has evolved (for better or worse, depending on your point of view) into a more character-driven form of literature, with more emphasis on the "why" of a crime's commission than on "who" or "how." The line between mystery fiction and general fiction has become increasingly blurred in recent years, producing fewer memorable detective stories but more significant literature.

It is a pleasure, as well as a necessity, to thank Carl Hiaasen for agreeing to be the guest editor for the 2007 edition of *The Best American Mystery Stories*. A regular presence on the bestseller list and one of the funniest writers who ever lived, he put aside virtually everything on his very crowded plate to deliver the work on schedule, thereby allowing a sigh of relief to emanate from the lips of one and all at Houghton Mifflin. And sincere thanks as well to the previous guest editors, beginning with Robert B. Parker, who started it all in 1997, followed by Sue Grafton, Ed McBain, Donald E. Westlake, Lawrence Block, James Ellroy, Michael Connelly, Nelson DeMille, Joyce Carol Oates, and Scott Turow.

While I engage in a relentless quest to locate and read every mystery/crime/suspense story published, I live in terror that I will miss a worthy story, so if you are an author, editor, or publisher, or care about one, please feel free to send a book, magazine, or tear sheet to me c/o The Mysterious Bookshop, 58 Warren Street, New York, NY 10007. If it first appeared electronically, you must submit a hard copy. It is vital to include the author's contact information. No unpublished material will be considered for what should be obvious reasons. No material will be returned. If you distrust the postal service, enclose a self-addressed, stamped postcard.

To be eligible for the 2008 edition, a story must have been written by an American or a Canadian, and it must first have been published in an American or Canadian publication in the calendar year 2007. The earlier in the year I receive the story, the more fondly I regard it. For reasons known only to the nitwits who wait until Christmas week to submit a story published the previous spring, this happens every year, causing much gnashing of teeth while I read a stack of stories as my wife and friends are trimming the Christmas tree or otherwise celebrating the holiday season. It had better be a damned good story if you do this. Because of the very tight production schedule for this book, the absolute firm deadline is December 31. If the story arrives two days later, it will not be read. Sorry.

O.P.

Introduction

MYSTERY IS THE NUT of all great fiction, so it seems superfluous and even a bit patronizing to promote a separate category for it. Yet the tag has stuck since the heyday of pulp, and now it seems unshakable.

The stories in this collection would do honor to any anthology of short literature. More than transcending the genre of crime, they blow away its nebulous boundaries. Good writing is good writing, period.

Oh, there's death in these pages. Death by shotgun, handgun, hammer, candlestick, Barlow knife, bayonet, golf club — even death by garage-door opener. But the stories are far more memorable for the characters than for the crimes.

"A plague set upon the world to cauterize and cleanse it" is our introduction to the menacing, grief-shattered Jeepster in William Gay's riveting "Where Will You Go When Your Skin Cannot Contain You?"

The Jeepster is hellbound, of course, which is not an uncommon fate in his neighborhood. There's nothing common about this story, though, a dark poetic torrent that makes vivid a state of almost unimaginable heartbrokenness.

The ability to deliver such complete and compelling tales in a couple of thousand words is an authentic gift, and the envy of writers who cannot pull it off.

When novelists pace themselves, they set their own clock. Sometimes the goal line is visible; other times it isn't. However long we take to get there is entirely up to us. Those who pick up our books can see how thick or thin they are, and adjust their expectations accordingly.

But readers of short stories arrive primed for a quick score, preferably in a single sitting. A writer must work essentially in a two-minute drill, trying to move the ball downfield quickly without fumbling. Such disciplined calibrations of plot and compressions of character development are difficult to do well.

In "Rodney Valen's Second Life," Kent Meyers's narrator sets the hook artfully: "Everyone figured Rodney, Shane's father, would end the Valen line. How the hell Rodney managed to find a wife's beyond anyone. Blame the freeway."

That funny line leads down a haunted road, though, and the shadows will be familiar to readers of Poe and even Faulkner.

In "Gleason," by Louise Erdrich, a philandering dreamer named Stregg tries to explain his recent life to his mistress's brother: "Until I met Jade last year, you understand, I was reasonably happy. Carmen and I had sex for twenty minutes once a week and went to Florida in the winter; we gave dinner parties and stayed at the lake for two weeks every summer. In the summer, we had sex twice a week and I cooked all our meals."

The kidnapping that follows is brilliantly incidental to the fate of that marriage. Think O. Henry channeling John Cheever.

While shored by tight structure, a mystery flops if the cast is uninteresting or fails to perform. The writers in this volume demonstrate zero tolerance for boring relationships, boring interludes, or boring endings.

Laura Lippman's soccer-mom call girl in "One True Love," Robert Andrews's homeless hero in "Solomon's Alley," Jim Fusilli's cuckolded Italian waiter in "Chellini's Solution" — all are splendidly galvanized from beginning to end.

As it does in life, evil abounds here in a variety of presentations. We expect to see it in a psychotic stalker, but not necessarily in a band of Texas volunteers on their way to battle the Mexican army of Santa Anna in 1836. Brent Spencer's "The True History" is one of the most chilling pieces in this anthology, and there's virtually nothing for a reader to sort out.

"Let it be said here and now that a Texian has no taste for discipline," the story begins, and soon it's as plain as day: something truly ugly is about to happen, and all we can do is be swept along with mounting dread.

No less powerful is Chris Adrian's "Stab," in which an autistic boy is first befriended and then recruited by a budding serial killer who moves "as slowly as the moon does across the sky." The search for a missing child leads to a sack of riled poisonous snakes in "Jakob Loomis," Jason Ockert's sinuous account of crossed paths and black luck. And in "The Timing of Unfelt Smiles," John Dufresne arranges the ultimate counseling session between a family therapist and a fellow who's just murdered his wife, his kids, and his parents. Obviously there are issues.

Sometimes there is no villain to blame, only fate or frailty — an accident of lust, distraction, or rotten judgment. Peter Blauner's "Going, Going, Gone" is about a man named Sussman who is separated from his six-year-old son on the subway — a parent's urban nightmare. Watching the boy's face in a window of the departing train, Sussman fills with desperation and thinks: *I have lost the only thing that matters.*

For those who prefer conventional pump fakes and behind-the-back passes, there's the redoubtable Lawrence Block and his droll, likable hit man, Keller. Having a killer for hire as a recurring protagonist must be challenging at times, but it doesn't hurt that this one lives in Greenwich Village, loves spicy food, and collects stamps as a hobby.

In "Keller's Double Dribble," he is sent to whack somebody in Indianapolis and finds himself killing time at a Pacers game, which for most assassins would be a pleasant diversion. However, basketball depresses Keller, so his attention wanders to other matters, such as why the stranger who hired him would kick in for two $96 seats. As Keller soon discovers, it was not an innocent gratuity.

Back in New York, a squad of detectives employs creative methods of interrogation on a Japanese businessman suspected of tossing a hooker from the window of his hotel room, in Robert Knightly's "Take the Man's Pay." Far away, in western Montana, a man oils his Winchester and prepares to hunt down the three marauding bikers who killed his sorrel mare. The rifle is brand-new, purchased at a Wal-Mart, and does not comfortably fit the hands of the avenging rancher in James Lee Burke's fine contribution, "A Season of Regret."

In "Meadowlands," Joyce Carol Oates takes us to a messy afternoon at the Jersey track, where the animals that break down are of the two-legged type. More gambling adventure is at play in "Pinwheel," Scott Wolven's story of an ex-con who takes a job at a private and very illegal Nevada racetrack where each day millions are won and lost. Mostly lost.

To the east, a peripatetic pimp known as Shank and a teenage prostitute called Meg contemplate the roaring enigma of Niagara Falls, in David Means's "The Spot." And in St. Louis, where Ridley Pearson sets "Queeny," a famous author of horror tales is trapped in a real one after his wife vanishes while jogging.

Up in Minnesota, territory long claimed by John Sandford, a golf pro turns up dead and plugged in a sand trap, making for a difficult lie in "Lucy Had a List." And way down in my own stomping grounds of South Florida, the most reliable freak show in America, a professional poker player gets lucky, laid, and then nearly lit up in "T-Bird," John Bond's hot deal on the Miami River.

All these pieces were originally published in story anthologies, distinguished magazines, and literary quarterlies that recognized them as fine fiction, not just fine mysteries. No single genre holds a special claim on grittiness and irony, blood-letting and remorse, betrayal and redemption — these are universal ingredients of art, and of the front page of your hometown newspaper; daily soul scrapings from back alleys, penthouses, suburbs, and farmlands.

Pulp is life. We are drawn to so-called mystery stories not only for anticipated thrills and surprises, but for the raw and reportorial light they shine on the human condition, which is mysterious indeed.

CARL HIAASEN

The Best American Mystery Stories 2007

CHRIS ADRIAN

Stab

FROM *Zoetrope: All-Story*

SOMEONE WAS MURDERING the small animals of our neighborhood. We found them in the road outside our houses, and from far away they looked like the victims of careless drivers, but close up you saw that they were plump and round, not flat, and that their bodies were marred by clean-edged rectangular stab wounds. Sometimes they lay in drying pools of blood, and you knew the murder had occurred right there. Other times it was obvious they had been moved from the scene of the crime and arranged in postures, like the two squirrels posed in a hug on Mrs. Chenoweth's doorstep.

Squirrels, then rabbits, then the cats, and dogs in late summer. By that time I had known for months who was doing all the stabbing. I got that information on the first day of June 1979, two years and one month and fourteen days after my brother's death from cancer. I woke up early that morning, a sunny one that broke a chain of rainy days, because my father was taking me to see Spider-Man, who was scheduled to make an appearance at the fourth annual Leukemia Society of America Summer Fair in Washington, D.C. I was eight years old and I thought Spider-Man was very important.

In the kitchen I ate a bowl of cereal while my father spread the paper out before me. "Look at that," he said. On the front page was an article detailing the separation of Siamese twin girls, Lisa and Elisa Johansen from Salt Lake City. They were joined at the thorax, like my brother and I had been, but they shared vital organs, whereas Colm and I never did. There was a word for the way we and they had been joined: thoracopagus. It was still the biggest word I knew.

"Isn't that amazing?" my father said. He was a surgeon, so these sorts of things interested him above all others. "See that? They're just six months old!" Colm and I were separated at eighteen months. I had no clear memories of either the attachment or the operation, though Colm claimed he remembered our heads knocking together all the time, and that he dreamed of monkeys just before we went under from the anesthesia. The Johansen twins were joined side by side; my brother and I were joined back to back. Our parents would hold up mirrors so we could look at each other — that was something I did remember: looking in my mother's silver-handled mirror, over my shoulder at my own face.

Early as it was, on our way out to the car we saw our new neighbor, Molly Matthews, sitting on the front steps of her grandparents' house, reading a book in the morning sun.

"Hello, Molly," said my father.

"Good morning, Dr. Cole," she said. She was unfailingly polite with adults. At school she was already very popular, though she had been there for only two months, and she had a tendency to oppress the other children in our class with her formidable vocabulary.

"Poor girl," said my father, when we were in the car and on our way. He pitied her because both her parents had died in a car accident. She was in the car with them when they crashed, but she was thrown from the wreck through an open window — this was in Florida, where I supposed everyone always drove around with their windows down and never wore seatbelts.

I turned in my seat so I was upside down. This had long been my habit; I did it so I could look out the window at the trees and telephone wires as we passed them. My mother would never stand for it, but she was flying that day to San Francisco. She was a stewardess. Once my father and I flew with her while she was working and she brought me a cup of Coke with three cherries in it. She put down the drink and leaned over me to open up the window shade, which I had kept closed from the beginning of the flight out of fear. "Look," she said to me. "Look at all that!" I looked and saw sandy mountains that resembled crumpled brown paper bags. I imagined falling from that great height into my brother's arms.

"Spider-Man!" said my father, after we had pulled onto Route 50 and passed a sign that read WASHINGTON, D.C. 29 MILES. "Aren't you excited?" He reached over and rubbed my head with his fist. Had my mother been with me, she would not have spoken at all, but my father talked the whole way, about Spider-Man, about the mall, about the Farrah Fawcett look-alike who was also scheduled to appear; he asked me repeatedly if the prospect of seeing such things didn't make me excited, though he knew I would not answer him. I hadn't spoken a word or uttered a sound since my brother's funeral.

Spider-Man was a great disappointment. When my father brought me close for an autograph, I saw that his Spider-Suit was badly sewn, and glossy in a gross sort of way; his voice, when he said, "Hey there, Spider-Fan," pitched high like a little mouse's. He was an utter fake. I ran away from him, across the mall; my father did not catch me until I had made it all the way to the Smithsonian Castle. He didn't yell at me. It only made him sad when I acted so peculiarly. My mother sometimes lost her temper and would scream out that I was a twisted little fruitcake, and why couldn't I ever make anything easy? She would apologize later, but never with the same ferocity, and so it seemed to me not to count. I always hoped she would burst into my room later on in the night, to wake me by screaming how sorry she was, to slap herself, and maybe me too, because she was so regretful.

"So much for Spider-Man," said my father. He took me to see the topiary buffalo, and for a while we sat in the grass, saying nothing, until he asked me if I wouldn't go back with him. I did, and though we had missed the Farrah Fawcett look-alike's rendition of "Feelings," he got to meet her, because he had connections with the Leukemia Society. She said I was cute and gave me an autographed picture that I later gave to my father because I could tell he wanted it.

When we got home I went up to my room and tossed all my Spider-Man comic books and action figures into the deepest recesses of my closet. Then I took a book out onto the roof. I sat and read *Stuart Little* for the fifth time. Below me, in the yard next door, I could see Molly playing, just as silent as I was. Every once in a while she would look up and catch me looking at her, and she would smile down at her plastic dolls. We had interacted like this before, me reading and her playing, but on this day, for some reason, she spoke to me. She held my gaze for a few moments, then laughed coyly and said, "Would you like to see my bodkin?" I shrugged, then climbed down and followed her into the ravine behind our houses. I did not know what a bodkin was. I thought she was going to make me look inside her panties, like Judy Corcoran had done about three weeks before, trying to make me swear not to tell about the boring thing I had seen.

But what Molly showed me — after we had gone down about thirty feet into the bushes and she had knelt near the arrow-shaped gravestone of our English sheepdog, Gulliver, and after she dug briefly in the dry dirt — was a dagger. It was about a foot long, and ornate, encrusted with what looked like real emeralds and rubies, with a great blue stone set in the pommel, and a rose etched in relief on the upper part of the blade.

"Do you like it?" she asked me. "My father gave it to me. It used to belong to a medieval princess." I did like it. I reached out for it, but she drew it back to her chest and said, "No! You may not touch it." She ran off down the ravine, toward the river; I didn't follow. I sat on Gulliver's stone and thought about all the little dead animals, and I knew — even a little mind could make the connection — that Molly had been murdering them. But I didn't give much thought to it, besides a brief reflection on how sharp the blade must be to make such clean wounds. I walked back to my house and went down to the basement to watch *The Bionic Woman*, my new favorite.

After Colm's death I got into the habit of staring, sometimes for hours at a time, at my image in the mirror. My parents thought it was just another of my new autistic tendencies, and they both discouraged it, even going so far as to remove the mirror from my bedroom. What they didn't know was that the image I was looking at was not really my own; it was Colm's. When I looked in the mirror I saw the face we had shared. We were mirror twins, our faces perfectly symmetrical, the gold flecks in my left eye mirrored in Colm's right, a small flaw at the right edge of his lips mirrored by one at the left edge of mine. So when I looked in the mirror, even the small things that made my face my own made my face into his, and if I waited long enough he would speak to me. He would tell me about heaven, about all sorts of little details, like that nobody ever had to go to the bathroom there. We had both considered that necessity to be a great inconvenience and a bore. He said he was watching me all the time.

There was a connection between us, he often said, even when he was alive, that the surgeons had not broken when we were separated. It was something unseen. We did not have quite two souls between us; it was more that we had one and a half. Sometimes he would hide from me, somewhere in our great big house, and insist that I find him. Usually I couldn't, but he always found me; I couldn't hide from him anywhere in the house, or, I suspected, anywhere on earth.

After he died I found him, not just in mirrors but in every reflective surface. Ponds and puddles or the backs of spoons, anything would do. And invariably the last thing he would say to me was, "When are you going to come and be with me again?"

Molly appeared that night at my window. I was still awake when she came. At first I thought she was Colm, until a flash of heat lightning illuminated her and I saw who she was. Glimpsing the dagger flashing in her hand, I was certain she had come to kill me, but when she came over to my bed, she said only, "Do you want to come out with me?" Another flash of lightning lit up the room. The lightning was the reason I had been awake — on hot summer nights Colm and I would stay up for hours watching it flash over the river. Sometimes our parents would let us sleep on the porch, where the view was even better.

She sat down on my bed. "I like your room," she said, looking around. There was light from the hall, enough to make out the general lay of the room. Our father had built it up to look like a ship for Colm and me, complete with sea-blue carpeting and a raised wooden deck with railings and a ship's wheel. Above one bed was an authentic-looking sign that read CAPTAIN'S BUNK; the other bed belonged to the first mate. While he lived we had switched beds every night, in the interest of absolute equality, unless one of us was feeling afraid, in which case we shared the same bed. The last time he slept in the room he had been in the captain's bed, and because the cycle could not go on any longer I had been in the first mate's bed ever since.

Molly pulled my sheets back, and while I dressed she looked around the room for my shoes. When she found them she brought them to me and said, "Come on."

I followed her — out the window, over the roof, and down the blue spruce that grew close to my house. She walked along our road, to the golf course around which part of our community was built. The site, once a Baptist girls' camp, had in the century since its founding turned into a place where well-to-do white people lived in rustic pseudo-isolation. It was called Severna Forest. You couldn't live there if you were Jewish or Italian, and in the summer they made you lock up your dog in a communal kennel. The golf course had only nine holes. It was a very hilly course, bordered by ravines in some places and in others by the Severn River. Molly took me to a wide piece of rough on the fourth hole, only about half a mile from our houses. Though the moon was down, I could see under the starlight that rabbits had gathered in the tall grass and the dandelions. I bent at my knees and picked a stalk. I was about to puff on it and scatter the seeds when Molly held my arm and said, "Don't, you'll frighten them."

For a little while we stood there, she with one hand on my arm and the other on her knife, and we watched the rabbits sitting placidly in the grass, and we waited for them to get used to us. "Aren't they lovely?" she said, letting go of my arm. She began to move, very slowly, toward the nearest one. She moved as slowly as the moon does across the sky. I couldn't tell she was getting any closer to the rabbit unless I looked away for a few minutes; when I looked back she was closer, and the rabbit had not moved. When she was about five feet away she turned and looked at me. It was too dark for me to see her face. I couldn't tell if she smiled. Then she leapt, knife first, at the little creature, and I saw her pierce its body. It thrashed once and was suddenly dead. I realized I was holding my breath, and still holding the dandelion in front of my lips. I blew into it and watched the seeds float toward her, to where she was stabbing the body again and again and again.

In school the next Monday, Molly studiously ignored me. The whole morning long I stared at her, thinking she must give some sign that a special thing had taken place between us, but she never did. I didn't really care if she never spoke to me again; I was used to people experimenting with me as a friend. I let them come and go.

After lunch, when we were all settling down again into our desks, in the silence after Mrs. Wallaby, our teacher, had offered up a post-luncheon prayer for the pope, Molly passed me a note. I opened it up, thinking for some reason that it might say, "I love you," because once a popular girl named Iris had passed me such a note, and when I blushed she and her friends had laughed cruelly. But Molly's note said simply, "You'd better not tell." I supposed she meant I had better not write a letter to the police. She did not really know me at all.

"What's that you've got there, Calvin?" Mrs. Wallaby asked, striding over to me, squinting at me through her glasses. Before she arrived I slipped the piece of paper into my mouth and began to chew.

"What was that?"

I swallowed. She brought her face so close to mine I could read the signature on her designer frame glasses: OSCAR DE LA RENTA.

"What was that?" she asked again. Of course I said nothing. She heaved a great sigh and told me to go sit in "The Judas Chair," which was actually just a desk set aside from the others, facing a corner. She was not a bad woman, but sometimes I brought out the worst in people. Once she saved me at recess from a crowd of girls who were pinching me, trying to make me cry out. She brought me inside and put cold cream from her purse on my welts; then, after she spoke for a while about how I couldn't go on like this, I just couldn't, she gave me a long grave look and pinched me herself. It was not so hard as what the girls were giving me, and it was under my shirt, where no one would see. She looked deep into my eyes as she did it, but I didn't cry out. I didn't even blink.

On the night of the first day of summer vacation, Molly came again and got me from my bed. She said nothing, aside from telling me to get dressed and to follow her. We passed the golf course and I started off to where the rabbits were; she grabbed my collar and pulled me back.

"No," she said. "It's time to move on." We spent the night hunting cats. It wasn't easy. We exhausted ourselves chasing them through the dark. Always they outran us or vanished up trees.

"We need a plan," she said at last. Closer to our houses, we found a neighbor cat named Mr. Charlemagne; we had chased him earlier and he escaped through a cat door into a garage. Molly positioned me in a bush by that door, while Mr. Charlemagne eyed us peacefully. Then she came at him. He took off for his door, but I jumped in front of it. For some reason he leapt right into my arms, looked up in my face, then turned to look at my companion. She had her knife out. He snuggled deeper into my arms, expecting, I think, that I would bring him inside to safety. I threw him down hard on the ground. Molly fell on him and stabbed him through the throat.

The authorities of Severna Forest —— the sheriff and the chairman of the community association and the president of the country club — had dismissed the squirrel and rabbit deaths as the gruesome pranks of bored teenagers. When Mr. Charlemagne was discovered, draped along a straight-growing bough of a birch tree, a mildly urgent sense of alarm spread over the community. "Sick!" people muttered to each other while buying vodka and Yoo-hoo at the general store. Not one bit of suspicion fell on Molly or me. Everyone considered me strange and tragic but utterly harmless. Molly was equally tragic yet widely admired, with her manners and her blond hair and her big brown eyes. Sometimes I thought it was only because she stabbed that she could play the part of her sweet, decent self so well.

A few days passed before she came for me again, in the early evening after lacrosse practice. The Severna Forest peewee team practiced every Saturday afternoon. I was one of its best players, because I had absolutely no fear of the ball. Others still ducked when the ball came flying toward them like a little cannon shot, or knocked it away with their sticks. I caught it. If it hit me, I didn't care. I scooped it up and ran with it, often all the way down the field because it rarely occurred to me to pass. I liked to run, and to be exhausted, and I thought one day the ball might fly at me with such force it would burst my head like a rotten pumpkin.

That day I got hit in the eye with the ball. Our coach, a college boy named Sam Corkle, hurled it at me with all his adult strength, thinking I was paying attention. When it struck my eye I saw a great white flash and then a pale afterimage of Colm's face that quickly faded. The blow knocked me down. I looked up at the sky and saw a passing plane and wondered, like I always did when I saw a plane in flight, if my mother was on board, though I knew she was at home that day. Sam came up with the other coach and they asked me all sorts of questions, trying to determine if I was disoriented and might have a concussion. Of course I didn't answer. Someone said I would throw up if I had a concussion, so they sat me on a bench and watched me to see if that would happen. When it didn't, they let me back onto the field. I went eagerly — though my eyeball was aching and starting to swell — hoping to get hit again, to catch another glimpse of my brother.

"What happened to you?" my mother asked when Sam brought me home. She was sitting at the dining room table, where my father held a package of frozen hamburger to his own swollen purple eye. He had gotten into a fight when someone tried to cut in front of him in a gas line. It was a bad week for gas. Stations were selling their daily allowances before noon. "You too, sport?" he said.

My father examined my eye and said I would be fine. As my mother pressed hamburger against the swelling, there was a knock at the door. Sam answered it, and I heard Molly's voice ask very sweetly, "Can Calvin come out and play?" I jumped from my mother's lap and ran toward the door. She caught me and said, "Take your hamburger with you." I stood at the door while she walked back to the dining room with Sam, and I heard her ask my father, "When did your son get a little girlfriend?"

Molly had an empty mayonnaise jar in her hands. "We're going to catch fireflies," she said, not asking about my eye. I followed her through the dusk to the golf course, dropping my hamburger in a holly bush along the way. We ran around grabbing after bugs. I was delighted she had come for me while there was daylight, thinking that must mean something. I grabbed at her flying blond hair as much as I did the fireflies; she slapped my hands each time.

I thought we were filling the jar so she could crush them mercilessly, or stick them with pins, or distill their glowing parts into some powerful, fluorescent poison with which she could coat her knife. But when it was dark, when about thirty of them were thick in the jar, she took off the lid and went running down the hill to the river, spilling a trail of bright motes that circled around her, rose up, and flew away.

Soon there weren't any cats left for us — not because we had killed them all, but because after the fourth one, a tabby named Vittles, was found stabbed twelve times on the front steps of the general

store, people started keeping their cats inside at night. Our hunts
were widely spaced, occurring only about once every two weeks,
but in between those nights Molly would come to the door for
me and take me out to play in the daylight. We did the normal
things that children our age were supposed to do, during the day.
We swam in the river and played with her dolls and watched television.

In late July Molly decided to change prey again. She took me
through the woods, out to the kennel. I could hear the dogs barking in the darkness long before we reached them. They knew we
were coming for them.

The kennel was lit by a single streetlamp, stuck in the middle of a
clearing in the woods. There was a little service road that ran under
the light, out to the main road that led to General's Highway and
Annapolis. I watched Molly stalk back and forth in front of the
runs. The dogs were all howling and barking at her. It was two A.M.
There was nobody around; nobody lived within a mile and a half of
the place. The whole point of the kennel was to separate the dogs
from the houses between June and September, so their barking
wouldn't disturb all the wealthy people in their summer cottages. It
was a stupid rule.

Molly had stooped down in front of a poodle. I did not recognize
it. It retreated to the back of its run and yipped at her.

"Nice puppy," she said, though it was full grown. She waved me
over to her, and then turned me around to take a piece of beef
from the Holly Hobbie backpack she had strapped on me at the beginning of our excursion. She took out my lacrosse gloves and told
me to put them on.

"Be ready to grab him," she said. She crouched down in front of
the bars of the cage and held the meat up in the meager light.
"Come on," she said. "Come and get your treat, baby. It's okay." She
held on to one end while the poodle nibbled, and with her free
hand she scratched its head. She motioned for me to come close
beside her. It was the closest I had ever been to a poodle in my life. I
tried to imagine the owner, probably a big fat rich lady with white
hair, who wore diamonds around her throat while she slept in a giant canopy bed.

"Just about . . . now!" said Molly. I reached through the bars with
my thick lacrosse hands and grabbed the dog by a foreleg. Immediately it started to pull away, just a gentle tug. "Don't let it escape!"

she said, scrambling in the bag for her knife. The poodle gave me a *What are you doing?* look, and I very nearly lost my hold.

It was an awkward kill, because the bars were in the way, and the poodle was a strong-willed little dog who wanted to live. It bit hard but ineffectively at my hands. It bit at the knife and cut its gums, and its teeth made a ringing sound against the metal. It snarled and yelped and squealed, and all around us the other dogs were all screaming. Molly was saying, "There! There! There!" in a low voice, almost a whisper. When she finally delivered the killing blow to the dog's neck, a gob of hot blood flew out between the bars and hit me in the eye. It burned like the harsh shampoos my parents bought for me, but I didn't cry out.

On the way back I let her walk ahead of me. I watched the glint of her head under the moon as she ducked between bushes and hopped over rotting logs. I felt bad, not about the poodle, which I had hated instantly and absolutely as soon as I had laid eyes upon it, but about the owner, the fat lady who I thought must be named Mrs. Vanderbilt because that was the richest name I knew. I thought about her riding down to the kennel in her limousine with a china bowl full of steak tartare for her Precious, and the way her face would look when she saw the bloody cotton ball on the floor of the cage and could not comprehend that this was the thing she had loved. Molly got farther and farther ahead of me, calling back that I should stop being so poky and hurry up. Eventually all I could see was the moonlight on her head, and on the white bag she had brought for my gloves, promising to clean them.

When we had gone about a mile from the kennel I heard a train whistle sounding. It was still far away, but I knew the tracks ran nearby. I went to them. In the far distance I could see the train light. I lay down in the middle of the tracks and waited. Molly came looking for me — I could hear her calling out, calling me a stupid boy and saying it was late. She was tired. She wanted to go to bed. As the train got nearer, I felt a deep, wonderful hum in the tracks that seemed to pass through my brain and stimulate whatever organ is responsible for generating happiness. I imagined my head flying from my body to land at her feet. Or maybe it would hit her and knock her down. She would, I imagined, give it a calm look, put it in the bag, and take it home, where she would keep it, along with my gloves, under her bed as a souvenir of our acquaintance. The train arrived and passed over me.

I suppose I was too small for it to take off my head. Or maybe it was a different sort of train that did that to Charlie Kelly, a fifteen-year-old who had died the previous summer after a reefer party in the woods when he lay down on the tracks to impress Sam Corkle's sister. The conductor never saw me. The train never slowed. It rushed over me with such a noise — it got louder and louder until I couldn't hear it anymore, until watching the flashes of moon between the boxcars I heard my brother's voice say, "Soon."

All Severna Forest was horrified by the death of the dog, whose name turned out to be Arthur. A guard was posted at the kennel. For the first few nights it was Sheriff Travis himself, but after a week he deputized a teenager he deemed trustworthy; that boy snuck off with his girlfriend to get stoned and listen to loud music in her car. While they were thus occupied we struck again, after two nights of watching and waiting for just such an opportunity. This time it was a Jack Russell terrier named Dreamboat.

After that the kennel was closed and the dogs sent home to owners who locked them indoors, especially at night. Sheriff Travis claimed to be within a hair's breadth of catching the "pervert," but in fact he never came near Molly or me. She never seemed nervous about getting caught. Neither did she gloat about her success. She was silent about it, as she was about why she went around stabbing things in the first place.

But she talked about her parents all summer. When I was not playing lacrosse, I was with her, sailing on the river in the Sunfish her grandparents had bought her in June, or soft-shell crabbing in the muddy flats off Beach Road, or riding around on our banana-seated bicycles. I envied her hers because it had long, multicolored tassels that dangled from the handlebars, and a miniature license plate on the back that read HOT STUFF. Floating in the middle of the river on a calm day, I dangled my hand in the water and listened to her talk about her parents; her father had been a college professor of history, and at night he would tell her stories about ancient princesses and tell her she herself had surely been one in a past life. Didn't she remember? Didn't she recognize this portrait of her antique prince? Didn't she recognize the dagger with which she had slain the beastly suitor who had tried to take her away to live in a black kingdom under the earth? Her mother, a cautious pediatrician, had protested when he gave her the bodkin, though

Molly was grave and responsible and not likely to hurt herself or others by accident. "A girl needs to defend herself," her father had said, but he was joking. The knife hung on her wall, along with an ancient tapestry and a number of museum prints of ancient princesses, and she was not supposed to touch them until she was older.

I listened and watched pale sea nettles drift by. Occasionally one would catch my hand with its tentacle and sting me. I wanted to tell her about my brother, about stories we had told each other, about our lighthouse game or our bridge game or our thunder and lightning game, or the fond wish we both had for a flying bed of the sort featured in *Bedknobs and Broomsticks,* except that ours would be equipped with a matter transporter, à la *Star Trek,* so we could hover over our favorite restaurant and beam up pizzas. But nothing could have made me talk, on that day or any of the days that stretched back to Colm's funeral. At the time I didn't know why I would not speak. I think now the reason my throat closed up was that I knew, that day in the funeral parlor, there was nothing I could ever say to equal the occasion of my brother's death. I should have spoken a word that would bring him back, and yet I could not, and so I must say nothing forever.

Molly's birthday came in the first week of August. My mother took me shopping for a present. She spent a lot of time in the Barbie section, agonizing over accessories, but I insisted silently on my own choice: a Bionic Woman combination beauty salon and diagnostic station. It was not the gift I really meant to give Molly, not the gift from my heart. I insisted on it because I knew she would disregard it, and I could then play with it myself. Her real gift from me was a wide, flat stone, taken from the Severn, with which she could sharpen her knife. I wrapped it in the Sunday funnies. When she opened it she smiled with genuine delight and said it was her favorite.

From her grandparents she got a Polaroid camera. Her grandfather, a man who had always believed in buying in bulk, gave her a whole carton of film and flashbulbs. In the evening after her birthday party we sat on my roof and she sent flashes arcing over the ravine, tossing aside the pictures that popped out. They were of nothing, and she was not interested in them. I picked them up and pressed them to my nose because I liked the developing-film smell.

Later that night she came to my window, her backpack on her

shoulders. I'd had a feeling she would come and so went to sleep fully dressed, right down to my shoes. To my surprise she removed my shoes, and my socks. While I sat with my feet hanging over the edge of the bed, she took a jar from her pack and scooped out a plum-size dollop of Vaseline, lathering it over my foot and between my toes.

"We have a long walk tonight," she said matter-of-factly. I closed my eyes while she did my other foot, enjoying the feeling. When I put on my socks and shoes and walked on my anointed feet, it was like walking on a pillow or on my father's fat belly, when he would play with Colm and me, all the while yelling, "Oh, oh, the elephants are trampling me!"

We went far past the kennel, three miles from our homes. We walked right out of Severna Forest, past the squat, crumbling brick pillars that marked the entrance to the forest road. We walked past the small black community, right at the edge of the gates, where families lived whose mothers worked as maids in our houses. Molly led me into the fields of a farm whose acreage ran along General's Highway.

"I want a horse," she said, standing still and eyeing the vast expanse of grass before us. In the distance I could see a house and a barn. I had seen the house countless times from my parents' car, when my mother was driving and I had to sit right-side up. I had always imagined it to be inhabited by bonneted women and bare-lipped, bearded men, like the ones in the coffee-table book on the Amish that sat in our living room and was never looked at by anyone but me. Molly started toward the barn. I followed her, looking at the dark house and wondering if some restless person was looking out the bedroom window, watching us coming.

No one challenged us, not even a dog or a cat. I wondered what she would do if a snarling dog came out of the darkness to get us. I did not think she would stab it. I had a theory, entirely unsubstantiated, that she was moving up the class chain, onward from birds to squirrels to cats to dogs and beyond, her destination the fat red heart of a human being, and I knew that once she had finished with an animal class she would not return to it. She was storing the life force of everything she stabbed in the great blue stone in her dagger's hilt, and when she had accumulated enough of it, the stone would glow like the Earth glowed in the space pictures that

hung on the wall in our third-grade homeroom, above the motto
NOTHING IS IMPOSSIBLE. When the stone glowed like that, I
knew, her parents would step from it and be with her again.

If the horse had a name, I never knew it. In the dim light of the
stable I might have missed it, carved on the stall somewhere. The
horse was a tall Appaloosa. Molly had brought sugar and apples.
She fed it and whispered to it. It was the only horse there. The
other stalls were empty but looked lived-in. Molly was saying to the
horse, "It's okay. It's all right. There's nothing to be afraid of." She
smiled at it a truly sweet smile, and it looked at her with its enormous brown eyes, and I could see that it trusted her absolutely, the
way unicorns in stories instinctively trust princesses. In her right
hand she held the knife, and her left was on the horse's muzzle.
"Touch it," she said to me. "It's like velvet." I put my hand on the
space just between its eyes. She was right. I closed my eyes and
imagined I was touching my mother while she wore her velvet
Christmas dress. When I opened them the horse was looking at me
with its great eyes, and in them I could see my brother touching the
horse, and behind him Molly striking with her dagger. The horse
did not even try to pull away until the blade was buried deep in its
throat. Then it rose up, jerking the blade out of her hand and trying to hammer us with its hooves, which clattered against the wood
of the stall. When it shook its head the knife flew out and landed at
my feet. The horse was trying to scream, but because of the wound
it could make only spraying, huffing noises.

I watched it jump and then stagger around the stall. I was still
and calm until Molly took the first picture — I jumped at the flash.
At thirty-second intervals another flash would catch in the horse's
eyes. At last it knelt in a wide pool of its blood, and then fell on its
side and was dead. All the time our surroundings seemed very
quiet, despite the whirring of the Polaroid, and the whooshing
and sucking noises of the wound, and the thumping. When those
noises stopped I could suddenly hear crickets chirping, and Molly's
frantic breathing, and my brother saying, "So soon!"

Molly took me home and made me get in the tub with my pants
rolled up. She washed the Vaseline from my feet, and the horse
blood from my hair, and then she put me back in my bed, not an
hour before the sun came up. I slept and dreamed of horses who
bled eternally from their throats, whose eyes held perfect images of

Colm, who spoke from their wounds in the voices of old women and said they could take me to him if I would only ride.

A real live police investigation inspired Molly to lie low for a while. While Anne Arundel County police cars cruised the night streets of Severna Forest, we lay most exceedingly low; and even after they were long gone, we still did not emerge. The summer ran out and school started again. Molly mostly ignored me while we were at school, but she still came by occasionally in the afternoons, or on weekends. We sailed in her boat and once went apple picking with her grandparents, in an orchard all the way down in Leonardtown. Outside my bedroom window the leaves dropped from the trees in the ravine, so I got my clear winter view of the river, all the way down to the bay. In the distance I could see the lights of the Naval Academy radio towers, blinking strong and red in the cold. I would watch them and wait for her, my window wide open, but she did not come again until the first snow.

That was in December, just before Christmas break. Earlier that evening, down by the general store, all the children of Severna Forest had gathered under an old spruce, where a false Santa sat on a gold-leafed wooden throne and handed out presents. I knew he was a false Santa, but most of the others there didn't. It was actually Sheriff Travis, handing out presents bought and delivered to him by the parents of all these greedy little kids. He sat in his chair, surrounded by bags of wrapped toys, and made a big fuss over whether or not this or that child had been good throughout the year. When he called my name I went up and dutifully received my present from his rough hands. It was a Fembot doll, the arch nemesis of the Bionic Woman doll that Molly had rejected. I was in my bed playing with my new toy when she appeared at my window.

"Go down and get your coat," she said. "It's cold out there." I did as she told me. My father had left for the hospital shortly after we got home from seeing Santa, and my mother was asleep in her room, exhausted by an all-night flight from Lima. But almost all the other Severna Forest adults were down at the clubhouse, having their Christmas party. Several of them were famous for getting drunk on the occasion, Sheriff Travis especially. He kept his Santa suit on all night, and people talked about his antics for weeks afterward. They were harmless antics, nothing crass or embarrassing.

He sang songs and said sharp, witty things, things he seemed incapable of saying at any other time of the year, drunk or not.

When we left my house, there was already about an inch of snow on the ground. The storm picked up as we climbed a tree outside the clubhouse. We waited there while the party began to die down. I could see my parents' friends dancing with each other, and Sheriff Travis standing on tables and gesticulating, or turning somersaults, or dancing with two ladies at once. Music and laughter drifted through the blowing snow every time someone opened the door. I got sleepy listening to the sounds of adult amusement, just like Colm and I always did when our parents had one of their dinner parties, something they did often back before he died.

I fell asleep in the tree, with my head on Molly's shoulder. We were wedged close to one another, so I was warm. It was snowing heavily when she jabbed me with her elbow and said, "Wake up, it's time to go." She climbed down the tree and hurried off. I jumped down, knocking the accumulated snow from my back and shoulders, and chased after her. She was moving back toward our houses, toward the tee of the seventh hole. When I caught up with her I could see another vague shape stumbling through the snow, about thirty yards before us. We had to get closer before I could make out the distinctive silhouette of the Santa hat.

Sheriff Travis lived down by the river, in a modest cottage that I imagine must have been lonely for all its smallness, because his children were gone and his wife was dead. He was taking a shortcut over the golf course. I knew he would cross through the woods beyond the green to Beach Road. He was singing "Adeste Fideles" in a loud voice and did not hear us come up behind him.

Molly had taken out her dagger and handed me a short length of lead pipe. "Be ready," she said. When we were less than ten yards away, she ran at him, looking slightly ridiculous trying to rush through the deepening snow with her short legs. But there was nothing ridiculous about the blow she struck, just above his wide black belt, about where his kidney would be. He fell to his knees and she struck again, this time at his back, almost right in the middle, and then again at his neck as he collapsed forward. He screamed at the first blow, just like I thought he would, a great, raw scream like the one my father let go in the hospital room when Colm finally stopped breathing. She stabbed him one more time,

in the right side of his back. In the dark his blood was black on the
snow. He lay on his face and was silent. I stood in the snow, clutching my pipe and wondering if I should hit him with it.

Molly grabbed my hand and dragged me after her. She ran as fast
as she could, through the woods, then along Beach Road to a point
just below our houses. "I got him," she was saying breathlessly, in a
high voice. "I got *Santa*." Twice we had to crouch down behind tree
trunks to escape the passing headlights of the party's last few strag-
glers. We tore up through the ravine, past Gulliver's headstone,
and she gave me a push up the tree by my house, saying only, "Put
your coat back downstairs!" before running off to her own house. I
did as she said. I would have anyway, and it grated on me that she
thought I would be careless. I still had the pipe. I put it deep in my
closet, where the Spider-Man toys were piled.

Back in bed I looked out my window at the storm, which was
still gaining strength. It would be almost a blizzard by morning.
School would be canceled. I lay watching the snow that I knew was
covering our child-sized footprints, covering Santa Travis's body. I
thought of him dying, the coldness of the snow penetrating in
stages through his skin and his muscle and his bone, a dark veil falling over his sight like somebody was wrapping his head in layer after layer of sweet-smelling toilet paper, like Colm and I used to do
when we played I Am the Mummy's Bride, or The Plastic Surgeon
Just Gave Me a New Face. I imagined Colm, waiting patiently by the
door to where he was, waiting and waiting, peering at the slowly approaching figure.

But Sheriff Travis did not die. A concerned citizen, worried because of the storm, had called his house. When he didn't answer,
people went looking for him. They found him where we left him,
alive. At the hospital my father operated to repair his lacerated kidney and fretted over his hemisected spinal cord.

When Sheriff Travis woke up he said he remembered everything. Despite the darkness of the night, and the falling snow, he
gave fairly detailed descriptions of his attackers. Two large black
men had done it, he said, one holding him while the other stabbed
him and called him "Honky Santa." Police called on the community just outside the Severna Forest gates, and two men were arrested after Sheriff Travis identified them in a lineup. I saw them in
the paper.

Molly was furious that Sheriff Travis hadn't died. She stood in my room, kicking my bed so hard that the wall shook and the FIRST MATE sign fell down with a clunk.

"Why?" she said in a loud voice. "Why couldn't he have died?"

I thought about her hungry blue stone while she kicked my bed some more, until my father came to the door and said, "Everything okay in here?"

"Yes, sir," she replied. "We were just kicking the bed."

"Well, please don't."

"Yes, sir," she said, blushing. I looked at the sunlight on the carpet and wanted my father to leave. *Don't make her angry,* I was thinking.

When he was gone she said, "It's just not fair."

I thought it would be many more months before she returned for me at night. I thought we would lie low, but she came back after only two weeks had passed, at the beginning of the second week of January. She had been in Florida with her grandparents over break, while a bitter cold descended over the Atlantic coast from New York to Richmond. The river and even parts of the Chesapeake were frozen over. She came for me the first night she was back.

When we went down the ravine to Beach Road, I thought for sure we were going to Sheriff Travis's house, to finish him off. But upon reaching the road she crossed it and stepped over the riverbank, onto the ice. She turned back to me. "Come on," she said, sliding over the ice in her rubber boots. She went past the pier and the boat slips, out to the wide center of the river. Her voice came drifting back to me: "Don't be such a slowpoke." I hurried after the place where I thought her voice was coming from, but I never caught up with her — perhaps she was hiding from me. It was a clear yet moonless night, and she was wearing a dark coat and a dark hat. I stopped after a while and wrapped my arms around myself. I was cold because my parents were both home and I had not dared go down for my coat. Instead I had worn two sweaters, but they weren't enough to keep me warm. I knelt on the ice and looked down at it, trying to catch Colm's image. I heard Molly's boots sliding over the ice out in the dark, and I thought about a story people told about the ghost of a girl who drowned skating across the river to Westport, to see her boyfriend. On nights like this, people said, you could see her, a gliding white figure. If you

saw her face you would die by water one day. I looked downriver,
searching for either the ghost or Molly but seeing only the lights of
the bridges down past Annapolis. There was a flash, and for a moment I thought it was the winter equivalent of heat lightning, until
I heard the Polaroid whirring.

   She took my picture again, and again, from different sides. I suppose she was trying to upset me, or make me afraid. Maybe she
thought I would run and slip on the ice. I just knelt there, and
then I lay down on my back and looked up at the stars. My father
had shown me the constellation of Gemini. It was the only one I
ever looked for; and though I didn't see it then, I made out my
brother's shape in any number of places. Molly came sliding up to
me. She stood behind my head; I could not see her, but I could see
her panting breath.

   I thought she would speak, then. In my mind I had heard her
speak this speech; I had played it out many times: "I need you," she
would say. "For my parents. They're stuck in here and I must let
them out. You don't mind, do you?" Of course I didn't. I would
have told her so, if I could have. I had been expecting her to say
this ever since she had stabbed the horse, because I didn't know
what animal she could turn to after that, besides me. That night
Colm had said to me, "So soon!" But it was not so soon, and I had
waited.

   She didn't say anything, though. She only knelt near me and put
a hand on my belly. She wasn't smiling, just breathing hard. The
camera hung around her neck and the dagger was in her hand.
She raised my sweaters and my pajama top so that I felt the cold
on my skin and the goose bumps it raised. She put the tip of
the dagger against my belly, and when she looked at me I was so
tempted to speak.

   "Goodbye," she said, and gently slipped it in. I heard my brother's
voice ring in my head: "Now!" For just a moment, as I felt the metal
enter me, I wanted it, and I was full of joy; but a tall wave of pain
crashed over me and washed all the joy away. A cresting scream
rose in me and broke out of my mouth, the loudest sound I had
ever heard, louder than Sheriff Travis's scream, louder than my father's scream, louder than any of the dogs or cats or rabbits. It flew
over the ice in every direction and assaulted people in their homes.
I saw windows lighting up in the hills above the river as I scrambled

to my feet, still screaming. Molly had fallen back, her face caught in a perfect expression of astonishment. I turned and ran from her, not looking back to see if she was chasing me, because I knew she was. I ran for my life, sliding on the ice, expecting at any moment to feel her bodkin in my back. I cried out again when I climbed over the sea wall and ran across the road, because of the pain as I lifted myself. I clambered up the ravine, hearing her behind me. On the spruce that led to my bedroom she caught me, stabbing my dangling calf, and I fell. She came at me again, and I kicked at her; she didn't make a sound. I held my hands out before me and she stabbed them. With a bloody fist I smashed her jaw and knocked her down. I got up the tree and into my room, too afraid to turn and close the window. I rushed down the stairs into my parents' bedroom, where I slammed the door behind me and woke them with my hysterical screaming. My mother turned on the light. Despite my long silence the words came smoothly, up from my leaking belly, sliding like mercury through my throat and bursting in the bright air of their room.

"I want to live!" I told them, though my heart broke as I said it; Colm's image appeared in the floor-length mirror on the opposite side of the bed. He was bloody like me, wounded. He looked at me as my parents jumped out of bed with their arms out, their faces white with horror at the sight of me. I cried great heaving, house-shaking sobs, not because of the pain of my wounds, or because my parents were crying, or because I knew Molly was on her way back to the river, where she would turn her knife on herself and at last take a human life for her soul-eating dagger. I didn't cry like that over the animals and people, now that I knew just how much a knife hurt, though I did feel guilty. And I wasn't crying at my pending betrayal of Molly, though I knew I would say I had no part in any of it and there would be no proof that I had. I cried because I saw Colm shake his head, then turn his back on me and walk away, receding into an image that became more and more my own until it was mine completely. I knew it would speak to me only with my own voice, and look at me with my own eyes, and I knew that I would never see my brother again.

ROBERT ANDREWS

Solomon's Alley

FROM *D.C. Noir*

SOLOMON'S ALLEY parallels M Street, Georgetown's main drag.
Running behind Johnny Rockets, Ben & Jerry's, Old Glory Barbecue, and the Riggs Bank, the alley connects Wisconsin Avenue on
the west to Thirty-first Street one block east.

Battered blue dumpsters line the alley. Solomon had puzzled
over the dumpsters for several years. Finally, he'd decided that
their BFI logo stood for *big fucking incinerators*. That job done, he'd
taken on thinking out the likely origins of the five ancient magno-
lia trees that shaded the stretch of alley where he parked his two
Safeway carts.

On this Tuesday morning in September, he sat in his folding canvas deck chair, part of him pondering the magnolias while another
part got ready for his day job, watching the Nigerian. At 10:00, like
clockwork, the white Dodge van pulled up across Wisconsin at the
corner of Prospect, by Restoration Hardware.

"Hello, Nigerian," Solomon whispered. He settled back to watch
the sidewalk come alive. Each morning's setup was a ballet, a precisely choreographed routine, and Solomon was a discriminating
critic.

Most mornings the performance went well: every move efficient,
rhythmic, smooth. Some mornings it didn't: some mornings everything fell apart in a cranky series of busted plays.

The driver eased the van forward so its front bumper toed the
white marks on the pavement. He switched off the ignition and got
out to go round to the back.

Waverly Ngame was a big man. Two-fifty, six feet and a couple of inches, Solomon figured. His skin blue-black . . . shiny . . . like the barrel of a .38.

First out, a long rectangular folding table, the kind you see in church basements. Ngame locked the legs open. With his toe and wood shims, he worked around the table until it rested solid on the uneven brick sidewalk.

He disappeared into the van and came out with racks of white plastic-coated wire-grid shelving under both arms and a grease-stained canvas bag in his left hand.

In swift, practiced motions, he picked the largest of the shelves and braced it upright on the side of the table facing the street. With one hand he held the shelf, with the other he reached into the canvas bag and came out with a large C-clamp. Twirling it with sharp snaps of his wrist, he opened the jaws just enough to slip over the shelf and the table edge. He tightened the clamp, and moved to repeat the process on the other side of the table.

More shelving and more C-clamps produced a display stand.

Now the van disgorged Ngame's merchandise in large nylon bags and sturdy blue plastic storage boxes. Soon, Gucci and Kate Spade handbags hung alluringly from the vertical shelving while Rolex watches and Serengeti sunglasses marched in neat ranks across the top of the church-basement folding table.

He slow today, said Voice.

"He did good," Solomon contradicted. He didn't want to give Voice shit. He did that, give Voice any slack, Voice start up. Voice need his pills? Solomon tried to remember the last time he trucked to the clinic, then gave it up. Long as it was only one Voice, he could handle it. It only got bad when he had to put up with the whole goddamn family yelling and screaming, scrambling things inside his head.

Ngame climbed into his van. That was Solomon's cue. He got out of his chair and walked to where the alley ran into Wisconsin. There, he could keep a closer eye on Ngame's stand.

Ngame eased the van across Wisconsin and into the alley, waving to Solomon as he passed by. He pulled the van into a slot by the florist shop on Thirty-first Street where he had a deal with the manager. Locking the van, he walked back up the alley toward Solomon.

"Nobody bother the stand, Waverly."

Ngame palmed Solomon a folded five.

"A good day, Solomon."

As a boy in Lagos, Ngame had learned his English listening to BBC. He sounded like a Brit announcer except that he had a Nigerian's way of softly rounding his vowels and stressing the final syllables of his sentences.

Solomon shook his head. "Watch yourself today."

Ngame gripped Solomon's shoulder.

"Voice tell you that?" he asked. He searched Solomon's face with clinical curiosity.

Ngame's concern irritated Solomon. "Hunh! Voice don't know shit," he said crossly. "Solomon telling you."

Something passed behind Ngame's eyes. He looked serious. "You hear anything?"

"Just feel," Solomon whispered to keep Voice from hearing, "just feel."

Ngame smiled. "You are a belt-and-suspenders man, Solomon."

Solomon pouted and tucked the five away. "You don't have belt and suspenders, Waverly, you lose your ass."

Ngame took that in with a laugh. He squeezed Solomon's shoulder, then turned and made his way across Wisconsin.

In the street by Ngame's stand, a crow worried at the flattened remains of a road-killed rat.

And down the block from the stand, Solomon saw two men get out of a maroon Crown Vic. One black, one white. Both big. Both cops.

With a little finger, Ngame made a microscopic adjustment, poking a pair of sunglasses to line them up just so with its neighbors. He didn't look up from putting fine touches to his display.

"Detectives Phelps and Kearney. Good morning, sirs."

"How's business, Waverly?" José Phelps asked.

Ngame gave the sunglasses a last critical look, then turned to face José and Frank. He smiled a mouthful of perfectly straight glistening teeth.

"This is America!" Ngame exploded with exuberance. *A-mare-uh-CUH!* "Business is *always* splendid!" A wave of his large hand took in the sidewalk. "One is free to sell and free to buy . . . buy and sell." He caressed a handbag. "This purse, for example —"

José pulled Ngame's string. "Mr. Gucci gets his cut?"

Ngame got the tired look of a long-suffering teacher with a slow student. "Detective Phelps! Do you suppose this is a real Gucci purse?" He swept a hand over the watches. "Or that these are real Rolexes?"

José's eyes widened. "They aren't?"

"And do you suppose that any of these good people who come to my stand *believe* they are buying real Guccis or real Rolexes?"

José opened his eyes wider.

Ngame spun up more. "And do you suppose that my customers could buy a *real* Rolex?"

"Oh?" José said, egging him on.

"So who is hurt?" Ngame was deep into it now, eyes wide in enthusiasm, hands held out shoulder-high, palms up. "Not Mister Gucci! Nor Mister Rolex! As a matter of fact, Mister Gucci and Mister Rolex ought to be pleased with me! Yes, pleased! My customers have learnt good taste here at my stand." Ngame's chin tilted up. "When they get wealthy, they'll buy the real Gucci and the real Rolex."

"Like Skeeter Hodges," Frank Kearney said.

Ngame gave Frank a heavy-lidded somber look. "He didn't buy here. He kept the real Mister Rolex in business."

"What's the talk?" José asked.

Ngame scanned the sidewalk. He did it casually, but he did it.

"Conjecture?" *Con-jec-TURE?*

Another glance, this time across the street. "The Puerto Ricans say it was the Jamaicans. The Jamaicans tell me it was the Puerto Ricans. And the American blacks" — Ngame shrugged — "they all point their fingers at one another."

"No names?" Frank asked.

Ngame shook his head. "No pretender to the throne. But then again, Detective Kearney, it was only last night."

Ngame paused a beat, then came up with a watch in his hand, gold-gleaming in the morning sun.

"A Rolex President? I will give a discount."

Solomon watched the two cops get in their car and leave. In the street the crow continued working on the dead rat.

"You watch yourself today, Waverly," he whispered, and swung his gaze along the alley, past Ngame's van, toward Thirty-first Street.

Motherfucker's runnin' late. Voice came up inside Solomon's head, peevish, accusing.

"He be along," Solomon told Voice, "he be along."

When?

As though on cue, tires squealed. A white Navigator roared in off Thirty-first. Sprays of gravel ricocheted off dumpsters. Partway down the alley the Navigator turned right and disappeared into the Hamilton Court garage.

"See?" Solomon whispered to Voice.

Moments later, Asad the Somali appeared, coming up the ramp carrying a large briefcase. A tall, thin man, he had a snaky, boneless way of moving. His tight-fitting yellow suit had a long jacket with five buttons and his skin was a light cocoa and his black hair lay slicked in thinning waves against his skull.

As usual, Asad's two goons flanked him. Gehdi and Nadif. Solomon had decided they were brothers. Maybe twins, whose orangutan mother had fallen out of an ugly tree.

Two weeks ago, Asad had come to Georgetown and leased a dingy storefront, paying cash. Solomon knew that storefront. A single window displayed garish men's clothes. The display had never changed. For years, players came and went. But he'd never seen any of them wearing those clothes. That shit only fools or Somalis would wear. Place never had sold anything legal. The Somali wasn't going to start now.

Asad didn't waste time setting up his network. He and his goons started with the street vendors. The vendors signed on to buy watches, sunglasses, and handbags from Asad. Asad gave his new partners discounts on the junk. C-phones came with the deal. In return, Asad got a cut on the profits and he would know what was going on in the streets. All the vendors had bought in except the Nigerian.

That first day, one of Solomon's carts had been sticking partway out into the alley. Gehdi misjudged his clearance and scraped the Navigator's fender.

Asad had stood there and watched with his hard black marble eyes while Gehdi and Nadif punched Solomon to the ground then kicked the shit out of him. They threw his carts out into the middle of Wisconsin Avenue. Things he'd collected, his precious things. The Nigerian had saved some, but the rest, his clippings, his notebooks, they'd been swept away with the street trash.

He'd been beaten before. But never in his alley. That they had done those things to him there shamed him. The alley had provided for him, and when danger came, he had been unable to defend the alley in return.

He gonna make the call?

"Sure he is." Voice didn't know its ass from apple butter sometimes.

Looking past Solomon and toward Ngame's stand, Asad reached into the briefcase and pulled out a fat c-phone/walkie-talkie. Flipping it open, he held it in front of his face.

Solomon saw Asad's lips move. A second or two passed and Solomon heard one crackling reply, then another.

"One more," he said to Voice.

Asad waited, holding the c-phone out from his face. Gehdi and Nadif swiveled their heads back and forth, searching the alley.

They expectin' Santy Claus?

A third crackle. Asad replied and stowed the c-phone away in the briefcase. He said something to the two goons and the three began walking toward Solomon.

They gonna hit you? Hurt you today?

Solomon got a tightness in his chest. How it had been came back to him like it had every day since.

Curled up on the alley bricks. Crying and slobbering and puking. Waiting for the goons to swing another steel-capped toe.

They had grunted with the effort and they had cursed Solomon because beating a man while he was down was hard work and it made them sweat and they blamed him for that.

He lowered his head and pretended to doze. Through slitted eyelids, he saw the shoes approach, then pass.

"Not today," he whispered to Voice. "Not today."

As soon as he thought it safe, he lifted his eyes and followed the three Somalis approaching Ngame's stand.

And along Wisconsin, the other vendors watched.

Ngame saw them cross Wisconsin. He turned and busied himself tightening a C-clamp. He started counting silently. At nine, he heard the sliding scuffle of shoe leather on the sidewalk behind him.

"I need a decision," he heard Asad say.

He didn't turn, but continued fiddling with the clamp.

"You got mine," he said. "I don't need a partner."

"Every businessman needs a partner. Suppose you get sick?"

"I am healthy."

A twisting, tearing at his shoulders, and his elbows were pinned behind him as he was spun around to face Asad.

Gehdi stood to Asad's right, and Nadif held him tight, the goon's sour breath on his neck.

"You may be healthy," Asad whispered, smiling, "but men have accidents."

Gehdi dropped his hand into his jacket pocket.

Ngame flexed his knees and sagged, loosening Nadif's grip. Then with a violent burst, he straightened up. He raised his heavy boot and brought it down with all his strength on the top of Nadif's foot. He felt bones grind as Nadif's arch collapsed.

Nadif was still screaming as Ngame swung his foot forward. His toe caught Gehdi in the crotch, lifting him off the pavement. Gehdi gasped. His hand flew out of his pocket. A switchblade clattered to the sidewalk.

Almost casually, Ngame clenched Asad's collar with one hand, twisting it tight around his neck. Stooping slightly, he scooped up Gehdi's switchblade. He held it up before Asad's bulging eyes. He pressed the release. Asad stared hypnotically as the silver blade flicked open. Ngame slammed Asad up against a lamppost and brought the blade against the Somali's throat just below the Adam's apple.

Gehdi lay curled on the sidewalk clutching his balls, and Nadif, sobbing, stood on his undamaged foot, hanging on to a parking meter.

In a swift motion, he pulled the blade away from Asad's throat, cocked his arm, and brought the knife forward in a stabbing motion.

Asad let out a high-pitched scream. The crotch of his trousers darkened.

A fraction of an inch from Asad's ear, Ngame drove the knife into the lamppost, snapping its blade.

"You're right," Ngame said to Asad in his best BBC voice, "men have accidents."

The rest of the morning, Solomon watched Ngame at his stand. The Nigerian went about his business as though nothing had happened. Asad and his goons had disappeared into the storefront. The other vendors in sight of Ngame's corner were careful not to be seen paying attention, but it seemed to Solomon they moved like men tiptoeing around a sleeping beast.

Around three o'clock, Solomon, eyes half-closed, was drowsing in his canvas deck chair. For seconds, he paid no attention to the car that pulled up to the curb by Ngame's stand, until the driver-side door opened and the black cop got out.

Oh shit, Voice said.

Solomon ignored Voice and sat up to get a better view of the cop and Ngame.

"You already find out who killed Skeeter?" Ngame asked.

José Phelps picked up a pair of Ray-Ban knockoffs and examined them. "Not yet."

"Those are ten dollars."

José put the shades back, taking care to line them up just so.

"Little while ago, we were over at Eastern Market," he said. "Buzz was, you had a run-in with Asad."

"News travels fast."

José didn't say anything but left the question on his face.

Ngame shrugged. "A discussion. A business proposition."

"You know," José threw in, "DEA's interested in him."

Ngame nudged the shades José had held. "That's good. I'm not."

"You ever thought to moving somewhere else?"

Ngame gave José a hard look. "I have been here almost ten years. I am somebody here."

José picked up the Ray-Ban knockoffs again. This time he tried them on. He leaned forward to check himself out in a small mirror hooked to the stand. He angled his face one way, then the other.

"Absolutely Hollywood," Ngame said.

José did another 180 in the mirror and handed over a ten. "You need anything . . ."

Toward evening the alley was getting dark. Solomon didn't need a watch to know Ngame would be closing up in an hour unless business was good. And today business hadn't been good. Not bad, but not good either. He saw Gehdi come out of Asad the Somali's store, stand in the doorway, and look down the block toward Ngame. Gehdi had a duffel bag slung over his shoulder. He stood there for a moment as though listening to a reply, then turned and said something to someone in the store. He shut the door and made his way across Wisconsin toward the alley. Solomon slouched in his canvas chair, pulled the American flag he used for a blanket up under his chin, and pretended to sleep.

Gehdi passed within a few feet of Solomon, and Solomon watched him disappear in the darkening alley toward the parking garage. Across the street, Ngame started disassembling his stand. Solomon began his night critique, judging how Ngame stowed the bulky handbags into the nylon sacks, taking care to dust each one carefully before putting it away.

Where Gehdi?

Voice surprised him. Feeling a flush of irritation and guilt, Solomon realized he hadn't been paying attention to his alley. If Gehdi was going to bring the Navigator around, why wasn't he out by now?

Minutes passed. Ngame was working on the last of the handbags. Solomon squinted down the alley, trying to pierce the deepening darkness.

What's that? Voice asked.

"What's what?"

That!

"You seeing shit," Solomon scolded, but even as he said it something moved, the slightest shift of black against the deeper black in the shadow of Ngame's van. And then nothing.

For a moment, stillness returned to the alley, then a figure crossed the sliver of light coming from between Old Glory and Johnny Rockets.

Paying no attention to Solomon, Gehdi walked by and returned to the store.

Solomon waited a moment or two, then slipped down the alley toward Ngame's van and the parking garage.

When he got back, Ngame was breaking down his stand, stacking the wire-grate shelving, and bagging the C-clamps. His merchandise was packed away in the nylon sacks and the blue plastic storage boxes.

Up the street, Asad came out, followed by Nadif. Nadif walked with a heavy limp. In one hand, an umbrella he used for a cane. His other cluched Gehdi's shoulder. Asad locked up, keyed the alarm, and the three made their way toward him.

Solomon smiled. One gimpy Somali. Man gonna remember this day, long as he live.

The three passed by him and soon headlights swept the alley as the Navigator came up the garage ramp. It stopped where the alley intersected Thirty-first, then took a right toward M Street and disappeared from view.

"Goodbye, Somalis," Solomon whispered. He got up, folded his flag carefully, and hung it over one of his Safeway carts. He crossed Wisconsin to stand guard over Ngame's goods while the Nigerian fetched his van.

It was 9:30 when Ngame slammed the doors of his van. He palmed Solomon their customary closing-of-the-day bill.

"This a twenty," Solomon said, offering it up.

Ngame waved it away. "We had a good day today."

"Business wasn't that good."

Ngame got into his van and started the engine. He leaned out the window and patted Solomon on the shoulder. "Business isn't all that makes a good day."

Canal Road runs northwest out of Georgetown along the Potomac River. Round a bend, the bright lights fade and it becomes a country road. After a mile, Waverly Ngame noticed headlights coming up behind him, speeding at first, then taking a position fifty yards or so behind and hanging in there. He checked his rearview. The lights behind him belonged to Asad's white Navigator.

And somebody in the passenger seat had an arm out the window, pointing something at him.

"Don't get so close," Asad said. "Drop back some."

Gehdi eased off the gas. He gave Asad a leer. "Fried Nigerian."

Asad laughed and pressed the button of the garage door opener. He imagined the sequence: the electronic command sent to the door opener's receiver, the receiver that would shoot thirty-six volts into the blasting cap, the blasting cap embedded in the quarter pound of C-4 plastic explosive that the magnet held to the gas tank of the Nigerian's van.

An hour later, José Phelps ducked under the police line tape.

Floodlights washed out color and turned the carnage two-dimensional: an axle with one wheel attached, its tire still smoldering, grotesque twists of metal strewn across the roadway and into the trees, a man's shoe obscenely lined up on the asphalt's center stripe, a portion of the owner's foot still in it.

Renfro Calkins huddled with two of his forensics techs at the far side of the road, looking into the drainage ditch.

José walked over. "ID?"

Calkins shook his head. "Gonna have to be DNA. All we gots is hamburger." He pointed into the ditch. "That's the largest."

José walked over and looked. It took him several seconds to make out the thing that had been an arm. "What's that in the hand?"

"Looks like a switch for a garage door. Best guess, these guys set off a bomb in their own vehicle."

"How'd they manage that?"

Calkins shrugged. "They not gonna tell you, José."

Gonna be a quiet day today.

Solomon looked down his alley, then across Wisconsin to where the Nigerian was setting up his stand.

"For once," he said to Voice, "you got your shit together."

PETER BLAUNER

Going, Going, Gone

FROM *Hard Boiled Brooklyn*

IT HAPPENS SO FAST. SUSSMAN ONLY TURNS his head for, *what,* maybe two seconds, to check out that hoochie mama in the low-slung ram-riders and the spaghetti-strand top and when he looks back, his six-year-old Ben is already on the Coney Island–bound F train and the shiny metal doors are closing between them.

Sussman pushes through the crowd of departing passengers, trying to pry the doors apart, but it's too late. The train is already starting to move. He runs alongside it, yelling *"STOP"* and gesturing wildly, as Ben stares through the scratchiettied glass in open-mouthed confusion.

But then the window slips past him, like a frame going through a film projector, and he almost collides with a pillar near the end of the platform. A seismic rumble fills the station and he sees the white F on the back of the train receding into darkness, going, going, gone, leaving him stranded.

He pictures his heart untethered from his body, falling through space but somehow still pulsing on its own.

The morning had begun on such a tremulous note of anticipation. This was supposed to be the day when he finally assumed his proper responsibilities and proved he wasn't such a schmuck after all. For the first time since the divorce, he'd managed to get away from work and set aside a full weekend for the kid. No phone calls from clients, no answering e-mails, just *quality* father-and-son time. Up until eleven on Friday night with a *Star Wars* DVD marathon (which, truth be told, he kept watching even after Ben fell asleep two-thirds of the way into *A New Hope*); field box seats from the corporate account at a Saturday afternoon Yankees game (half the innings spent at the souvenir stand, but that's what you get for taking a six-year-old), and dinner at Junior's (three-quarters of a strawberry cheesecake slice left uneaten).

But today was supposed to be the penultimate bonding experience, the maraschino cherry rescued from the bottom of the Shirley Temple glass: the long-awaited pilgrimage to Coney Island that Ben had been begging for. Sussman had been building it up for weeks, telling the kid about the trip he'd make to Astroland every summer with his father, who'd moved the family from Bay Ridge to Long Island back when he was seven. He'd told Ben about the Cyclone, the bumper cars, the shooting galleries in the midway, and of course, the Wonder Wheel. For some reason, the last attraction had meant the most to the kid; he woke up this morning to find Ben with his crayons in the kitchen, drawing a picture of a stick-figure man running after a spiny Ferris wheel as it rolled down a hill.

Now Sussman stands at the end of the platform, feeling a cold ripple of panic rise from the pit of his stomach. The murmur of the departed train still vibrates through the station.

The only thing that matters. I have lost the only thing that matters. His chest heaves and dread worms into his veins. He looks around — shouldn't there be a station manager on duty or a call box with a button you can push in case of emergencies? But it's still before noon on a Sunday morning in August and the place is desolate. He calls out, "Help," but his voice sounds thin and nasal echoing off the tiled walls. An old bag woman on the opposite platform, her jaw working like Popeye's from overmedication, glares at him furiously, as if she's seen everything that's just happened and knows he's at fault.

He starts to run, half-remembering a pay phone he'd once used way down at the other end of the platform for another hassled conversation with his ex. *Yes, I sent the check already. No, I can't take him next weekend . . .* What will she say about this time? *I knew it! I knew I couldn't leave him alone with you! You're such a fucking thoughtless asshole!* He grabs the phone's gummy yellow receiver, the rusted coil slithers, and then red and green wires spill from the chrome mainframe. Broken! Of course!

He drops the receiver in disgust and charges toward the stairs, blood throbbing in his ears. He pictures Ben alone on the train, a wan frightened child in a forest of strangers. Would he think to look for a policeman or another responsible adult? Who knew what his mother had taught him to do in an emergency? He was a fragile kid at the very best of times, and the divorce had shaken him badly. He'd cowered in his bedroom when his parents fought and had turned shy and withdrawn after the split; "a bully magnet" according to his kindergarten teachers, easily buffaloed away from the more popular toys. Sussman imagines a stranger taking the child's hand and leading him off the train at some unknown stop, saying Mommy and Daddy are waiting for him there. He leaps up the steps two at a time, the slap of concrete on the bottom of his loafers stinging the soles of his feet.

You're taking your son for the weekend? One of the other guys in sales gawked at him Friday afternoon. *Jesus, I never even knew you'd spawned.*

He stops a second on the landing to catch his breath, his belt buckle digging into a flabby roll. He's terribly out of shape these days, from eating junk food on the road and skipping the gym for weeks on end. *You think somebody's going to give you their account because you're the most relaxed rep they've ever met?* he'd asked one of the newbies just last week. He swallows and sees the token booth a football field and a half away. *No awards for the best excuse. He who hesitates is lunch.* He makes another run for it, his lungs already straining, his knees audibly squeaking. He realizes he's become the stick figure from Ben's drawing, chasing the giant wheel rolling down the hill. He lifts his thighs and digs for all he's worth. The future has narrowed to this barren gray stretch of concrete from here to the token booth.

But when he gets there the booth is empty. A small beige bag blocks the trench under the glass. For a second, he sees himself like Willem Dafoe on the poster for *Platoon,* falling to his knees as an enemy's bullet rips into his chest.

No. He doesn't even have the luxury of despair. Every wasted second holds the potential for disaster. What's the next stop on the train? His eyes find the map on the wall and start desperately searching for the right artery through Brooklyn. Up until this second, he's never bothered to study other routes besides the ones that take him back and forth to Manhattan.

The wilderness. Though he was born here and has been renting an apartment in Windsor Terrace for two years since the breakup, this borough is still the unexplored wilderness to him. Threatening swatches of Fort Greene and Williamsburg have only been glimpsed fleetingly through car service windows coming home from work late at night. He sees the train cuts through Borough Park and pictures mirthless bearded Hasidim glowering down at his boy. The stops have unfamiliar names like Church Avenue, Ditmas, Kings Highway. He sees "Avenue X," and somehow the starkness of those black letters on the bland beige background strikes terror into his heart.

He runs up the stairs for the street, drenched in sweat, his arteries beginning to constrict.

But the world above ground is oblivious. Just minding its own business and acting like this is just another peaceful Sunday morning on Fifteenth Street, by the park. The sidewalks are empty. Birds sing in the trees. Copies of the Sunday *New York Times* sheathed in blue plastic lie undisturbed on the doorsteps of prim Victorian-looking brownstones and limestones. How can the people upstairs still be sleeping, or having drowsy rollover sex, or scratching their butts on the way to the bathroom with a hangover, when his whole life is falling apart? How can they be so *complacent*?

He reaches for his cell phone but knows before his hand even touches his pocket that the thing is still sitting on the bedside table, where he'd deliberately left it this morning, so for once he wouldn't be answering calls about work instead of spending time with his son. He imagines it, blinking dumbly, its battery life slowly ebbing away. *Fuck.* Now he can't even call 911. Shouldn't there be one of those old-fashioned red fire department call boxes on this street? This is a nightmare in broad daylight. This is the beginning of a tragic story in the newspaper. He keeps seeing Ben's stunned little face pulling away from him. His heart squeezes and he feels a dull pain beginning in his left shoulder.

The wheel is rolling down the hill faster, picking up momentum. *Blame.* There must be someone else to blame. It can't *all* be his fault. At work, he's always had a talent for handling pressure and delivering in the clutch, but this is too much for anyone to carry. He pictures Ben surrounded by a roaming wolf pack on the train, a bunch of dead-eyed little thugs demanding the brand-new Game Boy Advance he had with him.

"Somebody help mee," his voice jiggles as he pounds on down the sidewalk, heading for Eighth Avenue, looking for someone, *anyone,* to make a call for him and stop the trains.

He sees a doughy-looking woman, gray hair sticking out from under a Yankees cap, on her way to the park with a saggy-faced mastiff on a leash.

"Cell phone?" he calls out to her.

She looks at him blankly. The pitch. He has to make a pitch to her, to sell her his terrible need.

"Ex*cuse me.*" He holds his hands out, beseeching. "Do you have a cell phone I could borrow? I'm having an emergency. My child is missing."

She tugs down on the bill of her cap, not meeting his eye as she starts to pass, a time-honored urban tradition for dealing with street crazies.

"Stupid bitch!"

A part of him is appalled, *he doesn't say this sort of thing,* but he can't stop himself. The wheel is spinning out of control. His whole life is on the brink of nullity, of meaninglessness, of total annihilation.

He sees one brownstone without a *Times* on its doorstep and decides the people inside must be awake. Maybe they even have children of their own. He runs up the stoop and starts ringing their buzzer.

"Hello?" A groggy female voice comes out of the intercom.

Automatically, he finds himself trying to picture her, like he's making a sales call. He sees a woman no longer young, not nearly old, on her first cup of coffee of the day. The type he could trap on the phone back when he was in telemarketing. He sees her in a flannel bathrobe, trying to make pancakes, moving around the kitchen with a three-year-old clinging to her leg like a little koala bear.

"Hi," he says, trying to modulate and sound reasonable. "I'm sorry to be bothering you. Something terrible has happened. I lost my child on the subway and I need to call 911."

"Oh."

For a moment, time stands still and the wheel stops turning, leaving him suspended at the top of the arc, rocking in the breeze. Everything depends on that one syllable. He tells himself that only someone who's known the joy and pain of childbirth could say "oh" in just exactly that way. Only someone who's stayed up at a feverish child's bedside until the bleak morning hours, with a damp washcloth and a dropper full of Children's Tylenol could draw the word out just so. Only someone who's filled a bathroom with shower steam at three A.M. for a croupy cough could be this empathetic. She understands. She knows he's telling the truth. He's going to close the deal with her. People are good. People are compassionate. This is a borough of neighbors, not a chilly collection of anonymous souls piled on top of each other in teetering stacks like Manhattan.

So he waits. And waits. Surely, she'll come back. But then he notices the tightness has moved down his shoulder to his arm now. Where'd she go?

"Hello?" He presses the talk button, knowing she couldn't have forgotten about him. "Are you still there?"

He can almost feel a waft of cool air issuing through the speaker holes.

"For God's sakes, at least make the call for me," he pleads, trying to get her back. "Tell them there's a little boy lost on the Coney Island F train . . ."

He's wasting his time, he realizes. The deal is off. She doesn't believe him either. No one could be that irresponsible, that criminally negligent, to just leave a child on a train, could they?

He runs for the corner, remembering a bodega there, one of those cramped little twenty-four-hour groceries, where cats chase mice around the produce and disenfranchised men hang around the pay phone outside. The dull pain in his shoulder has become a kind of tourniquet-like tightness. The only thing that matters. I have lost the only thing that matters. All the world could die now and he wouldn't care.

He arrives, gasping for breath, his thighs in flames from rubbing together. But somebody is already at the phone. A trim young man upholstered with muscles, wearing a white silky do-rag and a gold capped tooth that makes him look a little like a pirate. And with him, a girl. But not just any girl. A little sex grenade in a skimpy top and jeans low enough to reveal the jut of her hipbones. The very girl, Sussman realizes, with a sickening clench, he was ogling when Ben got on the train without him.

"Yeah, yeah, but what happened to my tape, son?" The pirate is ranting. "That was my tape, yo . . . Don't be playing me cheap . . ."

It's a performance — Sussman sees that right away. The boy is displaying his plumage, showing the girl that he is tough, a defender of his own rights, a man not to be trifled with.

"I'm a kick his ass, he tries to bite me. I'm serious, dawg . . ."

"Excuse me." Sussman stands before him, gulping, still trying to catch his breath. "I need to use that phone."

"What do you mean, you'll get back to me?" The pirate ignores him. "When does my copyright run out?"

How can anyone be so blindly selfish, Sussman asks himself, so wrapped up in themselves? How can anybody be so unaware there are other people in the world, going through their own private dramas? How can he just automatically assume that his needs are paramount and more urgent than anyone else's?

"I need that phone. *My son is missing.*"

"Say it again, man." The boy turns his back. "Some asshole was trying to talk to me."

Sussman stares at a spot between his shoulder blades, not quite believing what he's just heard.

Force of will, he tells himself. Nothing gets accomplished in this world, without force of will. He sees that every day in sales. Some people just won't move or react until you start to push.

Before he knows what he's doing, Sussman finds himself reaching over the boy's shoulder and pushing down on the pay phone's hook.

"What the fuck?" The boy spins around.

Sussman sees the girl flinch as the boy's gold tooth catches a glint of sun and he knows he's gone too far.

The gray receiver slams into the side of his head. His brain rings as he staggers sideways from the blow. But within the pain, there's something small, hard, and rightful. He knows this is what he deserves.

He clutches at the boy's forearm, to try to keep from falling, but it's too late. His muscles have lost their organizing principle. The back of his head hits the sidewalk. A flashbulb explodes inside his skull.

And in the fading light of the dying filament, he sees Ben alone on the train, drawing that picture of that stick-figure man chasing the wheel, as the Wonder Wheel looms into view against the gray ocean backdrop. It's over now. He's tried, given it everything he had, but he never got ahead of that wheel. It just kept spinning faster and faster, so that he could never catch up with it. And if the boy somehow survives this, his father wonders if he'll just end up chasing the same thing.

AVOID HEAD-ON COLLISIONS.

"Hi, Mrs. Sussman, you don't know me, but I have your son."

The woman in dreadlocks and flip-flops is talking on a cell phone while keeping an eye on the two small boys as they steer toward each other with the bumper cars, blatantly ignoring the safety sign on the wall.

"Yes, he's fine. I just gave him a hot dog and put him on one of the rides. He gave me your number and asked me to call. Apparently, he got separated from your husband on the train."

She watches the cars crash head-on as the kids jerk back convulsing with laughter.

"Well, I don't exactly know how it happened, but your boy's a real trooper," she says, holding the phone away from her ear a little as the voice on the other end turns sharp. "Some hairy puke started to bother him on the train so he got up and sat next to me because he saw I had a kid. There's grown men don't have that much sense."

The cars skitter and thump across the scuffed floor, barging heedlessly into one another's paths and slamming their front ends together again with joyful abandon.

"Don't worry about it, I'll keep him with me until you get here," she says. "The only thing is, he doesn't know what happened to his father. Maybe you ought to send somebody out to look for him."

LAWRENCE BLOCK

Keller's Double Dribble

FROM *Murder at the Foul Line*

KELLER, HIS HANDS IN HIS POCKETS, watched a dark-skinned black man with his shirt off drive for the basket. His shaved head gleamed, and the muscles of his upper back, the traps and lats, bulged as if steroidally enhanced. Another man, wearing a T-shirt but otherwise of the same shade and physique, leaped to block the shot, and the two bodies met in midair. It was a little like ballet, Keller thought, and a little like combat, and the ball kissed off the backboard and dropped through the hoop.

There was no net, just a bare hoop. The playground was at the corner of Sixth Avenue and West Third Street, in Greenwich Village, and Keller was one of a handful of spectators standing outside the high chainlink fence, watching idly as ten men, half wearing T-shirts, half bare-chested, played a fiercely competitive game of half-court basketball.

If this were a game at the Garden, the last play would have sent someone to the free-throw line. But there was no ref here to call fouls, and order was maintained in a simpler fashion: anyone who fouled too frequently was thrown out of the game. It was, Keller felt, an interesting libertarian solution, and he thought it might be worth a try outside the basketball court, but had a feeling it would be tough to make it work.

Keller watched a few more plays, feeling his spirits sink as he did, yet finding it oddly difficult to tear himself away. He'd had a tooth drilled and filled a few blocks away, by a dentist who had himself played varsity basketball years ago at the University of Kentucky, and had been walking around waiting for the Novocain to wear off so he could grab some lunch, and the basketball game had caught his eye, and here he was. Watching, and being brought down in the process, because basketball always depressed him.

His mouth wasn't numb anymore. He crossed the street, walked two blocks east, turned right on Sullivan Street, left on Bleecker. He considered and rejected restaurants as he walked, knowing he wanted something spicy. If basketball depressed him, highly seasoned food put him right again. He thought it odd, didn't understand it, but knew it worked.

The restaurant he found was Indian, and Keller made sure the waiter got the message. "You tone things down for Westerners," he told the man. "I only look like an American of European ancestry. Inside, I am a man from Sri Lanka."

"You want spicy," the waiter said.

"I want very spicy," Keller said. "And then some."

The little man beamed. "You wish to sweat."

"I wish to suffer."

"Leave it to me," the little man said.

The meal was almost too hot to eat. It was nominally a lamb curry, but its ingredients might have been anything. Lamb, beef, dog, duck. Tofu, shoe leather, balsawood. Papier-mâché? Plaster of Paris? The searing heat of the cayenne obscured everything else. Keller, forcing himself to finish every bite, loved and hated every minute of it. By the time he was done he was drenched in perspiration and felt as if he'd just gone ten rounds with a worthy opponent. He felt, too, a sense of accomplishment and an abiding sense of peace with the world.

Something made him call home to check his answering machine. Two hours later he was on the front porch of the big old house on Taunton Place, sipping a glass of iced tea. Three days after that he was in Indiana.

At the Avis desk at Indy International, Keller turned in the Chevy he'd driven from New York. At the Hertz counter, he picked up the keys to the Ford he'd reserved. He carried his bag to the car, left it in short-term parking, and went back into the airport, remembering to take his bag with him. There was a fellow waiting at baggage claim, wearing the green and gold John Deere cap they'd said he'd be wearing.

"Oh, there you are," the fellow said when Keller approached him. "The bags are just starting to come down."

Keller brandished his carryon, said he hadn't checked anything.

"Then I guess you didn't bring a nail clipper," the man said, "or a Swiss Army knife. Never mind a bazooka."

Keller had a Swiss Army knife in his carryon and a nail clipper in his pocket, attached to his key ring. Since he hadn't flown any-where, he'd had no problem. As for the other, well, he had never minded a bazooka in his life, and saw no reason to start now.

"Now let's get you squared away," the man said. He was around forty, and lean, except for an incongruous potbelly, as if he'd swal-lowed a small watermelon. "Quick orientation, drive you around, show you where he lives. We'll take my car, and when we're done, you can drop me off and keep it."

The airport was at the southwest corner of Indianapolis, and the man (who'd flipped the John Deere cap into the back seat of his Hyundai squareback, alongside Keller's carryon) drove to Carmel, an upscale suburb north of the I-465 beltway. He made a few efforts at conversation, which Keller let wither on the vine, whereupon he gave up and switched on the radio. He kept it tuned to an all-talk station, and right now two opinionated fellows were arguing about the outsourcing of jobs.

Keller thought about turning it off. You're a hit man, brought in at great expense from out of town, and some gofer picks you up and plays the radio, and you turn it off, what's he gonna do? Be im-pressed and a little intimidated, he thought, but decided it wasn't worth the trouble.

The driver killed the radio himself when they left the inter-state and drove through the tree-lined streets of Carmel. Keller paid close attention now, noting street names and landmarks and taking a good look at the house that was pointed out to him. It was a Dutch Colonial with a mansard roof, he noted, and that tugged at his memory until he remembered a real estate agent in Roseburg, Oregon, who'd shown him through a similar house years ago. Keller had wanted to buy it, to move there. For a few days, anyway, until he came to his senses.

When they were done, the man asked him if there was anything else he wanted to see, and Keller said there wasn't. "Then I'll drive you to my house," the man said, "and you can drop me off."

Keller shook his head. "Drop me at the airport," he said.

"Oh, Jesus," the man said. "Is something wrong? Did I say the wrong thing?"

Keller looked at him.

"'Cause if you're backing out, I'm gonna get blamed for it. They'll have a goddamn fit. Is it the location? Because, you know, it doesn't have to be at his house. It could be anywhere."

Oh. Keller explained that he didn't want to use the Hyundai, that he'd pick up a car at the airport. He preferred it that way, he said.

Driving back to the airport, the man obviously wanted to ask why Keller wanted his own car, and just as obviously was afraid to say a word. Nor did he play the radio. The silence was a heavy one, but that was okay with Keller.

When they got there, the fellow said he supposed Keller wanted to rent a car. Keller shook his head and directed him to the lot where he'd already stowed the Ford. "Keep going," he said. "Maybe that one . . . no, that's the one I want. Stop here."

"What are you gonna do?"

"Borrow a car," Keller said.

He'd added the key to his key ring, and now he stood alongside the car and made a show of flipping through keys, finally selecting the one they'd given him. He tried it in the door and, unsurprisingly, it worked. He tried it in the ignition, and it worked there, too. He switched off the ignition and went back to the Hyundai for his carryon, where the driver, wide-eyed, asked him if he was really going to steal that car.

"I'm just borrowing it," he said.

"But if the owner reports it —"

"I'll be done with it by then." He smiled. "Relax. I do this all the time."

The fellow started to say something, then changed his mind. "Well," he said instead. "Look, do you want a piece?"

Was the man offering him a woman? Or, God forbid, offering to supply sexual favors personally? Keller frowned and then realized the piece in question was a gun. Keller, relieved, shook his head and said he had everything he needed in his carryon. Amazing the damage you could inflict with a Swiss Army knife and a nail clipper.

"Well," the man said again. "Well, here's something." He reached into his breast pocket and came out with a pair of tickets. "To the Pacers game," he said. "They're playing the Knicks, so I guess you'll be rooting for your homies, huh? Tonight, eight sharp. They're not courtside, but they're damn good seats. You want, I could dig up somebody to go with you, keep you company."

Keller said he'd take care of that himself, and the man didn't seem surprised to hear it.

"He's a witness," Dot had said, "but apparently nobody's thought of sticking him in the Federal Witness Protection Program, but maybe that's because the situation's not federal. Do you have to be involved in a federal case in order to be protected by the federal government?"

Keller wasn't sure, and Dot said it didn't really matter. What mattered was that the witness wasn't in the program, and wasn't hidden at all, and that made it a job for Keller, because the client really didn't want the witness to stand up and testify.

"Or sit down and testify," she said, "which is what they usually do, at least on the television programs I watch. The lawyers stand up, and even walk around some, but the witnesses just sit there."

"What did he witness, do you happen to know?"

"You know," she said, "they were pretty vague on that point. The guy I talked to wasn't a principal. He was more like a booking agent. I've worked with him before, when his clients were O.C. guys."

"Huh?"

"Organized crime. So he's connected, but this isn't O.C., and my sense is it's not violent."

"But it's going to get that way."

"Well, you're not going all the way to Indiana to talk sense into him, are you? What he witnessed, I think it was like corporate shenanigans. What's the matter?"

"'Shenanigans,'" he said.

"It's a perfectly good word. What's the matter with 'shenanigans'?"

"I just didn't think anybody said it anymore," he said. "That's all."

"Well, maybe they should. God knows they've got occasion to."

"If it's corporate fiddle-faddle," he began, and stopped when she held up a hand.

"'Fiddle-faddle'? This from a man who has a problem with 'shenanigans'?"

"If it's that sort of thing," he said, "then it actually could be federal, couldn't it?"

"I suppose so."

"But he's not in the witness program because they don't think he's in danger."

She nodded. "Stands to reason."

"So they probably haven't assigned people to guard him," he said, "and he's probably not taking precautions."

"Probably not."

"Should be easy."

"It should," she agreed. "So why are you disappointed?"

"Disappointed?"

"That's the vibe I'm getting. Are you picking up on something? Like it's really going to be a lot more complicated than it sounds?"

He shook his head. "I think it's going to be easy," he said, "and I hope it is, and I'm not picking up any vibe. And I certainly didn't mean to sound disappointed, because I don't feel disappointed. I can use the money, and besides that, I can use the work. I don't want to go stale."

"So there's no problem."

"No. As far as your vibe is concerned, well, I spent the morning at the dentist."

"Say no more. That's enough to depress anybody."

"It wasn't, really. But then I was watching some guys play basketball. The Indian food helped, but the mood lingered."

"You're just one big nonsequitur, aren't you, Keller?" She held up a hand. "No, don't explain. You'll go to Indianapolis, you lucky man, and your actions will get to speak for themselves."

Keller's motel was a Rodeway Inn at the junction of Interstates 465 and 69, close enough to Carmel but not too close. He signed in with a name that matched his credit card and made up a license plate number for the registration card. In his room, he ran the channels on the TV, then switched off the set. He took a shower, got dressed, turned the TV on, turned it off again.

Then he went to the car and found his way to the Conseco Fieldhouse, where the Indiana Pacers were playing host to the New York Knicks.

The stadium was in the center of the city, but the signage made it easy to get there. A man in a porkpie hat asked him in an undertone if he had any extra tickets, and Keller realized that he did. He took a good look at his tickets for the first time and saw that he had a pair of $96 seats in section 117, wherever that was. He could sell one, but wouldn't that be awkward if the man he sold it to sat beside him? He'd probably be a talker, and Keller didn't want that.

But a moment's observation clarified the situation. The man in the porkpie hat — who had, Keller noted, a face straight out of an OTB parlor, a coulda-woulda-shoulda gambler's face — was doing a little business, buying tickets from people who had too many, selling them to people who had too few. So he wouldn't be sitting next to Keller. Someone else would, but it would be someone he hadn't met, so it would be easy to keep an intimacy barrier in place.

Keller went up to the man in the hat, showed him one of the tickets. The man said, "Fifty bucks," and Keller pointed out that it was a $96 ticket. The man gave him a look, and Keller took the ticket back.

"Jesus," the man said. "What do you want for it, anyway?"

"Eighty five," Keller said, picking the number out of the air.

"That's crazy."

"The Pacers and the Knicks? Section 117? I bet I can find somebody who wants it eighty-five dollars' worth."

They settled on $75, and Keller pocketed the money and used his other ticket to enter the arena. Then it struck him that he could have unloaded both tickets and had $150 to show for it, and gone straight home, spared the ordeal of a basketball game. But he was already through the turnstile when the thought came to him, and by that point he no longer had a ticket to sell.

He found his seat and sat down to watch the game.

Keller, an only child, was raised by his mother, who he had come to realize in later years was probably mentally ill. He never suspected this at the time, although he was aware that she was different from other people.

She kept a picture of Keller's father in a frame in the living room. The photograph showed a young man in a military uniform, and Keller grew up knowing that his father had been a soldier, a casualty of the war. As a teenager, he'd been employed cleaning out a stockroom, and one of the boxes of obsolete merchandise he'd hauled out had contained picture frames, half of them containing the familiar photograph of his putative father.

It occurred to him that he ought to mention this to his mother. On further thought, he decided not to say anything. He went home and looked at the photo and wondered who his father was. A soldier, he decided, though not this one. Someone passing through, who'd fathered a son and never knew it.

And died in battle? Well, a lot of soldiers did. His father might very well have been one of them.

Growing up in a fatherless home with a mother who didn't seem to have any friends or acquaintances was something Keller had been on the point of addressing in therapy, until a problem with his therapist put an end to that experiment. He'd had trouble deciding just how he felt about his mother, but had ultimately come to the conclusion that she was a good woman who'd done a good job of raising him, given her limitations. She was a serviceable cook if not an imaginative one, and he had a hot breakfast every morning and a hot dinner every night. She kept their house clean and taught Keller to be clean about his person. She was detached, and talked more to herself than to him — and, in the afternoons, talked to the characters in her TV soap operas.

She bought him presents at Christmas and on his birthday, usually clothing to replace garments he'd outgrown, but occasionally something more interesting. One year she bought him an Erector set, and he'd proved quite hopeless at following the diagrams in an effort to produce a flatbed railcar or, indeed, anything else. Another year's present was a beginner's stamp collecting kit — a stamp album, a packet of stamps, a pair of tongs to pick them up with, and a supply of hinges for mounting them in the album. The Erector set wound up in the closet, gathering dust, but the stamp album turned out to be the foundation of a lifelong hobby. He'd abandoned it after high school, of course, and the original album was long gone, but Keller had taken up the hobby again as an adult and cheerfully poured much of his spare time and extra cash into it.

Would he have become a stamp collector if not for his mother's gift? Possibly, he thought, but probably not. It was one more reason to thank her.

The Erector set was a good thought that failed, the stamp album an inspiration. The biggest surprise, though, of all the gifts she gave him was neither of these.

That would have to be the basketball backboard.

Keller hadn't bothered to note the seat number of the ticket he sold to the man in the porkpie hat. His own seat was 117, situated unsurprisingly enough between seats 116 and 118, both of them unoccupied when he sat down between them. Then two men came along and sat down in 115 and 116. One was substantially older than the other, and Keller found himself wondering if they were fa- ther and son, boss and employee, uncle and nephew, or gay lovers. He didn't really care, but he couldn't keep from wondering, and he kept changing his mind.

The game had already started by the time a man turned up and sat down in 118. He was wearing a dark suit with a subtle pinstripe and looked as though he'd come straight from the office, an office where he spent his days doing something no one, least of all the man himself, would describe as interesting.

The man in the porkpie hat had paid Keller $75 for that seat, which suggested that the man in the suit must have paid at least $100 for it, and perhaps as much as $125. But, of course, the fellow had no idea that Keller was the source of his ticket, and in fact paid no attention to Keller, devoting the full measure of his attention to the action on the court, where the Pacers had jumped off to an early lead.

Keller, with some reluctance, turned his attention to the game.

Across the street and two doors up from Keller's house, a family named Breitbart filled a large frame house to overflowing. Mr. Breitbart owned and ran a furniture store on Euclid Avenue, and Mrs. Breitbart stayed home and, for a while at least, had a baby every year. The year Keller was born she gave birth to two — twin sons, Andrew and Randall, the names no doubt selected so that their nicknames could rhyme. The twins were the family's only boys; the other five little Breitbarts, some older than the twins, the rest younger, were all girls.

Every afternoon, weather permitting, boys gathered in the Breitbart backyard to play basketball. Sometimes they divided into teams, and one side took off their shirts, and they played the sort of half-court game you could play with a single garage-mounted back-board. Other times, when fewer boys showed up or for some other reason, they found other ways to compete — playing Horse, say, where each player had to duplicate the particular shot of the first player. There were other games as well, but Keller, watching idly from across the street, was less clear on their rules and objectives.

One night at dinner, Keller's mother told him he should go across the street and join the game. "You watch all the time," she said — inaccurately, as he only occasionally let himself loll on the sidewalk watching the action in the Breitbart yard. "I bet they'd love it if you joined in. I bet you'd be good at it."

As it turned out, she lost both bets.

Keller, a quiet boy, always felt more at ease with grownups than with his contemporaries. On his own, he moved with an easy grace; in group sports, self-consciousness turned him awkward and made him ill at ease. Nonetheless, later that week he crossed the street and presented himself in the Breitbart backyard. "It's Keller," Andy or Randy said. "From across the street." Someone tossed him the ball, and he bounced it twice and tossed it unsuccessfully at the basket.

They chose up sides, and he, the unknown quantity, was picked last, which struck him as reasonable enough. He was on the Skins team, and shucked his shirt, which made him feel a little self-conscious, but that was nothing compared to the self-consciousness that ensued when the game began.

Because he didn't know how to play. He was ineffectual at guarding, and more obviously inept when someone tossed him the ball and he didn't know what to do with it. "Shoot," someone yelled, and he shot and missed. "Here, here!" someone called out, and his pass was intercepted. He just didn't know what he was doing, and before long his teammates figured out as much and stopped passing him the ball.

After fifteen or twenty minutes, the Shirts were a little more than halfway to the number of points that would end the game when a boy a grade ahead of Keller showed up. "Hey, it's Lassman," Randy or Andy said. "Lassman, take over for Keller."

And just like that, Lassman, suddenly shirtless, was in and Keller was out. This, too, struck him as reasonable enough. He went to the sidelines and put his shirt on, relief and disappointment settling over him in equal parts. For a few minutes, he stood there watching the others play, and relief faded while disappointment swelled. Well, I better be getting home now, he planned to say, and he rehearsed the line, rephrasing it in his mind, giving it different inflections. But nobody was paying any attention to him, so why say anything? He turned around and went home.

When his mother asked him about it, he said it had turned out okay, but he wouldn't be going over there anymore. They had regular teams, he said, and he didn't really fit in. She looked at him for a moment, then let it go.

A few days later he came home from school to see two workmen mounting a backboard and basket on the Keller garage. At dinner he wanted to ask her about it, but didn't know how to start. She didn't say anything either at first, and years later, when he heard the expression "the elephant in the living room that nobody talks about," he thought of that basketball backboard.

But then she did talk about it. "I thought it would be good to have," she said. "You can go out there and practice anytime you want, and the other boys will see you there and come over and play."

She was half right. He practiced, dribbling, driving toward the basket, trying set shots and jump shots and hook shots from different angles. He paced off a foul line and practiced foul shots. If practice didn't make perfect, it certainly didn't hurt. He got better.

And the other boys saw him there, she was right about that, too. But nobody ever came over to play, and before long he stopped going out there himself. Then he got an after-school job, and he put the basketball in the garage and forgot about it.

The backboard stayed where it was, securely mounted on the garage. It was the elephant in the driveway that nobody talked about.

The Pacers won in overtime, in what Keller supposed was an exciting game, although it didn't excite him much. He didn't care who won, and found his attention drifting throughout, even at the game's most crucial moments. The fact that the visiting team was the New York Knicks didn't make any difference to him. He didn't follow basketball, and his devotion to the city of New York didn't make him a partisan follower of the city's sports teams.

Except for the Yankees. He liked the Yankees and enjoyed it when they won. But he didn't eat his heart out when on rare occasions they lost. As far as he was concerned, getting upset over the outcome of a sports event was like getting depressed when a movie had a sad ending. I mean, get a grip, man. It's only a movie, it's only a ball game.

He walked to his car, which was where he'd parked it, and drove to his motel, which was where he'd left it. He was $75 richer than he'd been a few hours ago, and his only regret was that he hadn't thought to sell both tickets. And skip the game.

Grondahl had a backboard in his driveway.

That was the target's name, Meredith Grondahl, and when Keller had first seen it, before Dot showed him the photograph, he'd supposed it was a woman. He'd even said, "A woman?" and Dot had asked him if he'd become a sexist overnight. "You've done women before," she reminded him. "You've always been an equal-opportunity kind of guy. But all that's beside the point, because this particular Meredith is a man."

What, he'd wondered, did Meredith's friends call him for short? Merry? Probably not, Keller decided. If he had a nickname, it was probably Bud or Mac or Bubba.

Grondahl, he figured, meant *green valley* in whatever Scandinavian language Meredith's forebears had spoken. So maybe the guy's friends called him Greenie.

Or maybe not.

The backboard, which Keller saw on a drive-by the morning after the basketball game, was freestanding, mounted on a post just a couple of feet in front of the garage. It was a two-car garage, and the post was positioned so that it didn't block access to either side.

The garage door was closed, so Keller couldn't tell how many cars it held at the moment. Nor was anybody shooting baskets in the driveway. Keller drove off picturing Grondahl playing a solitary game, dribbling, shooting, all the while considering how his testimony might expose corporate shenanigans, making of basketball a meditative experience.

You could get a lot of thinking done that way. Provided you were alone and didn't have to break your concentration by interacting with somebody else.

South and east of downtown Indianapolis, tucked into a shopping mall, Keller found a stamp dealer named Hubert Haas. He'd done business with the man in the past, when he'd managed to outbid other collectors for lots Haas offered on eBay. So the name rang a bell when he came across it in the yellow pages.

He'd brought his Scott catalog, which he used as a checklist, so he could be sure he wasn't buying stamps he already owned. Haas, a plump and owlish young man who looked as though his chief exercise consisted of driving past a health club, was happy to show Keller his stock. He did almost all of his business online, he confided, and hardly ever had a real customer in the shop, so this was a treat for him.

So why pay rent? Why not work out of his house?

"Buying," Haas said. "I've got a presence in a high-traffic mall. That keeps the noncollectors aware of me. Uncle Fred dies, they inherit his stamp collection, who do they bring it to? Somebody they heard of, and they not only heard of Hubert Haas, they know he's for real, because he's got a store in the Glendale Mall to prove it. And then there's the walk-in who buys a starter album for his kid, the collector who runs out of hinges or Showgard mounts or needs to replace a lost pair of tongs. Helps with the rent, but buying's the real reason."

Keller found a comforting quantity of stamps to buy from Haas, including an inexpensive but curiously elusive set of Venezuelan airmails. He walked out imbued with a sense of accomplishment and took a few minutes to walk around the mall, to see what further accomplishments might be there for the taking.

The mall had the sort of stores malls usually have, and he found it easy enough to scan their window displays and walk on by. Until he came to the library.

Who had ever heard of a public library in a shopping mall? But that's what this was, occupying substantial space on the second and third levels, and complete with a turnstile and, yes, a metal detector, its purpose unapparent to Keller. Was there a problem of folks toting guns in hollowed-out books?

No matter. Keller wasn't carrying a gun or anything metallic but a handful of coins and his car keys. He entered without raising any alarms, and ten minutes later he was scanning back issues of the *Indianapolis Star,* learning all manner of things about Meredith Grondahl.

"It's pretty interesting," he told Dot. "There's this company called Central Indiana Finance. They buy and sell mortgages and do a lot of refinancing. The stock's traded on Nasdaq. The symbol is CIFI, but when people talk about it, they refer to it as Indy Fi."

"If that's interesting," she said, "I'd hate to hear your idea of a real yawner."

"That's not the interesting part."

"No kidding."

"The stock's very volatile," he said. "It pays a high dividend, which makes it attractive to investors, but it could be vulnerable to changes in interest rates, which makes it speculative, I guess. And a couple of hedge funds have shorted the stock heavily, along with a lot of private traders."

"Let me know when we get to the interesting part, will you, Keller?"

"Well, it's all kind of interesting," he said. "You walk around in a shopping mall, you don't expect to find out this stuff."

"Here I am, finding it out without even leaving the house."

"There's this class-action suit," he said. "Brought on behalf of the Indy Fi stockholders, though probably ninety-nine percent of them are opposed to the whole idea of the suit. The suit charges the company's management with irregularities and cover-ups, that sort of thing. It's the people who shorted the stock who are behind the suit, the hedge fund guys, and their whole reason for bringing it seems to be to destroy confidence in the company and further depress the price of the stock."

"Can they do that?"

"Anybody can sue anybody. All they risk, really, is their legal expenses and having the suit get tossed out of court. Meanwhile the company has to defend the suit, and the controversy keeps the stock price depressed, and even if the suit gets settled in the company's favor, the short interests will have had a chance to make money."

"I don't really care about any of this," Dot said, "but I have to admit you're starting to get me interested, although I couldn't tell you why. And our quarry's going to testify for the people bringing the suit?"

"No."

"No?"

"They subpoenaed him," he said. "Meredith Grondahl. He's an assistant to the chief financial officer, and he's supposed to testify about irregularities in their accounting procedures, but he's no whistleblower. He's more of a cheerleader. As far as he's concerned, Indy Fi's a great company, and his personal 401(k) is full of the company's stock. He can't really damage either side in the suit."

"Then why would somebody decide to summon you to Indianapolis?"

"That's what I've been wondering."

He thought the connection might have broken, but she was just taking her time thinking it over. "Well," she said at length, "even though this gets us interested, Keller, we're also disinterested, if you get my drift."

"It doesn't change things."

"That's my drift, all right. We've got an assignment and the fee's half paid already, so the whys and wherefores don't make any difference. Somebody doesn't want the guy to testify about something, and as soon as you nail that down, you can come on home and play with your stamps. You bought some today, didn't you tell me that earlier? So come on home and you can paste them in your book. And we'll get paid, and you can buy some more."

The next morning, Keller got up early and drove straight to Grondahl's house in Carmel. He parked across the street and sat behind the wheel of his rented Ford, a newspaper propped on the steering wheel. He read the national and international news, then the sports. The Pacers, he noted, had won last night, in double overtime. The local sportswriter described the game as thrilling and said the shot from half-court that fell in just as the second overtime period ran out demonstrated "the moral integrity and indomitable spirit of our guys." Keller wished he'd taken it a small step further, claiming the ball's unerring flight to the basket as proof of the Almighty's clear preference for the local heroes.

Reading, he kept an eye on Grondahl's front door, waiting for Greenie to appear. He still hadn't done so by the time Keller was done with the sports pages. Well, it was early, he told himself, and turned to the business section. The Dow had been up, he learned, in heavy volume.

He knew what this meant — he wasn't an idiot — but it was something he never followed because it didn't concern him or hold in-

terest for him. Keller earned good money when he worked, and he
didn't live high, and for years he had saved a substantial portion of
the money that came into his hands. But he'd never bought stocks
or mutual funds with it. He tucked some of it into a safe-deposit
box and the rest into savings accounts. The money grew slowly if it
grew at all, but it didn't shrink, and there was something to be said
for that.

Eventually he reached a point where retirement was an option,
and realized that he'd need a hobby to fill the golden years. He
took up stamp collecting again, but in a far more serious fashion
this time around. He started spending serious money on stamps,
and his retirement savings waned as his collection grew.

So he'd never managed to get interested in the world of stocks
and bonds. This morning, for some reason, he found the business
section interesting, not least because of an article on Central Indiana Finance. CIFI, which opened the day at $43.27 a share, had
fluctuated wildly, up five points at its high for the day, down as
much as seven, and finishing the day at $40.35. On the one hand,
he learned, the shorts were scrambling to cover before the ex-
dividend date, when they would be liable for the company's substantial dividend. On the other, players were continuing to short
the stock and drive the price down, encouraged by the pending
class-action lawsuit.

He was thinking about the article when the door opened and
Meredith Grondahl emerged.

Grondahl was dressed for the office, wearing a dark gray suit and
a white shirt and a striped tie and carrying a briefcase. That was to
be expected, it being a Thursday, but Keller realized he'd uncon-
sciously been waiting for the man to show himself in shorts and a
singlet, dribbling a basketball.

In the driveway, Grondahl paid no attention to the basketball
backboard but triggered a button to raise the garage door. There
was, Keller noted, only one car in the garage, and a slew of objects (he made out a barbecue grill and some lawn furniture) took
up the space where a second car might otherwise have been
parked.

Grondahl, given his position in the corporate world, could clearly
have afforded a second car for his wife. Which suggested to Keller
that he didn't have a wife. The fine suburban house, on the other

hand, suggested that he'd had one once upon a time, and Keller suspected she'd chosen to go away and had taken her car with her.

Poor bastard.

Keller, comfortable behind the wheel, stayed where he was while Grondahl backed his Grand Cherokee out of the driveway and drove off somewhere. Keller thought about following the man, but why? For that matter, why had he come here to watch him leave the house?

Of course, there were more basic questions than that. Why wasn't he getting down to business and fulfilling his contract? Why was he watching Meredith Grondahl instead of punching the man's ticket?

And a question that was, strictly speaking, none of his business, but no less compelling for it: why did somebody want Meredith Grondahl dead?

Thinking, he reminded himself, was one thing. Acting was another. His mind could go where it wanted, as long as his body did what it was supposed to.

Drive back to the motel, he told himself, and find a way to use up the day. And tonight, when Meredith Grondahl comes home, be here waiting for him. Then return this car to Hertz, pick up a fresh one from somebody else, and go home.

He nodded, affirming the wisdom of that course of action. Then he started the engine, backed up a few yards, and swung the car into the Grondahl driveway. He got out, found the button Grondahl had used to raise the garage door, pressed it, got back in the car, and pulled into the spot recently vacated by the Grand Cherokee.

There was a small boulder the size of a bowling ball standing just to the right of Grondahl's front door. It might have been residue from a local avalanche, but Keller thought that unlikely. It looked to him like something to hide a spare house key under, and he was right about that. He picked up the key, opened the door, and let himself in.

There was a chance, of course, that there was still a Mrs. Grondahl and that she was home. Maybe she didn't drive, maybe she was an agoraphobe who never left the house. Keller thought this was unlikely, and it didn't take him long to rule it out. The house was antiseptically clean, but that didn't necessarily signal a woman's presence; Grondahl might be neat by nature, or he might have someone who cleaned for him once or twice a week.

There were no women's clothes in the closets or dressers, and that was a tip-off. And there were two dressers, a highboy and a low triple dresser with a vanity mirror, and the low dresser's drawers were empty, except for one which Grondahl had begun to use for suspenders and cuff links and such. So there had indeed been a Mrs. Grondahl, and now there wasn't.

Keller, having established this much, wandered around the two-story house trying to see what else he could learn. Except he wasn't trying very hard, because he wasn't really looking for anything, or if he was, he didn't know what it might be. It was more as if he was trying to get the feel of the man, and that didn't make any sense, but then what sense was there in letting yourself into the house of the man you were planning to kill?

Maybe the best course of action was to settle in and wait. Sooner or later Grondahl would return to the house, and he'd probably be alone when he did, since he was beginning to strike Keller as your typical lonely guy.

Your typical lonely guy. The phrase resonated oddly for Keller, because he couldn't help identifying with it. He was, face it, a lonely guy himself, although he didn't suppose you could call him typical. Did this resonance get in the way of what he was supposed to do? He thought it over and decided it did and it didn't. It made him sympathize with Meredith Grondahl, and thus disinclined to kill him; on the other hand, wouldn't he be doing the poor bastard a favor?

He frowned, found a chair to sit in. When Grondahl came home, he'd be alone. And he'd be relieved to return to the safe harbor of his empty house. So he'd be unguarded, and getting taken from behind by a man with a club or a knife or a garrote — Keller hadn't decided yet — was the last thing he'd worry about.

It'd be the last thing, all right.

The problem, of course, was to figure out what to do with the day. If he just holed up here, it looked to be a minimum of eight hours before Grondahl returned, and the wait might well stretch to twelve or more. He could read, if he could find something he felt like reading, or watch TV with the sound off, or —

Hell. His car was parked in Grondahl's garage. That assured that the neighbors wouldn't see it and grow suspicious, but what happened when Grondahl came home and found his parking spot taken?

No good at all. Keller would have to move the car, and the sooner the better, because for all he knew, Grondahl might feel the need to come home for lunch. So what should he do? Drive it around the block, leave it in front of some stranger's house? And then he'd have to return on foot, hoping no one noticed him, because nobody walked anywhere in the suburbs and a pedestrian was suspicious by definition.

Maybe waiting for Grondahl was a bad idea altogether. Maybe he should just get the hell out and go back to his motel.

He was on his way to the door when he heard a key in the lock.

Funny how decisions had a way of making themselves. Grondahl, who had returned for something he'd forgotten, was insisting on being put out of his misery. Keller backed out of the entrance hall and waited around the corner in the dining room.

The door opened, and Keller heard steps, a lot of them. And a voice called out, "Hello? Anybody home?"

Keller's first thought was that it was an odd thing for Grondahl to do. Then another voice, pitched lower, said, "You better hope you don't get an answer to that one."

Had Grondahl brought a friend? No, of course not, he realized. It wasn't Grondahl, who was almost certainly doing something corporate at his office. It was someone else, a pair of somebody elses, and they'd let themselves in with a key and wanted the house to be empty.

If they came into the dining room, he'd have to do something about it. If they took a different tack, he'd have to slip out of the door as soon as the opportunity presented itself. And hide in the garage, waiting for them to emerge from the house and drive away, so that *he* could drive away, too.

"I think the den," one voice said. "House like this, guy living alone, he's gotta have a den, don't you think?"

"Or a home office," the other voice offered.

"A den, a home office, what the hell's the difference?"

"One's deductible."

"But it's the same room, isn't it? No matter what you call it?"

"I suppose, but for tax purposes —"

"Jesus," the first voice said. It was, Keller noted, vaguely familiar, but maybe that was just because the speaker had a Hoosier accent. "I'm not planning to audit his fucking tax returns," the man said. "I just want to plant an envelope in his desk."

Out the door, Keller told himself. Let them plant whatever they wanted in whatever they decided to call the room with the desk in it. He'd be gone, and they'd never know he'd been there in the first place.

But when he left the dining room, something led him not to the door but away from it. He tagged along after the two men and caught a glimpse of them as he rounded a corner into the living room. He saw them from the back, and only for a moment, but that was time enough to note that they were both of average height and medium build and that one was bald as an egg. The other might or might not have hair; you couldn't tell at a glance, because he was wearing a cap.

A green cap with gold piping, and when had Keller seen a cap like that? Oh, right. Same place he'd heard that voice. It was a John Deere cap, and the man wearing it had met him at the airport and given him tickets to that goddamn basketball game. Depressed the hell out of him, ruined his first evening in Indianapolis, and thanks a lot for that, you son of a bitch.

Keller, oddly irritated, padded silently after the two of them and lurked around a corner while they stationed themselves at Meredith Grondahl's desk. "Definitely a home office," the bald man said. "You got your filing cabinets, you got your desk and your computer, you got your Canon desktop copier, you got your printer and your fax machine —"

"You also got a big-screen TV and a La-Z-Boy recliner, which shouts den to me," the man in the Deere cap said. "Look at this, will you? The drawer's locked."

"This one ain't. Neither's this one. You got seven drawers, for chrissake, who cares if one of 'em's locked?"

"This is incriminating evidence, right? Dangerous stuff?"

"So?"

"You got a desk with a locked drawer, don't you think that's the drawer you're gonna keep the shit in?"

"The cops in this town," the bald man said, "they find a locked drawer, they might just decide it's too much trouble to open it."

"Point."

Keller, out of sight in the adjoining room, heard a drawer open and close.

"There," the Deere cap said. "Right where they'll find it."

"And if Grondahl finds it first?"

"I figure that's in the next day or two, because he's not gonna wait that long."

"The shooter."

"A real piece of work."

"You told me."

"I tell you how he walks up to a car in the airport lot and drives off with it? Has a master key on his ring, pops the lock like it was made for it. 'I'll just borrow it,' he tells me."

"Casual son of a bitch."

"But how long is he gonna drive around in a stolen vehicle? I'm surprised he hasn't made his move already."

"Maybe he has. Maybe we go to the bedroom, we find Grondahl sleeping with the fishes."

"That'd be in the river, wouldn't it? You don't find fishes sleeping in beds."

Oysters, Keller thought. In oyster beds. He retreated a few steps, because there was no longer any reason to stick around. These two worked for the client, and they were just planting evidence to support the same end as Grondahl's removal. They could have let him plant the stuff himself, all part of the service, but they hadn't thought of that, or hadn't trusted him, so —

The bald guy said, "It's not really finished until he's dead, you know."

"Grondahl."

"Well, that, obviously. No, I mean the shooter. He's killed, and he's the one took out Grondahl, and he's tied to Indy Fi's management. Then you got them good."

Jesus, Keller thought. And he'd almost walked away from this. They were moving, the two of them, and he moved, as well, so that he could wind up behind them when they headed for the door.

"All part of the plan," Deere Cap said.

"But if he just goes and steals another car and flies back to wherever he came from —"

"Portland, I think somebody said."

"Which Portland?"

"Who cares? He ain't making it back. What I did, I stuck a bug on the underside of his back bumper while he was showing me how slick his key worked. He went to that basketball game, incidentally. Guy loves basketball."

"Who won the game?"

"You'd have to ask him. That Global Positioning shit is wonderful. He's at the Rodeway Inn near the I-69 exit. That's our next stop. What we'll do, I got a pair of tickets for tomorrow night's game, and we'll leave 'em at the motel desk for him. What I figure —"

It might have been interesting to learn how the basketball tickets were part of the man's plan, but they were almost at the door at this point, and that was as far as Keller could let them get. Following them, he'd paused long enough to snatch a brass candlestick off a tabletop, and he closed the distance between him and them and swung the candlestick in a sweeping arc that ended at a patch of gold braid on the green John Deere cap. It caught the man in mid-stride and mid-sentence, and he never finished either. He dropped in his tracks, and the bald man was just beginning to take it in, just beginning to react, when Keller backhanded him with the candlestick, striking him right across his endless forehead. The scalp split and blood spurted, and the man let out a cry and clapped a hand to the spot, and Keller swung the candlestick a third time, like a woodsman with an ax, and brought it down authoritatively on the back of the bald man's neck.

Jack be nimble, he thought.

It took Keller a moment to catch his breath, but only a moment. He stood there still holding on to the candlestick and looked down at the two men lying a couple of feet apart on the patterned area rug. They both looked dead. He checked, and the bald man was every bit as dead as he looked, but the guy in the cap still had a pulse.

Keller, waiting for him to regain consciousness, did what he could to clean up. He washed and wiped the candlestick and put it back where he'd found it. He wasn't going to be able to do anything about the blood on the rug, and couldn't even make an attempt while the two of them were lying on it.

He stationed himself alongside them and waited. Eventually the Deere cap guy came to, and Keller asked him a couple of questions.

The man didn't want to answer them, but eventually he did, and then there was no need to keep him alive anymore.

The hardest part, really, was getting the two bodies out of the house and into their car, which turned out to be the same Hyundai squareback that had picked him up at the airport. It was parked in the driveway, and the keys were in the Deere cap guy's pocket.

He could see how it was all going to work out.

"Like we don't have enough to contend with," Dot said. "You do everything right and then you get killed by the client. This business isn't the bed of roses people think it is."

"Is that what people think?"

"Who knows what people think, Keller? I know what I think. I think you better come home."

"Not just yet."

"Oh?"

"One of the fellows gave me a name."

"Probably his very last words."

"Just about."

"And you want to get together with this fellow?"

"I probably won't be able to," he said. "My guess is he'll be overcome by fear or remorse."

"And he'll take his own life?"

"It wouldn't surprise me."

"And it wouldn't start me crying, I have to tell you that. All right, sure, why not? We can't let people get away with that crap. Do what you have to do and then come home. We got half in front, and I don't suppose there's any way to collect the back half, so —"

"Don't be too sure of that," Keller said. "I've been thinking, and why don't you see how this sounds to you?"

When Meredith Grondahl pulled into his driveway around five-thirty, Keller was parked halfway down the block at the curb. He got out of the car and stood where he could watch the Grondahl driveway, and after five minutes Grondahl emerged from the house. He'd changed from a suit and tie to sneakers and sweats, and he was dribbling a basketball. He took a shot, missed, took the ball as it came off the backboard, and drove for a layup.

Keller headed up the driveway. Grondahl turned, saw him, and tossed him the ball. Keller shot, missed.

They played for a few minutes, just taking turns trying shots, most of which failed to make it through the hoop. Then Keller sank a fadeaway jump shot, surprising both of them, and Grondahl said, "Nice."

"Luck," Keller said. "Listen, we should talk."

"Huh?"

"You had a couple of visitors earlier today. They got into an argument, and they bled all over your rug."

"My rug."

"That area rug with the geometric pattern, right when you come into the house."

"*That's* what was different," Grondahl said. "The rug wasn't there. I knew there was something, but I couldn't put my finger on it."

"Or your foot."

"You said there was blood on it?"

"Their blood, and you don't want that. Anyway, you get a lot of blood on a rug and it's never the same. So the rug's not there anymore."

"And the two men?"

"They're not there anymore, either."

Grondahl had been holding the basketball, and now he turned and flipped it at the basket. It hit the rim and bounced away, and neither man made any move toward it.

Grondahl said, "These men. They came into my house?"

"Right through the door over there. They had a key — not the one you keep under the fake rock, either."

"And then, inside my house, they got into an argument and . . . killed each other?"

"That's close enough," Keller said.

Grondahl thought about it. "I think I get the picture," he said.

"You probably get as much of the picture as you need to get."

"That's what it sounds like. Why did they come here in the first place?"

"They were going to leave an envelope."

"An envelope."

"In a desk drawer."

"And the envelope contained . . ."

"A motive for a murder."

"My murder?"

Keller nodded.

"They were going to kill me?"

"Their employer," Keller said, "had already hired someone else for that job."

"Who?"

"Some stranger," Keller said. "Some faceless assassin flown in from out of town."

Grondahl looked thoughtfully at him, the way one might look at a putative faceless assassin. "But he's not going to do it," he said. "At least I don't think he is."

"He's not."

"Why?"

"Because he happened to learn that once his job was done, they were planning to kill him."

"And pin everything on the Indy Fi management," Grondahl said. "I was killed to keep me from giving testimony I never had any thought of giving in the first place. Jesus, it might have worked. I can imagine what must have been in the envelope. Is it still around? The envelope. Or did it disappear along with the two men?"

"The men will turn up eventually," Keller said. "The envelope is gone forever."

Grondahl nodded, retrieved the basketball, bounced it a few times. Keller could almost see the wheels turning in the man's head. He was bright, Keller was pleased to note. You didn't have to spell things out for him, you gave him the first paragraph and he got the rest of the page on his own.

"I owe you," Grondahl said.

Keller shrugged.

"I mean it. You saved my life."

"I was saving my own at the time," Keller pointed out.

"When the two of them, uh, had their accident, I'll concede that was in your own self-interest. But you could have just walked away. And you certainly didn't have to show up here and fill me in. Which leads to a question."

"Why am I here?"

"If you don't mind my asking."

"Well, actually," Keller said, "I have a couple of questions of my own."

"I think I get it," Dot said. "This is a new thing for me, Keller. I wrote it down, and I'm going to read it back to you, to make sure I've got it all straight."

She did, and he told her she had it right.

"That's a miracle," she said, "because it was a little like taking dictation in a foreign language. I'll take care of it tomorrow. Can I do it all in a day?"

"Probably."

"Then I will. And you'll be . . ."

"Biding my time in Indianapolis. I switched motels, by the way."

"Good."

"And found the bug they put on my bumper, and switched it to the bumper of another Ford the same color as mine."

"That should muddy the waters nicely."

"I thought so. So I'll do what I have to do, and then I'll be a couple of days driving home."

"Not to worry," she said. "I'll leave the porch light on for you."

It was a full week later when Keller drove his rented Toyota through the Lincoln Tunnel and found his way to the National garage, where he turned it in. He went home, unpacked his bag, and spent two full hours working on his stamp collection before he picked up the phone and called White Plains.

"Come right on up," Dot said, "so I can turn the light off. It's attracting moths."

In the kitchen of the house on Taunton Place, Dot poured him a big glass of iced tea and told him they'd done very well indeed. "I was wondering at first," she said, "because I bought a big chunk of Indy Fi, and the first thing it did was go down a couple of points. But then it turned around and went back up again, and the last I checked it's up better than ten points from when I bought it. I bought options, too, for increased leverage. I don't understand how they work exactly, but I was able to buy them, and this morning I sold them, and do you want to know exactly how much we made on them?"

"It doesn't have to be exact."

She told him, down to the last decimal point, and it was a satisfying number.

"We're about that much ahead on the actual stock we bought," she said, "but I haven't sold that yet, because I kind of like owning it, especially the way it's going up. Maybe we can sell half and let the rest ride, something like that, but I figured I'd wait and see what you want to do."

"We'll work it out."

"My thought exactly." She sat forward, rubbed her hands together. "What really kick-started things," she said, "was when Clocker killed himself. His hedge fund had been shorting Indy Fi's stock all along, and he was behind the lawsuit they were going through, and when he was out of the picture, and in a way that put the cloud right over his own head, well, the price of Indy Fi's stock could go back where it belonged. And the price of his hedge fund . . ."

"Sank?"

"Like a stone," she said. "And we sold it short and covered our shorts very cheaply and made a killing. It's nice to make a killing without having to drive anywhere. How did you know how to do all this?"

"I had advice," he said. "From a fellow who couldn't do any of this himself because it would be insider trading. But you and I aren't insiders, so there's no problem."

"Well, I've got no problem with it myself, Keller. That's for sure. You know, this isn't the first time you've wound up killing a client of ours."

"I know."

"This one brought it on himself, no question. But usually it costs us money, and this time we came out way ahead. You're going to be able to buy a veritable shitload of stamps."

"I was thinking about that."

"And we're a giant stride closer to being able to retire, when the time comes."

"I was thinking about that, too."

"And you bonded with what's-his-name."

"Meredith Grondahl."

"What do his friends call him, did you happen to find out?"

"It never came up. I'm not sure he's got any friends."

"Oh."

"I was thinking I ought to send him something, Dot. I had an idea of how to make money in the market, but he spelled the whole thing out for me. I didn't know a thing about options, and I never would have thought of shorting the hedge fund."

"How big a share do you want to send him?"

"Not a share. He's pretty straight-arrow, and even if he weren't, the last thing he wants is cash he can't explain. No, I was thinking more of a present. A token, really, but something he'd like to have and probably wouldn't ever buy for himself."

"Like?"

"Season tickets to the Pacers home games. He loves basketball, and a pair of courtside season tickets should really do it for the guy."

"What's it cost?" Before he could answer, she waved the question away. "Not enough to matter, not the way we just made out. That's a great idea, Keller. And who knows? Next time you're in Indianapolis, maybe the two of you can take in a game."

He shook his head. "No," he said. "Leave me out of it. I hate basketball."

JOHN BOND

T-Bird

FROM *Miami Noir*

BEFORE POKER I was an insurance claims investigator, a corporate private eye with a short-sleeved white shirt and skinny tie,
sometimes catching scumbags but mostly helping big guys screw little guys out of benefits they were entitled to. I put ten years' experience to work on my own disability claim — a psych claim, though
you can't buy a decent psych policy anymore. Now I just open the
mail for my check once a month and play poker. I'm never wearing
a tie or watch again. The trick is to keep your head straight, not be
sucked in, not to want too much.

I play at McKool's, a sweet two-table poker room in a Miami
River warehouse, minutes from the Dolphin Expressway. Across the
bridge from the downtown ramps to I-95, it has easy access, drawing players from Boca to Homestead. McKool runs six nights a
week, says if you don't give players Saturdays with their wives, then
the wives won't let 'em play. I wouldn't know from wives, and with
any luck never will.

Texas Hold'em's hot, and I play it, but I prefer Omaha 8-or-
better high-low split, which McKool spreads on Fridays. There's
more to think about in high-low, and a lot of seductive starting
hands, trap hands that suck people in. I scoop both sides in split-
pot games more than anybody. That's why McKool calls me Bobby
Two-ways. Everybody has a nickname: Rebel, Bumper, Luckbucket,
Goombah. Everybody except McKool.

McKool's has a kitchen girl who knows how you take your coffee,
what you want on your sandwich, what snacks you like. I catch two
meals every play, and sometimes hit the fridge for a takeout bag at

the end of the night. There's a shower, for guys who play all night and then head straight to the office. McKool's got a smoking room in back with its own vent system, and another room with two computers so people can play online poker while waiting for a seat. Both rooms have queen-size beds — some guys take a little nap then get up to play more, or snooze for an hour before heading to work.

I met McKool when he first came back to Miami after twenty years in the army, before he opened up his room. We were playing in the big game at Black Jack's, down in Ocean Reef — $100–$200-limit Hold'em. We'd played all night and were down to the hard cores. Only four of us remained. Tommy Trash — he had the garbage contract for the Keys — had lost $20k-plus, and wanted to play a four-handed $25k freeze out, winner take all. McKool had gotten beat up pretty badly too, and didn't have the buy-in. I'd been the big winner. So I bought McKool's cherry red 1962 Ford Thunderbird Sports Roadster convertible with a 390 V-8 300-hp engine for twenty-five grand — a steal. The four of us played for the hundred thousand. It only took a couple of hours for McKool and me to bust out Tommy and Jack and get heads up. We played and played and played. And played some more. Fourteen hours later McKool busted me. His mental toughness and physical conditioning for the long sit made the difference. He won the hundred grand, and offered me $30k to buy back the T-bird. But I liked it and said no.

McKool used that win to bankroll opening his place. He's offered me forty, then fifty, and recently sixty grand for the car. I'm not much into things, but I love that ragtop. Besides, it's good when The Man wants something he can't have from you.

I don't really have friends, but McKool and I know we can rely on each other. I think I'm the only player in the game who has his private cell. I do a lot for McKool: recruit from the parimutuels; deal when somebody calls in sick; give up my seat when he needs to fit a live one in. Mostly I show up for the afternoon gin game before start time and stay through the last hand. Starters and finishers are key to running a profitable house game, getting games off early and keeping them going late.

My trouble started at McKool's Thursday game, No Limit Hold'em night, five hundred minimum/a thousand maximum buy-in, five and ten blinds. Rebel — Rebecca Ellen O'Shaunessy — strolled in after her shift as bartender at a trendy South Beach club, as she did a couple of nights a week.

Rebel's easy on the eyes, all natural. To see her is to want her. She'd sweetly turned me down more than once. Mid-twenties, about five-foot-six, maybe 115 pounds, green eyes, and auburn-almost-red hair, perfect spinner bod. The kind of girl men would leave their wives for in a heartbeat. McKool uses Rebel like he uses me, like he uses everybody — hustling here, cajoling there, pushing buttons, building up a stash of favors so butts are in seats and the cards are always in the air by seven o'clock, and the game goes on toward dawn and beyond. Knowing the hottie was coming kept early players hanging on late, and gave the late players reason to arrive early. We rarely broke before sunrise when Rebel played.

Poker's not a game where you have to be the best player in the world — just the best at the table. Winning players aren't welcome at most private games. We take cash from the game, use it to pay rent and buy groceries. A houseman wants action. Gambling fools. The suckers who look for any excuse to play a hand, who don't understand that more often than not the right play is to pass, not get involved. Live ones attract players, working pros drive them away. I've been barred from the weekly games at the Coconut Grove Yacht Club and Lauderdale Country Club. I help McKool not because I'm a nice guy, but so he'll let me play in his juicy lineup of fish.

Rebel did her grand-entrance thing, giving this one a wink, tousling that one's hair, stroking the other's arm. Escort Randy — he owns a low-rent Internet escort agency, buck-fifty-an-hour girls, mostly but not all skanks — asked her for the zillionth time if she'd work for him, and for the zillionth time she smacked him on the arm, then gave him a hug. I like Randy — he gives me a twenty-dollar discount on calls.

McKool had his usual crew on hand: three dealers, Lilith the kitchen girl, and Cartouche, the half-Senegalese half-Moroccan from Montreal McKool had hooked up with in some little jungle war. Cartouche didn't exactly have a job, though he sometimes dealt and even sometimes cooked. He just stood by McKool's side, a silent giant.

Rebel sat down and set off on a chip fry like she hated her

money. No Limit's a dangerous game for people who play fast. In limit games, when you make a mistake, you lose a bet or maybe a pot. In No Limit, when you make a mistake, you lose everything. Rebel got herself stuck fifteen hundred in less than twenty minutes, and soon had McKool pinned in a corner, stroking his arm, giving him that damsel-in-distress look.

McKool sometimes gives regulars a nickel or dime's credit juice-free, but only until the next play, up to a week max. Having players on the book is a necessary evil of the business. Problem is, when they owe you money, the next time they have a few bucks they take that money someplace else to play, instead òf paying you. McKool, after his twenty years in Special Forces, doesn't have a lot of collection problems. Plus he has Cartouche. McKool's rule is only lend to people who have money to pay you back right away. I knew Rebel wasn't getting a penny more out of McKool.

She looked around the room, caught me eyeing her. She stuck out her lower lip in a pouty way, and mouthed "please." I shook my head. She smiled and shrugged, then grabbed Skip Converse, one of Miami's slimiest shysters, and pulled him away from the table. A minute later he plopped his big butt back in his seat — Skip's a fish with no clue when to pass and hates to miss a hand. Reb sashayed over to the other table, draped her arms around Big Country's shoulders, and whispered something in his ear. He got up and they stepped into one of the back rooms.

"Chick already owes me five hundred," Skip said. "I told her the next nickel would require sex. Can't imagine why she passed."

Five minutes later they came out of the back, Big Country laughing like a schoolboy. He bought two racks of reds from McKool and handed them to Rebel. She gave him a full-contact hug, something more than affectionate, and a kiss on the cheek.

"Thanks, Country, you're a real gentleman," she said. "I'll crush these fuckers, but if for some reason they escape, I promise you'll have it back Sunday." Then she terrorized the game. One hand she came over the top on Big Country and moved him off a big pot. I knew from the way she stared him down she'd bluffed him off. Lending people money to play against you is a bad bet. If they lose, you won't see it anytime soon. If they win, you lose. But I understand not being able to say no to a pretty girl. What man doesn't? In a couple of hours Reb won back the fifteen hundred she'd lost, the dime she'd borrowed from Big Country, and seven hundred sugar. Then she did something she almost never does. She locked up her win.

While McKool counted her down, Rebel came over, rested her hand oh-so-lightly on my inside thigh, and blew gently on my neck, sending a shiver down my neck and making my dick hard. She whispered in my ear, "Two-ways, I need your help. Meet me upstairs at the Road in an hour?"

I hate being manipulated by anybody, especially women. "Make it an hour and a half," I said.

As she headed to the door, Skip called out to her: "Hey, Rebel, what about my five bills?"

She smiled sweetly. "Next week, Skip."

Cartouche gave Rebel a look; she understood that really meant next week.

Every eye in the room followed her as she walked out. If God had ever made a more perfect ass than Rebel's, he kept it for himself.

I cashed out then headed down South River, the full moon behind me. Downtown and Little Havana meet here in Riverside, not far from the Orange Bowl. I often play dominoes with the old Cubanos at Marti Park before heading to afternoon gin at McKool's.

Miami had been born along the river. South River Drive, with all its banyans, ficus, and palms, runs southeast-to-northwest by the riverbank, cul-de-sacs and dead ends off it on the river side. This once was a working river, but the fishing boats on the east end had given way to condos and office towers, though piles of lobster pots and crab traps lay stacked here and there along the banks. Scattered small freighter terminals serviced seedy tramps running back and forth to the Bahamas, Haiti, and other islands. Most of South Florida's stolen bicycles and chopped-up car parts found their way into these cargo holds, and more than a little of the area's dope came through here.

I parked by a sand yellow, two-story stucco building on the riverbank: Miami's oldest bar, Tobacco Road. During Prohibition, rumrunners out of Bimini had unloaded their wares from the river behind the building, under the protection of the local sheriff. The day Prohibition ended, the bar opened fully stocked and has never closed since. Most Miami bars close at two A.M., but the Road has a grandfathered late-night license. I arrived twenty minutes late, figured if Rebel wanted something then keeping her waiting a bit would establish negotiating control. I climbed the narrow staircase to the tiny upstairs bar, but she hadn't arrived. I sat at a cocktail table, ordered a mojito from Maidel, the-waitress-who-wrote-blues-lyrics-about-three-legged-dogs-and-lovelorn-artists, listened to a frumpy grad student reading incomprehensible poetry from the tiny stage, and waited.

She arrived ten minutes later, on her arm a handsome blond guy. I stood as they approached. She kissed me on the lips, almost but not quite tonguing me. "Bobby, this is my boyfriend Dmitri. Dima, this is Bobby Two-ways, the poker player who used to do insurance investigations."

Dmitri smiled, showing hillbilly teeth. "Rebecca tells me you are a man to be trusted," he said with a thick Russian accent. "That you do the right thing."

I shot a glance at Rebel. In an after-game bull session one night, I'd told her I could always be trusted to do the right thing. The right thing for me, that is. She'd laughed, and many times since had made sly comments about "the right thing" with a wink and a knowing smile. "What's this about, Reb?"

"How'd you like to fuck me, Bobby?"

"Fuck you out of what?"

She licked her lips. "Really."

"Really? Like in sex? How's Dmitri here feel about that?"

"It's his idea."

"I'm not big on audiences." I thought she was inviting me to do a three-way with them. "And he's cute, but definitely not my type."

Rebel shook her head. "No, no, nothing like that. I need money. Big money. Dima came up with a scam we can work. We need a third person. All you got to do is fuck me."

"It would have to be after two o'clock. I don't do mornings."

"You'd fuck me on I-95 in the middle of morning rush hour with your mother watching."

She was right, of course. I'd drag my dick through a mile of broken glass for a chance at her. Anyplace, anytime. "Why do you need money so bad?"

She laughed, not an amused laugh but a sharp one. "Why does anybody need money? And why do you care? We can score. Big money. Low risk. If this was a no-limit hand you'd shove your stack in. You get ten percent for a half hour's work." She pressed her breasts against my arm, rested her hand high on my thigh under the table, breathed on my neck, and said huskily, "If you call this work."

Dmitri leaned toward me, whispered the details — a lawsuit scam, like those teams that stage car accidents to rip off insurance companies. I'd sent my share of those scumbags to jail, back when. He'd cased the target well, had the timing down. Litigation potential hit seven figures, easy. A quick settlement was worth a half mill, minimum.

Poker players make fast decisions, always on incomplete information — hundreds, thousands of dollars won or lost in a blink. Good players make quality reads of situations. We get into our opponent's mind. What is he thinking? What does he think I'm thinking? What does he think I think he's thinking? Anticipate what he's going to do, what he wants you to do, make the play that uses his thoughts against him. Investigating this as a claim, what would I go after? As a scammer, how would I avoid what the investigator would look for? What would the investigator think a scammer would be thinking? How could I use those thoughts against him?

"It's probably a winner," I said. Solid poker players, like insurance companies, act on risk-reward ratio. But it's more than just the odds. If ninety-nine percent of the time you get a good result, but one percent of the time the result is horrendous, then even a 99-1 favorite can be a bad bet. Dmitri's scheme looked good, yet even a slim chance of winding up in the slam made this an easy fold for me. "But I like my life the way it is." I laid a twenty on the table for my drink and Maidel's tip, and stood up. "Sorry, I'm out."

Rebel grabbed my wrist and yanked me back into my seat.

"Twenty-five percent," Dmitri said.

I live well, but not fancy, in a nice one-bedroom a block from the beach in Surfside. I have my T-bird. I have $70k sitting in a box at Banque de Geneve in Nassau, $20k buried in coffee cans in the trees lining the seventh fairway at Doral, and my working bankroll of $10k stashed in a shoebox in my AC vent. If they hit for $1.5 mill, the lawyer took a third — $250k would make a gigantic difference in my life. Enough to bankroll me for a shot at the World Poker Tour, maybe the big one at Binion's. Maybe even buy a little condo. "No," I said.

Rebel moved her hand up under the table and unsnapped my

pants, pulled down the zip of my jeans, and slipped her hand into my boxers.

"All right," Dmitri said. "Even split. One-third each."

Rebel gently ran her nails up and down my rock-hard dick. She came close and whispered in my ear with hot breath, "Please, Two-ways?"

I shook my head no. "Okay. A third."

Friday I got up early, around noon, and drove up the Palmetto to Alligator Alley and cruised across the Everglades to Fort Myers in my T-bird with the top down. I found a Super Wal-Mart and bought a black long-sleeved shirt, two pairs of black socks, a Yankees cap, wraparound shades, a pair of flared black jeans a couple of inches longer in the in-seam than usual, four dog leashes, a roll of duct tape, a box of flesh-colored latex gloves, a box of safety matches, a $12 Casio watch, a dark blue bandanna, a shower cap, a small plastic waste bin, a five-gallon gas can, a bottle of Astroglide, a pack-age of three condoms, and a small backpack. Cash, of course. Then I went to Payless and purchased a pair of size-eleven shoes with four-inch cork platforms — told the nearly oblivious clerk they were a gift, to explain why a size-nine guy was buying elevens. I bought a roll of quarters at a beachfront arcade, then stopped into a Super-cuts for a buzzcut.

I drove home across the Alley, the winter sun setting behind me. I headed to the never-ending traffic construction on Biscayne, found a job on a deserted side street, hopped out of the T-bird, grabbed two orange traffic cones and a barricade, threw them in my trunk, then drove across the bay. I cruised South Beach waiting for a suitable parking space to open up on Washington. One finally did right where I wanted, just south of Lincoln Road. I pulled up alongside it, set the cones and barricade in it, and headed home.

I filled the T-bird and the five-gallon gas can at the Mobil on Har-ding around the corner from my apartment, then put the gas can in the trunk. In my apartment-house parking lot I looked about, found a perfect pebble — about a quarter-inch, rounded, with no sharp edges — and pocketed it. I placed my purchases in the back-pack in the order I'd need them, last items on the bottom, first on top, shoved in a big green trash bag, then set the radio alarm for 9:45 and settled in for a nap to catch up on my lost sleep.

Jimmy Buffett woke me singing "Margaritaville" on the classic rock station. I spent a half hour shaving every hair off my body from the eyes down. I trimmed my eyebrows, made sure I had no loose eyelashes, then showered, wiping every speck of hair off my body. I dressed in my usual blue jeans and tee, strapped on the Casio, grabbed the backpack, put the pebble, quarters, and a plastic hotel key card Dmitri had given me in my pocket, and headed out. In the parking lot I unscrewed the little light bulb over my license tag, put the trash can from Wal-Mart in the trunk with the gas, and threw the backpack on the passenger seat. I checked the Casio — an hour forty to go.

I drove past the Jackie Gleason across Lincoln Road to Washington Avenue, with all its spiffed-up deco buildings — pastel paint jobs and colored lights showing off the architectural accents. I pulled up to my space, threw the cones and barricade back in the trunk, and parallel parked. South Beach parking spaces on weekend nights are like gold. I filled the meter with four hours' worth of quarters, then ambled down to the 11th Street Diner. The 11th is famous for the best meatloaf sandwiches this side of your mom's kitchen and the best milkshakes anywhere. But it suited me this night because it's 24/7 and bustles with clubgoers from around ten P.M. to six A.M.

I made my way past the crowded booths to the john in back, stepped into a stall, and hung the backpack on the hook on the door. I pulled out the Wal-Mart black jeans, socks, and black shirt and changed into them. I put on the shower cap, tied the bandanna around my head so that not a single hair showed, pulled the Yankees cap over it, and slipped on the wraparounds. I shoved the extra socks into the toes of the platforms and set the pebble carefully so it rested just under my arch, and put on the shoes. I pulled on a pair of the flesh-colored latex gloves, shoved my sneaks, jeans, and T-shirt into the backpack.

Then I sat on the pot for five minutes so nobody who'd been in the bathroom still lingered, stepped out of the stall, through the diner, and back onto Washington. The SoBe party crowd milled about, just starting to cook. Teenagers wanting to be older, boomers wanting to be younger, loads of twenty-somethings wanting to be seen. Glitz, glamour, and grunge, hip-hoppers in baggy shorts with legacy hoops jerseys and hooded sweatshirts, supermodel-wannabes in short, slinky dresses, random retros in Goth, buffed-up boys in muscle shirts, bikers and beachboys and babes. I blended right in.

Rap, industrial, and hip-hop boomed from a parade of tricked-out cars circling through the Deco District, bass throbbing from overpowered woofers. Lines formed outside the most popular clubs. I ambled amid the throng up and across to Collins Avenue, the platforms making me a six-foot-one guy, not five-nine, with a marked limp from the pebble in my shoe. Poker players not only observe body language as part of the art of reading tells, but notice what their opponents observe, and then try to use that knowledge to deceive them. Real winners make this observation a habit of their lives. I'd discovered over years of watching what people see that you always notice, at least subconsciously, how people walk. The limp disguised me as much as the shades and the platform shoes.

Two blocks up Collins stood the former Hotel Roosevelt, a stream-lined, thirty-five-story art deco masterpiece, restored beyond its former glory, renamed the Delano and now owned by an over-the-hill rock diva struggling to stay cool. Right that moment I found myself in my own struggle to stay cool. My palms were sweating in the latex gloves, a sharp ache throbbed in my shoulders. I took a deep breath. Focus, I told myself. Think, don't react. Adjust as each card comes off the deck. I breathed deeply, put myself in game mode, all focus, focus, focus. Just keep on reading the situation and make the right play. One card after another, one hand then the next, one step after another, then the next, until I found myself walking past the valets and doormen into the Delano's ornate lobby. I checked the Casio — still running good.

Bodies ebbed and flowed through the lobby from the adjoining coffee shop and nightclub. Dmitri stood at the concierge's desk. As I made my way through the bustle to the elevators at the back, the concierge handed him a slip of paper and made some motions with his hands as if giving directions. Dmitri tipped the concierge and headed out the grand entrance I had just come through.

I rode the elevator alone to the fourth floor. Dmitri had scouted two cameras on every floor, each pointing toward the center, show-ing half the hallway to the elevator. If he'd done his job, the camera at the east end would be tilted upward, leaving a blind spot so that the doors to the last four rooms or so were out of view.

I turned west and stopped at the end of the hall, in clear camera view, and tried a random door with the Holiday Inn key card Dmitri had given me at the Road. It wouldn't open the door, of course, but I wanted the cameras to see. Then I tried another door. I slapped my forehead as if I'd screwed up and walked to the east end, and now out of camera view went through the fire-escape door and took the stairs down to the third floor.

The camera here should be tilted too, but ever so slightly, so just the last room was unwatched. I opened the fire-escape door a crack and peeked down the hall. A lone couple entangled in an embrace stood waiting for the elevator. I checked the room numbers on both sides of the fire escape door. On my left, 327, just as Dmitri had said. I pushed on the door and it gave way. The small piece of matchbook that Dmitri had stuck in the latch so it wouldn't catch fell to the floor. I shut the door quietly behind me, picked up the bit of matchbook, put it in my pocket, and slipped into the room.

Rebel didn't look up as the door latch clicked. She sat on the edge of the canopied, king-size bed wearing only her panties — pink bikini bottoms — sucking on a cigarette, clinking ice cubes in a cocktail glass. A half-empty bottle of Jack stood on the nightstand. The bedcovers had been tossed on the floor. She caressed the bed. "Never in my life have I slept on sheets this soft, Two-ways," she said. "But at five hundred a night, you should get nice sheets."

I couldn't think of anything to say, so I just nodded.

She stood and faced me. Near-naked she was as perfect as I'd imagined.

Rebel handed me a buck knife. "Dima said you should cut the panties off with this, then before you go, hold it against my throat hard enough to make a mark. And leave the knife when you're done. It leads someplace a million miles from any of us."

I took the knife from her, opened it, slipped the blade between the skin of her hip and the panties, and cut. They fell to the floor. Her pubes were shaved. Above her pussy, DIMA was tattooed in script, inside a heart. "You look nice."

"I don't look 'nice.' I'm fucking *hot*. So fucking hot that you lose all control and just fucking take me. So hot you can't think straight." She grabbed my crotch. "Jesus Christ. Here I am, the hottest woman you'll ever fuck as long as you live, standing buck-naked for you to take, and you don't even have a hard-on."

I'd wanted to bed Rebel since the first time I saw her. Here she stood naked in all her glory for me to have. I couldn't remember a less erotic moment with a beautiful girl in my life.

"Two-ways, let's do this. We're on a schedule."

I took the leashes, Astroglide, duct tape, and condoms from the backpack and set them on the bed.

"You're going to wear a condom? Rapists don't wear fucking condoms."

"It's the twenty-first century, Reb. Rapists worry about STDs as much as the next guy. And smart rapists don't leave a load of DNA inside you for some crime-lab geek to analyze. If I'm going to be a rapist, I'm going to be as smart a rapist as I can be."

"Dima won't like it."

"Screw Dima."

"No — screw me. Right fucking now! Get naked already."

I stripped clumsily, sure I looked foolish in the bandanna, platforms, and latex gloves.

"Jesus Christ, Bobby, you're still not hard." She grabbed my dick and squeezed. "Doesn't this thing work?" She pushed me onto the bed, deftly manipulated my dick until it finally stood at attention, then tore open a condom and slipped it on. She crawled on the bed and threw her arms and legs wide, spread-eagled.

I looped a dog leash around each of her wrists and ankles, then tied them to the feet of the bed, snapped the D-ring at the end of each into place.

She strained at the leashes. "Left arm's not tight enough," she said.

I adjusted the leash securing her left arm, then crawled atop her — and realized I had gone soft.

She laughed. "Do you have this problem often?"

"N-n-never."

"Jesus Christ, untie me."

I did as she said.

"You should have taken some Vitamin V." She pressed against me, kissed my neck while holding my dick, wrapped her legs around me, massaged my thigh with her pussy. My dick grew, this time with conviction. She went down on me, playing with my balls while she moved her mouth up and down my shaft, until I was about to come. She climbed up my body, whispered in my ear, "Hold that thought for five minutes."

I tied her again to the bed, opened another condom, pulled it on, climbed back atop her, and tried to slip myself into her. She was completely dry. I rolled off her and, rubbing my dick against her leg to keep my hard-on, began to massage her clit.

"That won't work," she said. "Use the Astroglide."

I squirted the lube on her pussy, massaged her insides with my fingers, filling her with wetness. I climbed on top again — but again I had gone soft.

"Listen, Two-ways, you don't have to come, but you do have to get it inside me. I know from experience the police rape kit will show whether or not you penetrated."

I untied her and she repeated her oral magic, bringing me once more to the edge of orgasm. This time I didn't tie her but let the animal in me take over — I threw her back on the bed and mounted her quickly, shoving and humping and grunting until I exploded. I rolled off her onto the bed and began to laugh, a little nervously — at myself.

"We're behind schedule," she said matter-of-factly. "Get me tied down."

I tied her to the bed for the third time, pulled the leashes tight as I could.

"Now hit me in the face. Hard."

I hesitated. "I've never hit a girl and I'm not going to start now."

"Goddamn it, Two-ways. The more I'm hurt, the more we can win. Hit me."

I shook my head no. "Sorry, Reb. I won't. Can't."

"Dima's going to be pissed."

"Screw Dima."

"You said that already. Don't ever say it to him. He's not one to be fucked with."

I dressed in my Wal-Mart outfit, shoved the used condoms and wrappers into the pockets of the jeans, and put the Astroglide in the backpack. I picked up the knife.

"At least hold the knife against my throat," Rebel said. "Cut me some."

I did as she said, leaning over her with the blade held tight against her throat, but away from her jugular.

"Harder," she said.

"Shit, Rebel, how the hell do I know how much is hard enough?"

"Just do it, Bobby. Harder!"

I pressed down harder, afraid that I might hurt her. I managed to break the skin without doing any more damage. A rivulet of blood trickled down her neck.

"Good," she said. "Now hit me, goddamn it, Bobby. Leave bruises."

"No, Reb."

"Don't be such a fucking wimp. There's big fucking money at stake here."

I cut a length of duct tape off the roll with the knife and slapped it across her mouth, perhaps the most satisfactory moment of the night so far. I stepped back and looked at her spread wide on the bed, helpless, her beauty almost perfect, her pussy glistening with the Astroglide. To see her was to want her.

Wanting is good. Even better than having.

I looked at the Casio. My bout of erectile dysfunction had put us behind schedule, even with the extra time Dmitri had built in for margin of error. He'd be coming up the elevator to discover his raped girlfriend any minute. I shoved the duct tape in the backpack, threw the knife on the bed. Fibers from generic Wal-Mart clothes, no prints or hairs, size-eleven footprints impressed on the lush carpet. I looked around the room to make sure I hadn't left anything incriminating behind. I'd done what I could to minimize risk.

I slipped into the hall and ran down the stairwell to the first floor, moseyed out into the lobby. The Delano's nightclub in full swing, even more people milled about the lobby than earlier. I saw Dmitri at the elevator. Then he saw me. He checked his watch, scowled. If looks could kill, I'd have been dead on the floor. The elevator dinged, the doors opened, and he stepped on. We'd cut it mighty close.

I walked briskly back to the 11th, changed back into my own clothes and sneaks, shoved the platforms and Wal-Mart clothes into the backpack, then again waited a few minutes before stepping out of the stall, through the diner, and onto the street. Less than ten minutes after leaving Rebel, I was driving west on Seventeenth Street, feeling empty but relieved, glad that it was over. I drove across the MacArthur past the parade of cruise ships waiting at dock to sail off for temporary island fantasies, and got on I-95 north. I exited at State Road 84 twenty minutes later, turned down a small street, then into an alley between two warehouses.

I poured some gas into the Wal-Mart waste bin and dumped in everything I'd used and worn — only the knife, a piece of duct tape across Rebel's mouth, and the four leashes that tied her to the bed remained. In life, as in poker, you can't control all the variables, but you do what you can. I poured in some more gas, struck a safety match against the box, and flicked it in, then dropped in the rest of the box. Flame whooshed upward. I watched it burn and visualized Rebel spread-eagle on the canopied bed. My dick hardened at the vision. I had to laugh at myself; oh well, what can you do?

The blaze left a goo of plastic slag. After the fire died, I shoved the mess into the green garbage bag, tied it off tight, and drove to a complex I'd once lived in on Marina Mile, where they had Saturday-morning trash pickup. I threw the bag into a dumpster; in a few hours it would be lost in the daily refuse of a million people, with only the vultures circling overhead and the never-ending parade of garbage trucks for company. I set the cones and barricade at a construction site, then took I-95 to the Kennedy Causeway, home across the bay into the pink dawn.

I slept later than usual Saturday. I went to Miami Jai-Alai, yakked with the $2 poker players, ate a breakfast of hot dogs and beer, then headed to Gulfstream, where I relaxed in the cheap seats, basking in the afternoon sun with the racing form. The hard work was now on Rebel — Monday she'd retain a lawyer. He'd file the suit for inadequate security resulting in Rebel's rape, and the settlement dance would begin. Most cases like this never went to trial, but rarely settled before the eve of trial. All I had to do now was live my life and wait for my payday.

I cashed a $220 ticket in the last race, then went to the Porterhouse up in Sunny Isles to have a nice steak and flirt with the waitresses. As I ate, my cell rang. I didn't recognize the number, and didn't answer. A few seconds later it rang again, from the same number. The third time, curious about who would be so persistent, I picked up.

"Bobby, thank God you answered. It's Rebel." She sounded as if she were crying. "I need your help." She started to babble — Dima

had gone crazy, beaten her. She was afraid. Could I meet her someplace private? No, not my place in Surfside, he'd check there.
Freighter terminal #9 on the river, a few blocks from McKool's. Just
get there and we could decide together what to do. An hour, please
hurry. She abruptly disconnected.

I didn't like it a bit, but I didn't see how I couldn't go. I took
163rd Street to the Spaghetti Bowl, then I-95 to downtown and
across the river. As I drove under the halogen-tinted sky, I slammed
my fist on the wheel, telling myself this was wrong, that I was an idiot. Whatever Rebel wanted from me, I wasn't going to want to do
it. Why couldn't my mother have raised a less chivalrous son?

Just past the Miami River Inn, I turned onto the street that dead-
ended at terminal #9. The gate to the pier was open, the streetlight
next to it burned out. I edged the T-bird past pallets loaded with
construction materials waiting for the next freighter out, turned
the corner along the warehouse, and saw Rebel's car parked by the
gantry crane. Lights from across the river cast oblong shadows. Rebel leaned on her car, smoking a cigarette. I climbed out of the T-
bird and saw in the glow of the burning ash that her face was all
mangled, bruised yellow and purple, one eye bandaged. "Holy shit,
Rebel."

"It pissed Dima off that you didn't beat me," she said. "The rape
didn't look real enough. So he added that touch himself." She
sobbed. "He likes hurting me too much. I'm scared, Bobby. I can't
go to the police. I don't know what to do." She stared into my eyes.

I stepped forward to take her in my arms. Something about that
look.

"I'm sorry, Bobby," Rebel whispered softly. "If it makes you feel
any better . . ."

It was the same way she stared when she was trying to run a bluff!

". . . Dima's next."

From behind me I heard the double click of a revolver's hammer
pulling back.

Oh shit, I thought. I grabbed Rebel by the shoulders, ducked,
and twirled around, holding her in front of me. Then came the explosion of a shot, the acrid smell of cordite, the blinding muzzle
flash. The bullet that had been intended for me took her square in
the chest, knocked her into me, came out her back, and hit me in
the belly, but its momentum spent, didn't penetrate. The slug clat-

tered to the ground. Blood seeped out Rebel's back all over my clothes. Dmitri stood in front of me, not ten feet away, a shocked look on his face that quickly turned to rage. It happened in seconds, but took forever.

He lunged toward me, screaming in Russian, pointing the pistol at my head. I pushed Rebel's limp body at him, dropped, and threw my weight at his knees; the three of us rolled to the ground in a tangle of arms and legs. The gun went off again, near my ear, the explosion deafening me. I grabbed Dmitri's hair, wrapping my fingers in tight, and smashed his head into the parking lot pavement with all my strength, and again and again and again and again, until he stopped moving.

I lay there covered in blood, entangled in two bodies, with no clue what to do next, where to turn. My head throbbed. How would I explain this to the cops? How did I know these people who had just reported a brutal rape? Any investigator worth a damn would toast me. Focus, I told myself. Think, don't react. Breathe deep. What are your options? What's the best play here?

I called McKool on his private cell. "McKool. Two-ways," I said. "What's that Explorer you drive worth?"

McKool started to say something, then started over. "Maybe 25, 30k. Why?"

"The Explorer and 25 for the T-bird," I said.

McKool hesitated a second. "Twenty."

"Deal. But I need your help with something right now . . ."

Less than ten minutes later he was there, with Cartouche. They quickly surveyed the scene. "Fine mess, Bobby," McKool said, as he tossed me his keys.

I pulled the keys to the T-bird from my pocket, pulled off my apartment key, then handed them to McKool. "She set us both up."

"Chicks can be that way," McKool said.

Cartouche bent over, felt Rebel's neck for a pulse. *"Mort,"* he said. Then he checked Dmitri and shook his head. *"Il n'est pas tout à fait mort."*

"She's dead. He's not quite dead," McKool translated for me. "This costs me. Rebel filled some seats." He thought a moment, then made a small flick of his finger across his throat.

Cartouche took a handkerchief from his pocket and picked up

the pistol, stuck the barrel in Dmitri's ear, and pulled the trigger, then handed McKool the gun.

"He was near dead anyway, and now he can't mention your name before he goes," McKool said. He stuffed the gun in his pocket. "We'll dispose of the bodies. Go home and get rid of those clothes."

"Thanks."

"Come before gin tomorrow," McKool said. "We'll do the car titles and talk."

I got the gas from the T-bird's trunk, then drove the Explorer home. I disconnected my apartment's smoke detector, threw my clothes in the bathtub, poured in the last of the gas, and burned my bloody clothes to ash. After making sure not a speck of fabric remained, I washed the ash down the drain, then stood under the shower until the hot water ran out, and fell into bed without even bothering to dry. I missed my T-bird.

Sunday afternoon, after a fitful sleep, I knocked on McKool's door. The peephole darkened, and Cartouche let me in. Lilith stood at the stove making dinner for the crowd to come, and one of the dealers, Lefty Louie, sat at a poker table making up decks.

"Step into my office," McKool said, and we went into one of the back rooms. He handed me the local section of Sunday's *Herald,* opened to page five. A story halfway down the page read:

POLICE SUSPECT RUSSIAN MOB HIT
Two dead bodies were found early Sunday on a bus bench off Brickell Avenue, near S.W. 10th Street. Dmitri Ribikoff, a Russian national in the U.S. on an expired visa, had been brutally beaten and shot in the head, execution-style. The victim was a distant cousin of Russian oil oligarch Sergei Petrov, and a spokeswoman for Miami PD said Russian organized crime might be responsible. Police are withholding the name of the other victim, a woman in her twenties, shot through the heart and also badly beaten, pending notification of her family.

"They won't find any family," McKool said. "She had nobody." There was a gentle tapping on the door. "Come."

Lilith stuck her head in. "Luckbucket and Bumper are here."

"We'll be right out," McKool said. He handed me a manila envelope full of hundreds rolled in rubber bands. I didn't need to count it, knew the twenty grand was there. "You understand you owe me," he said. "And last night never happened." He signed the title to the Explorer and handed it to me with the pen.

"Never happened."

"Make it out to Jean-Luc Cartouche."

I looked at him, puzzled. "Cartouche? Why?"

"He wants it. I'd rather he have it and me want it. Ready for gin?"

I signed the title over to Cartouche. "Yeah." Who knew wanting and having were so complicated?

We stepped into the main room, where Bumper and Luckbucket sat leafing through back issues of *Card Player*. Luckbucket's was opened to an article by Roy Cooke headlined: "Some Hands You Just Don't Play!"

Life is like the game, I thought. It's supposed to be the fish who play the trap hands.

"Let's gamble," Bumper said.

McKool turned to Lefty and said, "Shuffle up and deal."

And that's exactly what happened.

JAMES LEE BURKE

A Season of Regret

FROM *Shenandoah*

ALBERT HOLLISTER LIKES the heft of it, the coldness of the steel, the way his hand fits inside the lever action. Even though the Winchester is brand-new, just out of the box from Wal-Mart, he ticks a chain of tiny drops from a can of Three-in-One on all the moving parts, cocks and recocks the hammer and rubs a clean rag over the metal and stock. The directions tell him to run a lubricated bore brush down the barrel, although the weapon has never been fired. After he does so, he slips a piece of white paper behind the chamber and squints down the muzzle with one eye. The oily spiral of light that spins at him through the rifling has an otherworldly quality about it.

He presses a half-dozen .30-30 shells into the tubular magazine with his thumb, then ejects them one by one on his bedspread. His wife has gone to town with the nurse's aide for her doctor's appointment, and the house is quiet. The fir trees and Ponderosa pine on the hillside are full of wind, and a cloud of yellow dust rises off the canopy and sucks away over his barn and pasture. He picks up the shells and fits them back in the cartridge box, then puts the rifle and the shells in his closet, closes the door on them, and drinks a glass of iced tea on the front porch.

Down the canyon he can see the long roll of the Bitterroot Mountains, the moon still visible against the pale blueness of the sky, like a sliver of dry ice. He drains his glass and feels a terrible sense of fatigue and hopelessness wash through his body. If age brings wisdom, he has yet to see it in his own life. Across the driveway, in his north pasture, a large sorrel-colored hump lies in the bunch grass. A pair of magpies descend on top of it, their beaks dipping into their bloody work. Albert looks at the scene with great sorrow on his face, gathers up a pick and a shovel from the garage, and walks down the hillside into the pasture. A blond Labrador retriever bounds along behind him.

"Go back to the house, Buddy," Albert says.

The wind makes a sound like water when it sharks through the grass.

Albert had seen the bikers for the first time only last week. Three of them had ridden up the dirt road that splits his ranch in half, ignoring the PRIVATE ROAD sign nailed to the railed fence that encloses his lower pasture. They turned around when they hit the dead end two hundred yards north of Albert's barn, then cruised back through Albert's property toward the paved highway. They were big men, the sleeves of their denim jackets scissored off at the armpits, their skin wrapped with tattoos. They sat on their motorcycles as though they absorbed the throttled-down power of the engine through their thighs and forearms. The man in the lead had red hair and a wild beard and sweat rings under his arms. He seemed to nod when Albert lifted his hand in greeting.

Albert caught the tag number of the red-haired man's motorcycle and wrote it down on a scrap of paper that he put away in his wallet.

A half hour later he saw them again, this time in front of the grocery store in Lolo, the little service town two miles down the creek from his ranch. They had loaded up with canned goods and picnic supplies and sweating six-packs of beer and were stuffing them into the saddlebags on their motorcycles. He passed within three feet of them, close enough to smell the odor of leather, unwashed hair, engine grease, and wood smoke in their clothes. One of them gargled with his beer before he swallowed it, then grinned broadly at Albert. He wore black glasses, as a welder might. Three blue teardrops were tattooed at the corner of his left eye.

"What's happening, old-timer?" he said.

"Not much outside of general societal decay, I'd say," Albert replied.

The biker gave him a look.

Five days later, Albert drove his truck to the Express Lube and took a walk down toward the intersection while he waited for his truck to be serviced. It was sunset, and the sky was a chemical green, backdropped by the purple shapes of the Bitterroot Mountains. The day was cooling rapidly, and Albert could smell the cold odor of the creek that wound under the highway. It was a fine evening, one augmented by families enjoying themselves at the Dairy Queen, blue-collar people eating in the Mexican restaurant, an eighteen-wheeler shifting down for the long pull over Lolo Pass. But the voices he heard on the periphery of his vision were like a dirty smudge on a perfect moment in time. The three bikers who had trespassed on his private road had blundered onto a young woman who had just gotten out of her car next to the town's only saloon.

Her car was a rust-eaten piece of junk, a piece of cardboard taped across the passenger window, the tires bald, a child's stuffed animal inside the back window. The woman had white-gold hair that was cut short like a boy's, tapered on the sides and shaved on the neck. Her hips looked narrow and hard inside her pressed jeans, her breasts firm against her tight-fitting T-shirt. She was trapped between her car and the three bikers, who behaved as though they had just run into an old friend and only wanted to offer her a beer. But it was obvious they were not moving, at least not without a token to take with them. A pinch on the butt or the inside of her thigh would probably do.

She lit a cigarette and blew the smoke at an upward angle, not responding, waiting for their energies to run down.

"How about a steak when you get off?" the man with the red beard asked.

"Sorry, I got to go home and wash out my old man's underwear," she said.

"Your old man, huh? Wonder why he ain't bought you a ring," the man with the beard replied. When he got no response he tried again. "You a gymnast? 'Cause that's what you look like. Except for that beautiful pair of ta-ta's, you're built like a man. That's meant as a compliment."

Don't mix in it. It's not your grief, Albert told himself.

"Hey, fellows," he said.

The bikers turned and looked at him, like men upon whom a flashbulb had just popped.

"I think she's late for work," Albert said.

"She sent you a kite on that?" the red-bearded man said, smiling.

Albert looked into space. "Y'all on your way to Sturgis?"

The third biker, who so far had not spoken, stuck an unfiltered cigarette into his mouth and lit it with a Zippo that flared on his face. His skin looked like dirty tallow in the evening light, his dark hair hanging in long strands on his cheeks. "She your daughter? Or your wife? Or your squeeze on the side?" he said. He studied Albert. "No, I can see that's probably not the case. Well, that means you should butt out. Maybe go buy yourself a tamale up at the café. A big, fat one, lot of juice running down it."

The bikers grinned into space simultaneously, as though the image conjured up shared meaning that only they understood.

Walk away, the voice inside Albert said.

"What's wrong with you fellows?" he asked.

"What?" the bearded man said.

"You have to bully a young woman to know who you are? What the hell is the matter with you?" Albert said.

The three bikers looked at one another, then laughed. "I remember where I saw you. On that ranch, up the creek a couple of miles. You walk up and down the road a lot, telling other people what to do?" the bearded man said.

The young woman dropped her cigarette to the ground and used the distraction to walk between the bikers, onto the wood porch of the saloon.

"Hey, come on back, sweet thing. You got a sore place, I'll kiss it and make it well," the biker with black glasses said.

She shot him the finger over her shoulder.

"Show time is over," the bearded man said.

"No harm intended," Albert said.

"You got a church hereabouts?" the man with the black glasses said.

"There's a couple up the road," Albert said.

The three bikers looked at one another again, amused, shaking their heads.

"You're sure slow on the uptake," the bearded man said. "If you go to one of them churches next Sunday, drop a little extra in the plate. Thank the Man Upstairs he's taking care of you. It's the right thing to do." He winked at Albert.

But the evening was not over. Fifteen minutes later, after Albert picked up his truck at the Express Lube, he passed by the saloon and saw the three men by the young woman's car. They had pulled the taped cardboard from the passenger-side window and opened the door. The biker with the beard stood with his feet spread, his thighs flexed, his enormous phallus cupped in his palm, urinating all over the dashboard and the seat.

Albert drove down the state highway toward the turnoff and the dirt road that led to his ranch. The hills were dark green against the sunset, the sharp outline of Lolo Peak capped with snow, the creek that paralleled the road sliding through shadows the trees made on the water's surface. He braked his truck, backed it around, and floored the accelerator, the gear shift vibrating in his palm. The note he left under the young woman's windshield wiper was simple: "The Idaho tag number of the red-haired man who vandalized your car is —" He copied onto the note the number he had placed in his wallet the day the bikers had driven through his property. Then he added, "I'm sorry you had this trouble. You did nothing to deserve it."

He walked back toward his truck, wondering if the anonymity of his note was not a form of moral failure in itself. He returned to the woman's car and signed his name and added his phone number at the bottom.

On the way home the wind buffeted his truck, powdering the road with pine needles, fanning geysers of sparks out of a slash pile in a field. In the distance he saw a solitary bolt of lightning strike the ridgeline and quiver whitely against the sky. The air smelled of ozone and rain, but it brought him no relief from the sense of apprehension that seized his chest. There was a bitter taste in his mouth, like copper pennies, like blood, a taste that reminded him of his misspent youth.

It takes him most of the afternoon to hand-dig a hole in the pasture in order to bury the sorrel mare. The vinyl drawstring bag someone had wrapped over her head and cinched tight around her neck lies crumpled and streaked with ropes of dried saliva and mucus in the bunch grass. The under sheriff, Joe Bim Higgins, watches Albert fling the dirt off the shovel blade onto the horse's flank and stomach and tail.

"I checked them out. You picked quite a threesome to get into it with," Joe Bim says.

"Wasn't of my choosing," Albert replies.

"Others might argue that."

Albert wipes the sweat off his forehead with the back of his forearm. The wind is up, channeling through the grass, bending the fir trees that dot the slopes of the hills that border both sides of his ranch. The sun is bright on the hills and the shadow of a hawk races across the pasture and breaks apart at the fence line. "Say again?"

"In the last year you filed a complaint because some kids fired bottle rockets on your property. You pissed off the developers trying to build a subdivision down on the creek. You called the president a draft-dodging moron in print. Some might say you have adversarial tendencies."

Albert thought about it. "Yes, I guess I do, Joe Bim. Particularly when a lawman stands beside my dead horse and tells me the problem is me, not the sons of bitches who ran her heart out."

But Joe Bim is not a bad man. He removes a shovel from his departmental SUV and helps Albert bury the animal, wheezing down in his chest, his stomach hanging against his shirt like a water-filled balloon. "All three of those boys been in the pen," he says. "The one who hosed down the girl's car is a special piece of work. His child was taken away from him and his wife for its own protection."

Then Joe Bim tells Albert what the biker or his wife or both of them did to a four-month-old infant. Albert's eyes film. His clears his throat and spits into the grass. "Why aren't they in jail?" he says.

"Why do we have crack and meth in middle schools? The goddamn courts, that's why. But it ain't gonna change because you get into it with a bunch of psychopaths."

Albert packs down the dirt on top of his horse and lays a row of large, flat stones on top of the dirt. He cannot rid himself of the images Joe Bim's story has created in his mind. Joe Bim looks at him for a long time.

"How's the wife?" he asks.

"Parkinson's is Parkinson's. Some days are better than others," Albert says.

"You're a gentle man. Don't mess in stuff like this," Joe Bim says. "I'll get them out of town. They're con-wise. They know the hurt we can put on them."

You have no idea what you're talking about, Albert says to himself.

"What's that?" Joe Bim asks.

"Nothing. Thanks for coming out. Listen to that wind blow," Albert says.

Before his retirement he had taught at the state university in Missoula, although he did not have a Ph.D., and had managed to publish several novels that had enjoyed a fair degree of commercial success. Early on he had learned the secret of survival among academics, and that was to avoid showing any sign of disrespect for what they did. But in actuality the latter had never been a problem for him. He not only respected his colleagues but thought their qualifications and background superior to his own. His humility and Southern manners and publications earned him a tenured position and in an odd way gave him a form of invisibility. In the aftermath of the most bitter faculty meetings, no one could remember if Albert had attended the meeting or not.

In truth, Albert's former colleagues, as well as his current friends, including Joe Bim Higgins, have no idea who he really is.

He never speaks of the road gang he served time on as a teenager, or the jails and oil-town flophouses he slept in from Mobile to Corpus Christi. In fact, he considers most of his youthful experience of little consequence.

Except for one event that forever shaped his thinking about the darkness that can live in the human breast.

It was the summer of 1955, and he had been sentenced to seven days in a parish prison after a bloody, nose-breaking brawl outside a bar on the Texas-Louisiana line. The male lockdown unit was an enormous iron tank, perforated with square holes, on the third floor of the building. Most of the inmates were check writers, drunks, wife beaters, and petty thieves. A handful of more serious criminals were awaiting transfer to the state prison farm at Angola. The inmates were let out of the tank at seven A.M. each day and allowed the use of the bull run and the shower until five P.M., when they went back into lockdown until the next morning. By six P.M. the tank was sweltering, the smoke from cigarettes trapped against the iron ceiling, the toilets often clogged and reeking.

The treatment of the inmates was not deliberately cruel. The trusties ladled out black coffee, grits, sausage, and white bread for breakfast and spaghetti at noon. It was the kind of can where you did your time, stayed out of the shower when the wrong people were in there, never accepted favors from another inmate, and never, under any circumstances, sassed a hack. The seven days should have been a breeze. They weren't.

On Albert's fourth day a trailer truck with two huge generators boomed down on the bed pulled to a stop with a hiss of airbrakes and parked behind the prison.

"What's that?" Albert asked.

"This is Lou'sana, boy. The executioner does it curbside, no extra charge," an inmate wiping his armpits with a ragged towel replied. His name was Deek. His skin was as white as a frog's belly, and he was doing consecutive one-year sentences for auto theft and jailbreak.

But Albert was staring down from the barred window at a beanpole of a man on the sidewalk and was not concentrating on Deek's words. The man on the sidewalk was dressed western, complete with brim-coned hat, the bones of his shoulders almost piercing his snap-button shirt. He was supervising the unloading of a heavy, rectangular object wrapped with canvas. "Say that again?" Albert said.

"They're fixing to fry that poor sonofabitch across the hall," Deek replied.

The clouds above the vast swampland to the west were the color of scorched iron, pulsing with electricity. Albert could smell an odor like dead fish on the wind.

"Some night for it, huh?" Deek said.

Without explanation, the jailer put the inmates into lockdown an hour early. The heat and collective stink inside the tank were almost unbearable. Albert thought he heard a man weeping across the hall. At eight P.M. the generators on the truck trailer began to hum, building in velocity and force until the sounds of the street, the juke joint on the corner, and even the electric storm bursting above the swamp were absorbed inside a grinding roar that made Albert press his palms against his ears.

He would have sworn he saw lightning leap from the bars on the window, then the generators died, and he could smell rain blowing through the window and hear a jukebox playing in a bar across the street from the jail.

The next morning the jailer ran a weapons search on the tank and also sprayed it for lice. The inmates from the tank were moved into the hall and the room in which the condemned man had died. The door to the perforated two-bunk iron box in which he had spent his last night on earth was open, the electric chair already loaded on the trailer truck down below. When Albert touched the concrete surface of the windowsill, he thought he could feel the residue from the rubber-coated power cables that had been stretched through the bars. He also smelled an odor that was like food that had fallen from a skillet into a fire.

Then he saw the man in the coned hat and western clothes emerge from a café across the street with a masculine-looking woman and two uniformed sheriff's deputies. They were laughing — perhaps at a joke or an incident that had just happened in the café. The man in the coned hat turned his face up into the light and seemed to look directly at Albert. His face was thin, the skin netted with lines, his eyes as bright and small as a serpent's.

"You waving at free people?" a guard said. He was a lean, sun-browned man who had been a mounted gun bull at Angola before he had become a sheriff's deputy and a guard at the parish prison. Even though the morning was still cool, his shirt was peppered with sweat, as though his body heat created its own environment.

"No, sir."

"So get away from the window."

"Yes, sir." Then he asked the question that rose from his chest into his mouth before he could undo the impulse. "Was that fellow crying last night?"

The guard lifted his chin, his mouth down-turned at the corners. "It ain't none of your business what he was doing."

Albert nodded and didn't reply.

"Food cart's inside now. Go eat your breakfast," the guard said.

"Don't know if I can handle any more grits, boss. Why don't you eat them for me?" Albert said.

The guard tightened the tuck of his shirt with his thumb, his expression thoughtful, his shoulders as square as a drill instructor's. He inhaled deeply through his nostrils. "Let's take a walk down to the second floor, get you a little better accommodated," he said. "Fine morning, don't you think?"

Albert never told anyone of what the guard did to him. But sometimes he smells the guard's stink in his sleep, a combination of chewing tobacco and hair oil and testosterone and dried sweat that had been ironed with starch into the clothes. In the dream he also sees the upturned face of the executioner, his skin lit in the sunshine, his friends grinning at a joke they had brought with them from the café. Albert has always wanted to believe this emblematic moment in his life was regional in origin, born out of ignorance and fear and redneck cruelty, perhaps one even precipitated by his own recklessness, but he knows otherwise.

Albert has learned that certain injuries go deep into the soul, like a stone bruise, and that time does not eradicate them. He knows that the simian creature that lived in the guard and the executioner took root many years ago in his own breast. He knows that, under the right circumstances, Albert Hollister is capable of deeds no one would associate with the professor who taught creative writing at the university and whose presence at a faculty meeting was so innocuous it was not even remembered.

To the east the fog is heavy and white and hangs in long strips on the hills bordering Albert's ranch. When the early sun climbs above the crest, it seems to burst among the trees like a shattered red diamond. From the kitchen window, where he is drinking coffee and looking down the long slope of his southern pasture, he sees a rusty car coming up the road, its headlights glowing against the shadows that cover the valley floor. One headlight is out of alignment and glitters oddly, like the eye of a man who has been injured in a fight. The passenger window is encased with cardboard and silver duct tape.

The girl from the saloon knocks at his front door, dressed in colorless jeans and a navy-blue corduroy coat. She wears a cute cap and her cheeks are red in the wind. She is obviously awed by the size of his home, the massive amounts of quarried stone that support the two top floors, the huge logs that could probably absorb a cannon shell. Through the rear window of her vehicle, he can see a small boy strapped in a child's car seat.

"I wanted to tell you I'm sorry about what happened to your horse," she says.

"It's not your fault," Albert says.

Her eyes leave his, then come back again. He thinks he can smell an odor in her clothes and hair like damp leaves burning in the fall. He hears his wife call to him from the bedroom. "Come in," he tells the girl. "I have to see to Mrs. Hollister. She's been ill for some time now."

Then he wonders to himself why he has just told the girl his personal business.

"We're on our way to Idaho. I just wanted to thank you and to apologize."

"That's good of you. But it's not necessary."

She looks down the pasture at the frost on the barn roof and the wind blowing in the bunch grass. She sucks in her cheeks, as though her mouth has gone dry. "They got your name from me, not from the under sheriff."

In the silence he can hear his wife getting up from the bed and walking toward the bathroom on her own. He feels torn between listening to the young woman and tending to his wife. "Run that by me again," he says.

"One of them was my ex-husband's cellmate in Deer Lodge. They wanted to know your name and if it was you who called the cops. They're in the A.B. That's why I'm going to Idaho. I'm not pressing charges," she says.

"The Aryan Brotherhood?"

She sticks her hands in the pockets of her jacket and balls them into fists, all the time looking at the ground. Then Albert realizes she has not come to his home simply to apologize. He also realizes the smoke he smells on her clothes and person did not come from a pile of burning leaves.

"My boss is gonna send me a check in two weeks. At least that's what he says. My boyfriend is trying to get one of those FEMA construction jobs in New Orleans. But his P.O. won't give him permission to leave the state. I have enough money for gas to Idaho, Mr. Hollister, but I don't have enough for a motel."

"I see," he replies, and wonders how a man of his age could be so dumb. "Will fifty dollars help? Because that's all I have on me."

She seems to think about it. "That'd be all right," she says. She glances over her shoulder at the little boy strapped in the car seat. Her nails look bitten, the self-concern and design in her eyes undisguised. "The saloon will be open at ten."

"I don't follow you," he said.

"I could take a check. They'll cash it for me at the saloon."

He lets her words slide off his face without reacting to them. When he removes the bills from his wallet and places them in her hand, she cups his fingers in her palm. "You're a good man," she says.

"When are they coming?" he asks.

"Sir?"

He shakes his head to indicate he has disengaged from the conversation and closes the door, then walks down the hallway and helps his wife back to her bed. "Was that someone from the church?" she asks.

During the night he hears hail on the roof, then high winds that make a rushing sound, like water, through the trees on the hillsides. He dreams about a place in South Texas where he and his father bobber-fished in a chain of ponds that had been formed by sheets of twisted steel spinning out of the sky like helicopter blades when Texas City exploded in February of 1947. In the dream wind is blowing through a piney woods that borders a salt-water bay hammered with light. His father speaks to him inside the wind, but Albert cannot make out the words or decipher the meaning they contain.

In the distance he hears motorized vehicles grinding up a grade, throttling back, then accelerating again, working their way higher and higher up the mountainside, with the relentlessness of chainsaws.

He wakes and sits up in bed, not because of the engines but because they have stopped — somewhere above his house, inside the trees, perhaps on the ridgeline where an old log road traverses the length of the canyon.

He removes the rifle from his closet and loads it. He disarms the security system and steps out onto the gallery, in the moonlight and the sparkle of frost on the bunch grass. His hands and uncovered head and bare feet are cold. He levers a shell into the chamber, but releases the hammer with his thumb so that it cannot drop by accident and strike the shell casing, discharging the round. The fir trees are black-green against the hillside, the arroyo behind his house empty. The air is clean and smells of pine and snow melting on the rocks and wood smoke from a neighbor's chimney down the canyon. In the whisper of the wind through the trees he wants to believe the engine sounds in his dream are just that — the stuff of dreams. Far up the hill he hears a glass bottle break on stone and a motorcycle roar to life.

Inside the topmost trees three separate fires burst alight and fill the woods with shadows. The sound of motorcycle engines multiplies and three balls of flame move in different directions down the ridgeline. Inside the house, he calls 911, and through the back window he sees the silhouette of one rider towing a fireball that caroms off the undergrowth, the points of ignition fanning down the slope in the wind.

"What's the nature of your emergency?" the dispatcher asks.

"This is Albert Hollister, up Sleeman Gulch. At least three men on motorcycles are stringing fires down my ridgeline."

"Which way are they headed?"

"Who cares where they're headed? The wind is out of the southwest. I'll have sparks on my roof in a half hour. Get the goddamn pump trucks up here."

"Would you not swear, please?"

"These men are criminals. They're burning my land."

"Repeat, please. I cannot understand what you're saying."

His voice has wakened and frightened his wife. He comforts her in her bed, then goes outside again and watches a red glow spread across the top of the valley. The summer has been dry, and the fire ripples through the soft patina of grass at the base of the trees and superheats the air trapped under the canopy. A sudden rush of cold wind through the timber hits the fire like an influx of pure oxygen. Flame balloons out of the canopy and in seconds turns fir trees into black scorches dripping with sparks. He can hear deer running across rocks and see hundreds of bats flying in and out of a sulfurous yellow cloud that has formed above the flames. He connects a hose to the faucet on the back of the house and sprays the bib of green grass on the slope, his heart racing, his mouth dry with fear.

By noon the next day the wind has died and inside the smell of ash is another odor, one that reminds him of the small room on the third floor of the parish prison where a man was strapped down in a wood chair and cooked to death with thousands of volts of electricity. Joe Bim Higgins stands next to Albert in the south pasture and stares up the hillside at the burned rocks and great stands of fir that are now rust-colored, as though stricken by blight.

Joe Bim blows his nose into a handkerchief and spits into the grass. "We found a sow and her cub inside a deadfall. The fire was probably crowning when they tried to outrun it," he says.

"Where are they, Joe Bim?" Albert asks.

"Just up there where you see that outcropping." He tries to pretend his misunderstanding of Albert's question is sincere, then gives it up. "I had all three of them in a holding cell at seven this morning. But they got an alibi. Two people at their campground say they was at the campground all night."

"You cut them loose?"

Joe Bim is not a weak man or one who has avoided paying dues. He was at Heartbreak Ridge, and one side of his face is still marbled from the heat flash of a phosphorous shell that exploded ten feet from his foxhole. "I can't chain drag these guys down the Blackfoot highway because you don't like them. Look, I've got two deputies assigned to watch them. One of them throws a cigarette butt on the sidewalk —"

"Go back to town," Albert says.

"Maybe you don't know who your real friends are."

"Yeah, my wife and my blond Lab, Buddy. I'd include my sorrel, except the two of us buried her."

"You're like me, Albert. You're an old man, and you can't accept the fact you can't have your way with everything. Grow up and stop making life hard for yourself and others."

Albert walks away without replying. Later, he spreads lime on the carcasses of the bears that died in the fire and tries not to think the thoughts he is thinking.

That night, during a raging electrical storm, Albert leaves his wife in the care of the nurse's aide and drives in his pickup to the only twenty-four-hour public campground on the Blackfoot River in Missoula County, his lever-action rifle jittering in the rack behind his head. It's not hard to find the three bikers. Their sky-blue polyethylene tent is huge, brightly lit from the inside, the extension flaps propped up on poles to shelter their motorcycles. Lightning flickers on the hillside across the river, limning the trees, turning the current in the river an even deeper black. The smell of ozone in the air makes Albert think of the Gulf Coast and his youth and the way rain smelled when it blew across the wetlands in the fall. He thinks of his father, who died while returning from a duck-hunting camp in Anahuac, Texas, leaving Albert to fend for himself. He wonders if this is the way dementia and death eventually steal upon a man's soul.

Down the road he parks his truck inside a grove of Douglas fir trees that are shaggy with moss and climbs up the hill into boulders that look like the shells of giant gray turtles. He works his way across the slope until he can look down on the bikers' campsite. In the background the river is like black satin, the canyon roaring with the sounds of high water and reverberated thunder. The flap of the bikers' tent is open, and Albert can see three men inside, eating from GI mess kits, a bottle of stoppered booze resting against a rolled sleeping bag. They look like working men on a summer vacation, enjoying a meal together, perhaps talking about the fish they caught that day. But Albert knows their present circumstances and appearance and behavior have nothing to do with who they really are.

They could as easily wear starched uniforms as they do jailhouse tats. Their identity lies in their misogyny and violence and cruelty to animals and children, not the blue teardrops at the corner of the eyes or the greasy jeans or the fog of testosterone and dried beer-sweat on their bodies. These are the same men who operated Robespierre's torture chambers. They're the burners of the Alexandrian library, the brownshirts who pumped chlorine gas into shower rooms. They use religions and flags that allow them to peel civilizations off the face of the earth. There is no difference, Albert tells himself, between these men and a screw in a parish prison on the Louisiana-Texas border where a guard frog-walked a kid in cuffs down to an isolation area, shoved him to his knees, and closed the door on the outside world.

The rain looks like spun glass blowing in front of the open tent flap. The biker with the red beard emerges from the opening, fills his lungs with air, and checks his motorcycle. He wipes off the frame and handlebars with a clean rag and admires the perfection of his machine. Albert levers a round into the chamber and steadies his rifle across the top of a large rock. The notch of the steel sight moves across the man's mouth and throat, the broad expanse of his chest, the hair blossoming from his shirt, then down his stomach and scrotum and jeans that are stiff with road grime and engine grease and glandular fluids.

In his mind's eye Albert sees all the years of his youth reduced to typewritten lines written on a sheet of low-grade paper. He sees the paper consumed by a white-hot light that burns a hole through the pulp, curling through the typed words, releasing images that he thought he had dealt with years ago but in reality has not. In the smoke and flame he sees a stretch of rain-swept black road and his father's car embedded under the frame of a tractor-trailer rig; he sees the naked, hair-covered thighs of a former Angola gun bull looming above him; he sees the ax-bladed face of a state executioner, a toothpick in his mouth, his eyes staring whimsically at Albert, as though it is Albert who is out of sync with the world and not the man who cinches the leather straps tightly to the wrists and calves of the condemned. Albert raises the rifle sight to the red-bearded man's chest and, just as a bolt of lightning splits a towering Ponderosa pine in half, he squeezes the trigger.

The rifle barrel flares into the darkness and he already imagines the bullet on its way to the red-bearded man's chest. The round is copper-jacketed, soft-nosed, and when it strikes the man's sternum it will flatten and topple slightly and core through the lungs and leave an exit wound the size of Albert's thumb.

My God, what has he done?

Albert stands up from behind the boulder and stares down the hillside. The bearded man has taken a candy bar from his pocket and is eating it in the light from the tent flap while he watches the rain blowing.

He missed, thanks either to the Lord or the constriction in his chest that caused his hand to jerk or maybe just to the fact he's not cut out of the same cloth as the man he has tried to kill.

Albert grasps the rifle by the barrel and swings it against a boulder and sees the butt plate and screws burst loose from the stock. He swings the rifle again, harder, and still breaks nothing of consequence loose from either the wood or the steel frame. He flings the rifle like a pinwheel into the darkness, the sight on the barrel's tip ripping the heel of his hand.

He cannot believe what happens next. The rifle bounces muzzle-down off the roof of a passing SUV, arcing back into the air with new life, and lands right in front of the bikers' tent.

He drives farther down the dirt road, away from the bikers'

camp, his headlights off, rocks skidding from his tires into the canyon below.

When he gets back home, he strips off his wet clothes and sits in the bottom of the shower stall until he drains all the hot water out of the tank. His hands will not stop shaking.

The rains are heavy the following spring, and in May the bunch grass in Albert's pastures is tall and green, as thick as Kansas wheat, and the hillsides are sprinkled with wildflowers. In the evening white-tailed and mule deer drift out of the trees and graze along the edge of the irrigation canal he has dug from a spring at the base of the burned area behind his house. He would like to tell himself that the land will continue to mend, that a good man has nothing to fear from the world, and that he has put aside the evil done to him by the bikers. But he has finally learned that lying to oneself is an offense for which human beings seldom grant themselves absolution.

He comes to believe that acceptance of a wintry place in the soul and a refusal to speak about it to others is as much consolation as a man gets, and for some odd reason that thought seems to bring him peace. He is thinking these thoughts as he returns home from his wife's funeral in June. Joe Bim Higgins is sitting on the front steps of his gallery, the trousers of his dress suit stuffed inside his cowboy boots, a Stetson hat balanced on his knee, a cigarette almost burned down to a hot stub between two fingers. A pallbearer's ribbon is still in his lapel.

"The old woman wants me to invite you to dinner tonight," Joe Bim says.

"I appreciate it," Albert replies.

"You never heard no more from those bikers, huh?"

"Why would I?"

Joe Bim pinches out the end of his cigarette, field-strips the paper, and watches the tobacco blow away in the wind. "Got a call two days ago from Sand Point. The one with the red beard killed the other two and an Indian woman for good measure. The three of them was drunk and fighting over the woman."

"I'm not interested."

"The killing got done with an 1894-model Winchester. Guess who it's registered to? How'd they end up with your rifle, Albert?"

"Maybe they found it somewhere."

"I think they stole it out of your house, and you didn't know about it. That's why you didn't report it stolen." Joe Bim folds his hands and gazes at the hillside across the road and the wildflowers ruffling in the wind.

"They killed an innocent person with it?" Albert asks.

"If she was hanging with that bunch, she bought her own ticket. Show some humility for a change. You didn't invent original sin."

Albert starts to tell Joe Bim all of it — the attempt he made on the biker's life, the deed the sheriff's deputy had done to him when he was eighteen, the accidental death of his father, the incipient rage that has lived in his breast all his adult life — but the words break apart in his throat before he can speak them. In the silence he can hear the wind coursing through the trees and grass, just like the sound of rushing water, and he wonders if it is blowing through the canyon where he lives or through his own soul. He wonders if his reticence with Joe Bim is not indeed the moment of absolution that has always eluded him. He waits for Joe Bim to speak again but realizes his friend's crooked smile is one of puzzlement, not omniscience, that the puckered skin on the side of his face is a reminder that the good people of the world each carry their own burden.

Albert feeds his dog and says a prayer for his wife. Then he drives down the dirt road with Joe Bim in a sunset that makes him think of gold pollen floating above the fields.

JOHN DUFRESNE

The Timing of Unfelt Smiles

FROM *Miami Noir*

AT 9:15 ON THURSDAY MORNING, June 4, while Jordan Delreese was bludgeoning his two young children to death, I was sitting in Dr. Hamburger's consulting room at the Sunny Isles Geriatric Clinic with my father, who was just then at a loss for
words. He had been trying to explain to the doctor why he no
longer felt comfortable being in the same room with his shadow.
He'd said, If light can pass through the universe, why can't it pass
through me? But now he could only manage to hum and to shake
his head. I highlighted a speech in my script. Dad's contention,
as near as I could figure it, was that light had a mind of its own
and had taken to behaving arbitrarily and recklessly in the last
six months or so. After Dr. Hamburger clicked off his desk lamp,
Dad took off his eyeshade, blinked, rubbed his rheumy eyes, and
asked me who I was. Dr. Hamburger tapped the side of his pre-
scription pad on his desk blotter, leaned back in his squeaky Pos-
ture-Tech office chair, cast me a glance, raised his articulate brow,
and lifted his upper eyelids. Lid-lifters tend to be a tad melodra-
matic.

Dr. Hamburger had diagnosed Dad with Alzheimer's. Dad said
he was merely closing up shop. He hadn't lost his ability to make
metaphor, not yet. And he did have his lucid moments. He was in
and out, however, and he was hard to read. His expressions were often without nuance or blend. He was extremely angry, extremely
happy, or extremely vacant. He could remember what he had for
breakfast on June 15, 1944, in Guam (gumdrop candy, two cook-
ies), but not that he just turned on the gas without lighting the pi-

lot; which is why I had to move him into an all-electric, assisted-living facility.

Jordan Delreese walked down to the kitchen after slashing his wife's throat and changing out of his blood-soaked pajamas and into a maroon polo shirt and khaki chinos. He clapped his hands and told Davenport and Darchelle to finish up their Cap'n Crunch quick like bunnies. Darchelle said she thought she heard Mommy screaming before, but then it stopped.

Jordan said, You did, dumpling. Mommy and Daddy were playing Multiply and Replenish again.

In the morning? she said. That's silly.

Jordan asked the kids if they wanted to play a game too. They sure would. Okay, then you have to clean up your mess, put the bowls in the sink and the spoons in the dishwasher, handles up. Davenport wanted to know what the game was called. Just Rewards, Jordan said.

The kids giggled when Jordan blindfolded them. He told Darchelle to wait in her room and to count to two hundred. One Mississippi, she said. He locked her door and led Davenport to the children's bathroom. The tub was full. He asked Davenport to lie on his back on the floor. Yes, I know the tile is cold, but it won't be for long. Jordan took the hammer from the ledge of the tub, raised it above his shoulder, and brought it down on his son's right eye, and then the left eye, the mouth, the forehead, the forehead again. He wiped the slick face of the hammerhead on an aqua hand towel and walked to Darchelle's room. One hundred and eleven Mississippi, she said. Darchelle lay on the floor like her daddy asked her to. Jordan said, I saved you for last, dumpling, because you are my special angel. She did not get to say, Goody! or, Thank you, Daddy.

And then, to be extra certain that his buddy and his dumpling did not wake up in pain, Jordan laid the children face down in the bathtub. He washed his hands with antibacterial soap, singing "Happy Birthday" twice while he did. Dr. Sanjay Gupta on CNN said that's how long it takes to wash your hands properly. Jordan went downstairs and made himself breakfast. Scrambled eggs on a blueberry Pop-Tart, sausage links, a box of grape Juicy Juice. While he ate and read the *Sun-Sentinel,* he called his mother and asked her if she and Dad would be home this afternoon. He'd like to pay a visit. Do I have to have a reason? His mom told him she'd make gingerbread and whipped cream. Jordan said, I'll be there one-ish.

Jordan lifted the children out of the tub and dried them off. He noticed a small mole on Darchelle's left hip, examined it, touched it, figured it was probably nothing. He tucked them both into Davenport's bed, pulled the sheets to their chins, covered their faces with the lace doilies from Darchelle's vanity. He nestled cuddly toys next to their bodies and read them the Bible story about Abraham and Isaac. He sang their favorite lullaby. *Sweetest little baby, everybody knows. Don't know what to call her, but she's mighty like a rose.* He choked back tears. Jordan decided to drive to North Beach in Hollywood, stare at the ocean, clear his head. And then maybe surprise his parents by showing up early. He'd drive by Whole Foods and pick up lunch. Some of that tabouli he likes so much. And the grilled portobellos. He cleared the table, started the dishwasher, went up to the master bath, and hopped in the shower.

I told Dad I was still Wylie, the same old Wylie.

"Well, you look a little like my boy Winston."

"Winston was your bulldog."

"Like Cameron, I mean."

"Cameron's dead. I'm all you got."

"Where's Birute?"

"Mom's dead."

"I know she's dead. That's not what I asked you."

Dr. Hamburger had Dad take off his shirt — easier said than done — and climb up on the examining table. I turned my script toward the window light and read Willis's next speech. *It's like you're in ninth grade, and you die and go into high school. That's all death is.* I was playing Willis Harris in the Gold Coast Theatre's production of *Trailerville*. Willis is a true believer. I'm not. It was one week till dress rehearsal. *Or maybe you're humming along in a big rig, and you see a long straightaway up ahead and you shift gears and jam that pedal, and just like that the hum of the engine's an octave higher. Dying's like that, like shifting into a higher gear.* My cell phone vibrated. I excused myself and stepped out into the hall. Dr. Hamburger was trying to unknot Dad's T-shirt from around his neck.

The call was from my friend, Detective Carlos O'Brien of the Hollywood Police Department, requesting my immediate services.

He had a situation in the Lakes. Three bodies, two weapons, one missing suspect, much blood. "I need you here, Coyote. Now."

"I'll have to take my dad."

"How's he doing?"

"He's not himself."

"Ten minutes."

I couldn't leave Dad in the car with the keys in the ignition, so I opened the windows and gave him a Fifteen Puzzle, told him to slide the numbers around until they were all in order.

"In order of importance?" he said.

"In numerical order."

I'm not a police officer. That morning I was a forensic consultant. Sometimes I work for lawyers who are trying to empanel the appropriate jury for their clients. Sometimes I sit in my office and help my own clients shape their lives into stories, so the lives finally make some sense. A lack of narrative structure, as you know, will cause anxiety. And that's when I call myself a therapist. And that's what it says on my business card: *Wylie Melville, MSW, Family and Individual Counseling.* Carlos uses me, however, because I read minds, even if those minds aren't present. I say I read minds, but that's not it really. I read faces and furniture. I look at a person, at his expressions, his gestures, his clothing, his home, and his possessions, and I can tell you what he's thinking. I've always been able to do it. Carlos calls me an intuitionist. Dr. Cabrera at UM's Cognitive Thinking Lab tells me I have robust mirror neurons. I just look, I stare, I gaze, and I pay attention to what I see.

Carlos showed me the framed wedding photo they'd found on the slain wife's body. No, I said, I'd prefer not to see the victims. The photographer had posed the couple with Jordan's cheek on — "applied" might be a better word — with Jordan's cheek applied to Caroldean's temple, and he'd canted the shot at a thirty-degree angle. I wondered what he saw that suggested the pressure and the slant. Jordan's smile was thin, yet wide, as wide as he knew was appropriate to the occasion and pleasing to the photographer. Adequate but unfelt. His eyes were eager, yet slightly squinted. I guessed that the obvious accompanying brow lines had been Photoshopped out. You can't trust photos to tell you the truth anymore. Caroldean wore a diamond stud in her left ear and a thin silver necklace. She had a dimple on her right cheek, like she was used to smiling out one side of her face. This ingrained unevenness suggested a lifetime of feigned emotion.

Jordan River Delreese was a thirty-five-year-old graduate of FIU's College of Business Administration and the CEO of, and the creative force behind, Succeedingly Wealthy, Inc., a company that produced and sold motivational artwork. Like there's this photo of crashing waves on a rocky, forested coast, and beneath it, in case you think this is just an empty, if dramatic landscape, are Jordan's words: *Sometimes amidst the waves of change, we find our true direction.* Or maybe there's a lighthouse, its beacon shining above a roiling sea, and Jordan has printed: *The savage sea can pull our customers in many directions. Our duty is to light their way to safety — before the competition does.* Above his desk in his office at the back of the house hung his company's best-selling framed photo, a shot of a golf green in the brilliant light of early morning, dew still on the grass. The photo is titled *Success,* and beneath the photo, Jordan's inspiring words: *Some people only dream of success . . . other folks wake up early and work at it.*

You can lie with your possessions, of course. I suppose we all do this a bit, stash the Enya CDs in a drawer and leave the Chet Baker and the Louis Prima conspicuously on the coffee table. Jordan had lined his office bookshelf with the hundred-volume set from the Franklin Library of *The Collected Stories of the World's Greatest Writers, from Aesop to Thomas Wolfe.* Each book had gold decor on leather boards, gilt page edges, silky end pages, and a ribbon bookmark. None of the spines had been broken; none of the pages in those volumes I checked had been thumbed.

The neatness of the office, the precise arrangement of items on Jordan's desk — laptop computer, family photo, cherry wood and punched–black metal desk organizer, matching Rolodex and pencil cup, stapler, tape dispenser, wire mesh paper clip holder — told me that he was a man with a firm handshake, a pumper, not a wrist grabber, a man who numbered his arguments, asked and answered his own questions, and was given to proverbial expression. Tucked into the side rail of his mocha desk pad, a note on pink "while-you-were-out" message paper, presumably to himself: *Stumbling isn't falling.* I took a business card from the leather card holder. The *S* in *Succeedingly* was a dollar sign.

In the family photo, our four Delreeses are posed casually, sitting on a white rug against a white backdrop. They wear white, long-sleeved oxford shirts, white casual slacks, and white socks. Jordan's in the middle, one hand on his leg, looking up at Darchelle, who smiles back at him. Caroldean — there's that dimple again — has her arm around Davenport. His is the smile of a child about to drift away to sleep. You can always tell a happy marriage. People in love begin to acquire each other's traits, each other's styles — they begin to look and act alike. They want to please. They admire each other and, naturally enough, want to become what they esteem and cherish. That had not happened with the Delreeses.

Carlos handed me a sheet of lime-green stationery. "He left a note."

Jordan's writing was half print, half cursive; his words began with a flourish and ended with a flat line.

I killed the children. Five minutes of pain for a lifetime of suffering. I know that Jehovah will take care of my little ones in the next life. And if Jehovah is willing, I would love to see them again in the resurrection, to have my second chance. I don't plan to live much longer myself, not on this earth. I have come to hate this life and this unreasonable system of things. I have come to have no hope. I give you my wife, Caroldean, my honey, my precious love. Please take care of her.

I told Carlos that no person who has ever tried to be honest for even one second of his life could think like this.

Carlos said, "He's a deacon in his church."

"Of course he is. And he's probably a scoutmaster."

"Soccer coach."

"There you go."

"So you think the volunteer work is pretense? You don't think he's sincere?"

I shook my head. "I think sincerity is his honesty. And I think you'd better find Mr. Delreese soon. He's not finished. The family was just the flourish. He'll kill again. My guess is he's killed before."

Back at the car, I nudged Dad awake, strapped him in his seat belt, closed the windows, cranked up the AC, and drove toward Federal Highway. I told Dad about the victims, omitting the gruesome details. He shrugged. "Life is nothing," he said.

"But it's all we've got."

"Nothing's plenty for me."

"Did you finish your puzzle?"

"The zero was missing."

"So what did you do?"

"Killed some time." He picked up my script, fanned the pages, found a highlighted speech, and fed me my cue. *"You want to lose her too?"*

"A man belongs with his family, Arlis. Where we come from, the elderly are not discarded like old rags."

"Are you listening to yourself?"

"That's not in the script, Dad."

"What was her name?"

"Who?"

"Your ex-wife."

"Georgia. What about her?"

"On my mind is all. You lost her."

"She found someone else."

"So she's dead to you."

I dropped Dad at Clover House in North Miami, told him I'd pick him up on Sunday for the Marlins game.

On the way to rehearsal I took a chance. I checked Delreese's business card and called his cell. I told him who I was and said I was hoping he could design me a piece of art I could hang in my office. What I had in mind was one of those Hubble shots of distant space, maybe the one of the eagle nebula or some radiant spiral galaxy, and it'll say, *I love the light for it shows me the way. I endure the dark for it shows me the stars.* Something like that.

Jordan Delreese told his parents that the kids were swell, fit as fiddles, never been better. He asked his mother to pass the tabouli. She told him to leave room for dessert. Caroldean's busy with her scrapbook project, he said. He told them that when he was at the beach earlier he saw this cloud that looked like an angel. Did they see it too? Like Michael the archangel. They hadn't seen it. What do you think it means? he said.

Rain, his father said.

Jordan said, He makes the sun to rise on the evil and the good, and sendeth rain on the just and the unjust.

Amen, his mother said.

Jordan's BlackBerry played "You Are the Wind Beneath My Wings." He checked the number and punched *Ignore.*

*

Emotions don't lie, but you can lie about them. Of course, lying about them's not so easy. You're angry, but you say, I'm not angry, but then just for a moment, you draw your eyebrows down and together, flash those vertical wrinkles on your forehead, and press your lips together. Or maybe it's your body that leaks the truth. Your natural-born liar understands that everyone is watching his transpicuous face, and he knows that an easy smile is the cleverest mask. Gestures, however, may belie that smile. He brushes a nonexistent piece of lint from his slacks, drums his fingers, leans forward.

You can't command emotions to appear, but you can coax them, summon them. I learned that in acting class. Stanislavsky said if you move your hands in a tender way, you'll begin to experience tenderness. You move with the quality of tenderness, in other words, and the movement will evoke the sensation of tenderness, and that sensation will lead you to the true emotion, and now you're feeling it. No pretense. Change your expression and you change your nervous system. And you can use your own life experiences and your remembered feelings to help you understand your character. Work from an aroused emotion back to the source of it. In other words, to lie on stage, you need to be honest with yourself.

I was working on feeling Willis's exhilaration, his joy about life after death and the promise of eternal salvation. Easy enough to slap on the brilliant smile, brighten the bountiful eyes. I stood on my toes like I couldn't hold the good news inside, like I was bursting with beatific energy. I started hopping, pounding my fists in the air. Hiroshi, our director, asked me to take it down a notch, or several. "It's only life everlasting, Wylie; it's not a weekend with Madonna." I wondered if I had any exhilaration in my past to call on. When had I ever been so deliriously excited? Maybe on my wedding day, but the failure of that whole enterprise got me sad like it always does. When I was five or six I ran everywhere. I ran to school, ran to the kitchen. I couldn't wait to get to wherever I was going. And I was happy wherever I was. I ran down the stairs, over to the park. I ran to the swings. I ran to church. So what happened when I was seven? Hiroshi put his wrist to his forehead and told me he couldn't take another interruption. I said, "I'm ready," and then I saw Carlos backstage waving me over.

*

Jordan Delreese asked his father Calbert to tie him to the cyclone fence in the backyard. Calbert smiled and turned on the TV. *Let's Make a Deal* on the Game Show Network. Jordan said how that would be the best thing for all of us. Calbert told the contestant, a man in a hoop skirt and red baloney curls, to just take the cash and be happy with it. Cripes, he said, people don't know when they have it good. Calbert sucked on a sourball. The contestant went with whatever was behind Door #3. Greed, Calbert said. Jordan said, I have no way to control my stress. Jordan's mother said she'd like to serve dessert out by the pool. Calbert said, Put on your sunscreen, Vernal. The contestant seemed delighted with his six-piece gray mica bedroom suite, complete with platform bed and Serta Perfect Sleeper mattress and box spring. Jordan said, That way I won't fly way. Calbert said, What way? Tied to the fence with baling wire, Jordan said. And you'd better do it now.

While they ate, Jordan brought up the time his father had caught him masturbating into a tube sock while he was watching *Bewitched*. His mother said now what she had said then. About Onan spilling his seed. *And the thing which he did displeased the Lord: wherefore He slew him also.* Calbert said he couldn't remember what happened after he'd caught Jordan abusing himself, so Jordan reminded him. You took the TV cord off the old Motorola, plug and all, wet it, ran it through the sandbox, and put it in the freezer. Bringing back any memories, Dad? Then Mom filled a tub with ice-cold water and had me sit in it. Then you had me stand naked in the kitchen; you took out the cord and whipped me with it. I've still got the scars. Calbert said he wasn't proud, but it had to be done. You were committing an abominable sin, son. You were no better than a viper. And look how you've turned out, Jordan. A success. A God-fearing, law-abiding man, a solid citizen, and a pillar of the community. You should thank me. Jordan poured his parents two glasses of sweet iced tea and proposed a toast to discipline. Calbert said, You might want to try a little tough love with your own kids, Jordan. That grandson of mine has a sassy mouth on him.

Jordan finished his gingerbread and then his mother's gingerbread and his father's. He talked while his parents nodded off. He'd dissolved six Ambien in their tea. Worked like a dream. He told them about how if you wanted to get away with killing someone, you should kill them in a pool. Not that he was trying to get away with anything, you understand. Too late for that. Drowning is a diagnosis of exclusion, he said. It cannot be proven in an autopsy, cannot be disproved. He told them about the actor who drives a spaceship through the universe, how he drowned his wife in Beverly Hills, and everyone knows he did, but they can't prove it. You could see this guy any week on his new TV show, and he behaves like butter wouldn't melt in his mouth. That's acting.

Jordan slapped his mother awake. He told her what he'd done this morning. Vernal blinked, looked at Calbert with his face in the bowl, and laughed. This is the strangest dream, she said. He told her how he'd carved Caroldean's throat with a serrated kitchen knife, how it felt like slicing through a mango when he hit the larynx. Oh dear, Vernal said. Whee! Jordan reached out his foot and rested it on the seat of Calbert's chair. He kicked the chair over. Calbert hit his head on the concrete skirt of the pool. A floret of blood bloomed on his teal Marlins cap. Jordan stripped his parents to their undies and slid them into the pool. He sat under the umbrella and watched, saw those brief spasms when the water first hit the lungs, and then the flutter as the body fought for air. He watched them float, knock against each other, sink to the bottom of the pool. He knew it would take a couple of days for the bodies to bloat with gas and rise again. He knew they'd be discovered long before that. He fetched his dad's Sony Handycam, sat at the edge of the pool, and taped the bodies, looking like the last two pickled eggs in a jar. Then he turned the camcorder on himself and told his story.

Jordan explained how he had a crew in his office tearing up the place. So could we meet at your place? he said. That way he could take some measurements, note the color scheme, kill two birds with one stone. I gave him my address. That's over by the Fetish Box, isn't it? Yes, it is. Twenty minutes.

He said, "Determination is often the first chapter in the book of excellence."

"Excuse me?"

"Maybe the photo's of a long-distance runner on her last leg, gritting it out to the finish line."

"Do you have one for honesty?"

"I can give you serenity."

"I wish you could."

"Will truth do?"

"Close enough."

"Okay. An old man, red jacket, floppy cap, walks through the autumn woods in New England. Glorious colors. Clear, crisp. We can see the steam of his breath. His head's down. Below that the word *truth* — all caps — and below that, *Purity is born of virtue.*"

Jordan Delreese knocked shave-and-a-haircut-two-bits on my office door, pushed the door open with his shoulder, and poked his grinning face into the room. He held his BlackBerry to his ear, rolled his eyes, smiled at me, and told whomever he was speaking with or pretending to speak with that he'd get back to them with the figures ASAP. He scratched his nose. Okey-dokey. He nodded. Ciao!

He holstered the BlackBerry, clapped his hands, and stepped toward the desk where I sat. He said, "I pictured you bald, slight, with maybe a pitiful little mustache. Funny how a voice can fool you." He admired my autographed Marlins baseball, gripped it like he was pitching a curve. "Well, here we are, Mr. Melville."

"Call me Wylie. All my friends do."

"I pegged you for a sociable guy."

"Except Carlos. He calls me Coyote."

"And you call him The Jackal, I suppose."

"Have a seat, Mr. Delreese."

He pointed to the wall above the sofa. "We'll hang it there." He put his fists on his hips, swiveled and looked left, then right, looked at me, and shrugged. "No photos of the wife and kiddies."

"No wife and kiddies, I'm afraid."

"Fag?"

"Excuse me?"

"Are you a fag?"

"That's an inappropriate question, Mr. Delreese."

"If you say so."

"But a revealing one."

He sat, crossed his legs, folded his hands behind his head, smiled, and I knew that he knew that I knew. "No kids." He clicked his tongue and shook his head. "Fruitless." He raised an eyebrow, stuck out his lower lip, and cocked his head. "No regrets, Coyote?"

"Plenty."

He picked up the photo of Dad and me squinting into the sun at the News Café. "They fuck you up, don't they?"

"Who?"

"Your mom and dad."

"They did their best."

He smiled and aligned my Post-it note dispenser with my saucer of paper clips. Ordering his thoughts. He turned my little ceramic flamingo so she was facing me. He leaned back in his chair. I leaned back in mine.

He said, "I see what you're doing."

"You're a perceptive man."

"Why didn't you call the cops?"

"Who says I didn't?"

"Your need makes you transparent." He steepled his fingers, brought them to his lips. "So what do we do now?"

"You tell me your story."

"And you process my behavior and feed it back to me."

"I listen."

"Why should I tell you my story?"

"Why did you kill your family?"

"Why not?"

"Because it's barbaric, illegal, immoral —"

"Insane?"

"Did you think you'd get away with it?"

"I already did, dipshit." He laughed. "They're dead." He put his face in his hands. "My parents had outlived their usefulness. They disgusted me. They smelled like rancid milk."

"How do you feel right now?"

"Like I'm wasting my time. If you're looking for credible motivation, Melville, you won't find it here."

"Every lie is a victory for you, isn't it?"

"You want to make sense of this so badly, you'll believe anything I tell you so long as there's an element of horror and remorse. Am I right? You want the world to make sense, but it doesn't."

"It does if you bother."

"Most times nobody knows why they do anything."

"Most times they don't want to know."

"Don't you go to the movies? This is the twenty-first century,

Wylie, the Age of Unreason. Kill someone in the morning; go to
the theater at night. No reason, no resistance. Action is its own motivation. It's kind of funny if you think about it." Delreese pulled a
snub-nosed revolver out of a shoulder holster, said he bet I wasn't
planning on this, and I told him he was right about that, and he
told me he had nothing to lose, and I told him that I did. How
on earth had I missed the signals? Had his lips narrowed while I
blinked? Did the pitch of his voice rise, not in deceit, but in anger?

He said, "You know what's easy, Wylie? Lying to someone who
wants to be lied to." He aimed the pistol at my heart and asked me
if I was a religious man. I told him I was not. He said, "Too bad for
you then. You don't get saved."

"There's no salvation for you either, Delreese. Every child knows
that this is our only life. Every pig knows it. Every snake. Just people
like you who don't."

"People like me."

"People who feel that the world has let them down, who can't
imagine existence without their own presence. Dishonest people."

"The only honesty is a lie well acted."

I told him to put the gun away and let's talk. I said it like I was
soothing a feisty dog.

Delreese picked up the Marlins baseball, lobbed it across the
room, fired the pistol at it, and put a bullet through the window. "I
suspect we don't have much time now." He pointed the gun at my
face. I squeezed my eyes shut. I tried to breathe deeply to keep
my heart from exploding out of my chest. I trembled and held onto
my chair. I thought about my father waiting for me on Sunday, sitting with the cigarette-smoking attendants on the shady bench
outside the Clover House lobby, tapping his foot, chewing his lip,
trying to remember why the hell he was sitting there, and I understood that without me around to fight for him, the health-care system would swallow him up, strap him to a bed in some shadowy
ward, and let him waste away. When they told him I was dead,
would he know who they were talking about?

Delreese said, "Cat got your tongue?"

I thought if I could talk, maybe I could save my life, but in order
to talk I'd have to think; only I couldn't think; I could only remember. I saw my brother Cameron and me, and we're six and on the
floor in the den with Oreos and milk watching *The Lone Ranger.*

Dad's snoring over on the couch, and Mom's out on the patio smoking up a storm and reading another Harlequin romance. This bad guy from the Cavendish gang has the drop on the Lone Ranger and tells him to nice-and-easy-like take off his mask, which looks like my father's eyeshade, and which, of course, he will never do, even though I kind of want him to myself, which is sort of a betrayal, I know, and the Lone Ranger pretends that someone's behind the bad guy by making these not-so-subtle head and eye gestures that arouse the desperado's suspicion, and then the Lone Ranger says, "Get 'em, Tonto," and when the bad guy turns and fires, the Lone Ranger jumps him, grabs the six-shooter, and knocks the bad guy out with a single punch.

Delreese said, "I call this game Meet Your Maker." He laughed. "Ten Mississippi," he said. "Nine . . ."

Cameron changed the channel and told me to stop crying. I told him I wasn't crying, but I could taste the tears on my lips. Bugs Bunny aimed a pistol at Elmer Fudd, pulled the trigger, and a flag popped out of the barrel of the gun, unfurled, and said *Bang!* Bugs gave Elmer a big wet kiss. I couldn't remember my mother's face, just the back of her head. I knew I wouldn't hear the gunshot, wouldn't feel a thing. Everything would be over before I knew it. What would be the last thought I thought, the last picture I saw?

"Five Mississippi."

What I did remember about Mom was her silence, her ratty chenille robe, and her pink Deerfoam slippers. When she thought I was lying, she'd tell me to stick out my tongue, said that if I was lying it would be black. It was always black, even those times I was sure I wasn't lying. She'd wash my mouth out with Lifebuoy soap or spoon horseradish on my tongue. Cameron called her The Beast. Cameron, my twin, who looked exactly like me, people said, but was somehow more handsome, who always knew what I was thinking and could make me laugh at the drop of a hat, who fell into a life of drug addiction and robbed my parents blind, died in room 201 at the Pirate's Inn in Dania, beaten to death by his playmates with a studded mace and a stone war club. He was twenty-four.

I realized that Delreese had stopped counting, and I waited and thought maybe I was dead already, that this dark stillness was life after life, that I'd already been shot, that I'd been wrong about death too, and Willis had been right after all; there is no pain, no past, no present, no future, just the everything all at once, just a floating toward a resplendent and cleansing light, so I opened my eyes to see it, to let it wash over me, and I saw Delreese, who must have been waiting for this moment, with the black barrel of the gun in his mouth, saw him smile and wink. I reached for his arm, and he squeezed the trigger.

LOUISE ERDRICH

Gleason

FROM *The New Yorker*

JOHN STREGG OPENED his front door wide and there was Gleason, his girlfriend Jade's little brother. The boy stood, frail and skinny, in the snow with a sad look on his face and a gun in his hand. As the president of the New Otto Bank, of New Otto, North Dakota, Stregg had trained his employees to stay relaxed in situations like this. Small-town banks were vulnerable, and Stregg had actually been held up twice. One of the robbers had even been a methamphetamine addict. He did not flinch now.

"What can I do for you?" he said to Gleason. His voice was loud and calm. His wife, Carmen, was reading in the living room.

"You can come with me, Mr. Stregg," Gleason said, leading slightly to the left with the barrel of the gun. Behind him, at the curb, a low-slung Oldsmobile idled. Stregg could see no one else in it. Gleason was just nineteen years old, and Stregg now wished that he'd joined the army as Jade had said he was threatening to do. Except that, if he had, he might be carrying something better than an old, jammed-looking .22-caliber pistol. From the living room Carmen called, "Who is it?" and Gleason whispered, "Say 'Kids selling candy.'"

"Kids selling candy," Stregg called back.

"Tell them we don't want any," Carmen yelled.

"Say you're going for a little walk," Gleason said.

"I'm going for a little walk."

"In this snow?" his wife cried. "You're crazy!"

"Put your coat on," Gleason said. "So she doesn't see it still hanging on the rack. Then come with me. Shut the door."

As he headed down the walkway with Gleason behind him, Stregg began to hope that he would find Jade hidden in the car. That this was some odd kind of prank. Some desperate way for her to get to see him. It was evening, and the windows of his house cast a soft, golden light all the way down the landscaped twist of paving stones. There was a band of utter darkness where a stone wall and close-grown arborvitae cast a shadow onto the boulevard. The car sat beyond that, in the wintry shimmer of a street lamp.

"Get in," Gleason said.

Stregg stumbled a bit in the icy snow, then let himself into the passenger's side. The back seat was empty, he saw. Gleason held the pistol just inside the sleeve of his large topcoat, and kept it pointed at the windshield as he rounded the front of the car and ducked quickly into the driver's seat.

"I'm going to ease out of this light," he said.

Gleason kept his gun out and his mild eyes trained on Stregg as he put the car in drive and rolled forward into the darkness beyond the street lamp's glow.

"Time to talk." He put the car in park.

Gleason was a nervous-looking boy with large brown eyes, a thin face, and a mop of toast-brown hair flopping over one eye and bending into his collar. There were little wisps of down on his chin. He was artistic. This sort of behavior, Stregg knew, did not come naturally to Gleason. He'd probably had to get slightly drunk in order to drive to the Stregg residence with a gun and ring the bell. And what would he have done if Carmen had answered? Would he have pretended to be selling candy bars for some high-school trip? Did he have a Plan B? Stregg stared at Gleason's gaunt little face. The boy didn't seem likely to put a bullet in him. Plus, his hands looked too weak to pull back the slide. Stregg knew, too, that his presence in Gleason's car had depended on some implicit collaboration on his own part.

"So," Stregg repeated, in the patient voice he used with jumpy investors, "what can I do for you?"

"I think a hundred thousand dollars should be just about right," Gleason said.

"A hundred thousand dollars."

Gleason was silently expectant. Stregg shivered a little, then he pulled his coat tightly around himself and felt like crying. He had cried a lot with Jade. She had brought all his tears up to the surface. Sometimes they rushed out, and sometimes they trickled in long tracks down his cheeks.

She'd said that there was no shame in it, and she'd cried along with him until their weeping slowed erotically and sent them careening through each other's body, toward a dark peace. Stregg heard himself make a sound, an *Ah* of doubt. There was something about the monetary figure that struck him as wretched.

"It's just not enough," he said.

Gleason looked perplexed.

"Look, if she keeps the baby — and you know I want her to keep the baby — she's going to need a house. Maybe in Fargo, you know? A hundred thousand isn't enough for a decent house. And then there are clothes, and, what, car seats, that sort of thing. I've never had a child, but I know they need certain equipment. Also, she needs a good, safe car. A hundred thousand isn't enough for everything. It's not a future."

"OK," Gleason said, after a while. "What do you suggest?"

"Besides," Stregg went on, thinking out loud, "the thing is, in for a penny in for a pound. A hundred thousand would be missed just as much as a larger amount would be. My wife sees our accounts. It might as well be . . . Let me think. If it's under half a million, the papers will say nearly half a million anyway. So it might as well be over half a million. But not seven hundred thousand, because they'll call that three-quarters of a million. So let's say six hundred thousand."

Gleason was quiet. "That's just over half a million," he said finally.

Stregg nodded. "See? But that's a doable thing. Only there has to be a reason. A very good reason."

"Well," Gleason said, "maybe you were going to start some kind of business?"

Stregg looked at Gleason in surprise. "Well, yes, that's good, a business. Only then we'd need to actually have the business, keep it going, make a paper trail, and that'd lead to more deception, and the taxes . . . It'd all lead back to me. It's too complicated. We need one catastrophic reason."

"A tornado," Gleason said. "I mean, in winter, maybe not. A blizzard."

"And where does the money come in?"

"The money gets lost in the blizzard?"

Stregg looked disappointed, and Gleason shrugged weakly.

They both cast about for a time, mulling this over. Then Gleason said, "Question."

"Yes?"

"How come you don't just get divorced from your wife and marry Jade? The way you're talking, it sounds to me like you love her. So maybe I didn't have to come here and threaten you with this." He wagged the gun. "But I'm not getting why you don't just leave your wife and run off with Jade, or something, if you love her."

"I do love her."

"Then what's the problem?"

"Look at me, Gleason." Stregg put his hands out. "Do you think she'd stay with me just for me? Now, be honest. Without the money. Without the job. Just me."

Gleason shrugged again. "You're not so bad, man."

"Yes, I am," Stregg said. "I'm sixteen years older than Jade and I'm half bald. If I had my hair, then maybe, or if I was good-looking or athletic. But I'm a realist. I see what I am. The money helps. I'm not saying that that's the only reason Jade cares for me, not at all — Jade is a pure soul — but the money helps. If I divorced Carmen now, I wouldn't have a job. I took the bank over from her father, who is, yes, in his nineties and in a nursing home, but perfectly lucid. Carmen is a fifty-one-percent shareholder. Besides, here's the thing. Carmen has done nothing wrong. She has never, to my knowledge, betrayed me with another man, nor has she neglected me, within her own powers. Until I met Jade last year, you understand, I was reasonably happy. Carmen and I had sex for twenty minutes once a week and went to Florida in the winter; we gave dinner parties and stayed at the lake for two weeks every summer. In the summer, we had sex twice a week and I cooked all our meals."

Gleason looked uncomfortable.

"The thing is, we're the last small, independent bank in this part of the state and pretty soon we'll get bought out, swallowed up. That will change my situation. I'd like to be with Jade. I plan to be with Jade. When I can. If she'll have me."

Now Stregg leaned searchingly toward Gleason. "What does your presence here mean, exactly? Did she send you?"

"No."

"What happened? She won't talk to me right now, you know."

"Well, she told me about her being pregnant. She was kind of up-set, and I thought you were ditching her. That's what I thought. You know, it's always been just the two of us. She raised me after our mother OD'ed. I was only eleven when it happened, and she was twenty-one. I'd die for her."

"Of course," Stregg said. "Of course you would. Let that be our bond, Gleason. Both of us would die for her. But here's the thing. Only one of us — right now, anyway — only one of us can provide for her."

"So what should we do?"

"Something has come to me," Stregg said. "Now, I'm going to propose something that may surprise you. It may seem bizarre, but give it a chance, hear me out, Gleason, because I think it will work. Are you ready?"

Gleason nodded.

"Say you kidnap my wife."

Gleason gave a strangled yelp.

"No, just listen. Tomorrow night you do the very same thing as tonight. You come to the door. Carmen answers. You show her the gun and you come into the house. You have some strapping tape. A pair of scissors. At gunpoint, you order me to tie Carmen up. Once she's taken care of, you tie me up and say to me, in her hearing, that if I don't deliver six hundred thousand dollars in cash to you by the next day you'll kill her. You have to say that, I'm afraid. Then you bring her out to the car — not this car, a rental. Don't let her see the license plates."

"I don't think so," Gleason said. "I think you're describing a fed-eral crime."

"Well, yes," Stregg said. "But is it really a crime if nothing hap-pens? I mean, you'll be really, really nice to Carmen. That's a given. You'll take her to a secure out-of-town location, like your house. Keep her blindfolded. Put her in the back bedroom where you keep the freezer. Lay down a mattress so she's comfortable. It'll just be for a day. I'll drop off the money. Then you'll let her out somewhere on the other side of town. She may have a long walk — be sure she brings shoes and a coat. I don't think we should tell Jade."

"Jade's gone, anyway."

Stregg's heart lurched. He'd somehow known it. "Where?" he managed to ask.

"Her friend Bonnie took her to Bismarck, just to clear her head. They'll be back on Friday."

"Oh, then this is perfect," Stregg said.

Gleason looked at him with great, silent eyes. His and Jade's eyes were very similar, Stregg thought, and he suddenly felt extremely sorry for Gleason. He was so wimpy, so young, and what would he do with Carmen? She worked out on a stationary bicycle and lifted free weights. Gleason kept shifting the gun from hand to hand, probably because his wrist was getting tired.

"By the way, where did that gun come from?" Stregg asked.

"It used to belong to my mother's boyfriend."

"Is it loaded?"

"Of course it is."

"You don't have ammunition for it, do you?" Stregg said. "But that's good. We don't want any accidents."

When Gleason knocked on the door the following evening, John Stregg pretended to have fallen asleep. His heart beat wildly as the quiet transaction occurred in the entryway. Then Carmen walked into the room with her arms out in front of her and her square honest face blanched in shock. She made a gesture to her husband, asking for help, but Stregg was looking at Gleason and trying not to give everything away by laughing. Gleason wore a cinnamon-brown knitted ski mask with white piping around the mouth, nose, and eyes. His coat and his pants were a baked-looking brown. He looked like a scrawny gingerbread boy, except that he was wearing surgical gloves.

"I'm going to throw up," Carmen moaned when Gleason ordered Stregg to tie her up.

"No, you'll be OK," Stregg said. "You'll be OK." Tears dripped down his face and onto her hands as he tried firmly but gently to do his job. His wife's hands were so beautifully cared for, the nails lacquered with soft peach. Let nothing go wrong, he prayed.

"Look, he's crying," Carmen said accusingly to Gleason, before her husband tied a scarf between her teeth, knotting it tightly behind her head. "Nnnnnn!"

"I'm sorry," Stregg said.

"Now it's your turn," Gleason said.

The two of them suddenly realized that Gleason would have to put down the gun and somehow subdue Stregg, and their eyes got very wide. They stared at each other.

"Sit down in that chair," Gleason said at last. "Take the tape and loop it around your legs." He proceeded to instruct Stregg in how to do most of the work himself. He even had him cut strips to the appropriate length, all of which Stregg thought was quite ingenious of Gleason.

Once Stregg had secured himself to the chair and Gleason had gagged him, Gleason told Carmen to get on her feet. But she refused. Even as anxiety coursed through him, Stregg felt obscurely proud of his wife. She rolled around on the floor, kicking like a dolphin, until Gleason finally pounced on her and pressed the barrel of the gun to her temple. Straddling her, he untied the gag in her mouth and rummaged in his pocket. He drew out a couple of pills.

"You leave me no choice," he said. "I'm going to have to ask you to dry-swallow these."

"What are they?" Carmen asked.

"Just sedatives," Gleason said. Then he spoke to Stregg. "Leave six hundred thousand dollars in a garbage bag next to the 'Adopted by the Flickertail Club' highway sign. No marked bills. No police. Or I'll kill your wife. You're being watched."

Stregg was surprised that Carmen took the pills, but then for some reason she'd always been that way about taking pills — a willing patient. Now she turned out to be a willing hostage, and Gleason had no more trouble with her. He cut the tape on her legs and put a hobble on her ankles. She walked out dreamily, her coat draped over her shoulders, and Stregg was left alone. It took him about half an hour of patient wiggling to release himself from the tape, which he left looped around the chair. Now what? He wanted desperately to call Jade, to talk to her, to hear the slow music of her voice. But for some hours he sat on the couch with his head in his hands, replaying the whole scenario. Then he started thinking ahead. Tomorrow he would go in early. He would transfer money from their retirement account into the bank's general account. Then he would go into the safe and take out the cash and get into the car. He would drive out to the highway sign and make the drop. It would all be done before nine A.M., then Gleason would free Carmen west of town, where she could walk home or find a ride.

There would be police. An investigation. Newspapers. But no insurance was involved.

The amount wasn't excessive. It would use up most of their retirement account, but Carmen still had the bank. It would all blow over.

A blizzard came up and Carmen got lost and might have frozen to death had a farmer not pulled her from a ditch. Luckily, Gleason had scooped up her snow boots as they left, and her coat was one of those long down coats, quilted past her knees. She suffered no frostbite, and though she ran a fever for six days, she did not develop pneumonia. Stregg nursed her with care, waited on her hand and foot, took a leave from the bank. He was shocked by how the kidnapping had affected her. Over the next weeks, she lost a great deal of weight and spoke irrationally. To the police she described her abductor as quite large, muscular, with firm hands, a big nose, and a deep voice. Her kidnapper was stunningly handsome, she said, a god! It was all so strange that Stregg almost felt like correcting her. Though he was delighted, on the one hand, that she had the description so wrong, her embroidery disturbed him. And when he brought her home from the hospital she was so restless. In the evenings, she wanted to talk instead of watching television or reading the many magazines that she subscribed to. She had questions.

"Do you love me?"

"Of course I love you."

"Do you really, really love me? I mean, would you have died for me if the kidnapper had made you make a choice? 'It's her or you' — say he'd said that. Would you have stepped forward?"

"I was tied to the chair," Stregg said.

"Metaphorically."

"Of course, metaphorically. I would have."

"I wonder."

She began to look at him skeptically, measuring him. At night, now, she wanted lots of reassurance. She seduced him and scared him, saying things like "Make me helpless."

"He made me helpless," she said one morning. "But he was kind, very kind to me."

Stregg took her to the doctor, who said that it was posttraumatic stress and prescribed antidepressants and antianxiety medications, which didn't help much.

"Hold me tighter — squeeze the breath out of me."

"Look at me. Don't close your eyes."

"Don't say something meaningless. I want the truth."

It was terrifying, how she'd opened up. What had Gleason done?

Nothing, Gleason insisted on the phone. Stregg was ashamed to feel repelled by his wife's awkward need — it was no different from his own need. If she'd been this way before, he recognized, he might have responded. He might not have turned to Jade. He might have been amazed, grateful. But when Carmen threw herself onto him at night he felt only despair, and she could sense his distance. She grew bony and let her hair go gray, long, unruly, beautiful. She was strange. She was sinking. She looked at him with the eyes of a drowning person.

Stregg went to visit his father-in-law at the nursing home. The place did not depress him, though he could see how it might depress others. His father-in-law was resting on his single bed, on top of a flowered polyester coverlet. He'd pulled an afghan over himself, one that Carmen had knitted, in intricate stripes of green and blue. He was listening to the radio.

"It's me. It's John."

"Ah."

Stregg took his father-in-law's hand in his. The old man's skin was dry and very soft, nearly translucent. His face was thin, pale, almost saintly, though he'd been ruthless when he was younger, a cutthroat banker, a survivor.

"I'm glad you're here," Stregg's father-in-law said. "How's my little girl?"

"She's just fine." No one had told Carmen's father what had happened. "She has a cold," Stregg lied. "She's staying in bed today. She's probably curled up around her hot-water bottle, sleeping."

"The poor kid."

Stregg resisted telling Carmen's father, as he always used to, "I'll take good care of her." How wrong, and how ironic, would that be? The old man's hand relaxed, and Stregg realized that he had fallen asleep. Still, he continued to sit beside the bed holding his father-in-law's slender and quite elegant hand. It gave him time to con-

sider some things. The baby would be born in four months, and
Gleason and Jade were now living in a sturdy ranch-style house not
far from Trollwood Park, up in Fargo. Gleason was just about to
start college. The last time Stregg visited, Gleason had shaken his
hand but said nothing.

As for Jade, she spent a lot of time alone. Stregg couldn't get
away much because of Carmen. Jade understood. She was radiant.
Her hair was long, a lustrous brown. They went into her bedroom
in the middle of the day and made love in the stark light. It was very
solemn. He went dizzy with the depth of it. When he lay against
her, his perceptions shifted and he saw the secret souls of the objects and plants in the room. Everything had consciousness and
meaning. Jade was measureless, but she was ordinary, too. Afterward, Stregg drove back down to New Otto and arrived just in time
for dinner.

When he left the old man, Stregg usually patted his arm or made
some other vague gesture of apology. This time, still thinking of his
visit with Jade, he bent dreamily over Carmen's father. He kissed
the dry forehead, stroked back the old man's hair, and thought-
lessly smiled. The old man jerked away suddenly and eyed Stregg
like a mad hawk.

"You bastard!" he cried.

One day, Carmen was sitting in her bathrobe at lunch, tapping a
knife against the side of a soft-boiled egg. Suddenly she said, "I
know who he was. I saw him in a high-school play right here in New
Otto."

Stregg's guts turned to ice and he phoned Gleason as soon as he
could. Sure enough, Gleason had been in every single drama production in high school. Stregg put the phone down and stared at
it. Carmen was at the town library at that very moment, looking
through old high-school yearbooks.

This was how it happened that instead of starting college
Gleason bolted and joined the army. Jade was heartbroken and
cried day and night after he was shipped off for basic training. She
said that she couldn't feel anything anymore, and she turned away
from Stregg when he visited and wouldn't let him touch her. After
six weeks, Gleason sent a photograph of himself in military gear.
He didn't appear to have bulked up much. His helmet seemed to

balance on his thin head, shadowing those wide, soft brown eyes. He looked about twelve years old.

Stregg drove home after visiting Jade one afternoon, and put his car keys on the coffee table. "I'm leaving now," he said. "You keep everything. I have clothes. I have shoes. I'll make myself a sandwich and be going now." Jade's cold sorrow had finally driven him to this. Stregg was sure that he would lose her if he didn't take action.

He walked into the kitchen and made the sandwich and put it into a plastic bag. He walked out into the living room and stood in the center of the carpet. Carmen just looked at him. Then she raised her hand, swept it to the side, and let it fall. The gesture seemed to hang in the air, as if her arm had left a trail. Stregg turned and walked out the door and across town, and headed back to Fargo along the highway. There was only a slight wind, and the temperature was about forty-five degrees. The fields were full of standing water and ducks and geese swam in the ditches. He didn't take a ride until the sky darkened.

Shortly after John Stregg moved into the house in Fargo, his baby boy was born. In those dazzling moments after the birth, Stregg had a vision. The baby resembled Gleason, brave young Gleason, with his big feet and no ass to speak of, who looked as if he could hardly lift a water canteen. Gleason's heart was a pale and valiant little fish. Was there anyone more magnificent than Gleason? Stregg saw that Gleason was a kind of Christ figure, a martyr like those in the New Testament. Only he had been thrown to the lions in the name of his sister's happiness. It had occurred to Stregg that, in his new life, Gleason might grow in strength and valor and become exactly the person Carmen believed had abducted her. Now he saw that Gleason already *was* that person, and that Carmen had recognized it all along. He also saw that Gleason had told his sister about the kidnapping.

All of this was clear in the face of the tiny new baby. Stregg looked closer, and tried to see whether Gleason would live or die. But, just then, the baby opened his mouth and bawled. As Jade put the baby to her breast, Stregg sank back into the hospital chair, dizzy with spent adrenaline. For a long time, he just watched mother and son from across the room.

*

Only twice did Stregg visit New Otto. The first time, he brought a
U-Haul and loaded into it all that Carmen had not disposed of —
she'd thrown a lot of things away. But physical objects had ceased to
matter to Stregg. Jade argued with him every day, threatening to go
to the police, to turn him in for the kidnapping.

"You'll lose everything." Stregg waved his arm. "This house. And
Gleason will go to jail. Would you like that? You'll be out on the
street. And what about little Gleason?"

Jade had named the baby after her brother. There was no getting
away from Gleason; he would always control the situation, no matter where he was. Gleason, with his bristle-headed cut, with his
combat boots and rifle. In the months after his son's birth, Stregg
had come to understand that he would never be forgiven for engi-
neering the kidnapping scheme that had sent Gleason off to the
army. He had lost Jade's love. She kicked him out to sleep in the garage, where he curled up beside his car, in a sleeping bag spread
out on a little camp cot. Jade spent all day by herself, caring for the
baby and cleaning the house. Every so often, she would thrust a
shopping list at Stregg, or make him help with heavy lifting. Beyond that, she didn't want him to get close to her or the baby. He
moved around the small house like a ghost, never knowing where
to settle.

He'd found a job at the insurance agency he'd always used, a low-
level position assisting others in processing claims. One day, a home-
owner's claim from his old address landed on his desk. Carmen
had filed a claim on everything that he had taken from the house
— his own things, which she had agreed and even pressured him to
come and clear out. There were power tools, each with a serial
number and an identification code, and some stereo and other
electronic equipment, even a small computer. Looking at the list,
Stregg felt a glimmer of heat rise in his throat. He took his jacket
from the office door, went back to the house that his and Carmen's
retirement money had bought, and packed up everything he kept
in the garage. He drove to New Otto with a full car, and parked in
the driveway of his former home.

After a while, Carmen came to the window. She looked at him as
he got out of the car, and he looked at her, through the window,
which was like the glass of a dim aquarium. When she vanished, he
was not sure whether she would come to the door or be absorbed

into the gloom. But she did open the door at last, and beckoned him inside. They stood in the entry, quite close. Her hair had gone from gray to silver white. A pulse beat in her slender throat. Her arms were stick thin, but she seemed to generate an unusual light. Stregg could feel it, this odd radiance. It seemed to emanate from her translucent skin. It occurred to him that he should sink down at the feet of this beautiful, wronged woman and kiss the hem of the pearl velour jogging suit she was wearing.

"You filed a claim on all my stuff. I'm bringing it back," he said.

"No. I want the money. I need the money," she told him.

"Why?"

"We're sunk. They're not going to buy the bank out. They're opening a new one next to it."

"What about your father's accounts?"

"He'll live to be a hundred," Carmen said. "John, he told me that you were seeing another woman all along."

"I don't know where he got that idea," Stregg said.

Carmen waited.

"All right. Yes."

Her eyes filled with terrible tears and she began to shake. Before Stregg knew it, he was holding her. He shut the door. They made love in the entryway, on the carpet where so many people paused, and then on the bench where visitors sat to remove their boots. His remorse, and his shame, compelled him. And her need for him was so powerful it seemed as if they were going over a rushing waterfall together, falling in a barrel, and at the bottom Stregg cracked open and told her everything.

He had to, because of Gleason. Stregg clung to Carmen with blackness washing over him, and talked and talked.

"I know he violated you," Stregg said, after he'd spilled everything else. "I understand now."

"Who? That boy? He was just a twerp," Carmen said. "He never touched me. I said all that stuff out of desperation, to try to make you jealous. Why, I do not know."

She sat up and eyed him with calm assessment. "Possibly, I thought you still loved me, way deep down. I think I believed there was something in you."

"There is, there is," Stregg said, strangling on a surge of hope, touching her ankles as she got to her feet.

"When the snow was covering me, out in the ditch, I saw your face. Real as real. You bent over me and pulled me out. It wasn't the farmer, it was you."

"It *was* me," Stregg said, lifting his arms. "I must have always loved you."

She looked down at him for a long time, contemplating this amazing fact. Then she went upstairs and called the police.

In the years afterward, Stregg was sometimes asked by the friends he made behind bars what had caused him to confess what he'd done, and then take all the blame. Sometimes he couldn't think of a good reason. Other times, he said he had guessed that it would never end; he'd seen that he'd be kicked from one woman to the other until the end of time. But, after he gave his answer, he always came back to that moment when he'd first opened the door to Gleason, and thought of how, when he saw the boy standing in the glowing porch light, in the snow, with that dull gun and that sad face, he hadn't flinched.

JIM FUSILLI

Chellini's Solution

FROM *Death Do Us Part*

CHELLINI WAS MUCH YOUNGER than he seemed. A Sicilian wife, bubbly six-year-old twin daughters, and perpetually aching feet conspired to deprive him of the swagger customary to men from the Puglia region of Italy. So too did a rotund frame, legs that were slightly bowed, and a floppy gray mustache he grew shortly after his discharge from the U.S. Army Air Force in '46. At the time, just seven years ago, the mustache was a deep brown.

Chellini did his best to meet life with a shrug, as would befit a man from a sunny southern province, though life in postwar America was maybe a bit hectic for his tastes, what with his sharp-tongued Lydia, their mischievous daughters, and his job as a waiter in an Italian restaurant near the National Broadcasting Company in Rockefeller Center. Despite the hubbub, he himself kept quiet and sought what he would call uneventfulness. He had no ambitions, save a desire for abundant happiness for his daughters and for Lydia to love him as she once did.

Chellini had a pet bulldog, Ambrose, with whom he shared a slow, labored gait. Each night, after a clattering dinner during which Ava and Rita amused each other and Lydia reminded him of the dreary life he provided, Chellini would wander the cobblestone streets of his mile-square New Jersey town in search of serenity and equilibrium. With Ambrose at his side, he would drift into his own agreeable fantasies, which consisted of little more than sitting under an olive tree in Bovino, straw between his teeth, a manageable herd of goats feeding nearby, white almond blossoms blooming at the lip of the field, and his little family enjoying the stone house in which he was raised.

Chellini would often lose track of time during his nightly so-
journs and return home as Lydia slept, her back to his side of their
bed. While Ambrose slurped his water, Chellini would tiptoe toward his daughters' bed in the living room and kiss them on the
palm of the hand, which he would then close to a fist so they would
have a token of his devotion as soon as they awoke. Then he would
retire to his room and hope for streams of moonlight and tranquil
dreams of Lydia as the bright-eyed girl from Ragusa who had shyly
accepted his invitation to dance.

One night not long ago, Chellini found he had returned to the
Italian quarter much sooner than he had intended, and he passed
Tartuffo's, the cigar store where a group of neighborhood men
congregated. On such a pleasant, summerlike evening, the crowd
of hardscrabble brown-skinned thugs of one sort or another sat
outside the store and played penny-a-point gin and smoked che-
roots. Unlike Chellini, most of these dubious men had immigrated
to the United States after the war; some had served in Mussolini's
army and others remained at home and willingly suffered the in-
dignity of the German occupation.

Chellini preferred to avoid them, as they were not merely argu-
mentative but bitter. He considered them lazy malcontents who
pronounced big schemes but took no action when action was
needed, thus allowing the Nazis to steal their homes, their women,
and their pride.

A voice reached Chellini on the other side of the narrow street.

"Chellini, *dove andate?*"

Of course, it was the man he respected least who had addressed
him.

"Chellini, I'm speaking to you," said Emilio Marzano, whose accent revealed him to be from the Liguria region, though he sought
to portray a Sicilian tough. "What do you think? I want to talk to
your dog?"

The other men laughed with a dark, superior tone.

Under the street lamp's dull violet light, Chellini stopped, tipped
his fedora, and continued walking, Ambrose chugging along at his
side.

The men whispered to each other as if sharing a secret. Tartuffo,
the impossibly fat store owner and chief of the local numbers
racket, flicked his thumb dismissively at Chellini, shaking his mam-
moth head.

"Hey, war hero," Marzano said with an air of derision. "Wait."

Marzano climbed out of his chair and, though he was built as if cut from the same stubby, thickset mold as Chellini, he tried to affect a strut. On Marzano's skull was a brown cap festooned with colorful buttons of various trade unions and social organizations with which he was associated. He ran a carting business, and what needed removal ended up in his rattling truck for a trip to the city dump. This was said to include Mrs. Feduza's rabid dog, Benny, and the thieving iceman, Stucchi.

"Chellini, what's with you? You can't be a friend?"

As Ambrose sniffed disapprovingly at Marzano's soiled shoes, Chellini shrugged.

"Listen to me. It's about Lydia. Your wife."

Chellini scratched the underside of his chin. Lydia, he knew, bought her many movie magazines at the candy store, and her Chesterfields. With a nature as outgoing as Chellini's was not, she was bound to be known by Tartuffo, Marzano, and the others.

Marzano shifted to give his associates a better view. "I have to say it's not pleasant."

Chellini began to walk away, Ambrose in his wake.

Said Marzano, a snicker in his voice, "Don't you want to know his name?"

The following morning, after dropping his daughters at St. Francis, Chellini returned to the Italian quarter and sat in Columbus Park rather than taking the tubes to his job. As pigeons pecked at the dog biscuit he'd crumpled for their pleasure, he stared at the tattered brownstone in which he lived, and he considered a strategy.

To his mind, there was no doubt Marzano was telling the truth. Chellini knew a few small-minded sharpies in the Sixty-fourth Fighter Wing, and they took a wicked pleasure from others' misfortunes — far more than from a practical joke. These minor-league mafiosi sitting on their own kitchen chairs outside Tartuffo's seemed no different than those wise guys, and surely they were no better, even if they were Italian.

At a few minutes short of ten o'clock, the man who would turn out to be Hans Koppel arrived, and he kicked up the steps with a confidence that suggested he had been there before. A moment later, perhaps two, Lydia, still in the snug housedress she wore during their typically rancorous breakfast, pulled the shades on the third-floor window that faced the vest-pocket park. When she reappeared after thirty minutes had passed, she was wearing a slip Chellini didn't recognize, the kind that barely contained her ample breasts. Lydia's curly black hair was thoroughly disheveled, and Chellini thought he detected, beneath the veneer of caution, a hint of nefarious satisfaction that perhaps spoke of revenge.

As the pigeons happily fed, Chellini concluded that action was required — action of a kind that would provide a thorough solution to his unexpected dilemma. By the time his rival had departed the brownstone, Chellini had devised a plan.

Leaving the park, Chellini fell in behind Koppel, a thin man with blond, slicked-back hair who wore wire-rimmed glasses, an expertly cut brown double-breasted suit, and an apple red silk tie. Before flagging a bus to return him to the Port Authority in Manhattan, Koppel stopped briefly in a storefront with a State Farm sticker in the window and a ding bell on the door frame. Chellini watched as he was greeted warmly by a similarly dressed man, the proprietor, Aichberger, no doubt, who gave Koppel an accordion folder stout with papers. Their conversation ended with the proprietor's joke, and both men laughed as the blond secretary in kelly green tittered and blushed.

When Koppel took his seat on the New York–bound bus, Chellini was several rows behind him. When Koppel rode the subway uptown, Chellini was in the same car.

When Koppel left the IRT station, Chellini listened as he paused for a brief conversation with an elderly couple, conducted entirely in German. Crossing Eighty-sixth Street, Koppel greeted, in German also, the milky-eyed counterman at the Ideal Diner and took for lunch two eggs sunny-side up, a bauernwurst, and red cabbage, which he washed down with a Schlitz and a black coffee while Chellini waited, hidden by the hood of a '49 Buick Super, baby blue.

Now, as Koppel paid his tab, Chellini nodded knowingly and departed, calculating his return to the tubes at Herald Square so as to guarantee that he would arrive home as always, via the same route and unlocking the door at the same time, lifting Ava and Rita as they leaped into his arms, screaming, "Papa, Papa," one louder than the next.

*

Lydia said, "What? No tips?"

Three seconds in the door, and Chellini had already made his first mistake. The roll of bills and the loose coins he dropped into the cookie jar were no greater than they had been this morning, and in fact were short the cost of the bus, the hot dog, and orangeade Chellini consumed at Nedicks on Thirty-fourth, and a few pennies spent here and there.

The twins' cheery stampede relieved Chellini of constructing a lie.

"I know you don't gamble, Chellini," Lydia said in Italian, hands on her generous hips, bare feet clutching the linoleum. "You couldn't tolerate the excitement."

"Papa, Papa," yelled the gleeful twins.

Chellini went off to examine the drawings they'd made at school.

"That's right," Lydia squealed. "Go, go, why don't you? Why should you talk to me? I'm only your wife. Mother of those two . . . Those two! Go, Chellini. Just go."

The breaded pork chops she dropped before him that evening were especially leatherlike, and the Chianti was moments away from completing its conversion to vinegar. Fortunately, the bread was fresh and still had its two heels, so both girls were satisfied.

Lydia, not so.

"Chellini, I want to go to the Avalon on Friday night," she announced.

Chellini had put on a fresh undershirt and had applied a balm to the wounds from the strafing he'd suffered over the Adriatic.

"Kirk Douglas, Lana Turner, Gloria Grahame, Gilbert Roland. Dick Powell. *The Bad and the Beautiful.* Chellini."

Chellini shrugged. Perhaps now was not the time to tell his wife that the actor Powell sauntered over from NBC to eat at one of his tables at least twice a week. Powell tipped like he'd just won the sweepstakes. The fist-sized meatballs and bland sausages made him smile.

"Chellini. I am twenty-four years old, and I was not born to slave in this kitchen. I need to live, Chellini. To live!"

Her voice made the glasses ring, and when she shouted the veins in her neck threatened to burst.

Meanwhile, Rita frowned severely, comically, and mocked her mother's diatribe by bobbing her head and silently flapping her jaw. Ava put her hands over her eyes to prevent an outburst of laughter.

"Chellini, if you don't give to me a life, I am going to show you something you won't forget!"

Lydia had a skillet in her hand. Burned clumps of breading clung to its surface.

"Chellini. Speak to me!"

Chellini shrugged. He had nothing to say. New knowledge had put him in a weak position.

Resigned, Lydia resumed her chores, sprinkling soap powder onto the rushing water. Chellini pushed back his plate and threw down the last of the tart wine.

As if on cue, Ambrose rose up, shook himself awake, and waddled off to retrieve his leash.

Waiting in the shadows under the viaduct, Chellini watched as Marzano leaped from behind the driver's wheel to unlock and open the garage doors, then climbed back up to manipulate his empty truck until it was snug inside the bay.

As Chellini approached, Ambrose toddling too, he wondered if the blood of the missing Stucchi had once stained the concrete floor.

Marzano was more than surprised to find a visitor in the darkness. "Mother of God!" he shouted in Italian. "Chellini, you put a fright in me!"

Ambrose growled from his belly.

"And that dog of yours! What a disposition! Miserable!"

Marzano turned his back on Chellini as he secured the lock and yanked on the knob for good measure.

Not exactly Fort Knox, Chellini thought.

Adjusting his cap and hitching up his floppy slacks, Marzano shoved his hands in his pockets and started his walk south to the Italian quarter some six blocks away.

Chellini stood still, as did Ambrose.

Marzano stopped. "You want to talk, Chellini?"

Chellini looked at the rubbish beneath his feet.

Marzano tilted his head as he returned. "Has this to do with Lydia?"

Chellini nodded.

Marzano wiped his brown lips with the back of his grimy hand. "Well?"

Chellini said, *"Grupo Azione Patrioti."*

Marzano frowned. *"Grupo Azione Patrioti,"* he repeated. "The GAP?"

As he nodded, Chellini saw that Marzano had begun to understand.

"You're saying to me this motherless bastard is a Nazi?" Marzano asked, as he stepped into the black space Chellini and Ambrose now occupied. The smell of urine and gasoline surrounded them.

Chellini shrugged.

If the light had permitted, Chellini would have seen that Marzano's neck and ears were now bright red. His heart was racing inside his chest.

"The Nazis," he said, "they raped my sister."

Chellini thought this unlikely, though it was a tale Marzano repeated often in the neighborhood. His sister had no doubt taken a Nazi lover, if only for the food and security he could provide. Regrettably, many confused young women had, and not only in San Remo, Marzano's birthplace and former home.

"They made a mockery of us," he continued, jabbing himself in the chest with a stiff finger, which he then pointed toward the sky.

Ambrose was sniffing the dirt, exhuming messages from countless dogs who had preceded him to this spot.

Marzano put his right hand over his heart. "I pledged myself to the GAP," he said, adding, "even though I was too young to participate."

Also not true. Marzano was at least thirty-five years old, perhaps forty. The GAP, a unit of the marginally organized partisan movement in Italy, had recruited teenage boys when necessary to resist the Nazi occupation. Marzano would have been well into his twenties when the Nazis arrived.

"And now this godless pig is here! Taking our women again! And who knows how many?"

Chellini shrugged, though now the gesture suggested Marzano had summarized the situation with admirable insight.

"Leave everything to me," Marzano said, tapping Chellini on the shoulder. "It will be a pleasure. Hell, I do it for free."

Chellini nodded, but as Marzano began to walk away, he called to him.

Again, Marzano stopped and peered into the darkness.

Chellini said, *"Avrete bisogno di una lama splendida."*

Marzano stroked his chin. "A superb knife, eh?" He smiled knowingly. "Revenge with a twist, Chellini. Clever man!"

The following morning, Chellini took the tubes to Christopher Street in Greenwich Village and zigzagged until he arrived at Canal Street, avoiding Little Italy in case someone might recognize him as the bombardier who had returned to Puglia to dispatch the Germans.

The barber who shaved off his mustache was a Chinaman, and Chellini could not understand a single word he said. But the man knew his craft and Chellini left satisfied, a mysterious Oriental astringent causing the naked skin above his lip to tingle.

At an army surplus shop off Baxter Street, he bought a bayonet that had belonged to one of Mussolini's fascist troops. A restaurant supply store on the Bowery willingly sharpened it to a razor's edge for a modest fee that did not include a dizzying conversation with a Polish Jew who tried to sell Chellini an enormous refrigerator. Defeated by silence, the insistent salesman then pressed Chellini on the origins of the brown cap the Italian had placed on the counter and the meaning of its array of colorful buttons.

Escaping without comment, Chellini tossed his old hat under a beat-up Oldsmobile on Delancey Street, and the nonsensical buttons he'd purchased at Herald Square the day before went down a subway grate to rest among gum wrappers, beer bottle tops, and what seemed to be thousands of cigarette butts.

The IRT and a crosstown bus delivered Chellini to the restaurant a few minutes later than usual, but his missing mustache seemed to provide an excuse, especially when some gentle ribbing from his colleagues ensued, and so his accordion-playing boss said nothing. With the bayonet hidden in his locker, Chellini went to work and soon his section was crowded with visitors from Wisconsin, Pennsylvania, and even California, none of whom seemed to know that what they happily consumed bore no resemblance to what was served in any region of Italy.

Close to the end of his shift, the actor Powell arrived. He complimented Chellini on his altered appearance. In a voice familiar to millions of moviegoers and, these days, fans of radio's *Richard Diamond, Private Detective,* Powell told Chellini he looked like a new, younger man.

Powell's customary generous tip more than covered the cost of the shave, the bayonet, the sharpening, and the additional transportation.

"Papa, Pa —"

Ava and Rita stopped as if suddenly frozen. They glared at their father's face. Never before had they seen him without his mustache.

Lydia, meanwhile, looked at Chellini and was impressed. He seemed almost handsome, and certainly younger. But she would not admit it.

"Big experiment," she muttered in Italian.

Ambrose opened one eye and, unmoved, immediately shut it.

Chellini dropped the money in the cookie jar and went to his knees so his daughters could examine his new face. They did so with warm, curious fingers.

A moment later, Chellini stood. "Going out," he said, as he went toward the bedroom.

Lydia's voice followed him as he reached into his tool chest, stored at the rear of his clothes closet.

"Such an outburst, Chellini! A new face and now you are a talking man! But Chellini, the door is the other way if you're going to go."

Now he had in his jacket a screwdriver, a bayonet, and a few slips of paper, and he was grateful his daughters didn't ask if they could accompany him. They were busy discussing his appearance. Rita seemed in favor, Ava opposed.

"Go, Chellini. Go before you change your mind!" added Lydia.

And Chellini went.

Chellini rarely recalled his years in the Army Air Force, though he served in the war with a valor he saw as customary among the men of the Sixty-fourth stationed in San Severo. His bombs struck harbors, submarine pens, bridges and trains and fuel dumps — entirely a team effort, of course — and a strafing by a Messerschmitt Bf 109 had ripped open his shoulder. But his wounds were minimal, and he did not consider himself a hero. Their copilot was killed on that fateful run: a convivial boy from Iowa named Leonard McMillan with whom Chellini had taken coffee before the mission began. Chellini considered the redheaded McMillan a hero: he suffered the night sweats and was terrified at takeoff, and yet he fought with courage and ferocity for his country and family back home.

Once the men and women in Puglia learned that Chellini, one of their own, was serving to protect them and give them back their homeland, the legend of the Hero of San Severo was born. The army heard of it, and while Chellini recovered from his wounds, his mother was brought from Bovino to his bedside, where she served him chicken with turnip tops, his boyhood favorite. A photo, provided by Army Public Relations, appeared in the *Journal-American* and soon the gaunt Chellini, swaddled in bandages, was famous stateside too, if only among natives of Italy who lived in or near New York City.

Now, as he approached Marzano's garage, Chellini recalled that Lydia had put the newspaper clipping in her hope chest. It had been given to her by Father Gregorio, who introduced them at the dance at St. Francis. Removing the Phillips head screwdriver from his pocket, Chellini wondered if the yellowing newspaper clipping was still there, tucked among her linens and the white lace of her secondhand wedding dress.

Following a few twists of the wrist, Chellini stepped inside the darkened bay. Calculating where the truck's headlights would shine, he affixed the bayonet to the wall — also an easy task since a protruding nail allowed him to hang it at eye level. The scent of motor oil and the rumble of traffic on the viaduct enveloping him, Chellini then buried in a crowded trash can the receipts from the army surplus and restaurant supply stores. Returning to the twilight, he put the lock plate back in its place and he departed, dusting his hands. Despite his aching feet, he walked at a pace that would have taxed Ambrose had he accompanied Chellini on his task.

They found Hans Koppel with his throat slashed — "ear to ear," according to a grisly story on page five of the morning edition of the *Daily News* — in his apartment on Eighty-ninth Street, between First and York avenues. The German's blood had oozed through the floorboards and saturated the ceiling of the apartment below. The New York City police were notified after Koppel's downstairs neighbor found vivid red stains on the white fur of her Turkish Angora cat, Geli.

That very same evening, the tabloid carried the headline "Italian Resistance Fighter Nabbed," and made note of an anonymous tip received by police. The receipts were located at Marzano's garage, and the countermen at the army surplus and restaurant supply stores remembered a squat, clean-shaven Italian man with a brown cap festooned with buttons.

Marzano's fingerprints were found on the bayonet, which he foolishly kept at his apartment. Koppel's blood had splattered onto his already soiled shoes.

Marzano told the cops he had no regrets. He killed the German, the *Daily News* reported, to restore the honor of all Italian women. Marzano declared that he had been a passionate partisan in San Remo, where the Nazis raped and defiled women, and his taste for revenge did not end with the armistice.

This seemed to explain, at least to the satisfaction of the *Daily News*, why Marzano carved the letters "GAP" into Koppel's forehead.

Toward the end of its article, the newspaper speculated that there would be a faction among New York City's Italian community that would declare Marzano a hero for his bold determination, and suggested Hans Koppel was active in the movement to revive the Bund in the neighborhood where the Brownshirts had once paraded.

The Hero of Yorkville, Chellini mused. *Emilio Marzano.*

The man had served his purpose. *Let him be a champion, as long as he remains behind bars.*

Later that night, as magenta clouds streaked the starless sky, Chellini, with Ambrose in tow, concluded his walk by passing the cigar store. As he peered across the street at the rabble playing cards, sipping jug wine, and avoiding conversation about Marzano, the man all of them now would claim never to have met, Chellini allowed his tired eyes to find the fat crook Tartuffo.

After a moment's consideration, Tartuffo bowed his enormous head.

Chellini silently accepted the gesture, and he and Ambrose moved on, man and bulldog with an almost imperceptible bounce of pride in their step.

Any illusion Lydia harbored that the murder of Koppel by Marzano had been a coincidence was dispatched by the time Chellini returned.

Though it was after eleven o'clock, espresso brewed on the stove, and fried bow ties dusted with powdered sugar sat in a dish at the center of the kitchen table. The frilly tablecloth was one Chellini had not seen in years.

"Chellini?" said Lydia, hopefully.

While Ambrose glugged his water, Chellini visited his daughters, gently closing their fingers around his kiss. For a moment, he allowed himself the pleasure attendant in the thought that he had saved his family.

By the time he returned, a tiny cup of the rich, aromatic coffee sat in front of his seat.

Chellini took his place. With a sweep of his hand, he gestured for his wife to join him.

She did so, humbly.

"Chellini."

He took no satisfaction from her fear — in Chellini's mind, love could not exist where trepidation reigned — but he did not immediately reply.

The circular lamp overhead flickered unevenly, and soon they both could hear its buzz.

Chellini took a sip of the espresso.

He nodded his approval and gestured for his bride to take some coffee for herself.

"*Grazie,* Chellini," she said as she filled her cup, all the while keeping her eyes on his.

Chellini waited.

"Lydia," he said finally, as he reached into his vest pocket.

He withdrew a slip of paper and he slid it toward his wife, whose solemnity dominated the little room.

She unfolded the sheet.

"*Lydia,*" it read, "*your husband loves you.*"

Chellini watched as she read the salutation and signature.

"Your friend, Dick Powell."

Chellini reached for a cookie.

"Your Friday movie," he said. "At what time do we go?"

Stunned, Lydia could not respond.

As she stared at the note, young Chellini dropped his hand under the table.

Ambrose happily licked the sugar from his fingertips.

WILLIAM GAY

Where Will You Go When Your Skin Cannot Contain You?

FROM *Tin House*

THE JEEPSTER COULDN'T KEEP STILL. For forty-eight hours he'd been steady on the move and no place worked for long. He'd think of somewhere to be and go there and almost immediately suck the life from it, he could feel it charring around him. He felt he was on fire and running with upraised arms into a stiff cold wind, but instead of cooling him the wind just fanned the flames. His last so-called friend had faded on him and demanded to be left by the roadside with his thumb in the air.

The Jeepster drove westward into a sun that had gone down the sky so fast it left a fiery wake like a comet. Light pooled above the horizon like blood and red light hammered off the hood of the SUV he was driving. He put on his sunglasses. In the failing day the light was falling almost horizontally and the highway glittered like some virtual highway in a fairy tale or nightmare.

His so-called friend had faded because The Jeepster was armed and dangerous. He was armed and dangerous and running on adrenaline and fury and grief and honed to such a fine edge that alcohol and drugs no longer affected him. Nothing worked on him. He had a pocket full of money and a nine-millimeter automatic shoved into the waistband of his jeans and his T-shirt pulled down over it. He had his ticket punched for the graveyard or the penitentiary and one foot on the platform and the other foot on the train. He had everything he needed to get himself killed, to push the borders back and alter the very geography of reality itself.

On the outskirts of Ackerman's Field the neon of a Texaco station bled into the dusk like a virulent stain. Night was falling like some disease he was in the act of catching. At the pumps he filled the SUV up and watched the traffic accomplish itself in a kind of wonder. Everyone should have been frozen in whatever attitude they'd held when the hammer fell on Aimee and they should hold that attitude forever. He felt like a plague set upon the world to cauterize and cleanse it.

He went through the pneumatic door. He had his Ray-Bans shoved onto the top of his shaven head and he was grinning his gap-toothed grin. Such patrons as were about regarded him warily. He looked like bad news. He looked like the letter edged in black, the telegram shoved under your door at three o'clock in the morning.

You seen that Coors man? The Jeepster asked the man at the register.

Seen what? the man asked. Somewhere behind them a cue stick tipped a ball and it went down the felt in a near-silent hush and a ball rattled into a pocket and spiraled down and then there was just silence.

The Jeepster laid money on the counter. I know all about that Coors man, he said. I know Escue was broke and he borrowed ten bucks off the Coors man for the gas to get to where Aimee was working. Where's he at?

The counterman made careful change. He don't run today, he said. Wednesday was the last day he's been here. And what if he did run, what if he was here? How could he know? He was just a guy doing Escue a favor. He didn't know.

He didn't know, he didn't know, The Jeepster said. You reckon that'll keep the dirt out of his face? I don't.

They regarded each other in silence. The Jeepster picked up his change and slid it into his pocket. He leaned toward the counterman until their faces were very close together. Could be you chipped in a few bucks yourself, he finally said.

Just so you know, the counterman said, I've got me a sawed-off here under the counter. And I got my hand right on the stock. You don't look just right to me. You look crazy. You look like you escaped from prison or the crazy house.

I didn't escape, The Jeepster said. They let me out and was glad to see me go. They said I was too far gone, they couldn't do anything for me. They said I was a bad influence.

The Jeepster in Emile's living room. Emile was thinking this must be the end times, the end of days. The rapture with graves bursting open and folk sailing skyward like superheroes. There was no precedent for this. The Jeepster was crying. His shaven head was bowed. His fingers were knotted at the base of his skull. A letter to each finger, LOVE and HATE inscribed there by some drunk or stoned tattooist in blurred jailhouse blue. The fingers were interlocked illegibly and so spelled nothing. The Jeepster's shoulders jerked with his sobbing, there was more news to read on his left arm: HEAVEN WON'T HAVE ME AND HELL'S AFRAID I'M TAKING OVER.

Emile himself had fallen on hard times. Once the scion of a prosperous farm family, now he could only look back on long-lost days that were bathed in an amber haze of nostalgia. He'd inherited all this and for a while there were wonders. Enormous John Deere cultivators and hay balers and tractors more dear than Rolls-Royces. For a while there was coke and crank and wild parties. Friends unnumbered and naked women rampant in their willingness to be sent so high you couldn't have tracked them on radar, sports cars that did not hold up so well against trees and bridge abutments.

Little by little Emile had sold things off for pennies on the dollar and day by day the money rolled through his veins and into his lungs, and the greasy coins trickled down his throat. The cattle were sold away or wandered off. Hogs starved and the strong ate the weak. It amazed him how easily a small fortune could be pissed away. Money don't go nowhere these days, Emile said when he was down to selling off stepladders and drop cords.

Finally he was down to rolling his own, becoming an entrepreneur, slaving over his meth lab like some crazed alchemist at his test tubes and brazier on the brink of some breakthrough that would cleanse the world of sanity forever.

The appalled ghost of Emile's mother haunted these rooms, hovered fretfully in the darker corners. Wringing her spectral hands over doilies beset with beer cans and spilled ashtrays. Rats tunneling in secret trespass through the upholstery. There were man-shaped indentations in the Sheetrocked walls, palimpsest cavities with out-flung arms where miscreants had gone in drunken rage.

JESUS IS THE UNSEEN LISTENER TO EVERY CONVERSATION, an embroidered sampler warned from the wall. There were those of Emile's customers who wanted it taken down or turned to the wall. Emile left it as it was. He needs an education, Emile would say. He needs to know what it's like out here in the world. There's no secrets here.

The Jeepster looked up. He took off his Ray-Bans and shook his head as if to clear it of whatever visions beset it. Reorder everything as you might shake a kaleidoscope into a different pattern.

You got to have something, he said.

I ain't got jack shit.

Pills or something. Dilaudid.

I ain't got jack shit. I'm out on bond, and I done told you they're watchin this place. A sheriff's car parks right up there in them trees. Takin pictures. I seen some son of a bitch with a video camera. It's like bein a fuckin movie star. Man can't step outside to take a leak without windin up on videotape or asked for a autograph.

What happened?

I sent Qualls to Columbia after a bunch of medicine for my lab. He kept tryin to buy it all at the same drugstore. Like I specifically told him not to do. He'd get turned down and go on to the next drugstore. Druggists kept callin the law and callin the law. By the time they pulled him over it looked like a fuckin parade. Cops was fightin over who had priorities. He had the whole back seat and trunk full of Sudafed and shit. He rolled over on me and here they come with a search warrant. I'm out on bond.

I can't stand this.

I guess you'll have to, Emile said. Look, for what it's worth I'm sorry for you. And damn sorry for her. But I can't help you. Nobody can. You want to run time back and change the way things happened. But time won't run but one way.

I can't stand it. I keep seeing her face.

Well.

Maybe I'll go back out there to the funeral home and see her.

Maybe you ought to keep your crazy ass away from her daddy. You'll remember he's a cop.

I have to keep moving. I never felt like this. I never knew you could feel like this. I can't be still. It's like I can't stand it in my own skin.

Emile didn't say anything. He looked away. To the window where the night-mirrored glass turned back their images like sepia desperadoes in some old daguerreotype.

You still got that tow bar or did you sell it?

What?

I'm fixing to get that car. Aimee's car. Pull it off down by the river somewhere.

This is not makin a whole lot of sense to me.

They wouldn't let me in out there, they won't even let me in to see her body. I went and looked at her car. Her blood's all in the seat. On the windshield. It's all there is of her left in the world I can see or touch. I aim to have it.

Get away from me, Emile said.

Aimee had turned up at his place at eight o'clock in the morning. The Jeepster still slept. It took the horn's insistent blowing to bring him in the jeans he'd slept in out onto the porch and into a day where a soft summer rain fell.

Her battered green Plymouth idled in the yard. He stood on the porch a moment studying it. In the night a spider had strung a triangular web from the porch beam and in its ornate center a single drop of water clung gleaming like a stone a jeweler had set. The Jeepster went barefoot down the doorsteps into the muddy yard.

He was studying the car. Trying to get a count on the passengers. He couldn't tell until she cranked down the glass that it was just Aimee. He stood with his hands in his pockets listening to the rhythmic swish of the windshield wipers. The dragging stutter of a faulty wiper blade.

I need a favor, she said.

It had been a while and he just watched her face. She had always had a sly, secretive look that said, I'll bet you wish you had what I have, know what I know, could share the dreams that come for me alone when the day winds down and the light dims and it is finally quiet. She was still darkly pretty but there was something different about her. The grain of her skin, but especially the eyes. Something desperate hiding there in the dark shadows and trying to peer out. She already looked like somebody sliding off the face of the world.

I don't have a thing. I'm trying to get off that shit.

Really?

I've had the dry heaves and the shakes. Fever. Cramps and the shits. Is that real enough for you? Oh yeah, and hallucinations. I've had them. I may be having one now. I may be back in the house with baby monkeys running up and down the window curtains.

She made a dismissive gesture, a slight curling of her upper lip. Will you do me a favor or not?

Is Escue all out of favors?

I've left him, I'm not going back. He's crazy.

No shit. Did a light just go on somewhere?

He stays on that pipe and it's fucked him up or something. His head. You can't talk to him.

I wouldn't even attempt it.

I don't understand goddamned men. Live with them and they think they own you. Want to marry you. Eat you alive. Jimmy was older and he'd been around and I thought he wouldn't be so obsessive. Sleep with him a few times and it's the same thing over again. Men.

The Jeepster looked away Blackbirds rose from the field in a fury of wings and their pattern shifted and shifted again as if they sought some design they couldn't quite attain. He thought about Aimee and men. He knew she'd slept with at least one man for money. He knew it for a fact. The Jeepster himself had brokered the deal.

What you get for taking up with a son of a bitch old enough to be your daddy.

I see you're still the same. The hot-shit macho man. The man with the platinum balls. You'd die before you'd ask me to come back, wouldn't you?

You made your bed. Might as well spoon up and get comfortable.

Then I want to borrow a gun.

What for?

I'm afraid he'll be there tonight when I get off work. He said he was going to kill me and he will. He slapped me around some this morning. I just want him to see it. If he knows I've got it there in my purse he'll leave me alone.

I'm not loaning you a gun.

Leonard.

You'd shoot yourself. Or some old lady crossing the street. Is he following you?

He's broke. I don't think he's got the gas.

I hope he does turn up here and tries to slap me around some.

I'll drop him where he stands and drag his sorry, woman-beating ass inside the house and call the law.

Loan me the pistol. You don't know how scared I am of him. You don't know what it's like.

The loop tape of some old blues song played in his head: *You don't know my, you don't know my, you don't know my mind.*

No. I'll pick you up from work. I'll be there early and check out the parking lot and if he's there I'll come in and tell you. You can call the cops. You still working at that Quik Mart?

Yes. But you won't come.

I'll be there.

Can I stay here tonight?

You come back you'll have to stay away from Escue. I won't have him on the place. Somebody will die.

I'm done with him.

The Jeepster looked across the field. Water was standing in the low places and the broken sky lay there reflected. Rain crows called from tree to tree. A woven-wire fence drowning in honeysuckle went tripping toward the horizon, where it vanished in mist like the palest of smoke.

Then you can stay all the nights there are, he said.

The murmur of conversation died. Folks in the General Café looked up when The Jeepster slid into a booth but when he stared defiantly around they went back to studying their plates and shoveling up their food. There was only the click of forks and knives, the quickstep rubber-soled waitresses sliding china across Formica.

He ordered chicken-fried steak and chunky mashed potatoes and string beans and jalapeño cornbread. He sliced himself a bite of steak and began to chew. Then he didn't know what to do with it. Panic seized him. The meat grew in his mouth, a gristly, glutinous mass that forced his jaws apart, distorted his face. He'd forgotten how to eat. He sat in wonder. The bite was supposed to go somewhere but he didn't know where. What came next, forgetting to breathe? Breathing out when he should be breathing in, expelling the oxygen and hanging onto the carbon dioxide until the little lights flickered dim and dimmer and died.

He leaned and spat the mess onto his plate and rose. Beneath his T-shirt the outlined gun was plainly visible. He looked about the room. Their switchblade eyes flickered away. He stood for an awkward moment surveying them as if he might address the room. Then he put too much money on the table and crossed the enormity of the tile floor and went out the door into the trembling dusk.

So here he was again. The Jeepster back at the same old stand. On his first attempt he'd almost made it to the chapel where she lay in state before a restraining hand fell on his shoulder, but this time they were prepared. Two uniformed deputies unfolded themselves from their chairs and approached him one on either side. They turned him gently, one with an arm about his shoulders.

Leonard, he said. It's time to go outside. Go on home now. You can't come in here.

The deputy was keeping his voice down but the father had been waiting for just this visitor. The father in his khakis rose up like some sentry posted to keep the living from crossing the border into the paler world beyond. A chair fell behind him. He had to be restrained by his brothers in arms, the sorriest and saddest of spectacles. His voice was a rusty croak. Crying accusations of ruin and defilement and loss. All true. He called curses down upon The Jeepster, proclaiming his utter worthlessness, asking, no, demanding, that God's lightning burn him incandescent in his very footsteps.

As if superstitious, or at any rate cautious, the cops released him and stepped one step away. One of them opened the door and held it. Doors were always opening, doors were always closing. The Jeepster went numbly through this opening into the hot volatile night and this door fell to behind him like a thunderclap.

In these latter days The Jeepster had discovered an affinity for the night side of human nature. Places where horrific events had happened drew him with a gently perverse gravity. These desecrated places of murder and suicide had the almost-nostalgic tug of his childhood home. The faces of the perpetrators looked vaguely familiar, like long-lost kin he could but barely remember. These were places where the things that had happened were so terrible that they had imprinted themselves onto an atmosphere that still trembled faintly with the unspeakable.

The rutted road wound down and down. Other roads branched off this one and others yet, like capillaries bleeding off civilization into the wilderness, and finally he was deep in the Harrikin.

Enormous trees rampant with summer greenery reared out of the night and loomed upon the windshield and slipstreamed away. All day the air had been hot and humid and to the west a storm was forming. Soundless lightning flickered the horizon to a fierce rose, then trembled and vanished. The headlights froze a deer at the height of its arc over a strand of barbed wire like a holographic deer imaged out of The Jeepster's mind or the free-floating ectoplasm of the night.

He parked before the dark bulk of a ruined farmhouse. Such windows as remained refracted the staccato lightning. Attendant outbuildings stood like hesitant, tree-shadowed familiars.

He got out. There was the sound of water running somewhere. Off in the darkness fireflies arced like sparks thrown off by the heat. He had a liter of vodka in one hand and a quart of orange juice in the other. He drank and then sat for a time on a crumbling stone wall and studied the house. He had a momentary thought for copperheads in the rocks but he figured whatever ran in his veins was deadlier than any venom and any snake that bit him would do so at its peril. He listened to the brook muttering to itself. Night birds called from the bowered darkness of summer trees. He drank again and past the gleaming ellipse of the upraised bottle the sky bloomed with blood-red fire and after a moment thunder rumbled like voices in a dream and a wind was at the trees.

He set aside the orange juice and went back to the SUV and took a flashlight from the glove box. Its beam showed him a fallen barn, wind-writhed trees, the stone springhouse. Beneath the springhouse a stream trilled away over tumbled rocks and vanished at the edge of the flashlight's beam. You had to stoop to enter the stone door; it was a door for gnomes or little folk. The interior had the profound stillness of a cathedral, the waiting silence of a church where you'd go to pray.

This was where they'd found the farmer after he'd turned the gun on himself. Why here? What had he thought about while he'd waited for the courage to eat the barrel of the shotgun? The Jeepster turned involuntarily and spat. There was a cold metallic taste of oil in his mouth.

Light slid around the walls. Leached plaster, water beading and dripping on the concrete, the air damp and fetid. A black-spotted salamander crouched on its delicate toy feet and watched him with eyes like bits of obsidian. Its leathery orange skin looked alien to this world.

Against the far wall stood a crypt-shaped stone spring box adorned with curling moss like coarse, virid maidenhair. He trailed a hand in the icy water. In years long past, here was where they'd kept their jugged milk. Their butter. He'd have bet there was milk and butter cooling here the day it all went down. When the farmer walked in on his wife and brother in bed together. The Jeepster could see it. Overalls hung carefully on a bedpost. Worn gingham dress folded just so. Did he kill them then or watch a while? But The Jeepster knew he was in the zone. He killed them then. And lastly himself, a story in itself.

When The Jeepster came back out, the storm was closer and the thunder constant and the leaves of the clashing trees ran like quicksilver. He drank from the vodka and climbed high steep steps to the farmhouse porch and crossed it and hesitated before the open front door. The wind stirred drifted leaves of winters past. The oblong darkness of the doorway seemed less an absence of light than a tangible object, a smooth glass rectangle so solid you could lay a hand on it. Yet he passed through it into the house. There was a floral scent of ancient funerals. The moving light showed him dangling sheaves of paper collapsed from the ceiling, wallpaper of dead, faded roses. A curled and petrified work shoe like a piece of proletarian sculpture.

The revenants had eased up now to show The Jeepster about. A spectral hand to the elbow, solicitously guiding him to the bedroom. Hinges grated metal on metal. A hand, pointing. There. Do you see? He nodded. The ruined bed, the hasty, tangled covers, the shot-riddled headboard. Turning him, the hand again pointing. There. Do you see? Yes, he said. The empty window opening on nothing save darkness. The Jeepster imagined the mad scramble over the sill and out the window, the naked man fleeing toward the hollow, pistoned legs pumping, buckshot shrieking after him like angry bees, feets don't fail me now.

The Jeepster clicked out the light. He thought of the blood-stained upholstery strewn with pebbled glass and it did not seem enough. Nothing seemed enough. He stood for a time in the darkness, gathering strength from these lost souls for what he had to do.

He lay in the back seat of the SUV and tried to sleep. Rain pounded on the roof, wind-whipped rain rendered the glass opaque and everything beyond these windows a matter of conjecture. The vodka slept on his chest like a stuffed bear from childhood. It hadn't worked anyway, it might as well have been tap water. Things would not leave him alone, old unheeded voices plagued his ears. Brightly colored images tumbled through his mind. An enormous, stained-glass serpent had shattered inside him and was moving around blindly reassembling itself.

He'd concentrate on more pleasant times. His senior year in high school, he saw his leaping body turning in the air, the football impossibly caught as if by legerdemain, he heard the crowd calling his name. But a scant few years later he was seated alone in the empty stands with a bottle between his feet. A winter wind blew scraps of paper and turned paper cups against the frozen ground and the lush green playing field had turned brittle and bare. He wondered if there was a connection between these two images and, further, what that connection might be.

A picture of himself and Aimee the first time, try to hold on to this one. Fooling around on her bed. Her giggling against his chest. A new urgency to her lips and tongue. Leonard, quit. Quit. Oh quit. Oh. Then he was inside her and her gasp was muffled by applause from the living room and her father chuckling at the Letterman show. Other nights, other beds. The Jeepster and Aimee shared a joint history, tangled and inseparable, like two trees that have grown together, a single trunk faulted at the heart.

Drink this, smoke this, take these. Hell, take his money, you won't even remember it in the morning. You'll never see him again. Ruin, defilement, loss. One pill makes you larger, one pill makes you small, one pill puts you on the road to Clifton with a Ford truck riding your bumper.

For here's what happened, or what happened on the surface, here's what imprinted itself on the very ether and went everywhere at once, the news the summer wind whispered in The Jeepster's sleeping ear.

The truck pulled up on Aimee past Centre. Escue blew the truck horn, pounded on the steering wheel. She rolled down the glass and gave him the finger. She sped up. He sped up. She could see his twisted face in the rearview mirror. The round O of his mouth seemed to be screaming soundlessly.

When she parked on the lot before the Quik Mart he pulled in beside her. He was out of the Ford before it quit rocking on its springs. He had a .357 magnum in his hand. As he ran around the hood of his truck she was trying to get out of her car on the passenger's side. Just as he shot out the driver's-side window the passenger door on the Plymouth flew open and she half fell onto the pavement. She was on her back with her right elbow on the pavement and a hand to her forehead.

She looked as if she might be raking the hair out of her eyes. He shot her twice in the face. Somebody somewhere began to scream.

Hey. Hey goddamn it.

A man came running out of the Quik Mart with a pistol of his own. His feet went *slap slap slap* on the pavement. Escue turned and leveled the pistol and fired. The running man dropped to his palms and behind him the plate-glass window of the Quik Mart dissolved in a shimmering waterfall.

The man was on his hands and knees feeling about for his dropped weapon when Escue put the barrel of the revolver in his own mouth with the sight hard against his palate and pulled the trigger.

Now The Jeepster opened the door of the SUV and climbed out into the rain. He raised his arms to the windy heavens. All about him turmoil and disorder. Rain came in torrents and the thunder cracked like gunfire and lightning walked among the vibratory trees. His shaven head gleamed like a rain-washed stone. He seemed to be conducting the storm with his upraised arms. He demanded the lightning take him but it would not.

Mouse-quiet and solemn, The Jeepster crossed the rich mauve carpet. Who knew what hour, the clock didn't exist that could measure times like these. This time there were no laws stationed to intercept him and he passed unimpeded into another chamber. Soft, indirect lighting fell on purple velvet curtains tied back with golden rope. He moved like an agent provocateur through the profoundest of silences.

This chamber was furnished with a steel gray casket, wherein an old man with a caved face and a great blade of a nose lay in state. Two middle-aged female mourners sat in folding chairs and watched The Jeepster's passage with fearful, tremulous eyes.

He parted another set of purple curtains. Here the room was empty save for a pale pink casket resting on a catafalque. He crossed the room and stood before it. Water dripped from his clothing onto the carpet. A fan whirred somewhere.

After a while he knew someone was standing behind him. He'd heard no footsteps but he turned to face an old man in worn, dusty black hunched in the back like a vulture, maroon tie at his throat. His thin hair was worn long on the side and combed over his bald pate. The Jeepster could smell his brilliantined hair, the talcum that paled his cheeks.

The Jeepster could tell the old man wanted to order him to leave but was afraid to. The old man didn't want to be here. He wanted to be ten thousand miles away, in some world so far away even the constellations were unknowable and the language some unintelligible gobbledygook no human ear could decipher. He wished he'd retired yesterday.

For The Jeepster looked bad. He was waterlogged and crazed and the pistol was outside his shirt now and his eyes were just the smoking black holes you'd burn in flesh with a red-hot poker.

He laid a hand on the pink metal casket. Above where the face might be. He thought he could detect a faint, humming vibration.

I can't see her, The Jeepster said.

The undertaker cleared his throat. It sounded loud after the utter silence. No, he said. She was injured severely in the face. It's a closed-casket service.

The Jeepster realized he was on the tilted edge of things, where the footing was bad and his grip tenuous at best. He felt the frayed mooring lines that held him part silently and tail away into the dark and he felt a sickening lurch in his very being. There are some places you can't come back from.

He took the pistol out of his waistband. No it's not, he said.

When the three deputies came they came down the embankment past the springhouse through the scrub brush, parting the undergrowth with their heavy, hand-cut snake sticks, and they were the very embodiment of outrage, the bereft father at their fore goading them forward. Righteous anger tricked out in khaki and boots and Sam Browne belts like fate's gestapo set upon him.

In parodic domesticity he was going up the steps to the abandoned farmhouse with an armful of wood to build a fire for morning coffee. He'd leaned the girl against the wall, where she took her ease with her ruined face turned to the dripping trees and the dark fall of her hair drawing off the morning light. The deputies crossed the stream and quickened their pace and came on.

The leaning girl, The Jeepster, the approaching law. These scenes had the sere, charred quality of images unspooling from ancient papyrus or the broken figures crazed on shards of stone pottery.

The Jeepster rose up before them like a wild man, like a beast hounded to its lair. The father struck him in the face and a stick caught him at the base of the neck just above the shoulders and he went down the steps sprawled amid his spilled wood and struggled to his knees. A second blow drove him to his hands, and his palms seemed to be steadying the trembling of the earth itself.

He studied the ground beneath his spread hands. Ants moved among the grass stems like shadowy figures moving between the boles of trees and he saw with unimpeachable clarity that there were other worlds than this one. Worlds layered like the sections of an onion or the pages of a book. He thought he might ease into one of them and be gone, vanish like dew in a hot morning sun.

Then blood gathered on the tip of his nose and dripped and in this heightened reality he could watch the drop descend with infinitesimal slowness and when it finally struck the earth it rang like a hammer on an anvil. The ants tracked it away and abruptly he could see the connections between the worlds, strands of gossamer sheer and strong as silk.

There are events so terrible in this world their echoes roll world on distant world like ripples on water. Tug a thread and the entire tapestry alters. Pound the walls in one world and in another a portrait falls and shatters.

Goddamn, Cleave, a voice said. Hold up a minute, I believe you're about to kill him.

When the father's voice came it came from somewhere far above The Jeepster, like the voice of some Old Testament god.

I would kill him if he was worth it but he ain't. A son of a bitch like this just goes through life tearin up stuff, and somebody else has always got to sweep up the glass. He don't know what it is to hurt, he might as well be blind and deaf. He don't feel things the way the rest of us does.

ROBERT KNIGHTLY

Take the Man's Pay

FROM *Manhattan Noir*

SERGEANT THOMAS CIPPOLO, desk sergeant at Midtown South, peers over his half-moon reading glasses at Detective Morrie Goldstein and his handcuffed prisoner as they enter the precinct.

"What's up wit' Charlie Chang?" he asks.

"Chang?"

"Yeah." Cippolo starts his various chins in motion with a vigorous shake of his head. "Charlie Chang. The dude made all those movies with Number One Son."

"That's *Chan,* ya moron," Goldstein replies without relaxing his grip on the arm of his prisoner. "Charlie Chan." Goldstein is a massive man, well over six feet tall with broad sloping shoulders that challenge the seams of an off-the-rack suit from the Big & Tall shop at Macy's. "Anyway, he's not Chinese. He's a Nip. Hoshi Taiku."

"A Nip?"

"Yeah, like Nipponese. From Japan." Goldstein notes Cippolo's blank stare, and sighs in disgust. "The Japanese people don't call their country Japan. They call it Nippon. Ain't that right, Hoshi?"

Taiku does not speak. Though he's been in the United States for three days and has only the vaguest notion of the American criminal justice system, he's heard about Abner Louima and wouldn't be surprised if the giant policeman strung him up by his toes.

Goldstein steers Taiku around Cippolo's desk and up a flight of stairs to a large room jammed with desks set back to back. A few of the desks are occupied by detectives who look up from their paperwork to watch Goldstein direct his prisoner to a small interview room. They do not speak. The windowless interview room contains a table and two metal chairs, one of which is bolted to the floor.

The table and chairs are gray, the floor tiles brown, the walls a dull institutional yellow. All are glazed with decades of accumulated grime, even the small one-way mirror in the wall opposite the hump seat.

"That feel better?" Goldstein removes Taiku's handcuffs, then flips them onto the table, where they settle with an echoing clang. "Okay, that's your chair." He points to the bolted-down chair. "Take a seat."

Hoshi Taiku is a short middle-aged man with a round face that complements his soft belly. From his seated position, looking up, Goldstein appears gigantic and menacing. Curiously, this effect remains undiminished when Goldstein draws his own chair close, then settles down with an appreciative sigh.

"My back," he explains. "When I gotta stand around, it goes into spasm. I don't know, maybe I should get myself one of those supports. I mean, standing around is all I ever fuckin' do." He removes a cheap ballpoint pen, a notebook, and a small tape recorder from his jacket pocket and sets them on the table.

"First thing I gotta do is explain your rights. Understand?"

Taiku does not reply. Instead, his gaze shifts to the wall on the other side of the room, a small act of defiance that elicits a triumphant smile from Goldstein. Goldstein has bet Sergeant Alex Mowrey twenty-five dollars that Taiku will crack before one o'clock in the afternoon. It is now ten thirty in the morning.

Goldstein lays his hand on Hoshi's shoulder, and notes a barely detectable shudder run along the man's spine. "Hoshi, listen to me. You chatted up the desk clerk, the bartender in the Tiger Lounge, and a barmaid named Clara. I know you know how to speak English, so please don't start me off with bullshit. It's inconsiderate."

After a moment, Hoshi bows, a short nod that Goldstein returns.

"Okay, like I already said, you got certain rights which I will now carefully enumerate. You don't have to speak to me at all if you don't want to, plus you can call a lawyer whenever you like. In fact, if you're broke, which I doubt very much, the court will appoint a lawyer to represent you. But the main thing, which you should take into your heart, is that whatever you say here is on the record. Even though you haven't been arrested and you might never be. You got it so far?"

Goldstein acknowledges a second bow with a squeeze of Taiku's bony shoulder, then releases his grip, leans back in the chair, and scratches his head. In contrast to his body, Goldstein's oval skull is very small and rises to a definite point in the back, a sad truth made all the more apparent by a hairline that stops an inch or so above his ears.

"So it's up to you, Hoshi," he finally declares. "What you're gonna do and all. You say the word, tell me you don't wanna clear this up, I'll put you under arrest, and that'll be that."

"No lawyer." Despite a prodigious effort, the words come out "'No roy-uh.'"

"Okay, then you gotta sign this." Goldstein takes a standard Miranda waiver from the inside pocket of his jacket, then spreads it on the table as if unrolling a precious scroll. "Right here, Yoshi. Right on the dotted line."

A moment later, after Yoshi signs, a knock on the door precedes the entrance of Detective Vera Katakura.

"The lieutenant wants you in his office."

"Now?" Goldstein is incredulous.

"Not now, Morris. Ten minutes ago."

When he returns a few minutes later, Hoshi Taiku, though unattended, is sitting exactly as Goldstein left him, has not, in fact, moved at all.

"I'm gonna be a while," the detective explains. "I gotta take you downstairs. Stand up."

Recuffed, Hoshi is led across the squad room to a narrow stairway at the rear of the building, then down two flights to the holding cells in the basement.

"What you got here, Morrie?" Patrolman Brian O'Boyle asks when Goldstein approaches his desk. O'Boyle has been working lockup since he damaged his knee chasing a suspect ten years before. He sits with his feet on his desk, perusing a worn copy of *Penthouse* magazine.

"Gotta stash him for a while," Goldstein explains. He lays his service automatic on O'Boyle's desk, then grabs a set of keys. "Don't get up."

Goldstein leads Taiku through a locked door, then down a corridor to a pair of cells. The cells are constructed of steel bars, two cages side by side.

"Yo, Detective Goldstein, wha'chu doin'? You bringin' me some candy?"

"That you, Speedo Brown? Again?"

"Yeah. Ah'm real popular these days."

Taiku's arm tightens beneath Goldstein's grip and his steps shorten. Speedo Brown is every civilian's nightmare, a bulked-up black giant with a prison-hard glare that overwhelms his bantering tone.

"Put your eyes back in your head, Speedo. I'm stashin' Hoshi outta reach."

"That the bitch cell," Speedo protests as Goldstein unlocks the cell adjoining his. "Can't put no man in the bitch cell lessen he a bitch. You a bitch, man? You some kinda Chinatown bitch? You Miss Saigon?"

Goldstein pushes Taiku into the cell, locks the door, then turns to leave. "C'mon, baby," he hears Speedo coo as he walks off, "bring it on over here. Let Speedo bus' yo cherry."

Hoshi Taiku perches on the edge of a narrow shelf bolted to the wall at the rear of his cell. He stares out through the bars, his face composed as he studiously ignores the taunts of Speedo Brown. But he cannot compose his thoughts. He has disgraced his family and betrayed his nation. In the ordinary course of events, he would already have lost everything there is to lose. But not here in this land of barbarians. No, in the land of the barbarians there is a good deal more to lose, as Speedo Brown's words make clear.

"You come to Rikers Island, ah'm gonna own yo sorry ass. I got friends in Rikers, git you put up in my cell. You be shavin' yo legs by sunrise."

Taiku thinks of home, of Kyoto, of his wife and children. If he is arrested, they will be shunned by their neighbors, his disgrace falling on them as surely as if they'd committed the act themselves. But he has not been arrested, has not, in fact, even been questioned, a state of affairs he finds unfathomable. In Japan, in Kyoto, he would already have done what is expected of anyone arrested for a crime. He would have confessed, then formally apologized for upsetting the harmony of Japanese society. That was what you did when you were taken into custody: you accepted your unworthiness, took it upon yourself, the consequences falling across your shoulders like a yoke.

But he is not at home, he reminds himself for the second time, and there are decisions to make, and make soon. Should he speak to the detective? If so, what should he say? Is it dishonorable to lie to the barbarians who bombed Hiroshima and Nagasaki? Who occupied Japan? Who humiliated the emperor? Taiku no longer believes that Goldstein will hurt him, not physically. That's because Goldstein has made the nature of his true threat absolutely clear: Talk or face immediate arrest and Speedo Brown, or someone just like him. Well, talk is one thing, truth another . . .

Taiku's thoughts are interrupted by the appearance of Patrolman O'Boyle. He is walking along the hallway, a prisoner in tow, a female prisoner.

"Up ya go, Taiku," O'Boyle orders. "You're movin'."

"Thank you, Lord," Speedo Brown cries.

O'Boyle cuffs his prisoner to the bars of Taiku's cell, then unlocks the door and motions Taiku forward. Already on his feet, Taiku finds that his legs do not respond to his will, that his heart has dropped into his feet, that he has a pressing need to immediately void his bladder. He has never known such fear, has not, prior to this moment, known that human beings had the capacity to be this afraid.

"You wanna hustle it up, Tojo? I don't got all day."

Again, Taiku wills himself to move, again he fails.

"Lemme put it this way, Taiku. If I gotta call in backup and extract you from that cell, I'm gonna carve your little Jap ass into sushi. You *comprende?*"

Taiku's mouth curls into a little circle, then he finally speaks, "Man threaten me."

The word "threaten" emerges as "fletta," which only adds to the humiliation Taiku feels at that moment. He has begged an inferior, a foreigner, to protect him.

"What?"

"Man threaten me."

"Who *fletta,* you? Speedo?" O'Boyle glances at Speedo Brown, then laughs before answering his own question. "Little Speedo? He wouldn't hurt a fly. Would ya, Speedo?"

"Never hurt a fly in my life, but I'm hell on Japanese beetles."

"I am Japanese citizen. You must . . . protect me." Taiku chokes on his own demand. A shudder runs through his body. If he'd had the means, he would have killed himself before speaking those words.

"Whatta ya think, Speedo? Should I *ploteck* him?"

"You jus' leave the boy in my hands, officer. Ain' nobody gonna hurt him. Leastways, nobody but me."

O'Boyle chuckles and shakes his head. "Awright, Tojo. You can wait for Goldstein out by the desk. Bein' as you're a Jap citizen and you ain't been charged with a crime, I guess it's my beholden duty to save you from the big bad wolf."

"I'm really sorry," Goldstein apologizes for the second time. "A couple of uniforms picked up a rapist I been after for six months. I hadda make sure he got hit with enough counts to catch a high bail. The asshole, he goes out on the streets, he's gonna rape someone else."

They are sitting in the interview room they left an hour before, on either side of the gray table. Goldstein's pen, pad, and tape recorder are laid out in a neat row. "We're goin' on the record now." Goldstein sets the tape recorder on end, starts it running, then suddenly shuts it off and pushes it to the side.

"Ya know something, Hoshi? I don't think we need to get formal. For right now, let's just keep this between the two of us. Whatta ya say?"

Goldstein acknowledges Hoshi Taiku's nod with one of his own, then gets to work. "Okay, why don't we start at the beginning. Why don't you tell me, in your own words, exactly what happened at the hotel this morning."

Taiku draws a breath and feels his command of English, modest at the best of times, slip away. He fears that when he speaks, he will appear a clown to the detective whose eyes never leave his own. Still, he knows he must speak.

"Girl jump," he finally says. "She whore."

"Whore?"

"She whore," Taiku repeats.

"A prostitute? That's what you're saying?"

"Yes."

"You devil. So, how'd you meet her?" Goldstein shakes his head and mock-punches Taiku's arm. "And by the way, her name was

Jane Denning. She was twenty-eight years old and had a kid in fourth grade at Holy Savior in Brooklyn."

Bit by bit, with Goldstein in no seeming rush, Taiku's story emerges. First, before leaving Japan, he was handed a business card from the Monroe Escort Service by a superior who'd been quick to explain that Monroe's specialty was large-breasted, blond-all-over blonds. Taiku had accepted the business card, not because he wished to enjoy the favors of a blond-all-over blond, but only because a refusal would result in his superior's losing face. He'd bowed, put the card in his wallet, and had forgotten about it until a dinner meeting was canceled at the last second and he found himself consigned to a long evening in his room at the Martinique Hotel. Jane Denning (who'd called herself Inga Johannson) had arrived an hour later.

"Did you get what you paid for?" Goldstein asks. He hasn't stopped grinning (nor have his eyes strayed from Taiku's) since Taiku began his story.

"What you say?"

"You know." Goldstein cups his hands against his chest. "Did she have a big pair? Was she blond all over?"

Taiku recoils. He cannot divine the motive behind the question; the cultural differences are too vast. Policemen in Japan maintained a supremely disapproving countenance at all times. Goldstein looks as if he's about to drool.

"*Hai*. Girl okay."

"How many times you do her?" Goldstein arches his back and grunts. "I mean, it was an all nighter, right? You took her for the whole night?"

"Yes. All night."

"So, how many times you do her?"

Taiku has had enough. He expects foreigners to be offensive, and knows he has to make allowances. But this is too much. Next Goldstein will ask him to describe what they did. "This not your business."

Goldstein's eyes narrow, but do not waver. "Awright." He waves his hand in a vague circle. "Go on, Hoshi."

They'd had sex, Taiku admits, then he'd gone to sleep. He'd slept through the night and when he'd awakened the next morning, found himself alone in the bed. His first thought was that he'd been robbed, but his wallet, with his cash and credit cards, was where he'd left it in the pocket of his trousers. Then a cool breeze had drawn his attention to an open window, which he'd closed without thinking to look down. It was only after he'd showered and dressed, after Goldstein knocked on his door, after a long, repeated explanation, that he'd finally understood. Inga Johannson had used the window to make her final exit.

The story is simple and carefully rehearsed, but Taiku's voice drops in pitch and volume as he proceeds. He is lying and certain that Goldstein knows it, certain also that he has to maintain the lie if he hopes to see his country and his family any time in the near future. But the need to confess, prompted by shame and disgrace, is very strong as well. And then there is the likelihood that even should he be released, he will neither be welcomed in his country nor embraced by his family.

"Look," Goldstein declares after a long moment of silence, "just for the record, is this the woman who came to your hotel room?"

Goldstein dips into the breast pocket of his jacket to remove a small photo of a young woman kneeling behind a toddler. The child, a boy, is looking over his shoulder and up at his mother while she faces the camera squarely. The broad smile on her face appears to be spontaneous and genuine.

Taiku stares at the photo, remembering the heavily made-up prostitute who'd emerged from the bathroom in her transparent lingerie, who'd run her tongue over her lips and her fingertips over her belly as if possessed. "Tell me what you want me to do," she'd said. "Just tell me."

"*Hai.* This her."

"We found it in her wallet. Good thing, too, because the way she came down on her face . . . Wait a second." Goldstein's fingers return to his breast pocket, this time removing a Polaroid taken a few hours before. He lays the photo on the table. "A fuckin' mess, huh?"

At first, Taiku sees only a large pool of blood spreading from a headless torso. But as he continues to stare down, he finally discerns the outlines of a flattened human skull made even more obscure by a semidetached scalp.

Goldstein's tone, when he begins to speak, is matter-of-fact. "You did okay for an amateur, Hoshi. First, you washed up the bathroom pretty good. Then you dumped the dirty towels, her makeup, and her syringe in a plastic bag which you took from the waste basket.

Then you carried the bag down two flights, and you tossed it in a service cart without being seen. The only problem is, it's not gonna help ya, not one bit, and what you're doin' here, lyin' to me and all, is only makin' things a lot worse."

Taiku finds that he can't tear his eyes from the photo on the table. Not because the gore holds him prisoner, but because he can no longer face Goldstein's steady gaze. It's ridiculous, of course; sooner or later he will have to look up. Still, he's relieved, at least initially, when Goldstein continues to speak.

"The way I see it, you wake up, find the bed empty, maybe check your wallet, then head into the bathroom, where you discover Jane Denning overdosed on heroin. Giving you the benefit of the doubt, you think she's dead. Maybe she's not breathing, maybe her skin is cool to the touch, maybe you can't find a pulse. Either way, you don't want her discovered in your room. Call it a culture thing. A dead whore brings dishonor on your company, your country, your family, yourself. You just can't let that happen. You tell yourself that nobody saw her come up to your room, that the cops will take it for a suicide, that nobody will lose any sleep over a dead whore, that by the time the police figure it out, you'll be ten thousand miles away.

"Not a bad plan, when I think about it. And if Jane hadn't been tight with the hotel detective, it might've worked, too. But she was well known to Mack Cowens, who was most likely bein' paid off, and she told him where she was goin'."

Goldstein pauses long enough to yawn. The squeal had come through at seven thirty, at the end of his tour, and it's now a little after noon. He wants his home and his wife and his bed, but the way it is, he won't finish the paperwork for many hours.

"Awright, back to the ball." He leans closer to Taiku, until his mouth is within a few inches of the smaller man's ear. "What you did, Hoshi, you bad boy, after due consideration, was open the window, haul her across the room, and toss her out. Then you closed . . ." Goldstein stopped, rubbed his chin, and nodded to himself. "Oh, yeah, something we couldn't figure out and I been wantin' to ask you. Did you wait for the crunch before you closed the window? You know, did you wait for her to hit the sidewalk? And another thing: Did you think about what would've happened if Jane landed on a pedestrian? I mean, it was pretty early, but what if some little kid had been walkin' along, mindin' her own business, maybe thinkin' about school or goin' to a party, and . . . *splat*? As it was, Hoshi, the few people down there who saw it happen, they're gonna carry that image into the grave. It's not fair and —"

The door opens at that moment, cutting Goldstein off in mid-sentence. He jerks back as though slapped. "What the fuck is this? I'm workin' here."

Vera Katakura endures the outburst without altering her stern expression. "You're wanted," she announces.

Goldstein's eyes squeeze shut for a moment, then, with a visible effort, he slowly gets to his feet. "Keep an eye on this jerk," he commands. "I'll be back in five minutes."

Taiku watches the door close behind Goldstein, then turns to Vera Katakura. Though clearly Asian, she might be from any of a dozen countries. He guesses Chinese, maybe Korean, but it doesn't matter because . . .

"Stand up."

The simple demand, spoken in perfect Japanese, runs up Taiku's spine, an ice cube settling onto the back of his neck. As in a dream, he feels the muscles in his thighs flex, his knees bend, his body rising until he stares directly into Vera Katakura's unyielding black eyes. She doesn't speak, but she doesn't have to speak. He can see his disgrace at the very center of her pupils, a tiny shadow, a smudge, and he knows that his dishonor extends to all — and to each — of the Japanese people. He wants to bow, to bend forward until his back is parallel to the ground; he wants to acknowledge his shame, to shrivel up and die, a cockroach in a fire. Instead, though his knees tremble, he continues to stare into Vera's eyes until, without changing expression, she lifts her open palm to her shoulder, then cracks him right across the face.

"*Hai,*" he says.

"She reduced him to a puddle," Goldstein declares, not for the first time. "The poor schmuck just melted on the spot." He turns to Vera Katakura, his partner for the last three years, and lifts his glass.

They are drinking in a hole-in-the-wall bar on Ninth Avenue, one of the last of its kind this close to Lincoln Center. Goldstein, Katakura, Brian O'Boyle, and First Grade Detective Speedo Brown.

It's been a very good day. A signed statement in hand before one o'clock, the paperwork completed by two o'clock, a crowded press conference at three thirty with Captain Anthony Borodski taking full credit for the successful investigation, though he hadn't arrived until after Hoshi Taiku was formally charged with murder. Mowrey had stood alongside his captain, there to field the questions that followed Borodski's official statement, while Goldstein and Katakura lounged at the rear of the dais, trying to appear at least vaguely interested.

"You were definitely right about one thing," O'Boyle says to Katakura. "You told me the poor bastard would beg to confess and beg he did."

Vera glances at Speedo Brown, who earned his nickname when he appeared at Captain Borodski's annual pool party in a tiny crimson bathing suit that fit his buttocks like a condom. "As you would, Brian, if you were in Taiku's position. For a Japanese male, Speedo Brown is the worst nightmare imaginable."

"I resent that," Speedo declares. "I'm really a very nice person when you get to know me."

They go on this way for another hour, with only Vera Katakura, who holds herself responsible, lending a passing thought to Hoshi Taiku. With malice aforethought, she'd signed, sealed, and delivered him into the hands of the state, plucking his strings as though playing a harp, effectively (and efficiently) consigning him to whatever nightmare awaited him on Rikers Island. Well, in fairness to herself, she hoped he'd asked for protective custody, or to get in touch with a lawyer, or with the Japanese embassy. An outraged embassy official had called the precinct ten minutes after the press conference ended. By that time, Taiku had already been arraigned and bail denied.

The saddest part, though it didn't seem to sadden her comrades, was that if Jane Denning was dead before Taiku pushed her out the window, the worst charge he faces is unlawful disposal of a body, an E felony for which he will likely receive probation. It all depends on the autopsy results. If Hoshi catches a break, he'll be out within a week. If not, he'll sit until he is indicted and rearraigned, until his lawyer makes an application for reduced bail, an application very likely to be denied.

"C'mon, Vera." Goldstein nudges his partner. "You got nothin' to say?"

Vera Katakura thinks it over for a moment, then sips at her third vodka tonic and shrugs. "You take the man's pay," she declares in a tone that brooks no contradiction, "you do the man's job."

LAURA LIPPMAN

One True Love

FROM *Death Do Us Part*

HIS FACE DIDN'T REGISTER at first. Probably hers didn't either.
It wasn't a face-oriented business, strange to say. In the early days,
on the streets, she had made a point of studying the men's faces
as a means of protection. Not because she thought she'd ever be
downtown, picking someone out of a lineup. Quite the opposite.
If she wasn't careful, if she didn't size them up beforehand, she'd
be on a gurney in the morgue and no one would give a shit. Certainly not Val, although he'd be pissed in principle at being de-
prived of anything he considered his property. And though Brad
thought he loved her, dead was dead. Who needed postmortem devotion?

So she had learned to look closely at her potential customers.
Sometimes just the act of that intense scrutiny was enough to fluster
a man and he moved on, which was the paradoxical proof that he
was okay. Others stared back, welcoming her gaze, inviting it. That
kind really creeped her out. You wanted nervous, but not *too* nervous; any trace of self-loathing was a big tip. In the end, she had
probably walked away from more harmless ones than not, guys
whose problems were nothing more than a losing card in the great
genetics lottery — dry lips, a dead eye, or that bad skin that always
seemed to signal villainy, perhaps because of all the acne-pitted bad
guys in bad movies. Goes to show what filmmakers knew; Val's face
couldn't be smoother. Still, she never regretted her vigilance, although she had paid for it in the short run, taking the beatings that
were her due when she didn't meet Val's quotas. But she was alive
and no one raised a hand to her anymore, not unless they paid
handsomely for that privilege. She had come a long way.

Twenty-seven miles, to be precise, for that was the distance from where her son had been conceived in a motel that charged by the hour and the suburban soccer field where he was now playing forward for the Sherwood Forest Robin Hoods. He was good, and not just motherly pride good, but truly skilled, fleet and lithe. Over the years she had convinced herself that he bore no resemblance to his father, an illusion that allowed her to enjoy unqualified delight in his long limbs, his bright red hair and freckles. Scott was Scott, hers alone. Not in a smothering way, far from it. But when he was present no one else mattered to her. At these weekend games, she stayed tightly focused on him. It was appalling, in her private opinion, that some other mothers and fathers barely followed the game, chatting on their cell phones or to one another. And during the breaks, when she did try to make conversation, it was unbearably shallow. She wanted to talk about the things she read in the *Economist* or heard on NPR, things she had to know to keep up with her clientele. They wanted to talk about aphids and restaurants. It was a relief when the game resumed and she no longer had to make the effort.

She never would have noticed the father on the other side of the field if his son hadn't collided with Scott, one of those heart-stopping, freeze-frame moments in which one part of your brain insists it's okay even as another part helpfully supplies all the worst-case scenarios. Stitches, concussion, paralysis. Play was suspended and she went flying across the still-dewy grass. Adrenaline seemed to heighten all her senses, taking her out of herself, so she was aware of how she looked. She was equally aware of the frumpy, overweight blond mother who commented to a washed-out redhead: "Can you believe she's wearing Tods and Prada slacks to a kids' soccer game?" But she wasn't the kind to go around in yoga pants and track suits, although she actually practiced yoga and ran every morning.

Scott was all right, thank God. So was the other boy. Their egos were more bruised than their bodies, so they staggered around a bit, exaggerating their injuries for the benefit of their teammates. It was only polite to introduce herself to the father, to stick out her hand and say: "Heloise Lewis."

"Bill Carroll," he said. "Eloise?"

"Heloise. As in 'hints from.'"

He shook her hand. She had recognized him the moment he said his name, for he was a credit card customer, William F. Carroll. He had needed a second more, but then he knew her as Jane Smith. Not terribly original, but it did the job. Someone had to be named Jane Smith, and it was so bogusly fake that it seemed more real as a result.

"Heloise," he repeated. "Well, it's very nice to meet you, Heloise. Your boy go to Dunwood?"

His vowels were round with fake sincerity, a bad sign. Most of her regulars were adequate liars; they had to be to juggle the compartmentalized lives they had created for themselves. And she was a superb liar. Bill Carroll wasn't even adequate.

"We live in Hamilton Point, but he goes to private school. Do you live —"

"Divorced," he said briefly. "Weekend warrior, driving up from D.C. every other Saturday, expressly for this tedium."

That explained everything. She hadn't screwed up. Her system simply wasn't as foolproof as she thought. Before Heloise's company took on a new client, she always did a thorough background check, looking up vehicle registrations, tracking down the home addresses. (And if no home address could be found, she refused the job.) A man who lived in her Zip Code, or even a contiguous one, was rejected out of hand, although she might assign him to one of her associates.

She hadn't factored in divorce. Perhaps that was an oversight that only the never married could make.

"Nice to meet you," she said.

"Nice to *meet* you," he replied, smirking.

This was trouble. What kind of trouble, she wasn't sure yet, but definitely trouble.

When Heloise decided to move to the suburbs shortly after Scott was born, it had seemed practical and smart, even mainstream. Wasn't that what every parent did? She hadn't anticipated how odd it was for a single woman to buy a house on one of the best cul-de-sacs in one of the best subdivisions in Anne Arundel County, the kind of house that a newly single mother usually sold post-divorce because she couldn't afford to buy out the husband's 50 percent stake in the equity. Heloise had chosen the house for the land, almost an acre, which afforded the most privacy, never thinking of the price. Then she enrolled Scott in private school, another flag: What was the point of moving here if one could afford private school? The neighbors had begun to gossip almost immediately, and their speculation inspired the backstory she needed. A widow — *yes.* A terrible accident, one of which she still could not speak. She was grateful for her late husband's pragmatism and foresight when it came to insurance, but — she'd rather have him. Of course.

Of course, her new confidantes echoed back, although some seemed less than convinced. She could almost see their brains working it through: *If I could lose the husband and keep the house, it wouldn't be so bad.* It was the brass ring of divorced life in this cul-de-sac, losing the husband and keeping the house. (The Dunwood School district was less desirable and therefore less pricy, which explained how Bill Carroll's ex maintained her life there.) Heloise simply hadn't counted on the scrutiny her personal life would attract.

She *had* counted on her ability to construct a story about her work that would quickly stupefy anyone who asked, not that many of these stay-at-home mothers seemed curious about work. "I'm a lobbyist," she said. "The Women's Full Employment Network. I work in Annapolis, Baltimore, and D.C. as necessary, advocating parity and full benefits for what is traditionally considered women's work. So-called pink-collar jobs."

"How about pay and benefits for what we do?" her neighbors inevitably asked. "Is there anyone who works harder than a stay-at-home mom?"

Ditch diggers, she thought. Janitors and custodians. Gardeners. Meter readers. The girl who stands on her feet all day next to a fryer, all for the glory of minimum wage. Day laborers, men who line up on street corners and take whatever is offered. Hundreds of people you stare past every day, barely recognizing them as human. Prostitutes.

"No one works harder than a mother," she always replied with an open, honest smile. "I wish there was some way I could organize us, establish our value to society in a true dollars-and-cents way. Maybe one day."

Parenting actually was harder than the brand of prostitution that she now practiced. She made her own hours. She made top-notch wages. She was her own boss and an excellent manager. With the help of an exceptionally nonjudgmental nanny, she had been able to arrange her life so she never missed a soccer game or a school concert. If sleeping with other women's husbands was what it took, so be it. She could not imagine a better line of work for a single mother.

For eight years, it had worked like a charm, her two lives never overlapping.

And then Scott ran into Bill Carroll's son at the soccer game. And while no bones cracked and no wounds opened up, it was clear to her that she would bear the impact of this collision for some time to come.

"We have to talk," said the message on her cell phone, a number that she never answered, a phone on which she never spoke. It was strictly for incoming messages, which gave her plausible deniability if a message was ever intercepted. His voice was clipped, imperious, as if she had annoyed him deliberately. "We have to talk ASAP."

No, we don't, she thought. *Let it go. I know and you know. I know you know I know. You know I know you know. Talking is the one thing we don't have to do.*

But she called him back.

"There's a Starbucks near my office," he said. "Let's meet accidentally there in about an hour. You know — *Aren't you Scott's mom? Aren't you Billy Jr.'s dad?* Blah, blah, blah, yadda, yadda, yadda."

"I don't think we really need to speak."

"I do." He was surprisingly bossy in his public life, given his preferences in his private one. "We need to straighten a few things out. And, who knows, if we settle everything, maybe I'll throw a little business your way."

"That's not how I work," she said. "You know that. I don't take referrals from clients. It's not healthy, clients knowing each other."

"Yeah, well, that's one of the things we're going to talk about. How you work. And how you're going to work from now on."

He wasn't the first bully in her life. That honor belonged to her father, who had beat her when he got tired of beating her mother. "How do you stay with him?" she had asked her mother more than once. "You only have one true love in your life," her mother responded, never making it clear if her true love was Heloise's father or some long-gone man who had consigned her to this joyless fate.

Then there was Heloise's high school boyfriend, the one who persuaded her to drop out of college and come to Baltimore with him, where he promptly dumped her. She had landed a job as a dancer at one of the Block's nicer clubs, but she had gotten in over her head with debt, trying to balance work and college. That had brought Val into her life. She had worked for him for almost ten years before she had been able to strike out on her own, and there had been a lot of luck in that. A lot of luck and not a little deceit.

People who thought they knew stuff, people on talk shows, quack doctors with fake credentials, had lots of advice about bullies. *Bullies back down if you stand up to them. Bullies are scared inside.*

Bully-shit. If Val was scared inside, then his outside masked it pretty well. He sent her to the hospital twice, and she was pretty sure she would be out on the third strike if she ever made the mistake of standing up to him again. Confronting Val hadn't accomplished anything. Being sneaky, however, going behind his back while smiling to his face, had worked beautifully. That had been her first double life — Val's smiling consort, Brad's confidential informant. What she was doing now was kid stuff, compared to all that.

"Chai latte," she told the counterwoman at the Starbucks in Dupont Circle. The girl was beautiful, with tawny skin and green eyes. She could do much better for herself than a job at a coffee shop, even one that paid health insurance. Heloise offered health insurance to the girls who were willing to be on the books of the Women's Full Employment Network. She paid toward their health plans and Social Security benefits, everything she was required to do by law.

"Would you like a muffin with that?" Suggestive selling, a good technique. She used it in her business.

"No, thanks. Just the chai, tall."

"Heloise! Heloise Lewis! *Fancy* seeing you here."

His acting had not improved in the seventy-two hours since they had met on the soccer field. He inspected her with a smirk, much too proud of himself, his expression all but announcing, *I know what you look like naked.*

She knew the same about him, of course, but it wasn't an image she wanted to hold on to.

Heloise hadn't changed her clothes for this meeting. Neither had she put on makeup, or taken her hair out of its daytime ponytail. She was hoping that her Heloise garb might remind Bill Carroll that she was a mother, another parent, someone like him. She did not know him well, outside the list of preferences she had cataloged on a carefully coded index card. Despite his tough talk on the phone, he might be nicer than he seemed.

"The way I see it," he said, settling in an overstuffed chair and leaving her a plain wooden one, "you have more to lose than I do."

"Neither one of us has to lose anything. I've never exposed a client and I never will. It makes no sense as a business practice."

He looked around, but the Starbucks was relatively empty, and in any event he didn't seem the type capable of pitching his voice low.

"You're a whore," he announced.

"I'm aware of how I make my living."

"It's illegal."

"Yes — for both of us. Whether you pay or are paid, you've broken the law."

"Well, you've just lost one paying customer."

Was that all he wanted to establish? Maybe he wasn't as big a dick as he seemed. "I understand. If you'd like to work with one of my associates —"

"You don't get it. I'm not paying anymore. Now that I know who you are and where you live, I think you ought to take care of me for free."

"Why would I do that?"

"Because if you don't, I'm going to tell everyone you're a whore."

"Which would expose you as my client."

"Who cares? I'm divorced. Besides, how are you going to prove I was a customer? I can out you without exposing myself."

"There are your credit card charges." American Express Business Platinum, the kind that accrued airline miles. She was better at remembering the cards than the men themselves. The cards were tangible, concrete. The cards were individual in a way the men were not.

"Business expenses. Consulting fees, right? That's what it says on the bill."

"Why would a personal injury lawyer need to consult with the Women's Full Employment Network?"

"To figure out how to value the lifelong earning power of women injured in traditional pink-collar jobs." His smile was triumphant, ugly, and triumphant. He had clearly put a lot of thought into his answer and was thrilled at the chance to deliver it so readily. But then he frowned, which made his small eyes even smaller. It would be fair to describe his face as piggish, with those eyes and the pinkish nose, which was very broad at the base and more than a little upturned. "How did you know I was a personal injury lawyer?"

"I research my clients pretty carefully."

"Well, maybe it's time that someone researched *you* pretty carefully. Cops. A prosecutor hungry for a high-profile case. The call girl on the cul-de-sac. It would make a juicy headline."

"Bill, I assure you, I have no intention of telling anyone about our business relationship, if that's what you're worried about."

"What I'm worried about is that you're expensive and I wouldn't mind culling you from my overhead. You bill more per hour than I do. Where do you get off, charging that much?"

"I get off," she said, "where you get off. You know, right at that moment I take my little finger —"

"*Shut up.*" His voice was so loud that it broke through the dreamy demeanor of the counter girl, who started and exchanged a worried look with Heloise. A moment ago, Heloise had been pitying her, and now the girl was concerned about Heloise. That was how quickly things could change. "Look, this is the option. I get free rides for life or I make sure that everyone knows what you are. Everyone. Including your cute little boy."

He was shrewd, bringing Scott into the conversation. Scott was her soft spot, her only vulnerability. Before she got pregnant, when she was the only person she had to care for, she had done a pretty shitty job of it. But Scott had changed all that, even before he was a flesh-and-blood reality. She would do anything to protect Scott, anything. Ask Brad for a favor, if need be, although she hated leaning on Brad.

She might even go to Scott's father, not that he had any idea he was Scott's father, and not that she was ever going to inform him of that fact. But she didn't like asking him for favors under any circumstances. Scott's father thought he was in her debt. She needed to maintain the equilibrium afforded by that lie.

"I can't afford to work for free."

"It won't be every week. And I understand I won't have bumping rights over the paying customers. I'm just saying that we'll go on as before, once or twice a month, but I don't pay for it anymore. It will be like dating, without all the boring socializing. What do the kids call it? A booty call."

"I have to think about this," she said.

"No, you don't. See you next Wednesday."

He hadn't even offered to pay for her chai, or buy her a muffin.

She called Brad first, but the moment she saw him, waiting in the old luncheonette on Eastern Avenue, she realized it had been a mistake. Brad had taken an oath to serve and protect, but the oath had been for those who obeyed the laws, not those who lived in flagrant disregard of them. He had already done more for her than she had any right to expect. He owed her nothing.

Still, it was hard for a woman, any woman, not to exploit a man's enduring love, not to go back to that well and see if you could still draw on it. Brad knew her and he loved her. Well, he thought he knew her, and he loved the person he thought he knew. Close enough.

"You look great," he said, and she knew he wasn't being polite. Brad preferred daytime Heloise to the nighttime version, always had.

"Thanks."

"Why did you want to see me?"

I need advice on how to get a shameless, grasping parasite out of my life. But she didn't want to plunge right in. It was crass.

"It's been too long."

He placed his hands over hers, held them on the cool Formica tabletop, indifferent to the coffee he had ordered. The coffee here was awful, had always been awful. She was not one to romanticize these old diners. Starbucks was taking over the world by offering a superior product, changing people's perceptions about what they deserved and what they could afford. In her private daydreams, she would like to be the Starbucks of sex for hire, delivering guaranteed quality to business travelers everywhere. No, she wouldn't call it Starfucks, although she had seen that joke on the Internet. For one thing, it would sound like one of those celebrity impersonator services. Besides, it wasn't elegant. She wanted to take a word or reference that had no meaning in the culture and make it come to mean good, no-strings, quid-pro-quo sex. Like . . . *zephyr.* Only not *zephyr,* because it denoted quickness and she wanted to market sex as a spa service for men, a day or night of pampering with a long list of services and options. So not *zephyr,* but a word like it, one that sounded cool and elegant, but with a real meaning that was virtually unknown and therefore malleable in the public imagination. Amazon.com was another good example. Or eBay. Familiar yet new.

But that fantasy seemed more out of reach than ever. Now she would settle for keeping the life she already had.

"Seriously, Heloise. What's up?"

"I missed you," she said lamely, yet not inaccurately. She missed Brad's adoration, which never seemed to dim. For a long time she had expected him to marry someone else, to pursue the average family he claimed he wanted to have with her. But now that they were both pushing forty with a very short stick, she was beginning to think that Brad liked things just the way they were. As long as he carried a torch for a woman he could never have, he didn't have to marry or have kids. Back when Scott was born, Brad had dared to believe he was the father, had even hopefully volunteered to take a DNA test. She had to break it to him very gently that he wasn't, and that she didn't want him to be part of Scott's life under any circumstances, even as an uncle or Mommy's "friend." She couldn't afford for Scott to have any contact with her old life, no matter how remote or innocuous.

"Everyone okay? You, Scott? Melina?" Melina was her nanny, the single most important person in her employ. The girls could come and go, but Heloise could never make things work without Melina.

"We're all fine."

"So what's this meeting about?"

"Like I said, I missed you." She sounded more persuasive this time.

"Weezie, Weezie, Weezie," he said, using the pet name that only he was allowed, given its horrible associations with that old sitcom. "Why didn't things work out between us?"

"I always felt it was because I wanted to continue working after marriage."

"Well, yeah, but . . . it's not like I was opposed to you working on principle. It was just — a cop can't be married to a prostitute, Weezie."

"It's my career," she said. It was her career and her excuse. No matter what she had chosen as her vocation, Brad would never have been the right man for her. He had taken care of her on the streets, asking nothing in return, and she had taken him to bed a time or two, grateful for all he did. But it had never been a big passion for her. It had, in fact, been more like a free sample, the kind of thing a corporation does to build up community goodwill. A free sample to someone she genuinely liked, but a freebie nonetheless, like one of those little boxes of detergent left in the mailbox. You might wash your clothes in it, but it probably didn't change your preferences in the long run.

They held hands, staring out at Eastern Avenue. They had been sweeping this area lately, Brad said, and the trade had dried up. But they both knew that was only temporary. Eventually, the girls and the boys came back, and the men were never far behind. They all came back, springing up like mushrooms after a rain.

Her meeting with Scott's dad, in the visiting room at Supermax, was even briefer than her coffee date with Brad. Scott's father was not particularly surprised to see her; she had made a point of coming every few months or so, to keep up the charade that she had nothing to do with him being here. His red hair seemed duller after so many years inside, but maybe it was just the contrast with the orange DOC uniform. She willed herself not to see her boy in this man, to acknowledge no resemblance. Because if Scott was like his father on the outside, he might be like his father on the inside, and that she could not bear.

"Faithful Heloise," Val said, mocking her.

"I'm sorry. I know I should come more often."

"It takes a long time to put a man to death in Maryland, but they do get around to it eventually. Bet you'll miss me when I'm gone."

"I don't want you to be killed." *Just locked up forever and forever. Please, God, whatever happens, he must never get out. One look at Scott and he'd know. He was hard enough to get rid of as a pimp. Imagine what he'd be like as a parent. He'd take Scott just because he can, because Val never willingly gave up anything that was his.*

"Well, you know how it is when you work for yourself. You're always hustling, always taking on more work than you can handle."

"How are things? How many girls have you brought in?"

Unlike Brad, Val was interested in her business, perhaps because he felt she had gained her acumen from him. Then again, if he hadn't been locked up, she never would have been allowed to go into business for herself. That's what happened when your loan shark became your pimp. You never got out from under. Figuratively and literally.

But now that Val couldn't control her, he was okay with her controlling herself. It was better than another man doing it.

"Things are okay. I figure I have five years to make the transition to full-time management."

"Ten — you continue taking care of yourself. You look pretty good for your age."

"Thanks." She fluttered her eyelashes automatically, long in the habit of using flirtation as a form of appeasement with him. "Here's the thing . . . there's a guy who's making trouble for me. Trying to extort me. We ran into each other in real life and now he says he'll expose me if I don't start doing him for free."

"It's a bluff. It's fuckin' cold war shit."

"What?"

"The guy has as much to lose as you do. He's all talk. It's like he's the USSR and you're the USA back in the 1980s. No matter who strikes first, you both go sky high."

"He's divorced. And he's a personal injury lawyer, so I don't know how much he cares about his reputation. He might even welcome the publicity."

"Naw. Trust me on this. He's just fucking with you."

Val didn't know about Scott, of course, and never would if she could help it. The problem was, it was harder to make the case for how panicky she was if she couldn't mention Scott.

"I've got a bad feeling about this," she insisted. "He's a loose cannon. I always assumed that guys who came to me had to have a certain measure of built-in shame about what they did. He doesn't."

"Then give me his name and I'll arrange for things to happen."

"You can do that from in here?"

He shrugged. "I'm on death row. What have I got to lose?"

It was what she wanted, what she had come for. She would never ask for such a favor, but if Val volunteered — well, would that be so wrong? Yet the moment she heard him make the offer, she couldn't take it. She had tested herself, walked right up to the edge of the abyss that was Val, allowed him to tempt her with the worst part of himself.

Besides, if Val could have some nameless, faceless client killed from here, then he could — she didn't want to think about it.

"No. No. I'll think of something."

Not my son's face, she told herself as she bent to kiss his cheek. *Not my son's freckles. Not my son's father.* But he was — she could never change that fact. And though she visited Val in part to convince him that she had nothing to do with the successful prosecution that had been brought against him when the undercover narc Brad Stone somehow found the gun used to kill a young man, she also came because she was grateful to him for the gift of Scott. She hated him with every fiber of her being, but she wouldn't have Scotty if it weren't for him. She wouldn't have Scott if it weren't for Val.

Maybe she did know something about divorce, after all.

Five days went by, days full of work. Congress was back in session, which always meant an uptick in business. She was beginning to resign herself to the idea of doing things Bill Carroll's way. He was not the USSR and she was not the USA. The time for cold wars was long past. He was a terrorist in a breakaway republic, determined to have the status he sought at any cost. He was a man of his word and his words were ugly, inflammatory, dangerous. She met with him at a D.C. hotel as he insisted, picking up the cost of the room, which was usually covered by her clients. He left two dollars on the dresser, then said, "For housekeeping, not for you," with a cruel laugh. Oh, he cracked himself up.

She treated herself to room service, then drove home in a funk, flipping on WTOP to check traffic, not that it was usually a problem this late. A body had just been discovered in Rock Creek Park, a young woman. Heloise could tell from the flatness of the report that it was a person who didn't matter, a homeless woman or a prostitute. She grieved for the young woman, for she sensed automatically that the death would never be solved. It could have been one of hers. It could have been her. You tried to be careful, but nothing was foolproof. Look at the situation she was in with Bill Carroll. You couldn't prepare for every contingency. That was her mistake, thinking she could control everything.

Bill Carroll.

Once at home, she called her smartest girl, Trini, a George Washington University coed who took her money under the table and didn't ask a lot of questions. Trini learned her part quickly and well, and within an hour she was persuading police that she had seen a blue Mercedes stop in the park and roll the body out of the car. Yes, it was dark, but she had seen the man's face lighted by the car's interior dome and it wasn't a face one would forget, given the circumstances. Trini gave a partial plate — a full one wouldn't have worked, not in the long run — and it took police only a day to track down Bill Carroll and bring him in for questioning. By then, Heloise had Googled him, found a photo on the Internet, and e-mailed it to Trini, who subsequently had no problem picking him out of a lineup.

From the first, Bill Carroll insisted that Heloise Lewis would establish his alibi, but he didn't mention that their assignation was anything more than two adults meeting for a romantic encounter. Which it technically was, after all. No money had exchanged hands, at his insistence. Perhaps he thought it would be a bad idea, confessing to a relationship with one prostitute while being investigated in the murder of another. At any rate, Heloise corroborated his version. She told police that they had a date in a local hotel. No, the reservation was in her name. Well, not her name, but the name of "Jane Smith." She was a single mother, trying to be careful. Didn't Dr. Laura always say that single parents needed to keep their kids at a safe distance from their relationships? True, hers was the only name on the hotel register. He had wanted it that way. No, she wasn't sure why. No, she didn't think anyone on the staff had seen him come and go; she had ordered a cup of tea from room service after he left, which was why she was alone in the room at eleven P.M. She spoke with many a hesitation and pause, always telling the truth yet never sounding truthful. That's how good a liar Heloise was. She could make the truth sound like a lie, a lie sound like the truth.

Still, her version was strong enough to keep police from charging him. After all, there was no physical evidence in his car and they had only two letters from the plate. Witnesses did make mistakes, even witnesses as articulate and positive as the wholesome young GW student. That was when Heloise told Bill she was prepared to recant everything, go to the police and confess that she had lied to cover up for a long-time client.

"I'll go to them and tell them it was all made up, that I did it as a favor to you, unless you promise to leave me alone from now on." They were meeting in the Starbucks on Dupont Circle again, but the beautiful girl had the day off. That, or she had moved on.

"But then they'll know you're a whore."

"A whore who can provide your alibi."

"I didn't *do* anything." His voice was whiny, put-upon. Then again, he was being framed for a crime he didn't commit, so his petulance was earned.

"I heard there's a police witness who picked you out of the lineup, put you at the scene. And once I out myself as a whore — well, then it's an established fact that you traffic in whores. That's not going to play very well for you. In fact, I'll tell the police that you wanted me to do something that I didn't want to do, an act so degrading and hideous I can't even speak of it, and we argued and you went slamming out of the room, angry and frustrated. Maybe that poor dead girl paid the price for your aggression and hostility."

He very quickly came to see it her way. He muttered and complained, but once he left the Starbucks she was sure she would never see him again. Not even back in the suburbs, for she had signed Scott up for travel soccer, having ascertained that Bill Carroll's son was not skilled enough to make the more competitive league. It was a lot more time, but then, she had always had time for Scott. She had set up her life so she was always there for her son. If there was a better gig for a single mother, she had yet to figure it out.

Her only regret was the dead girl. Heloise's debts to the dead seemed like bad karma, mounting up in a way that would have to be rectified one day. There had been that boy Val had killed for a crime no greater than laughing at his given name — Valery. She had told the boy, a drug dealer, Val's big secret and the boy had let it slip, so Val killed him. Had killed him, then driven off in the boy's car, just because it was there and he could, but it was the theft of the car that made it a death penalty crime in Maryland. And even as

Heloise had soothed Val and carted shoeboxes of money to various lawyers, skimming as much as she had dared, she was giving Brad the information they needed to lock him up forever. She had used a dead boy to create a new life for herself, and she had never looked back.

And now there was this anonymous girl, someone not much different from herself, whose death remained unsolved. If it had been Baltimore, Heloise could have leaned on Brad a little, pressed to know what leads the department had. But it was D.C. and she had no connections there, not in law enforcement, and Congress's relationship with the city was notoriously rocky. The Women's Full Employment Network offered a reward for any information leading to an arrest in the case, but nothing came of it.

Finally, there were all those little deaths, as the French called them, all those sighing, depleted men slumping back against the bed — or the carpet, or the chair, or the bathtub — temporarily sated, briefly safe, for there was no one more harmless than a man who had just orgasmed. Even Val had been safe for a few minutes in the aftermath. How many men had there been now, after eight years with Val and nine years on her own? She did not want to count. She left her work at the office, and when she came home she stood in her son's doorway and watched him sleep, grateful to have found her one true love.

DAVID MEANS

The Spot

FROM *The New Yorker*

JACK DUNHILL, AKA BONE, aka the Bear, aka Stan Newhope, aka Winston Leonard, aka Michigan Pete, aka Bill Dempsey, aka Shank, said, Not those waves but that little pucker on the surface out there is where the Cleveland water supply is drawn in, right there, and if you were to dump enough poison on that spot you'd kill the entire city in one sweep. Believe me, I've thought it out. You'd just have to hit right there, he said, pointing again, and then he turned to examine her gaze, and in doing so presented his face, weathered from years of picking blueberries and cherries in Michigan, and, after that, a merchant-marine gig during Vietnam. You see, the water is unsuspecting until it hits that spot. It has no idea it's gonna be collected, drawn under the streets, cleaned up, and piped into homes. Not a clue. But when it touches that suck its future vanishes. No chance of becoming a wave after that, no kissing the shore and yearning back out into the lake. Instead, it ends up pooled on somebody's lawn, or slipping down a throat, or spooned into a bowl of baby cereal. That's the mystery of chance. One minute you're one thing, the next you're another, and choice had nothing at all to do with it. He paused, pointed one last time at the spot, shook himself free of his reverie, and pulled her close while she searched the water, tried to find the spot, and, failing to do so, said, I see it. I do. It's right where you said it would be.

. . . All this while killing time in Cleveland, waiting for the Mansfield john to show up to collect the girl, because against all odds he had sent payment in advance for an evening of pleasurable escort after succumbing to Shank's well-polished pitch:

The girl's name is Meg. Hell, name her whatever you want, but I'd like you to call her Meg when you greet her for the first time, my friend. Said girl being in the prime of her youth, fresh as a daisy and raring to go. She'd practically escort you for free if I weren't around to mediate her desires, my friend, he said from a phone booth outside Ypsilanti, watching the girl as she sat in the car, fixing her face in the mirror. The Mansfield john's number had come from a list of potential clients he'd been keeping, names and numbers whispered to him as he and Meg rambled aimlessly around the Great Lakes. OHIO MEN IN NEED, it said at the top in block lettering. Below were six names. He'd tried four of them already, with no luck, but this time he felt the guy taking the bait — a sense of urgency formed at the other end of the line as the Mansfield john succumbed to the image he had painted: a bright young girl entwined in a skein of sexual confusion, open to just about anything. A girl born out of the loins of Akron, smothered by a father's touch, and then cast out to fend for herself. (He'd left out the boring details: the way he had come upon her small body curled up, asleep, beneath an overpass outside Port Huron; the long journey they'd taken around the rim of the state of Michigan, following the mitten, staying as close as possible to the waterline. He'd left out her delicate neckline and the shallow hopelessness of her gaze and the way he'd educated her in how to make use of her flesh to earn funds. He'd left out his former religious training at the Grand Rapids Bible Institute and the way God had failed to give him a precise indication of His will.)

After that, he'd begun to zero in on a price, speaking to the image he had conjured of a somewhat dainty man in neat trousers, with the kind of studied, dreamy comportment you'd expect from a farmer who had gone into the seed business and left field work behind for good; there was a hint of yokel in the Mansfield john's voice, a bit of hick around his tongue tempered by churchgoing and Sunday-school teaching. Yes, there was most certainly some Bible study in the formality of his elocutions, and there was fear in the amplitude of his voice — just loud enough to sound natural. In the phone booth, Shank imagined Mansfield as a man with neat hair, parted clean on the left-hand side, held with a shellac of brilliantine, cut tight above the ears. His wife would be in the family room watching television, aware of her husband in the kitchen, maybe even listening in to his side of the conversation, which to her would seem naturally cryptic because he often made deals on the phone, talking about seed prices, the best hybrids to plant, the way to intercrop carrots with corn. With this in mind, Shank took care when the dickering began and told Mansfield, Just say soy if you're going to bid lower on Meg, and alfalfa if we hit the magic number. Eventually the john said, softly, Yes, alfalfa is the way to go because it's a versatile crop, alfalfa will do just fine in your soil if you're lucky with the weather, and Shank said, Good, we've got a deal and you'll be saving this little girl's life, Mansfield, you understand, because she's putting money away for college after being kicked out of her home for no good reason. Then he instructed the man where and when to meet, adding, Just give us a nod. You'll see us standing around outside the Holiday Inn, and then go on up and check in and I'll send her up to you. You'll know us when you see us. I'll be the one with the big shoulders, and she'll be the one with the sweet derrière.

Here we are, Shank thought (or maybe said) outside the hotel, waiting out yet another john delayed by his guilt and his doubts and the time it takes to check his morality at the door, driving north, praying for forgiveness, taking a rain check on his deeper principles while the dull fields fly eagerly past the bug-speckled windows. As Mansfield drives, alone in the car, his face will be composed — the same look he might have when teaching his Sunday-school class — as he reaches up once or twice to straighten his cuffs, or his tie, and assures himself that if he maintains a certain formality he'll be able to justify anything he might do in this good world. When he gets to the hotel, he'll be so enthralled by his own desire — acute, as solid as carved stone — that the rest of his life, the house and the business and his upstanding place in the community, will become nothing but a small white dot behind him, zipping away like the last of an old television image.

A bolo tie at his throat, fresh-pressed plaid shirt tucked smartly into his chinos, the john will unchain the door, let it swing open, throw his arms wide, and say, Come on in, Meg, offering up a room truncated and narrow, papered in gold foil, periscoping to a view of Lake Erie from fifteen stories up. She'll go directly to the window and stay there, with her back to him, as long as possible, looking out, trying to fashion some drama. From the violent johns she's learned that it's best to build up an assemblage of gestures, somewhat vaudevillian and slapstick, around the act itself in order to preëmpt the hard, cold dynamics that otherwise set in naturally. (She would've got that from her father, an old tool-and-die guy: an awareness of the importance of the fine gradients, of using a micrometer, measure twice, cut once, and all that. . . .) Most johns were as hard as tungsten, as square inside as an unworked block. Behind her, Mansfield will cough a couple of times, unhitch his belt, and then approach her hesitantly. Beneath his façade of neat and upstanding morals will be a horrible goatlike presence, a humping energy that will arrive musky and damp, pressing up against her, moaning, reaching around to tweak her breasts. That much is certain. This john's a connoisseur of dry, Shank had warned her. He likes it sandpapery and rough, no lubrication, none, nada.

As Shank waited for her down in the hotel lobby, he began to feel himself edging into pure speculation. He knew little about what really went on up in the room, but he had a basic idea and he could imagine, in general terms, how she coped. Most likely she'd:

1) Find a crass rigidity, all bone and sinew, in the brashness of survival.

2) Abolish the formality of her own flesh. Reduce herself down to an essence — hips, the arch of her foot and shoulder blades, the part in her hair, the fine down on her earlobes, the nape of her neck.

3) Assume a protoplasmic mobility; the creep of the protozoa, one-celled hydra, primal and original and eager to consume itself for lunch.

In due course, Mansfield will tell her that he sells seed and some heavy equipment wholesale, just outside of town proper, and then he'll let his pants fall to the floor, step out of them, and move behind her as he places his cold, bloodless hands around her belly and tries to turn her while she resists slightly, and then some more, until he has to use a little force, and then they'll do a give-and-take shuffle to the bed, where he'll push her down and take her clothing off a bit at a time until finally they'll be doing it, and then he'll completely embody that goatlike carnality, grunting and groaning, while she keeps her eyes closed and concentrates on the spot Shank had pointed out to her on the water earlier, and she'll think about how it would feel to be devoured by darkness and then spat out somewhere, startled and renewed, fresh and tight from a spigot into a bucket or out onto a lush lawn somewhere pleasant — yes, she'll use that image, hold to it, and it will make things easier for her, he thought down in the lobby, waiting for her to emerge from the elevator, which she did, about forty-five minutes later, raising her hand to adjust her hair, glancing around for him with a bit too much eagerness.

There was something in her face: a slackness in her jaw that foretold the confession she'd give an hour later, driving through the moonlit suburb of Lakewood, speaking softly, saying: He had that string tie on the whole time, and it kept bugging me. You know, those cold metal tips kept brushing me, and it was like they were saying, Here I am, yank me. We're ready to go. Just grab hold. Cross the line, he said. Not out loud, but with his hands and his you-know-what. I said no. He struck me and said, Cross it. I said no. He hit me again. Then those strings told me: Draw me tight. And so I did. I did. It took all my might. I dug a knee into his ribs, tightened the bolo tie around his throat, and rode him like a bronco until he stopped moving, she said.

Shank could just barely make out the shape of her face in the pale Ohio light. Go on. Go on, he said, and she said, Well, what do you want to hear? Give me the nitty-gritty, he said. Give me the sick parts that this country ain't ready for, the bits folks would never believe. He waited, listening to the engine shudder. Well, she said, his teeth popped out during the fight. His bridge, I guess you'd call it, the four front ones, and when I was done I popped them into my mouth and said, What's up, doc? You didn't, he said, feeling the laugh come up from his ribs and then listening as she laughed in response.

Eventually they were up on the beach road, passing sensible homes, locked tight and frowning out at the lake with mute but unshaded windows while the first light came along the edge of the lake and he explained to her how even Erie would ignite if you touched a match to it correctly, and then he rambled on (trying to stop himself at first) about the time he'd witnessed the Cuyahoga River burn, a calico blanket of shimmering flames elbowing its way into the heart of Cleveland, and how the sight of it had changed everything and made him aware that his calling wasn't with the Lord, because there hadn't been a single recognizable sign of prophesy in that water, even as it burned.

After a swing up to Detroit for no good reason except to pay off a gambling debt and to cast a glance at Lake St. Clair, they headed east along the dreary tedium of Canada, Highway 401, the staggering dull flatness and repetition. This part of Canada's nothing but a feeble reflection of U.S. glory, he said. Then he carried on about old draft-dodger buddies who'd gone nuts from missing the American stuff. Guys who hallucinated burger joints, strip clubs, and billboards behind their eyelids. I avoided that. I skirted that issue, he said. I went into the merchant marine to get around running to Canada, and I got around it easy while my buddies went over and came back fucked up, or dead. Do I feel the guilt that comes from that? I certainly do. Do I live each day pondering it? I certainly do. Do I lament the way history chewed my best buddies up? I certainly do. Do I wonder at the great forlorn gravity of the way things went in the past? I most certainly do. Do I spend my days in a state of total lament? I certainly do. Do I tell the same old threadbare stories over and over as a way to placate the pain that is stuck between my rib bones? I do indeed. Am I just another lost sixties soul who dropped one tab too many and can't extricate myself from a high? I certainly am. And then, from that point, he kept talking, unable to help himself, until his discourse expanded (while she dozed and slept fitfully, rising from her dreams to catch fragments of his voice) and he fell into a reverie and told a long story as he drove, keeping close to the speed limit because the Mounties were out, their hats aslant. Here's the story, verbatim, as he told it:

There was this guy named Ham. This was just after my buddy Billy-T came back from his first tour of duty. You had to surmise Ham's story, because otherwise he was pretty much a blank slate. A big guy, the son of a pipe fitter from the Upper Peninsula, he was living in that shantytown I told you about, the old hobo hangout near the Kalamazoo River, a spot beneath the railroad tracks, not far from a gravel pit. Anyway, Ham had this wigwam setup, an assemblage of old sheet iron, tarpaper, birch bark, leather, nylon, deer hides, and bearskins laid over the original Potawatomi wigwam frame, arched branches twined with petrified deer hide, and the old smoke hole, too — and there was another shack, which had originally been a sweat lodge or something. You went in and smoked some hash and listened for the spirits to call. And they did call, man. Those spirits came in all forms and sizes and said things you'd never forget, at least not for a while.

Anyway, Ham had this girl, Maggie, a street kid from Detroit, a real looker, with those baby blues, bright blond hair, and a lispy little pair of lips that had trouble around polysyllabic words. Naturally, I took a shine to her, but she was Ham's, and you couldn't so much as look her way without getting him on your case. I snuck a glance anyhow, when I could. One day, I took her by the hand and led her down to the river and told her I'd baptize her right there if she wanted, and she said she did, go on, do it to me, make me clean or whatever. My study at the Bible institute was a year or so behind me then, but the words were still around, and I could still utter them in a convincing way. Full immersion, I told her. The works. Right down to an evocation of the Holy Spirit, which would pass into her soul, and so on and so forth, and her soul flying upward, skyward, I said, and so on and so forth. I admit, I laid it on thick, talking about the purity of her heart this, and the salvation of the soul that, and so on and so forth, and she listened to me attentively while her hands, tiny things, fluttered like hummingbirds sipping from her ears. Even now, when I think about it, I can imagine them fluttering on my shoulders and breastbone. (Here he lifted his hands from the steering wheel and waved his fingers.) Anyway, the Kalamazoo was one of the most polluted rivers in the world at the time. You could've walked across it if you'd had the will to do so. That sounds like an exaggeration, I know, but it was loaded with pulp waste from the paper mills, along with whatever Checker Cab felt like adding to the mix. In any case, I led her through the bush to the shore and we stood there looking at the water. This was early evening, or maybe dawn, or maybe early afternoon, late fall, perhaps, but a warm day for sure. The sky tried to reflect itself in the water but failed. Clouds and trees fell against the surface and were lost forever. The fish in the Kalamazoo begged for the hook. You'd flip them onto the shore and they'd flex their gills as a way of saying thanks. A few hardy bugs stalked the surface, yanking their gummy feet. You'll do better, I mean gracewise, without those garments, I told her.

Meanwhile, during all of this, Ham was in his wigwam, sleeping.

He slept like a mule. You could hear his snores all the way down to the shore. At least I thought you could. I knew he'd eventually get up, find her gone, and start looking. I knew he'd come down the trail noisily, heaving from side to side, unsteady on his feet, coughing and wheezing, because he was a grizzly of a man, and he snorted and snuffled even when he was still. You wanted to give him fair warning if you came up to him from behind. One was inclined to wear a bear bell around the guy.

Anyway, in her full, naked glory there was a shame in her that made her put her hands up, and then down, and then up. I said, I'm going to hold you under and speak the words, and you'll be down there in the depths, where it's dark and dreary, amid the detritus and waste for a moment, and you'll panic, most likely, feeling my hand here, I said, putting my hand on the back of her head. But you must resist the panic because I'll keep you under just as long as it takes me to say the words. Then I'll release you and you'll come up sputtering into newborn light brighter than anything you've seen before. And she said, I'm right for it, I'm in need, I've got blemishes that must be washed away, and I said, Good, good, you're ready. But one more thing. When you see that newborn light, take a long look before it fades when your eyes adjust. You only get a glimpse before it goes away, and then you have to rely on memory, and if your memory isn't strong you'll lose your grip on salvation. Then I took her into the water and started, pushing her under, and at some point I heard Ham on his way down, heaving through the brush. He must've seen me through the trees. What did he see? A man gripping his girl's head, holding her down while she wiggled with the Holy Spirit, splashing a froth into the air. Naturally, from his vantage, he misconstrued my actions and became wild with rage, dancing his way bowlegged through the brambles, held back only by his fear of water. Ham's terror of water was incredible. He could hardly find it in himself to splash his own face from the tap. He found brushing his teeth impossible. You could see his fear in the way he came in up to his toes and then backed out quickly. There were huge forces at play. He'd gone up against them as far as he could, and then he drew a line. He cursed the water, the river, and then yours truly. Against this backdrop, I tried to keep to the task at hand, and if anyone's to blame for my failings, for holding her under a beat too long, it's Ham himself for proving such a distraction. Timing is everything when it comes to the work of baptism. One wrong move and God enters the world at a weird angle. Take my word for it. I kept to the task at hand. After I released her body to the currents, Ham raced along the shore. I can't account for her spirit, but her body swung in wide windmill loops as it was drawn downstream, just out of Ham's reach. For a moment he stood still, quivering in a force field between his rage toward me and his lust for her. Lust won the prize, and he moved downstream, trying to lure her in with the end of a branch. But the currents were too strong.

Long story short, I went back to Ham's wigwam and sacked his food. Long story short, I ate his food while he followed her body all the way to Lake Michigan, where he stood on the shore and rolled his shoulders, as if bracing for a fight. He stood on the shore and bellowed. He was a grand, operatic bellower. His voice spiraled out over the water, as if blown from a conch shell. A big fat bellow that came five miles up the river to his wigwam, where by the time the sound got to me it was weak and feeble but still as clear as day. I sat, held off on my chewing as long as I could, and listened, clenching my teeth against the ringing in my ears, and the soft breeze that was coming through the leaves as evening approached. I was happy, because when the evening light met the Kalamazoo it did so on equal terms, and then for a while, until night fell and it was too dark to see, the river looked clean and even drinkable, Meg, as pure as anything you've seen in the world up until now.

He talked and then fell silent and then talked some more, until a few hours later they were in Niagara Falls and he nudged her awake so she could see the mist plume over the horizon. Then they drove along the river and up to the observation station and got out to stretch their legs. That river goes the wrong fucking way, it goes north instead of south, he explained, taking her hand. Then he climbed onto the fence and sat, patting the wooden railing. It goes against the grain of gravity heading that way, Meg. And it did. To their right the Niagara's water tore along the bank, groped hard, forming small eddies in which leaves and bits of trash pooled. To their left all fury and wonder until the river got close to the edge and then grew smooth and calm, thin with hesitation. You'll be able to walk out there if you're careful enough and stick with the harder surface near the edge, he said, and if I tell you to do it, you'll do it, won't you? You'll step right out there on your beautiful little feet when I give you the command, and you'll be just fine.

One more textbook case of discard and loss, another suicide fished out of the waters. Bodies were pushed to the bottom initially — for a few minutes — and then, unless snagged on the rocks below, they bobbed up and twirled around, unable to catch the outflow, which made it easy for the man named Kit Wilson, who took his Zodiac out with the collecting nets, to catch hold of her body and draw it up against the hull. Another slipper, he thought. Another foolish tourist who got too close. Another drunkard unable to resist the lure of danger. Another kid who went in too deep and couldn't get out of the rage. Another American testing the edge. (Canadians rarely went over.) Another girl skinny-dipping with her boyfriend, swimming too far out into the tangle of currents, taking the long trip down with plenty of time to think over her life and to consider the mistakes she'd made in one form or another. Maybe she simply couldn't live up to the expectations that life had, and decided that this was the best way to go, majestic and grand, united with the great drive of the water that had been coming over this escarpment for a million years (with the exception of that wonderful time, years ago, when just a trickle came over the scarred jawbone of rock while the rest of the mighty river was surprised to find itself diverted through the power-plant intake pipes). It seemed that at least once a year the same girl came over the falls to give him a bit role in the large drama that would culminate when the news crews showed up and asked him to speak. His Canuck voice would be clear and exact: We don't know where she came from. No idea why she did it. The falls aren't something to fool with. And, No, I don't get used to pulling them out like this.

He fished her out and saw that she was maybe fourteen or fifteen, with a thin, malformed rump, tiny arms, and a bruised face, cut along her brow, from which stared a pair of mute blue eyes. Her lips were pulled back in a grimace, exposing a gap between her two front teeth. Looking down at the body, flexing along with the hull, he got a hint of her story. (Later he'd hear her name, Meg Allen, and learn that her history could be traced back as far as a hotel in Cleveland, where she had murdered a seed dealer from a place called Mansfield, and then a bit further back, to a hell-on-earth childhood in Akron.) Whatever produced these bodies with regularity would go on, he thought. If there was a way to stop it, it had been forgotten long ago. He held the tiller and got the motor going full throttle and watched as the wake dug surprisingly straight and clean out of the torment. He loved the feel of the boat when its stern cut deep and, in turn, the bow lifted toward the sky, slapping over the waves. He loved the way the wake spread itself out — even in the foam and rage — and how, when he was past the washup, as they called it, the water gathered itself into order and smoothed quickly, as if eager to be done with all the noise and to get back to a more settled existence on the way down to the whirlpool, where it would spin mindlessly for a few minutes before being released into the relative calm of the river as it headed toward the merciful breadth of Lake Ontario.

KENT MEYERS

Rodney Valen's Second Life

FROM *The Georgia Review*

WE ALWAYS KNEW the crazy sonofabitch was out there. Don't know how many times people told me of waking at night to the sound of his rifle. Hell of a way to be jerked out of dreaming. Shane Valen was a weird son of a bitch from a long line of weird sons-abitches. Not that anyone ever went out and caught him in their headlights bending over an antelope or mulie he'd just poached. Just guts stinking and shining in a cloud of flies some hot, bright afternoon. We all knew who'd done it. *Goddamn it, Greggy,* they'd say to me, *can't you do something about that goofy bastard?*

Tried once. Turned on my rack and pulled the sonofabitch over — this was in the middle of the afternoon — just for a friendly chat. Shane, I said, I been hearing reports you're driving at night without headlights. Reports you're trespassing on land all over the county. Lot of people complaining, Shane.

He stared out his windshield so long I wondered was he deaf. So long I wondered if I'd really spoke. Finally he says, Anyone cut me?

Cut you? I asked.

Trespassin'? Anyone cut me trespassin'?

Hell, wasn't nobody in the goddamn county hadn't come across Shane's pickup parked along some back road at night with Shane behind the wheel and his rifle across his chest. Crazy bastard'd stare right into your headlights, never look away, so your lights'd bounce up and down on washboards, say, and his eyes'd be going on and off red, like a snapshot from a cheap camera. Spooky as hell. And you knew damn well he'd been creeping along, poaching, and saw your headlights from miles away, so he pulled off the road like that. A piece of the darkness. You knew damn well, too, if you'd go over the next hill and cut your own lights and come back, you'd find that sonofabitch moving along slow, feeling the edges of the road in the dark like one of his goddamned snakes, and seeing things out there in the night no one else can see.

Well, Shane, I said, they ain't so much caught you, but —

You cut me?

No, I ain't caught you either. Point is, though, you got neighbors, and —

You ketch me, we kin speak agin. I'm goin' now.

And he did. Put his pickup in gear and left me standing there — the only person ever did that. And hell, I let'm go. I hadn't *cut* Shane doing anything. Couldn't even catch the sonofabitch actually driving at night without headlights. He always saw me first.

Wish I could've caught him, though. Maybe this last mess wouldn't have happened. That's the trouble with being a peace officer — you're always after-the-fact.

Everyone figured Rodney, Shane's father, would end the Valen line. How the hell Rodney managed to find a wife's beyond anyone. Blame the freeway. Couple years after they finished it, Rodney got on it and ended up in Minneapolis, comes back telling about a woman he met in a bar. Dream on, broomstick cowboy. But two weeks later a car with Minnesota plates shows up here, and not some hippie girl looking for a sweat lodge. Of course, this is all before my time. I'm just telling what I been told, filling in the story that makes the rest of it make sense — if any of it makes sense at all.

In the car is Sarah Cornwall from Minneapolis, asking directions to the Valen ranch. And — no one could believe it — she marries Rodney and takes eight years to figure out what everyone else already knew, then gets back in her car and returns to Minneapolis, leaving seven-year-old Shane to Rodney's care — in other words, not much care at all.

I was a few years older than Shane, and what I remember most about him is how little there is to remember. Never knew if he was going to be in school or not, it was all haphazard with him, so I remember him more by his absence than his presence. Even then, stories were, he was out prowling. Spent more time with animals than with people, slept outside more than he slept in. Those stories about rattlesnakes crawling into sleeping bags for warmth? Shane maybe had that happen enough he figured it was normal. And maybe the snakes did, too.

Not too surprising he'd grow up and decide on a career in poaching, even if we can't prove that's what he did. But his letter writing — no one knew a goddamn thing about that until his mother returned and the whole business burst out of that ramshackle house of his into the light of day. Crazy thing. You think you know a man, but it turns out what you think's his secret's just keeping anyone from thinking he's got others. Like a black hole. So goddamn invisible it's gone right through to being visible again. To where everything is pointing to it, things warping around it, deforming. But unless you got a notion of what a black hole is, a theory of why, you just think, hell, ain't that an odd region of space.

Shane always had his pickup lights off and his house lights on. You could see the damn thing lit up, every room, off the Red Medicine Creek road. Didn't matter what time of night. Didn't matter if Shane's pickup was there or not. Lights were always on. So what the hell was the crazy sonofabitch doing?

She brought the letters back with her. I found them inside her car, tied up in a ribbon. Trying to figure it out, you don't know how far back to go. Maybe back to when Sarah up and left Shane. Or maybe to whatever the hell in Rodney appealed to her that got her here from Minneapolis. Or maybe you got to go clear back down the Valen line, to when Rodney's great-grandfather came out here and managed to wrest that patch of land away from the Indians and the government and claim it as his own. *There's* a sonofabitch still being talked about. Story is, he once whipped his wife with barbwire for not having a meal ready on time. And you look at the old records, it's goddamn odd how many kids in that family died young. All over that Valen ranch, kids buried. Little bundles of baby planted. Like saplings dead in a dry wind. You go out there, you wonder what you're stepping on.

It wasn't just Shane himself spooked people, wasn't just those red eyes behind that windshield. It was his whole family history — like that old ancestor never had been wholly buried. It ain't pretty, thinking of a woman whipped with wire. There's stories she's still seen, with children following her, none of them speaking a word. I can't afford to put much stock in them stories. That's in the past. Had nothing to do with Shane. Maybe. Just ghosts in the night, maybe. Bleeding mothers and dead children and an old man who finally got his hot meal, by God. I don't know. All I've really got are the letters.

Here's the first one:

july 15, 1961

dear mom

   how are you. I ben fine. dad to. thank you for the birthdee card. and the mony. I bot shotgun shels. I got a grows. there harder then fezzant.

Shane

A few things about that letter could intrigue you. For instance, the year: Shane was only eight years old when he wrote it — his first birthday after she left. She sends him money. She can't even imagine something he'd like.

And then the month: grouse season don't open till October. No sense waiting till you're grown to get started on your career, I guess.

But what gets me is how, even way back then, he's got that "Dad to."

Story is, on Shane's seventh birthday, Rodney handed him a loaded 12-gauge, and his mother left. Rodney wasn't what you'd call eloquent, but he had a couple guys he used to drink with, so we got these bits of quadruple-drunk story: Rodney drunk when he told it, his friends drunk when they heard, then drunk again when they retold it to a bunch of drunks. So Rodney gave Shane that 12-gauge, and you can imagine Sarah watching from the window, though that detail's not supplied. Been watching for eight years. All that hope she loaded into her car in Minneapolis is about to crumble into dust. The last straw's about to get loaded onto that goddamn overworked camel's back. She sees her son lift that shotgun, taller than he is, while her husband shows him the features. Points to the pump, crooks and uncrooks his elbow, imitating how it works. Points to the bead on the end of the barrel. To the trigger. Then stands back, looks around, shrugs his shoulders, opens his hands. I can just see it: *Whatever the hell you can find, son. Whatever the hell you can find.*

Shane's skinny arm straightens, works the pump. She's watching. Her little boy. Then the gun swings up and the barrel sweeps toward her, there's that sickening moment when its black dot is winking right at her and she's not sure what he's finding to shoot at, doesn't even know if he knows she's behind the window, and then it's gone up and by and then BOOM! She jumps and crams her fist in her mouth to tamp her scream down; she's afraid if she lets it out she'll never stop, she'll become the kind of thing they put on display at Wall Drug for tourists to see, the Screaming Woman, right next to that piano-playing gorilla with the grody knuckles, him playing and her screaming, a real duet. The weathervane on top of the barn — one of them old rooster things, half rusted-out and pointing the same way for as long as she's been Rodney's wife, don't matter how strong a different wind's blowing — she sees it rise off the roof. For just a moment it looks like that metal rooster's going to fly right up and away. But then it tumbles and falls, and clanks down the shingles on the other side, where I found the damn thing still laying in a patch of leafy spurge forty years later.

And her seven-year-old — she's just seen him stagger and damn near fall down, she can't imagine he isn't somehow wounded — he cries out, *Wow, Dad! Can I shoot it again?*

And you can just hear Rodney: *Good shootin', son. Damn good. Now you know how, you shoot that gun anytime you want. Shells're in the broom closet.*

She leaves that afternoon. Just gets in her car and leaves. Shane's prowling the pastures looking for nonmetal birds to shoot, and Rodney's she doesn't know where. She throws a suitcase of clothes in her car, the same one she drove out here eight years earlier. Takes nothing that wasn't hers when she came, including her son.

Here's the two that got me thinking:

July 15, 1973

Dear Mom,

Thank you for the money. Yeah, I turned 21. It ain't a big difference to me, though I been doing pretty much what I want for kind of forever anyway. It ain't like 21 and there you are like I hear with college kids. Dads doing fine. Cattle prices been OK.

Shane

July 17, 1974

Dear Mom,

Thank you for the money. My birthday was real good this year. Cattle prices was better than maybe ever least what I can remember. Dad said we oughta celebrate so we drove down to Rapid had dinner at the Howard Johnsons. I dont know if you was ever there but its got good food let me tell you. Dad makes about the best pies ever but that Howard maybe has even him beat. The waitress kept flirting with him and he was joking all night maybe I shouldn't be telling you that kind of stuff. Even people at the next table was laughing at Dads jokes and wondering if he was a professional comedian come to do a show at that Civic Center they just built in Rapid. Anyway Dads doing real good and my birthday was real good and the money you sent, well, Ill get something real nice with it dont know what yet but itll be nice. Something youd like and Dad too.

Shane

Look at them two letters. I'm leafing through them in my patrol car about a week after the whole thing happened, passing the time while I keep an eye on the radar, and wondering what I should do with the things, when I come to those two, one after the other like that. I stop and read them again. I can see how Sarah, getting them a year apart, might not have noticed anything. But me, I'm reading along and I got thirteen letters where Shane hardly says a damn thing, and then all of a sudden, in 1974, Rodney's all over the place — taking Shane to Rapid, flirting with the waitress, telling jokes, making pies. Where the hell'd this come from? Wasn't the Rodney Valen I ever knew.

Maybe I shouldn't have been reading them letters at all. There was nothing to investigate and no one to indict if there was. So those letters was private. On the other hand, there wasn't nobody to protest or care. I was about to read the next one when it hit me: Rodney Valen died in 1973. Collapsed on the sawdust of the Ruination Bar. It was talked about for some time, the dust his body raised, a regular cloud some people said, that had the shape of an old-time woman. That's drunk bullshit, of course. But that kind of story stays with you whether you believe it or not.

Only reason anyone called me was her car sat outside Shane's house for two days with the door open. Her car and Shane's pickup both. Shane's neighbor down the road finally calls me, he keeps driving by and gets to wondering. The thing about weird sons-abitches is they stick to their weird. You can trust them. Normal people keep their weird hid, so if it ever gets out you have no idea where it's going to go. But Shane Valen — I knew if he wasn't crawling around the county in his pickup with his lights off, something was serious wrong.

I got out there and parked behind her car, which at the time I didn't know was hers. Wasn't a sound out there, and that house with its blank windows waiting. I opened my door, called out, Shane! It's Greggy Longwell.

Wasn't even an echo.

I didn't think Shane'd actually shoot me, but no one I knew had ever actually drove up to his house, really tested his paranoia, so I got out of the car low but not so low I'd look like I was sneaking. In other words, I looked damn precisely like I was sneaking, and I made myself a good target besides, which shows how valuable compromise is.

I shouted, I'm coming up to the house, Shane!

Not a sound. But there wasn't nothing to do now but do it, so I shut the car door and started walking forward slow, up past her car. And then . . . Jesus!

I'm standing by that open car door, looking at this old lady, and she's got a big hole in her chest, and there's blood spattered all over the far window and a big smear through it like she reached up with her hand and then gave up. She's laying horizontal, her legs in the driver's seat, her shoulders in the passenger's. The shotgun blast must have lifted her right up and knocked her over. Her eyes, staring at the velour of the car roof, are blue and blank as marbles. But I can handle all that. Even the two-day stink I can handle. What froze my blood, what goddamn paralyzed me, was the goddamn snakes.

I mean, I know snakes will crawl into an open car for the warmth. Brock Morrison still talks about that time his wife drove fifty miles with a snake on her lap while he's snoozing in the back seat. Damn thing crawled in the car when they stopped for a break and left the door open. But that was just one of the sonsabitches. I was looking at snakes everywhere, twisted around like some puzzle that wouldn't never unravel. Snakes on the floorboards, the dash, slung over the backs of the goddamn seats, and that wasn't the worst of it. There was snakes all over her body, twisted in figure eights around her almost-nothing breasts, snakelaces wrapped around her withered, rotting neck and snakelets around her bony ankles and wrists. Snakes in her hair, vined around her feet. Jesus! She was crowned and booted with snakes.

*

Wasn't a soul in the county knew Shane well enough to confirm he actually had rattlesnakes living with him, even though talk was he let them curl around his feet while he drank his evening coffee before he went out poaching. But who the hell'd believe that kind of shit? Sure as hell not me. I got enough to do sorting out the bizarre from the just plain strange without adding in the implausible. But shit! Now I had to wonder just what was in that house. When I was finally able to move again I went toward it real slow, watching every goddamn grass blade and every goddamn shadow under every goddamn grass blade.

I stood on the cinder blocks Shane used for steps, wondering if there was snakes curled up inside them. I moved to the side of the door and turned the knob and pushed. The door swung in, but nothing else happened. Now I had me a hell of a fix. If I walked in slow, the crazy bastard might shoot me standing up, and if I barged in rolling on the floor like on some goddamn TV show, I might be rolling into a dozen rattlers. I eased away from the door and ducked under the kitchen window, then peered in sideways through it. It was so goddamn grimy and streaked and dotted with dirt I couldn't hardly see a thing, and I didn't want to get too close. So I'm peering and peeking at an angle, trying to see through that dirty glass, when my eyes adjust, and instead of seeing past the glass I look right at it. Them smears ain't dirt blocking my view. They're old blood turned dirt brown, and specks of dried-out tissue and little slivers of bone.

Shane! I called. You stupid sonofabitch, Shane, you get your ass out here, hear?

Nothing. Just a constant, swishing sound I'd been hearing awhile already, and right then I realized what it was. It was snakeskin moving against itself, so goddamn many of them sonsabitches in that house it sounded like wind in a forest in there.

Goddamn it, Shane! If you don't get your ass out here, I'll —

But I didn't have any idea what I'd do. I looked at that dried blood on the windowpane and thought, *There's someone besides that woman dead here, and there ain't but two vehicles, and one of them's hers and the other's Shane's, so it don't take no Dick Tracy to figure out whose blood's on this window.*

But I had a hell of a time steeling myself to walk slow into that dim kitchen where Shane Valen was perched on a ladder-back chair without his face, a 12-gauge on the floor next to him, the back of his head blown against the far wall and against that window, and the biggest goddamn rattlesnake I'd ever seen coiled in his lap, shaking its tail when I walked through the door.

May 23, 1989

Dear Mom,

    I been well, Dad too. He bought another section of land in order hes raising more horses. People said to him you aint never going to make a go of it raising arabians here but Dad said what its less rain here than in arabia? If you can raise arabians in arabia why cant you raise them in south dakota? Maybe we need to import some sand is that it? And I guess he proved right. We got people from foreign places like france and new york come out to buy dads horses. Them colts sure is cute. Long skinny legs cant hardly stand but you ought to see them run. You wouldnt hardly believe it. Aint nothing more peaceful of a evening then watching them mares and colts and the sun setting and the grass so green and some of Dads coffee and pie. He added onto the house maybe I told you that already last year or before and sometimes people will stay with us buying horses and all and Dad will just invite them to stay overnight so well sit on the deck and watch the sun go down and its about the finest thing they ever seen they say. And Dad hes been everywhere buying horses and he talks about them places and its something to hear him talk. Anyways thanks and I hope your well.

Shane

Check the date on that letter. First, Shane's writing more often. He ain't just waiting for his birthday thank-you in July. Second, Rodney's been dead fifteen years — and look at him, by God, still making pies but now he's also traveling around the country, raising horses, entertaining guests, adding onto his goddamn house. He sure as hell started to live the good life after he died. And every single letter's like that — Rodney rescuing people stranded in snowstorms, Rodney talking at public meetings, Rodney in one letter even learning to speak some goddamn Japanese. Jesus Christ, he couldn't hardly speak English when he was alive.

Goddamn mess getting her out of that car, with them damn snakes everywhere. We opened the doors and poked at them with sticks. It was noisy as hell, all them rattles going off. But we finally got them out. It was just up to me, I'd have had guys with shovels smacking the damn things, but news of Shane and Sarah had made it to Rapid, and the county commissioners was afraid the *Rapid City Jour-*

nal would show up and report a rattlesnake massacre, and then
who the hell knows what'd happen? Get them goddamn PETA
freaks out here telling us rattlesnakes have rights, too. So I had orders: no bad press, just get them sonsabitches out of the car, and
get this whole mess over with.

Which is just what I would have done if I hadn't found them letters. We got her body out, and there on the passenger seat under
where she'd fallen is that packet tied with a ribbon. By now I've got
her ID and figured out Shane murdered his own mother. But them
letters — they're all in the original envelopes, all addressed to her,
with Shane's return address on them. I throw them in an evidence
bag, but I ain't thinking I'm going to have to produce them as evidence in any trial, unless Shane can resurrect himself — like I later
found out he did his dad.

The whole thing's at first so goddamn clear, not a shred of doubt
what happened. And since there wasn't going to be a trial, there
didn't really have to be a motive, and there wouldn't have been if
I'd just left them damn letters alone. But I read a few of them at
random, just kind of officially perusing what I had, and they pissed
me off just like when any dumbshit brags. Rodney Valen raising
Arabian horses? Japanese businessmen sitting on his deck — which
he didn't have? It was too much, and I read some more just to find
out what other bullshit Shane would invent, and then I couldn't
stop reading, and then I got to wondering why the hell she came
back here anyway.

I mean, twist this sonofabitch around and look at it from her
view. She might have believed every one of them letters. Years and
years of bullshit piling up, but she doesn't know it. Her memory
of Rodney's not strong enough, maybe, to fight off the Rodney
that Shane's inventing. So, when she comes back to visit, who's she
coming to see? Hell! — her little boy and her breeder-of-Arabian-
horses and pie-maker husband. A goddamn dream, that's what. A
goddamn world that ain't and a person who never was.

And then, Shane looks just like his father. Both got that stare like
their old ancestor's, you can see it in the county historical book.
There the old guy is, staring out, dressed in his best clothes, surrounded by his wife and kids, them in white and him in black, like
they're froth floating up on the surface of something dark, though
there's no entry about him whipping his wife to shreds like cheese

or the kids who ain't in the picture. But all I'm getting at is Shane and Rodney look enough alike you could mistake one for the other if you forgot one was thirty years older.

And those letters of Shane's could make you forget. Hell, if anything, Rodney gets younger and younger after he dies — more and more who she must have wanted him to be in the first place. It's like time stopped for her, maybe. She looked in the mirror every day and saw, sure enough, she was getting older, but them damn letters were making Rodney younger. Like in a goddamn fairy tale, damn near unbelievable — except people believe in fairy tales all the time as long as they ain't written down and called that. So what's she thinking, really, when she pulls up to that dry-rot house out there?

It ain't nothing like the horse ranch she's been imagining. Hell, it's worse than when she left. But Rodney himself steps out the door, looking like she imagined him — maybe dirtier, but hell, he's a working man. There he is, by God. Ever since she left she's been half guilty and wondering what would've happened if she'd stayed. Wondering if Rodney would've been the man she imagined she married, the man them letters made him into. And now, there he is, real as life, walking out of the house holding a 12-gauge.

Wasn't till I had to figure out who the place belonged to, though, that I put it all together. End of the Valen line, so where's the land go now? How far do I have to go to find the uncles or cousins or whoever of the Valens who got as far from their past as they could but still got rights to the place? I knew something was up the moment I went in to see Orley Morgan. It ain't like a high-class lawyer is going to come to Twisted Tree to advance his career, but Orley got even shiftier than usual when I asked him about the Valen estate. Oh, hell, Orley didn't know a damn thing. Shit no! Jesus! That was so long ago when Rodney died, how the hell could Orley remember?

I ain't said a word about Rodney, I pointed out. And I ain't testing your memory. Just check your records. You keep records, I suppose?

Orley started babbling then. He'd been in charge of the Valen estate when Rodney died. And Rodney and Sarah hadn't never actually got around to divorcing. One of those things just never got done, like cleaning behind the refrigerator. So they were still legally married when Rodney up and raised that dust in the Ruination Bar. And who do you suppose estate law gives damn near the entire estate to? The surviving spouse, that's who.

Orley explains this to Shane. And ain't it odd that every goddamn letter Orley writes to Sarah Cornwall Valen comes back addressee unknown? *She musta moved agin,* is what Shane tells Orley. *Goddamn movingest mother I ever had.* And then, shit, seems Sarah Cornwall Valen spends half her time outta the country. *Ain't no goddamn use writin to her now, she's in Europe. She likes that kinda thing.* Orley couldn't keep track of all the places Sarah traveled. Every phone call he made, the number was disconnected or someone else answered the phone. *Moved agin. Even the goddamned phone company can't keep up with her.* I can just hear Shane handing out this bullshit, and Orley just lazy enough to believe it. He ain't gonna be able to buy that much Glenlivet anyway off what he'll make handling the Valen estate.

Jesus Christ, Orley, I said. You never got suspicious he was feeding you a line?

Dammit, Greggy, he named cities in Europe. Named buildings. Described 'em, even, how they looked. Named people she was seein'. With foreign names.

Guess those are the same people came to visit Rodney later, I said. Orley just looks at me, don't know what I'm talking about.

He says, It's just.

He picks up this paperweight on his desk, one of them water and fake-snow things that are supposed to make you think there's a whole other world in there. He looks at it like maybe there actually is, then gives it a shake and sets it back down.

Just, Shane didn't have that kind of imagination. Did he? Orley asks.

Well, ain't that the question right there? Shane never once let on he didn't want Orley to find his mother. Just the reverse. Gave Orley so much help he wore him out. And pretty soon the Valen file gets covered up with other files, and then one day I suppose Orley come across it and just kind of put it in a cabinet to keep from being reminded about it, telling himself he'd get back to it when Sarah settled down, and with that decided, had himself a drink. And Shane was careful to make just enough money to pay the taxes on that ranch, and there you got it: he gets to go on living out there and no one the wiser.

Seems Shane had more imagination than about anyone else around here, and enough left over to keep us thinking he didn't have none. And once he discovered he had it, he couldn't put an end to it. He's worried someone's going to figure out what he done, and he gets more paranoid every year, imagining his mother out there somewhere, antennas up to sense Rodney's dying so she can come back and snatch that land away, which is all he's got. Without that land he's nothing, don't even have no friends. He's imagining her, and that gets him to resuscitate his father and imagine *him*, a counter-imagination to keep his imagined mother at bay. Jesus Christ! And all that time alone, sitting in that truck, no one to interrupt his thoughts, bring him back to reality and tell him, *Shane, the garbage is starting to stink*. Hell, for all I know he might have started to believe his own bullshit, might've half thought his father was actually alive.

Here's my favorite:

May 19, 1990

Dear Mom,

How are things with you? Were fine. Its spring like I suppose its spring where you are to aint a lot of difference between here and there far as springs concerned I guess. The colts is wobbling around following there mothers like colts do and the meadowlarks is singing how they do I aint never been sure whether its a bell or its a whistle they got in there throats. And the swallows and the hawks is flying. National park service people been out talking to Dad about the blackfooted ferret I think I told you about that once. Dad got to studying about them ferrets and by god if he didnt up and make himself a expert on them critters. He convinced them national park service guys they ought to put some ferrets on our land and you oughta see how Dad watched over them things. They was having trouble with some they put in the badlands so they come out and talked to Dad to see what they was doing wrong. So Dads been gone some this spring off in the badlands with them national park guys keeping them ferrets there alive. Ferrets eat prairie dogs maybe you know that and prairie dogs sure make a mess of the grass aint hardly none left for cattle weather dry as it is. And theres some people think the prairie dog should be an endangered animal now what sense does that make? Like rats should be endangered. In fact the railroad thats coming here I told you about that too. Some people was mad because it was going to go through a prairie dog town like hows that not a good thing? Anyway Dad likes them ferrets so much he says thats how we ought to be controlling prairie dogs not with poison or railroads. Poison now that stuff kills them. Theres times Dads ideas go a bit screwy far as Im concerned but maybe hes right you get enough ferrets they could handle the job OK. But that manyd be as bad as prairie dogs.

Shane

Ain't that something else? It's not just Rodney's a goddamn expert on ferrets, and it's not just Shane's making up letters he didn't goddamn *write* — hell, he never once before so much as mentioned ferrets, or railroads either for that matter — but now he's even inventing what Rodney thinks and then, Jesus Christ!, *arguing* with him. It's just layers and layers of bullshit. It's bullshit about bullshit! And Sarah's getting this stuff year after year, and I don't know a damn thing about her, but she couldn't have been all that much in touch with reality if she came out here to marry Rodney in the first place, and she's probably guilty about leaving her little Shaney — wouldn't even occur to her that her little boy could lie, so hell yes she believes this stuff, maybe she even gets her memories mixed up with the letters, starts thinking she actually remembers Rodney being the kind of guy Shane's bullshit's making him into. So she ties those letters up and forgets what's in them, except not really — she remembers it as memory. Jesus Christ! That's the kind of mumbo jumbo Shane's got me talking. *Remembers it as memory* — what kind of bullshit is that? All I'm trying to get at is, I'm thinking Sarah got to where she couldn't tell the difference between what she remembered and what she read.

Like I said, to come out here and marry Rodney after meeting him in a goddamn bar, if Rodney was telling the truth about *that,* she had to be one of those women believes love's a goddamn abracadabra that whooshes the past away to some never-been and leaves only the goddamn shining future, unattached, like some Santa Claus gift. And who the hell's going to tell her she's stepping onto pockmarked land and into a family strange as a three-dollar bill? Love's a magic act all right, but that kind of thing don't finger snap away. It's like the elephant that disappears: only a goddamn idiot actually believes it went anywhere.

So one day her son blasts a wind-vane rooster off the barn, and she sees eight years of elephant dung she's been refusing to notice. Poof! She's gone. But that doesn't erase anything any more than love did. Elephant just goes on eating and crapping. And then in Shane's letters, by God, the Rodney she met in that bar in Minneapolis starts to come back to life: the Rodney she come out here to marry, the cowboy who'd take her away from whatever she didn't like about her life or herself, the Rodney who's going to give her everything pure, green grass and big skies and horse rides in the sunset — and none of that goddamn city pollution and traffic and dealing with people who don't want to deal with you. It ain't like Shane creates someone new for her. Hell no! He justifies her falling in love with Rodney in the first place. And how guilty does that make her feel? Without Rodney's surly-turtle real self around to remind her, she convinces herself she actually remembers the Rodney Shane's inventing for her. The man of her dreams, and her baby boy. She has to go back. Has to make amends before she dies.

And Shane never saw her coming. The only person ever he didn't see coming. Only one ever caught him by surprise. His own stories were making too goddamn much light around him, so he couldn't see past them. He thought it was Rodney's dying would bring her back, never thought it was his getting more alive would. I don't know what Shane thought she'd do if she owned the land — sell it out from under him I guess. And there he'd be — no house, no land, no grass, no snakes. It's goddamn pathetic thinking how little that sonofabitch had and how desperate he was to keep it.

He writes in one letter about this murder out here made the national news — this is part of his technique of putting in some true stuff along with all the bullshit. *You probably heard on the news about that girl out here got picked up and murdered. Dad says that must be about the loneliest you can ever be, in a car with someone like that and knowing where that cars going. Dad says that girl must have been thinking keep going car keep going. Because when it stops. Dad thinks about those kinds of things her thinking about that car when it stops.*

It ain't hard to figure out Shane's not just talking about that girl, he's talking about himself. He was one pure lonely sonofabitch. I found dozens of them stick pens all over the house. Empty, not a drop of ink in them. Scattered around. Husks of dreams ripened into letters. I can see it — Shane rolling into his place at two or three in the morning, no headlights, rolling in by feel with some new-dressed deer or antelope in the back of his pickup, and pulling into that shed that I can't figure how it managed to stand, and hoisting that animal out of the pickup with the come-along he had hooked to the rafters, and then walking out of the shed with those dead eyes swiveling behind him, groundward-facing, the come-along creaking in the beams. But Shane's already gone, he's been inventing his father for his invented mother the whole goddamn night, and now he walks into the light leaking from that shot-through house carpeted with snakes, stepping between them, his clothes all bloodstained from his work, sits down at that kitchen table that the varnish's been wore off for years, and maybe he's got to shoo a snake off the chair, and he picks up one of them stick pens and licks the end and grips that sonofabitch like it was a chisel, and he starts digging words into a notebook like the pen was a goddamn shovel, pressing some of them letters so hard I could see imprints of the previous ones in the paper and maybe the ones previous to that, too. Maybe the last letter has the whole goddamn dreaming pressed into it, and you could get the entire story out of that one page if you knew how to read it.

I don't know. It could be I'm bullshitting myself, and all that really happened is Shane was one paranoid son of a bitch, and when someone he don't know shows up at his place he blasts away without thinking or asking questions. I could be a bigger bullshitter than Shane. But I keep seeing him in that house, snakes sleeping around him or hunting in the walls where mice claws are clicking, and he's inventing Rodney's life. For her. For himself. And maybe both of them started believing it, memory and bullshit so mixed up that years back and now were the same damn thing, and little things like time and dying just didn't matter.

So she comes back to surprise them, her husband and her son. She doesn't call first. They might refuse to see her. So she pulls into that driveway, and even though she's old herself, in her mind Rodney hasn't changed and Shaney's still her little boy. But some serious confusion surely went on when she looked at that house, which isn't no Arabian horse ranch where foreigners from New York sit on the deck and sip bourbon. This is the place she left years ago, this is her real memory trying to get back inside her head. But she ain't got room for it, her head's so full of Shane's imaginings.

Before she can even get out of the car, who's she see walking out but Rodney. Her cowboy. Hasn't aged a bit, walking out with a shotgun in his hands, squinting through the glare off the windshield,

trying to figure out what this car is doing in his yard. She's not seeing the blades of grass moving all around him. Christ! It gives me
the willies. Here he comes. She's got her window open, thinks she's
hearing wind.

Rodney? she says. She almost recognizes something's wrong, but
she can't unlock it. *Rodney. It's me. Sarah? Remember?* She opens her
door.

Then she sees his eyes widen, recognition blooming like a goddamn flower. But what her husband says doesn't make any sense.

Mom? he says.

And even as the shotgun's sweeping up, everything's collapsing.
The house of cards that's her life is falling down around her, winds
are blowing it over, and she's a goddamn weathervane that in
spite of those winds ain't never turned any direction but one, never
pointed anywhere but where she's at right now. She's knocked
backward by the blast, lifted clear off the seat and into the passenger side onto that packet of letters she preserved and carried with
her. Time ain't never passed. She's right back in the moment she
left, her baby swinging that gun up past her face, the black hole of
that barrel turned toward her.

Shane stares at her. He had to kill her. Wasn't no reason she'd
come back but she'd found out the truth and wanted the ranch.
Never mind that to anyone but him that ranch would be a goddamn albatross around your neck. And Jesus, Shane couldn't never
live in town, with a street out his window and a lawn needs water-
ing. It was his land, goddamn it. His great-great-grandfather fought
for it and took it, and wasn't no woman, not even a mother, going
to take it away.

He turns back to the house and goes in, sits in that chair and
pumps the action of the shotgun. The spent shell goes somersault-
ing through the air and clucks onto the floor against the baseboard
where I found it, and he knocks the pump forward and sticks the
barrel in his mouth and puts the stock on the floor and leans for
the trigger. He's been *cut,* cut bad, and there's only one way out.
And then there's nothing in that house but rattle and alarm and
hazard, the singing of a hundred snakes in a concert you'd never
want to hear.

I'm tempted to go out some night with a can of gasoline and
burn that sonofabitching house down, just thinking of them rat-

tlesnakes out there — Shane's family they were, sprawled on the floors at night, coiled on the floors in the day waiting for mice to wander by, or slithering out under the doors, through various cracks, coming and going. He might actually have felt something for them, but I know goddamn well they didn't feel a damn thing for him. Ain't nothing but a den to them. Go out there and burn it down, all of them, and throw that damn pack of letters in and walk away.

But the letters got a grip on me. I can't stop reading them. I wouldn't be surprised if someday I'll be looking into my headlights, and the Valen women will parade across in front of me, one cut up and with children clinging, and the other with a hole in her chest and snakes swirling up and down her, looking at her empty hands, trying to read the letters I'm reading and not knowing where they've gone.

JOYCE CAROL OATES

Meadowlands

FROM *Murder at the Racetrack*

BRING YOUR DRIVER'S LICENSE, sweetheart. You're driving."
Fritzi's new car? He was letting her drive?

Smiling his easy smile. Reaching over to squeeze her arm in that
way of his, which sent a sensation like a mild electric shock through
Katie's body. Even as Katie warned herself, *Don't fall for it. You'll be
hurt.*

Fritzi Czechi was known for his upscale but tasteful cars. This
new-model steely-silver BMW with the mulberry leather interior
and teakwood dash, he'd purchased only two weeks before, he was
asking Katie Flanders to drive to the Meadowlands racetrack, handing over the keys to her as if they were husband and wife, not a man
and a woman in an undefined if romantic relationship. Katie stared
at the keys quivering on the palm of her hand. *Don't! Don't fall for it.*

"Look, Fritzi: Why exactly am I driving, and not you? I missed the
reason."

"Because I need to concentrate, sweetheart."

This was so. On the way to Meadowlands, while Katie, always a
careful driver, drove the elegant new car at exactly the Turnpike
speed limit, Fritzi studied what appeared to be racing forms, frowning, making notations with a stubby pencil. After a while he shifted
in his seat to stare out the passenger's window, frowning as if pain-
ful-sized thoughts were working their way through his brain, and
Katie glanced over at him wondering, what was Fritzi thinking?
(Probably not of what had happened between them the night before, as Katie was. A warm dreamy erotic memory intensified by the
smell of the new-car interior.) Fritzi was part owner of one of the

horses scheduled to race this Friday evening at Meadowlands, a three-year-old stallion named Morning Star who was returning to serious racing after being sidelined for months with a hairline fracture of his right front knee. Katie understood that Fritzi was worried about his horse, but also Fritzi was a gambler, which meant he dealt in odds, in numerals, and probably he had a mathematical mind and could "see" figures in his head in a way Katie could only imagine, it was so alien to her way of perceiving the world. Once, when she'd asked Fritzi how much one of his horses had cost, Fritzi had told her, "A racehorse is beyond computation, sweetheart," which had been a mysterious answer yet made sense.

It was a way of telling Katie Flanders, too, that Fritzi's private professional life was beyond her comprehension.

So Katie drove, and liked it that Fritzi so trusted her with his car, which wasn't like Fritzi Czechi in fact, or any man she'd ever known, asking or allowing a woman to drive his car while he sat in the passenger's seat staring out the window. Katie wondered if maybe Fritzi was in one of his moods: captured by the look of the mottled, marbled early-evening sky like the usual sky over northern New Jersey, clouds like chunks of dirty concrete shot with veins of acid yellow and sulfur red. This Jersey sky they'd been seeing all their lives, Katie thought. Familiar as a ceiling of some room you could die in.

The last time Fritzi had taken Katie to Meadowlands to see one of his horses race had been a year ago, or more. That year had passed slowly! Fritzi's horse then was Pink Lady, a four-year-old who hadn't won her race but hadn't lost badly, in Katie's opinion. Pink Lady had galloped so hard, Katie's heart had gone out to the shuddering mare, whipped by her scowling little jockey but unable to overtake the lead horses who'd seemed to pull away from the rest immediately out of the gate as if by magic. Pink Lady had come in third, out of nine. That wasn't bad, was it? Katie had seemed to plead with Fritzi, who'd said little about the race, or about Pink Lady, and he hadn't encouraged Katie's encouragement, still less her emotions. Always Katie would remember *A racehorse is beyond computation* and understand it as a rebuke.

A gentle rebuke, though. Not like somebody telling you to shut up and mind your own business, you don't know shit.

Fritzi Czechi was one of those men in Katie's life — Katie didn't

want to think how many there were, and that some of them knew
one another from Jersey City High where they'd all gone — who'd
been in and out of her life since the early 1970s. Now it was 1988
and they were fully grown, no longer high school kids, yet when
you looked closely at them, as at yourself in a mirror, frankly, un-
sparingly, you saw that they were still kids trying to figure what the
hell it was all about, and what they were missing out on, they were
beginning to realize they'd never get.

Except Fritzi Czechi. But for his broken-up marriages, Fritzi
hadn't done badly. He exuded a certain glamour. He dressed in
style. He was a fair-skinned, lean, ropy-muscled man of about five
feet nine, not tall, carrying himself with a certain confidence, at
least when people were likely to be watching. Fritzi had strangely
luminous stone-colored eyes, fair hair thinning at the crown he
wore slightly long so that it curled behind his ears; he had a habit of
stroking his hair, the back of his head, a medallion ring gleaming
on the third finger of his right hand. (Katie recalled Fritzi had
once worn a wedding band. But no longer.) Fritzi was a good-looking man, if no longer as good-looking as he'd been six or seven
years before when his smiling picture had been printed in Jersey papers as the part owner of a Thoroughbred that had won
$500,000 in the Belmont Stakes. (Katie had saved these clippings.
She hadn't been going out with Fritzi at that time, Fritzi had been
married then. If he'd been seeing other women, which probably he
had been, Katie Flanders wasn't one of these women.)

As well as horses, Fritzi was known to have invested in a number
of restaurants, clubs, and bowling alleys in Jersey, though he rarely
spoke of his business life; it was part of Fritzi's glamour that he was
so reticent, so elusive you might say, keeping his private life to himself, so if you were Katie Flanders you'd have to hear from other
sources that things were going well for Fritzi, or not so well. "Invest-
ments," horses, marriages. (Three marriages. Children, both boys,
from the first, long-ago marriage when Fritzi had thought he'd
wanted to be a New Jersey state trooper like his oldest brother. So
far as Katie knew, Fritzi was separated from his third wife, not yet legally divorced. But it was only an assumption. She couldn't ask.)
Definitely it was part of Fritzi Czechi's glamour that he did unpre-
dictable things like giving money to bankrupt Jersey City High for
new uniforms for both the boys' and the girls' varsity basketball

teams, or he'd send boxes of expensive chocolate candies to the mothers of certain of his old friends for their birthdays, or hospitalizations, or a dozen red roses to a woman friend like Katie Flanders he was sorry about not having seen in a while, as a token of his "esteem." Fritzi was known to pick up tabs in restaurants and clubs, and he was known to lend money to friends, if they were old friends, without asking for interest, and often without much hope of getting the money back.

He'd "lent" money to Katie, too. When there'd been a medical crisis in her family. When she'd tried to return it he'd told her, "Someday, sweetheart, you can bail me out. We'll wait."

Katie was a secretary at Drummond Tools, Ltd., in Hackensack. One of those temporary jobs, she'd thought, until she got married, started having babies. But just to be a secretary these days you had to know computers, and computers are always being upgraded, which is scary as hell when you're on the downside of thirty and not getting any younger or smarter while the new girls being hired look like junior high kids. The thought chilled Katie. She reached out to touch Fritzi's arm, needing to touch him, and liking the fact that it was Katie Flanders's privilege to touch Fritzi Czechi in this casual intimate way since they were more than lovers, they were old friends. "This BMW, Fritzi, is *very nice.*"

Fritzi said, "Well, good."

He wasn't listening. He'd put away his racing forms and was staring now at his watch, which he wore turned inward, the flat oval disc of digital numbers against his pulse. As if, with Fritzi Czechi, even the exact time was a secret.

"'Specially compared to my own." Katie drove a 1985 Ford compact, not a new model when she'd bought it. After this roomy number it would feel about the size of a sardine can.

Katie was suddenly quiet, realizing how she sounded. Like she was hinting that Fritzi give her this car, or another like it. She didn't mean that at all. She only just wanted to talk. She was lonely, and she wanted to talk. After last night, she wanted to be assured that Fritzi cared for her, that he wasn't already forgetting her, his mind flying ahead to the Meadowlands racetrack, to that blur of frantic movement out of the gate and around the dirt track and back to the finish line that would involve less than two minutes, yet could decide so much. She was frightened: If things turned out badly for

Morning Star, as, she'd gathered, they hadn't turned out all that wonderfully for Pink Lady, Fritzi would be plunged into one of his moods. If he didn't call her, she could not call him. He'd never exactly said, but that was her understanding. Wanting to tell him, *It's lonely being the only one in love.*

She wondered: Maybe Fritzi wasn't driving because his license had been suspended? Or maybe: nerves?

If they were living together, or married, Katie had to concede, Fritzi would be like this much of the time: distant, distracted. If — why not be extravagant, in fantasy — they had children, he'd never be home. Yet she felt tenderness for him. She wanted to forgive him, for hurting her. Katie's father, now deceased, a machine shop worker in Jersey City through his adult life, had been the same way. Probably most men were. So much to think about, a world of numbers, odds that always eluded them. So much, they couldn't hope to squeeze into their heads.

Lonely? That's life.

The night before, in her apartment, in her bedroom where he'd rarely been, Fritzi had showed Katie snapshots of Morning Star, taken at the Thoroughbred farm where the horse was boarded and trained in rural Hunterdon County. The way Fritzi passed the snapshots to her, Katie could sense that he felt strongly about the horse; the way he pronounced "hairline fracture," with a just-perceptible faintness in his voice, allowed Katie to know that Fritzi felt this injury as painfully as if it had been his own. "Beautiful, eh?" was all Fritzi could say. Katie marveled over the silky russet red horse with a white starlike mark high on his nose, the high-pricked ears and big shiny black protuberant eyes, for Morning Star was in fact a beauty, and maybe the knowledge that such beauty was fragile, so powerful an animal as a horse can be so easily injured, was a part of that beauty, as pain was part of it: the pain of anticipated loss.

"Oh yes. Oh Fritzi! Beautiful."

Two of the snapshots had been bluntly cropped. A third party, posed with Fritzi and Morning Star, had been scissored out of the picture. Katie wouldn't ask: It had to be the third wife. (Her name was Rosalind. Very beautiful, people said. A former model. And younger than Katie Flanders by several years.) In the snapshots, Fritzi Czechi was smiling a rare wide smile, one of his hard-muscled arms slung around the horse's neck, through the horse's thick chestnut red mane. Fritzi was wearing a sports shirt open at the throat, his stone-colored eyes gleamed like liquid fire; clearly he'd been happy at that moment, as Katie had to concede she'd never seen him.

Carefully Katie asked, "Was this last summer?"

"Was what last summer?"

". . . These pictures taken."

Fritzi grunted what sounded like yes. Already he'd taken the snapshots back and put them away in his inside coat pocket, with his narrow flat Italian leather wallet that was so sleek and fine.

Later, making love in Katie's darkened bedroom, Fritzi had gotten so carried away he'd almost sobbed, burying his heated face in Katie's neck. She'd been surprised by his emotion, and deeply moved. Katie wasn't the kind of girl who could make love with a man without falling in love with him, or, it was fair to say, she wasn't the kind of girl to make love with a man without preparing beforehand to fall in love with him, and deeply in love with him, like sinking through a thin crust of ice and you discover that, beneath the ice, there's quicksand. She'd been wondering if she would ever hear from Fritzi Czechi since the last time she'd seen him, months before, and now he was with her and in her arms, and he was saying, "You're my good, sweet girl, Katie Flemings, aren't you?" and Katie pretended she hadn't heard the wrong name, or maybe she could pretend she'd heard, but knew that Fritzi was teasing. She said, "I am if you want me, Fritzi." She hadn't meant to say this! It sounded all wrong. Holding Fritzi's warm body, stroking his smooth tight-muscled back, kissing the crown of his head where his hair was thinnest, as, half consciously, you might kiss an infant at such a spot, to protect it from harm, she teased, "Are you my 'good, sweet guy,' Fritzi Czechi?"

Fritzi was most at ease in banter. The way an eel squirms, so you can't get hold of it.

Fritzi said, "Exit after next, sweetheart."

The Meadowlands exit was fast approaching. Traffic was becoming congested in the northbound lanes. Katie, who'd been cruising at fifty-five miles an hour, was wakened from her reverie by her lover's terse voice. The BMW handled so easily, you could forget where you were, and why. *Maybe he's testing me. Like a racehorse.*

"Looks like lots of people have the same idea we do." Katie
meant the other vehicles, headed for the racetrack. "Coming to see
Morning Star win his race!"

Again, this sounded wrong. Childish. Katie knew better. Men
who followed the horses, especially men like Fritzi Czechi who were
professionally involved in the business, didn't require vapid emo-
tional support from women; probably they resented it. All that they
required was winning, which meant good luck, beating the odds,
and no woman could provide that for them.

Except for the Meadowlands complex, which covered many acres,
this part of Jersey wasn't developed. The land was too marshy.
There were dumps, landfills. Long stretches of sere-colored coun-
tryside glittering with fingers of water like ice. Toxic water, Katie
supposed. All of northeast Jersey was under a toxic cloud. Yet there
was a strange beauty to the meadowlands, as it was called. Even the
chemical-fermenting smell wasn't so bad, if you were used to it.
Katie remembered how once when she'd driven along this northern stretch of the Turnpike, into a wasteland of tall wind-rippled
rushes and cattails that stretched for miles on either side of the
highway, traffic had been routed into a single, slow lane, for there
were scattered fires burning in the area; mysterious fires they'd
seemed at the time, which Katie would learn afterward had been
caused by lightning. The season had been late summer; much of
the marshland was dry, dangerously flammable. Clouds of black,
foul-smelling smoke drifted across the highway, making Katie choke,
stinging her eyes. There were fire trucks and emergency medical
vehicles, teams of fire workers in high boots in the marsh, Jersey
troopers directing traffic. Katie had tried not to panic, forced to
drive her small car past fires burning to a height of ten feet, brilliant flamey orange, some hardly more than a car length from the
highway. Like driving through hell, you took a deep breath and
held it and followed close behind the vehicle in front of you, hoping the wind (yes, it was windy, out of the northeast) wouldn't blow
a spark or a flaming piece of vegetation against your car, and after a
mile or so you were out of the fire area and you could see again,
and you could breathe again, and you felt the thrill of having come
through, a sudden stab of happiness. "I'm alive! I made it."

Fritzi was directing Katie to exit, and where to turn at the top of
the ramp. As a horse owner he had a special parking permit. Again

Katie wondered why he wasn't driving the BMW and would afterward think, *It was all so deliberate! Like life never is.*

They went to the long open barn behind the racetrack where the
horses were stalled before their races. This part of the Meadowlands complex, hidden from view of spectators, was bustling with
horse activity. Katie stared: So many horses! A local TV camera crew
was filming the noisy disembarkment of a Thoroughbred stallion
from his van, led blinkered and whinnying down a ramp by his elderly trainer. Photographs were being taken. Katie was struck, as
she'd been at her previous visit, by the number of what you'd call
civilians in the barn: families, including young children, hovering
about their horses' stalls. And everywhere you looked, horses were
the tallest figures: their heads looming above the heads of mere human beings, who appeared weak and inconsequential beside them.
Even Fritzi Czechi looked diminished, his face suddenly creased
with an expression you wouldn't call worry, more like concern, an
intense concern, as he was approaching Morning Star's stall.

For this warm June evening at Meadowlands, Fritzi was wearing
designer sports clothes: an Armani jacket, jeans that were fitted to
his narrow hips like a cowboy's attire, and dark canvas shoes with
crepe soles. The jacket was sleekly tapered, though boxy at the
shoulders, with large, stylish lapels; the fabric was a soft pale gray,
the color of a dove's wings, and only if you looked closely could you
see the fine, almost invisible stripes in the cloth. Beneath, Fritzi was
wearing a black T-shirt: but a designer T-shirt. Fritzi Czechi always
dressed with a certain swagger, unlike most guys from Jersey City of
any age or class, and his hair was styled to appear fuller and wavier
than it was. Katie saw he wasn't tinting it, though. A fair faded
brown beginning to turn nickel-colored, like his eyes.

A photographer for the Newark *Star-Ledger* recognized Fritzi and
asked to take his picture with Morning Star, but Fritzi shrugged
him off, saying he was too busy. Usually, in public, Fritzi Czechi was
smoothly smiling and accommodating, so Katie knew: this race
meant a lot to him.

And if to Fritzi, then to Katie Flanders. *My future will be decided tonight.* Suddenly she was scared! On all sides she could feel the excitement of the races, like tension gathering before a thunder-
storm, and this evening's Meadowlands races were ordinary events,
no large purses at stake. Katie didn't want to imagine what it might

be like at the Belmont Stakes, the Kentucky Derby. Millions of dollars at stake. Was this where Fritzi Czechi was headed, or thought
he might be headed? Or was Fritzi just a small-time Jersey horse
owner, hoping for luck? Katie felt how deeply her life was involved
with his, or might be. She wanted him to win, if winning was what
he wanted, and if he wanted badly to win, she wanted this badly,
too. A man is the sum of his moods, it was moods you had to live
with. If he had a soul, a deeper self, that was something else: his
secret.

The tips of Katie's fingers were going cold. She clutched at Fritzi's
arm, but he was getting away from her, walking so quickly she
nearly stumbled in her two-inch cork-heeled sandals with the open
toes and tropical-colored plastic straps. Katie was a soft-bodied fleshy
girl, and she was wearing a candy-striped halter-top nylon dress that
showed her shapely breasts to advantage; the skirt was pleated, to
obscure the fullness of her hips and thighs, about which she felt
less confidence. Her dark blond hair was tied back in a gauzy red
scarf, and around her neck she wore a tiny jade cross on a gold
chain, a gift from Fritzi Czechi on the occasion of some long-ago
birthday he hadn't exactly remembered when Katie showed it to
him.

Fritzi, see? I love it!

What?

This. That you gave me. This cross.

Quickly Katie had kissed Fritzi, to cover his confusion. She was
skilled at such maneuvers with men. Always, you wanted a man to
save face: Never did you want a man to be embarrassed by you, still
less exposed or humiliated. Unless you were dumping him. But
even then, tact was required. You didn't want to end up with a split
lip or a blackened eye.

Right now, Fritzi was practically pushing Katie away. He'd forgotten who she was. At Morning Star's stall, talking in an earnest, lowered voice with a fattish gray-haired man who must have been the
horse's trainer, while Katie was left to gaze at the horse, marveling
at his beauty, and his size. She would play the wide-eyed admiring
glamorously made-up female hiding the fact she'd been rebuffed,
and was frightened: "Morning Star! What a beauty. So much depends upon you . . ." Katie was trying to overhear what Fritzi and
the trainer were talking about so urgently. This was a side of Fritzi

unknown to her: anxious, aggressive, not so friendly. It might have been that he and the other man, who was old enough to be Fritzi's father, were taking up a conversation they'd been having recently, in which the words *she, her, them* were predominant. (Fritzi's wife Rosalind? His ex- or separated wife who was a part owner of Morning Star? Was Fritzi wanting to know if she was at the track, if the trainer had seen her?) Fritzi had only glanced at his horse, immense and restless in his stall, being groomed by a young Guatemalan-looking stable hand, and must have thought that things looked all right. Morning Star would be racing in a little more than an hour. When she'd visited Pink Lady before her race, Katie had been encouraged to stroke the horse's damp velvety nose, and to stroke her sides and back, astonished at how soft and fine the hair was, but Morning Star was a larger horse, a stallion, and coarser, and when Katie lifted her hand to stroke his head as he drank from a bucket, he raised his head swiftly and made a sharp wickering noise and nipped at her fingers quick as a snake. "Oh! Oh God." Katie stared at her hand, her lacquered fingernails, that throbbed as if they'd been caught in a vise. Within seconds there was a reddened imprint of the horse's teeth across three of her knuckles. Fritzi called over sharply, "Katie, watch it," and the trainer said, with belated concern, "Ma'am, don't touch him, Mister can bite." Katie quickly assured them she was all right. (Later she would realize: The stallion might have severed three of her fingertips, in that split second. If he'd bitten down a little harder. If he'd been angry. If Katie had been due for some very bad luck.)

Katie was hurt the young Guatemalan groom hadn't warned her she might be bitten. He was rubbing Morning Star's sides, he'd been combing his mane, must have been aware of Katie putting out her hand so riskily, yet he'd said nothing, and was ignoring her now. And Morning Star was ignoring her, though baring his big yellow teeth, stamping, switching his tail. Ready to race? Did a horse know? Katie supposed yes, the horses must know. But they didn't know how risky their race could be, how they might be injured on the track, break a leg and have to be put down. At one of the races the previous year, a horse and jockey had fallen amid a tangle of horses, and the horse had been "put down," as Fritzi spoke of it, right out on the track beneath a hastily erected little tent. Katie had been appalled, she'd wanted to cry. You came to watch a race and

you witnessed an execution. "Morning Star! That won't happen to
you."

Fritzi came to inspect his horse. Fritzi dared to stroke the stallion's head, talking to him in a low, cajoling voice, but not pushing
it, and not standing too near. Always he was aware of the stallion's
mouth. He spoke with the groom, and a short, stunted-looking
man who was Morning Star's jockey, not yet in his colorful silk cos-
tume. It was a measure of Fritzi's distraction, he hadn't introduced
Katie to either the trainer or the jockey. She stood to one side feeling excluded, hurt. Embarrassed! She would make a story of it to
amuse her girlfriends, who were eager to hear how things had gone
with Fritzi Czechi. *That damned horse! — it almost bit off three of my
fingers. And you know Fritzi, all he does is call over, Katie, watch it.*

Or maybe she wouldn't tell that story. It wasn't very flattering to
her. Maybe, looking back on this evening at Meadowlands, in Fritzi
Czechi's company, Katie Flanders wouldn't carry away with her any
story she'd want to recall.

Of the nine races at Meadowlands that evening, Fritzi was interested in betting on the second, third, and fourth. Of the fifth race,
in which Morning Star was racing, he seemed not to wish to speak.
Maybe it was superstition. Katie knew that gamblers were superstitious, and touchy. She knew that being in a gambler's company
when he failed to win could mean you were associated with failing
to win. Still she blundered, asking a question she meant to be an in-
telligent question about Morning Star's jockey, and Fritzi replied in
monosyllables, not looking at her. They were in the clubhouse before the first race, having drinks. Katie had a glass of white wine.
Fritzi drank vodka on the rocks, and rapidly. He was too nerved up
to sit still. Men came over to greet him and shake his hand and he
made an effort to be friendly, or to seem friendly, introducing
Katie to them by only her first name. Katie smiled, trying not to
think what this meant. (She was just a girl for the evening? For the
night? Expendable, no last name? Or, Fritzi had forgotten her
name?) Many in the clubhouse for drinks were nerved up, Katie
saw. Some were able to disguise it better than others. Some were
getting frankly drunk. In other circumstances Katie would have
asked Fritzi to identify these people, whom he seemed to know,
and who knew him, at least by name. Fritzi ordered a second drink.

He was looking for someone, Katie knew. *The wife. Ex-wife? Rosalind.* Fritzi was smoking a cigarette in short, rapid puffs like a man sucking oxygen, for purely therapeutic reasons. When forced to speak with someone he smiled a bent grimace of a smile, clearly distracted. Compulsively he stroked the back of his head, his hair curling behind his ears. Katie would have liked to take his nervous hand in hers, as a wife might. In an act of daring, she did take his hand, and laced her fingers through his. She told him she was very happy to be with him. She told him she was very happy about the previous night. "And I won't ask about the future," she said, teasing, "because Fritzi Czechi isn't a man to be pinned down." Fritzi smiled at this, and stroked her hand, as if grateful for the bantering tone. Yet always his gaze drifted to the entrance, as a stream of customers, strikingly dressed women, came inside. Katie asked if he'd stake her at betting, as he had the previous year, and Fritzi said sure. "Not only am I going to stake you, sweetheart, you're going to place bets for me, too." Katie didn't get this. Must be, there was logic to it. She wasn't going to question him. She wished she could take chloroform and wake after the fifth race, when the suspense was over, and Morning Star had either won, or had lost; if he'd lost, had he lost badly; if badly, how badly. Katie had a sudden nightmare vision of the beautiful roan stallion crumpled and broken on the track, medics rushing toward him, the sinister canvas tent erected over the writhing body . . . It would be Katie Flanders's broken body, too.

Except Katie wasn't worth as much as Morning Star, whose bloodlines included Kentucky Derby winners. Katie had no life insurance, for there was no one for whom her life was precious.

After his third vodka, Fritzi took Katie to place their bets at the betting windows. The first race was shortly to begin. This wasn't a race in which Fritzi was much interested, for some reason he hadn't explained. Only the next three. And in each, he was calculating they'd win the exacta, which seemed to Katie far-fetched as winning a lottery: not only was your bet on the winning horse, but on the horse to place. (What were the odds against the exacta? Katie's brain dissolved into vapor, thinking of such things.) The money Fritzi gave her to bet with was in crisp twenty-dollar bills. Katie wasn't paying much attention to the odds on the horses. How much could they win, if they won? Especially she didn't want to know the exact sums of money they'd be losing, if they lost. Of course, all the money was Fritzi's. Yet, if they won, Katie would win, too.

She thought, *He does love me. This is proof!*

Fritzi led her to their reserved seats, in a shady section of the stadium, at the finish line, three rows up. Drinking seemed to have steadied Fritzi's nerves. He was still smoking, and looking covertly around. Whoever he was looking for hadn't arrived yet. Katie was beginning to tremble. (All the money she'd bet! And the fifth race, Fritzi's race, beyond that.) The first knuckles of her right hand were reddened, swollen, and throbbing.

Katie said, "I'm just so — anxious. Gambling makes me nervous."

Fritzi said, "Horse racing isn't gambling, it's an art."

He told her if you knew what you were doing, you didn't risk that much. And if you didn't know what the hell you were doing, you shouldn't be betting.

"My way of betting," Katie said, meaning to be amusing in the little-girl way she'd cultivated since childhood, "would be to bet on the horses' names."

Fritzi let this pass. "A name means nothing. Only the bloodline means anything. At the farm, young horses are identified by their dams' names. Until they demonstrate they're worth something, they don't have any identity."

Katie was grateful that Fritzi was talking to her again. Taking her seriously. She wanted to take his hands in hers and lace their fingers together to comfort him. Horses were at the starting gate, the crowd was expectant. A voice in her head, mellowed by wine, reminisced, *That time at Meadowlands! Remember how nervous we were, Fritzi? I didn't want to tell you how badly my hand was hurting . . .*

Fritzi was saying, as if arguing, "Horse racing isn't a crap shoot. It isn't playing the slots. You figure how the horse has done recently. You figure the horse's history, meaning the bloodline. You figure who the jockey is. You figure who the other horses are, he'll be racing. And the odds. Always, the odds. There's people who believe, and maybe I'm one of them, there's no luck at all. No luck. Only what has to be, that you can figure. Or try to." Katie was silenced by this speech of Fritzi's, which was totally unlike him. He seemed almost to be speaking to someone else. Not the slightest trace of banter here, or irony.

It was during the first race that Fritzi's wife, unless the woman was his ex-wife, came to sit a row down from them, twelve seats to Fritzi's right. Katie saw, and recognized her immediately. Or maybe Katie was reacting to Fritzi's sudden stiffness. Rosalind was with a tall sturdily built man of about Fritzi's age with olive-dark skin and ridged, graying hair. She was a striking young woman, as she'd been described to Katie, stylishly dressed in a lilac pantsuit with a loose, low-cut white blouse, and wearing a wide-brimmed straw hat. Her long straight dyed-looking black hair fell past her shoulders. Her skin was geisha white, and her mouth very red. She was theatrical-looking, eye-catching. Katie felt a pang of jealousy, resentment. Rosalind was said to have been a model even while attending East Orange High School, and at the peak of her brief career she'd appeared in glossy magazines like *Glamour* and *Allure*. She'd married Fritzi Czechi and gotten pregnant and had a miscarriage and within a few years the marriage was over and it was Rosalind who'd sued for divorce. All Fritzi had ever said about this third marriage in Katie's presence was that mistakes were made on both sides: "End of story."

Katie knew better. Not a single guy she'd ever dated, or even heard of, no matter how long divorced, if he hadn't been the one to initiate the divorce, he never forgot. A man never forgets, and never forgives.

Katie wondered what it would be like: a former husband still wanting you, when you didn't want him. A former lover still loving you even as he hated you. A man you'd slept with, and hoped to have children with, fantasizing how he might kill you, for betraying him.

There had to be money involved, too, with Fritzi's marriage. He'd signed over the house to Rosalind, and the house was reputedly worth a half-million dollars. And there was Morning Star, and maybe other horses. Common property. Katie felt how Fritzi was holding himself so still he was almost trembling, as if their seats and the stands and the very earth beneath them were vibrating, shaken by horses' pounding hooves as they galloped around the track. Katie stared, seeing nothing. A blur. People were on their feet, shouting. Katie hadn't bet on any horse in this race; none of the names meant a thing to her. She and Fritzi had no stake in the outcome. She scarcely glanced up when the winner was declared. The

time: 1.46.41. The purse was $17,000. (The purse for the fifth race
would be $34,000.) Katie brushed her hand against Fritzi's and felt
his icy fingertips.

High overhead, drifting across the red-streaked sky, was a lighted
dirigible advertising a brand of cigarettes. Katie glanced upward,
startled. Though she didn't exactly mean it, she heard herself saying to Fritzi, "These big open stadiums! They scare me. Somebody
could drop a bomb. Some sniper could shoot into the stands. On
TV I saw this soccer riot somewhere in South America. Think if
people panicked, how you could be trampled . . ."

Fritzi said, "There's cops here. Security cops. Things like that
don't happen in the U.S." Fritzi was forcing himself to speak in a
normal-sounding voice. But still he sat stiffly, turned slightly to the
left to prevent him seeing the strikingly dressed young woman
who'd been his third wife, and the man who was with her. Katie
thought, dismayed, *He loves her. He'll never get over it.* She had a vision
of Morning Star winning his race, and Fritzi and Rosalind coming
together to hug each other, united in victory. Reconciled. Was that
how this evening at Meadowlands would turn out?

Ruefully Katie rubbed her throbbing fingers. She saw, shocked,
that one of her meticulously manicured fingernails, lacquered ivory
pink, was broken and jagged. The nail was splitting vertically, into
her flesh.

After the first race, in which they had no stake, things would happen swiftly.

In the second race, Katie had placed bets on Sweet Nougat to win
and Iron Man to place. They came through. Katie was on her feet
screaming and flailing the air as the horses raced around the track.
All of it happening so fast: like a speeded-up dream. The horses'
rushing legs, pounding hooves, the jockeys crouched over their
backs in colorful silk costumes, little monkey-men wielding whips
— "Oh my God! Oh my God we won! We won, Fritzi, we *won!*" Like
an overgrown child Katie flailed the air with her arms, hardly able
to contain her excitement. The color was up in her face, her pulse
beat in a delirium of hope. Fritzi remained seated. With his stub of
a pencil he made a check on the racing form. When Katie tried to
hug him he stiffened, keeping her at a little distance with his left
forearm; not a forcible gesture, and in no way hostile, but Katie
would recall it afterward. *Didn't want me to touch him. Oh Fritzi!*

In that first race, clocked at 1.25.01, Katie and Fritzi won $1,336 each.

"Honey, you don't even seem much surprised," Katie said, lightly chiding. She dabbed at her overheated face with a tissue. "*I'm* surprised. I never win things!"

Fritzi shrugged, and smiled. As if to say that, with him, now she would.

In the third race, they'd bet on Hot Ott to win and Angel Fire to place. Another time Katie was on her feet flailing the air and screaming and another time their horses pulled away from the pack, Hot Ott by a length ahead of Angel Fire, the two horses racing headlong and furious in the homestretch, and Angel Fire was overtaking Hot Ott, had almost overtaken Hot Ott, but had not, and so it was Hot Ott to win and Angel Fire to place. "He won! Our picks won!" Perspiration glowed on Katie's skin; her eyes were radiant with innocence and hope. In this race they hadn't won quite so much as they'd won in the first, but it would be $834 apiece. Katie sat close beside Fritzi wanting to hug, hug, hug the man, but content with just nudging knees. She fanned herself with the track program. Tendrils of hair clung to her forehead. She was trying not to glance to the side, to observe the third Mrs. Czechi in her elegant wide-brimmed straw hat, calm and beautiful in profile; though she was wishing she'd worn a straw hat herself, it conferred such class to the wearer. "Some days, they seem to last forever. I mean, you remember them forever. It's like eternity. This is one of them, for me, Fritzi, it *is*." Katie spoke happily, heedlessly. She was one to speak her heart, when she believed she spoke truthfully, and when what she said would be heard, and valued, by another whom she trusted. Stiff and unyielding as a man who has been wounded and is trying not to betray pain, Fritzi was observing Katie with his stone-colored eyes that were oddly moist, sympathetic. That was what Katie believed: sympathetic. Fritzi Czechi was her friend, he'd always be her friend, not only her lover. "It's like at certain times in our lives, rare times, God peers into time out of His place in eternity and it's like a —" Katie paused, blushing, not knowing what she was saying: A flash of lightning? A spotlight in a theater? An eclipse of the sun, as the sun is easing free of the shadow over it? Probably she was making a fool of herself, chattering like this. Fritzi squeezed her hand as if to calm her. "Katie, you're my good, sweet girl, aren't you?" he said, and Katie murmured "Yes, yes!" and Fritzi said, "You and I go 'way back. We're old buddies." Katie shut her eyes to be kissed, and Fritzi did kiss her, but only on the nose, wet and playful as you'd kiss a child.

It was like Fritzi was amused by her, for her caring so much that they'd won a couple of thousand dollars. But Katie was feeling, well — like a winner should. Flying high! Drunk! That happy airy floating kind of drunk before you start to stumble, and find yourself puking into a toilet. She'd had just one glass of dry white wine in the clubhouse but it was as if she'd been drinking champagne all evening. She had a quick warm flash of being married to Fritzi Czechi and the two of them living somewhere suburban; no, they were living in Fair Hills, or was it Far Hills, Jersey horse country; Fritzi could raise Thoroughbreds, champion racehorses. In the barn, she'd liked the smell of the horses. Even the horses' droppings. It was mixed with an overlying smell of hay. And that was sweet. She would learn to ride a horse: It wasn't too late. Tall and elegant in the saddle she would take equestrian lessons, lose eighteen pounds and be slender again, and Fritzi would love her, and possibly he'd be faithful to her. But always, Fritzi Czechi would be her friend.

The fourth race! In the fourth race, Fritzi and Katie won the lottery: the trifecta.

Heavenly Jewel to win, Billy's Best to place, Sam the Man to show. They'd picked them all.

Another time Katie was on her feet, squealing, radiant with excitement. It was like she was back in high school those frenzied Friday nights cheering for the Jersey City team to win. Except here were nine horses, and of these nine any one could win, all the more triumphant their victory when Heavenly Jewel thundered across the finish line by a nose ahead of Billy's Best, and there came Sam the Man behind, and this time even Fritzi registered a smile, a small smile of surprise, yes Fritzi was surprised to have won the trifecta. (So maybe he did believe in luck, after all.) Katie cried, "Fritzi, it's *magic*. You are *magic*." Magic meant they'd collect $3,799 each.

Still Fritzi seemed not himself, somehow. Katie nudged his knees. Why wasn't he sexier, funnier? "You don't always win like this, honey, do you?" Katie asked, and Fritzi shrugged, "No. I have to admit." It was like Fritzi that, though he was visibly warm, he wouldn't unbutton the Armani jacket. A film of perspiration gleamed on his fair, flushed skin like miniature jewels. Slowly he stroked his hair behind his ears, a man in a trance.

The next race was the fifth.

Morning Star, and eight others. Katie was so scared, she hoped she wouldn't faint. She could see that Fritzi was in some zoned-out space, very quiet, very still, just staring at the starting gate. Morning Star was second to inside, his jockey wore yellow silks. There was a hush of expectation through the stands. Covertly Katie glanced to Fritzi's right and saw the beautiful black-haired young woman in the wide-brimmed straw hat also sitting very straight, very still, and gripping the arm of the man beside her.

Katie was trying not to think *hairline fracture, beyond computation, put down.* Was there a more devastating term than *put down!* She remembered the tangle of horses and jockeys in that race last summer, a horse had balked coming out of the gate, and swerved sideways into another, and horses had fallen, and jockeys, and the race was jinxed from the start though other horses had pulled away in the clear, and Pink Lady had galloped so hard, you could see the filly was running her heart out, yet the evil little monkey-man hunched over her neck continued to use his whip, and shuddering and in a lather she'd galloped over the finish line not first, not second, but third — and wasn't that enough? Wasn't that good enough? Though that evening, Katie had to concede Fritzi had been in an irritable mood, waving away Katie's elation, and the well-intentioned congratulations of others. For third place wasn't good enough. Third place at Meadowlands, a weekday race that's one of nine races, the purse is only $21,000 to win, no: not enough. Not for Fritzi Czechi. Gallop your heart out, it isn't enough.

For a melancholy time then Katie hadn't heard from Fritzi Czechi. He was back with his wife, Rosalind. If she'd begun divorce proceedings, these were halted. Temporarily. Katie made inquiries about Pink Lady and learned that the filly had lost races, hadn't qualified for some high-stakes handicap in Florida, and Fritzi had sold her.

What happens then, Katie asked, dreading to know. Whoever it was telling her this, a jokey kind of guy, he'd run his fingers across his throat. "Dog food."

Katie didn't believe that, though. She did not.

Not Pink Lady who'd been so comely, of whom, for a while, Fritzi
Czechi had been so proud.

At the gate, one of the horses was stamping its feet, misbehaving;
there was a delay and the horse was led off and an announcement
made, Duke II was "scratched." Katie thought: *This was good luck,
what might have gone wrong in the race went wrong before the race, and
Morning Star was safe.*

"Morning Star": Katie murmured the name aloud. She squinted
to see where he was positioned. The tall horse, beautiful russet red
coat, white starburst high on his nose, was lost amid the others at
the starting gate. All nine horses were large, beautiful, powerful
beasts with muscled haunches. Each was prized by its owners. Each
was worth a lot of money. It was like seeing someone you think you
love, unexpectedly in a public place, and you realize he isn't extraordinary, isn't that good-looking, nothing special about him but
you've invested your heart in him, you love him and want to love
him and to withdraw that love would be to violate your own heart,
to turn traitor.

The race began. So fast! Sudden! Katie was on her feet, blinking in confusion. Somehow it was more than the usual confusion
of horses' flying hooves, the gaily colored costumes of the jockeys; Katie's eyes were dazzled, hardly could she catch her breath.
Morning Star! Where was he? Another horse was in the lead? By a
length? Pulling away? She saw the roan stallion thudding along behind, caught in the pack, struggling to break ahead. A horse did
break ahead, but it wasn't the roan stallion. On Morning Star, the
monkey-man in the yellow silks wielded his whip. All the monkey-
men were wielding their cruel little whips. Katie was too frightened
to scream, to squeal, to flail her arms this time. For this was the race
of her life.

She saw Morning Star, her lover's horse who'd bitten her, galloping into the turn, straining to pull away from the others. Almost,
Katie had an evil thought: wished there would be an upset: a spill:
two horses tangled together, three horses, and falling, and Morning Star would pull away, free. In her trance of oblivion she was
praying, *God, let him win. God, God, let him win I will never ask another
thing of You.* The lead horses were in the backstretch. Morning Star
was among the lead horses now. Was Morning Star pulling for-

ward? He was! The lead horse, a big purely black stallion, had begun to wobble, other horses would overtake it. Swift and pitiless other horses would overtake it. There was the yellow-clad jockey easing his horse faster, always faster. Katie was screaming now, unaware. Screaming herself hoarse. She had no awareness of Fritzi, who was on his feet beside her, but very quiet, only just staring, his arms slightly lifted, elbows at his sides. She had no awareness of others in the stands shouting, screaming. There came horses into the homestretch, Morning Star on the inside of the track, in fourth place, now in third place, galloping furiously, now overtaking the front-running horses, in second place close behind the lead horse and edging closer, ever closer, to passing that horse; and if the track had been longer, if only the track had been longer! — the roan stallion would have passed the lead horse, thundering across the finish line only just a half-length behind the winner.

The race was clocked at 1.10.91. It would be the fastest race of the evening. Anchor Bay the winner, Morning Star second, and Blue Eyes third. Katie's cheeks were damp with tears. She had never been so happy. She cried to Fritzi, "Oh, honey, that was good, wasn't it? Wasn't it? His first time back, with his knee hurt? We came in second, we didn't lose, he did real well, didn't he? Honey?" In her excitement Katie was pawing at Fritzi, wanting badly to hug him, and he gripped her elbows to calm her, to steady her; he was himself in a daze though not smiling, not delirious with relief and happiness like Katie, more like a man waking from a dream of heart-stopping intensity not knowing where he was, but knowing what he must do. His face that was usually flushed was ashen, a rivulet of sweat ran down his forehead, his stone-colored eyes were shimmering with moisture. What was wrong with Fritzi Czechi? Telling Katie, with a small fixed smile like a mannequin's smile, "We did real well, sweetheart. Right. This is our lucky day."

Into Katie's still-shaking hand Fritzi was placing — what? An envelope?

He'd taken it out of his inside coat pocket. It was the size of a greeting card, it was sealed. On the front hand-printed KATIE FLANDERS. Fritzi said, "Don't open this till later. Promise."

"Promise — what?"

"Don't open this till later."

"Later, when?"

But Fritzi was walking away from her. Fritzi was leaving her behind. Like a sleepwalker, she would remember him. Ashen-faced,
and sweaty, and his damp hair curling and lank behind his ears.
And the back of the sexy Armani jacket sweated through between
his shoulder blades. Katie called, "Fritzi? Wait." Tried to follow him
but there were too many others in the aisle. Damn, Katie was stumbling in her ridiculous high-heeled shoes. "Fritzi?" Trying to follow
the man she loved, and always she would remember: it was one of
those nightmares where you are trying, trying desperately, to get
somewhere, but can't, like making your way through quicksand, a
bog that's sucking at your feet, and she could see Fritzi only a few
yards away, quickly descending the steps in the center aisle; for
a few confused seconds her vision was blocked, then again she
saw, she would be a witness, as Fritzi Czechi made his swift and unerring way to the woman in the wide-brimmed straw hat and eye-
catching lilac pantsuit, this woman and her male friend who were
also on their feet, dazed and exhilarated by the outcome of the
race, which for them, too, would seem to have been unexpected,
more than they'd hoped, and then Katie was seeing the woman
glance around, at Fritzi, her geisha-white face not quite so young as
Katie had thought, and frightened, yet she was trying to smile, for a
woman's first defense is a smile, and her companion beside her
who was just lighting a cigarette turned to see Fritzi, too, and possibly there was a glimmer of recognition here, too, but no time for
alarm, for there was a flash of something metallic in Fritzi's upraised right hand, and the man staggered and fell back, and there
was a second flash, and the young woman screamed and fell, the
straw hat knocked from her head, there came one, two, three more
shots and now in the crowd there were isolated screams, shouts, a
wave of panic that sucked all the oxygen from Katie's lungs and
brain and left her paralyzed unable to believe she'd seen what she
had seen, for it had happened too swiftly, nothing like a movie or
TV scene for in fact she couldn't see, all was confusion, the backs of
strangers, the flailing arms of strangers, a man beside her elbowing
her in his desperation to escape, a woman behind her beginning to
sob, and Katie was frantic to get to Fritzi, but shoved to the side, her
leg bruised against a seat, and now there came another shot, a single shot, and more screams, on all sides strangers were shoving and

pushing to escape, while others were ducking down into their seats, and Katie from Jersey City understood it was wisest to imitate these, huddling in her seat with her face pressed against her knees, her arms crossed over the tender nape of her neck, praying to God another time for help, as if in these moments of terror not knowing who the shooter was, and what he'd done, and that, with that last shot, it was probably over.

He'd killed them with a handgun that would be identified as a .380-caliber semiautomatic pistol with a defaced serial number that would be traced to a shipment of several hundred similar pistols that had been illegally sold in the New York City area in the mid-1980s. He'd killed his estranged wife and her companion with two shots and three shots respectively. From a distance of less than eighteen inches. Both had died within seconds. He'd then turned the gun on himself, as witnesses watched in horror, placing the barrel precisely at the back of his head, aiming upward, and pulling the trigger with no hesitation. It was a stance, it was an act, Fritzi Czechi had clearly rehearsed many times in solitude.

Katie identified herself to police. Katie Flanders, who'd been Fritzi Czechi's companion. Dazed and exhausted yet not hysterical (not yet: that would come later) she'd answered their questions, all that she knew. Suddenly sick to her stomach, vomiting what tasted like hot acid. She was fainting, medics attended her, her blood pressure dangerously low, yet she recovered within a few minutes and was strong enough to refuse to be taken to the hospital. Refused an ambulance. No, no! She searched for the envelope that had fallen beside her seat. With badly shaking fingers she opened it as police officers looked on. Yet, she opened it. Inside were keys to the BMW, and registration papers, and a document that looked legal, deeding the car to "Katie Flanders." A terse hand-printed note on a stiff white card:

> *Dear Katie*
>   *This is for you. Also the things in the trunk.*
> *A token of my esteem.*
>   *Fritzi C.*

Esteem! Fritzi C.! Katie began to laugh shrilly, helplessly, swiping at her eyes. Fritzi Czechi had eluded her, as she'd always known he

would. It had not mattered that she loved him. It had not mattered
what old, good buddies they were, from Jersey City. Like the roan
stallion with the white starburst on its forehead overtaking, passing
the other horses, galloping furiously, unstoppable, continuing in
his ecstatic head-on plunge away from the dirt track, out of Meadowlands park, out of your vision and into eternity.

JASON OCKERT

Jakob Loomis

FROM *The Oxford American*

THERM IS IN THE WOODSHED rubbing gasoline on his blood-stained sneakers when he sees a handcuffed man break from the woods and amble toward the house. Hefting an ax, Therm calls out, and the man, surprised, arms defeated behind his back, freezes.

The men consider each other over the short distance of semi-mowed backyard lawn in the cool prerain breeze. The mower hunkers to the bloodied ground between the woodshed and the house. For a moment the men feel the weight of their guilt, and then the moment breaks.

What the hell are you doing? Therm asks, stepping forward with the ax.

Hoping I could get a little water, the handcuffed man says, nodding to a green hose heaped next to the house.

Therm is a big man with broad shoulders and a measurable gut. He isn't a fighter, but he can defend himself if he has to. Especially with an ax. And if his potential opponent is handcuffed. There is nothing threatening about the restrained man; he is a foot shorter than Therm and has wiry hair, sun-browned skin, and a long chin. What makes Therm uncomfortable are the man's eyes. There is something off about them — not crossed exactly, just crooked.

Looks like you've gotten yourself into some trouble, Therm says, squaring himself against the other man.

The man raises his eyebrows, cocks his head back, and gazes down his chin at the bloodied patch of lawn. You too, he responds.

What, that? That was an accident. I hit a snake, Therm says.

A lot of blood for a snake.

A nest of them, I guess.

Therm was new to his house, just out of a wasted marriage to a woman who cheated on him with several of the felines in a low-budget theater troupe who performed an interpretation of *Cats* in town for a season. Therm discovered a long whisker on the stairs and thought nothing of it because of Molly and Digger, both big, nervous cats. Then whiskers started turning up everywhere. Whiskers on the love seat, in the hamper, next to the lava lamp, in the trunk of their Suburban: brown, blond, green. Green, of course, made Therm suspicious. Then, because his wife considered herself an amateur actress, and because he wanted to make an effort to understand her passions more, Therm bought two tickets to the show. He was shocked by the performance; the unitard-clad men with unrealistic bulges in their crotches meowing and fawning across the stage didn't impress him. When the green cat came out, Therm's wife had emitted a low purr of sorts, and that was that. Therm didn't make a fuss. She kept the property, he was rewarded a significant check her family could afford if the reason for the divorce stayed discreet. Molly and Digger remained with the wife.

Therm moved south and into the country where he wouldn't be bothered. He was a contract cartographer and worked at the drafting table he erected in the family room. The missing boy, though he wasn't missing yet, let his pet parrot free. The bird flew to Therm's property, landed in a tree infested with gnats, and started squawking. Therm went outside to look at the pretty bird thinking that maybe parrots were native to this neck of the woods. He tried talking to it. He said, *Hi birdie, birdie, hi, birdie, birdie,* and so on. The parrot squawked and sometimes bobbed its head. Therm retired back inside for work on the rivers of the Middle East. The parrot kept at its racket. Therm tried to ignore the bird. He put cotton in his ears. Music didn't help. Outside, he talked reason; *Okay, bird, enough. Shoo or shut up, birdie, birdie.* The parrot preened its feathers and continued screeching. Gnats were abundant. Therm tossed rocks. When he called Animal Control they said that a noisy bird wasn't an animal they considered a nuisance. He had been put on hold for a minute. When the operator came back, he said to Therm, We'll send a rescue squad over immediately, you're in grave danger, whatever you do, don't let it hit you on the head with its lethal crap. You wouldn't believe how many people die from parrot dookie every year. There was laughter in the background. Therm hung up.

All that night the parrot made its noise. The next day, more of the same. Therm couldn't concentrate on the complicated tributaries of the Euphrates River. He took a long hike and disrupted a fox chasing a rabbit. The fox hid behind a slash pine and angrily glared at Therm as the rabbit dashed away.

A half-mile from home, Therm heard the parrot. When he listened hard, Therm detected a squawking pattern that he imitated for a while for fun. Then the pattern broke.

In bed that night, trying to ignore the bird, Therm thought of Madeline, his ex-wife. They had been an attractive couple in college, lost their virginity together, wrote their own marriage vows, enjoyed the mall on late afternoons. Damn her for throwing that all away, he thought.

In the morning, Therm started drawing irrational parallels between the parrot and Madeline and frequently yelled for Maddy to *pipe down* or *put a sock in it*. This made him feel a little better.

The bird kept calling and eating gnats and staring at Therm with sidelong eyes as Therm stood below it with the old rifle his grandfather had left him in the will. Therm figured he'd scare the damned thing by firing near its head. But the parrot didn't budge, just twittered uncomfortably and changed to a higher pitch. A couple shots later, Therm knew he wasn't trying to warn the bird anymore. Still, he couldn't get a bead on the multicolored beast as it hopped from branch to branch.

At Food 4 U, Therm bought fruit he knew his ex-wife enjoyed; grapes, strawberries, and bananas. On the front door of the store was a black-and-white picture of the missing boy, smiling, that the clerk had just posted. Therm paid for his food. At home, he diced the fruit and laced it with rat poison from a bottle he kept under the sink. He placed the concoction on a paper plate and set it on a stump beneath the trees. He hid himself in the shed with the door cracked and waited all afternoon for something to happen. The bird squawked. A squirrel nosed the fruit but left it alone. Finally, just before the sun set, the parrot glided down to the fruit and investigated. It ate a grape and spat it out. It overturned the paper plate and shat. Therm rushed out of the shed with the ax, but the parrot was too quick and settled itself back in the tree.

Therm couldn't get Madeline out of his head as he smudged the Tigris River. She had really whipped him good. She never let him eat spicy foods and complained when he walked around the living room naked. She wore wool socks to bed and rubbed her feet over his legs at night. Some mornings, he'd wake up with a rash. Then she sleeps with a clowder of cat-men? She didn't even like sex, he thought. She had a bevy of excuses when he was in the mood; *I'm tired, I've got cramps, Molly's in heat, I just washed these sheets,* and so on. Supposedly, one of the actors had a SAG connection and Madeline was going to be an extra in some romantic comedy coming out next fall. She screws me, Therm thought, finds success doing something she loves, and I'm here with the loudest parrot in the world.

Therm decided to call Madeline's house and let the parrot bark its brains out over the answering machine.

In the morning, Therm went to Widgit's Hardware and asked a Widgit employee for the most powerful nozzle they had. Next to the register was the black-and-white picture of the missing boy, smiling.

Are we talking fifty feet? the Widgit employee asked.

A hundred and fifty, Therm replied.

That's a specialty item, it'll cost you.

Charge it.

Therm attached the high-powered nozzle to the hose and tested it against the side of the house. It chipped the paint. Satisfied, Therm unwound the hose and stalked up next to the parrot-tree. The parrot quieted and watched suspiciously. Therm let it rip. The parrot was caught off-guard and fell from the tree. It started to fly, but Therm kept the water steady and knocked it from the sky onto his lawn where it lay stunned.

Therm stood over the bird and sprayed it again for good measure. He bent down to flick the parrot's head and it snipped his hand. Blood welled up around his knuckles. There was a rag in the shed. Also in the shed, the ax. By the time the bleeding stopped, he had convinced himself to chop the bird to pieces. He raised the ax. The parrot blinked a few times and made a feeble chirp. It kind of pouted like he'd seen his ex-wife pout. Therm couldn't follow through. He went back into the shed, noticed that his hand was bleeding again, and fired up the lawn mower. The bird raised its voice. Therm set the mower on course, closed his eyes, told himself, *This won't hurt a bit,* and pushed the machine forward.

Jakob Loomis was told to be home before dinner. That gave him plenty of time, he figured. He was meeting Tommy Tucker at the baseball diamond and the two of them were going to take Tommy's pellet gun to the pond and shoot tadpoles. When Jakob got to the baseball field, Tommy was already there, waiting in the dugout. He had a worried look on his face.

Can't do it today, man, Tommy said.

Why not? Jakob asked.

Mrs. Pratt called my mom and told her I cheated on our math test.

Dumb Mrs. Fat, Jakob said.

My mom grounded me. I told her I had to meet you and get the homework assignment, but I have to get back now. I brought the pellet gun if you want it.

Sure. Jakob took the gun.

See you in school tomorrow, Tommy said, and ran away.

The pond was located between two mounds of sand that Jakob had to walk over to get to the bank. The water was green and full of cattails and lily pads. Jakob spotted a tadpole, took aim, but decided not to fire. He couldn't figure out why he should. When Tommy had the pellet gun, he took careful aim, his tongue lolling out of his mouth, and fired. Nine out of ten times, the tadpole floated to the surface. This was impressive. But Jakob thought differently. There was no need to kill baby frogs, or any animal. He even set his pet parrot free because it seemed to complain about being caged all the time.

Your hand's bleeding, the handcuffed man says. Snakebite?

No. I must have cut it on the ax.

Therm lets his hand hang loosely and bleed. A thin rain begins to slant down over the men. The handcuffed man tilts his head back and lets the water cool his face. Droplets of moisture linger on his eyelashes and a fine layer of precipitation forms on his forehead and chin.

Therm glances down at his stained sneakers. When he tried to clean them with the hose, the blood had merely smeared. Therm had washed the pulpy remains of the parrot from the mower down to the fringe of the woods. A cloud of gnats hangs over the remains. In a wicked moment, Therm tries to imagine Madeline's face opening a package with the dead bird in it. Her jaw would drop and she'd cover her mouth with her ringless hand. She'd probably shriek something dramatic like, *Oh, Christ, no!* and ask her cat-boyfriends what to do. They'd say call the police. Therm would send the package anonymously, of course, and he'd use gloves so that fingerprints weren't an issue. But there was a problem, Therm remembered. When the police asked Maddy about anything suspicious lately, she'd recall the odd message on her answering machine. The police would replay the tape with the recorded squawking and use a forensics team to determine that the pulpy mess had been a parrot and that the cawing on the tape had been a parrot. They'd trace the call somehow, arrest Therm, and he'd spend time in the slammer, humiliated. Better let the bird decompose in the rain and not make a big deal out of it.

If you're not going to give me a drink of water, I think I'm going to move on, the handcuffed man says.

You can't drink from that hose. There's a high-powered nozzle that'd shake your teeth. The rain should be enough.

The handcuffed man licks his lips.

As far as letting you just walk off, Therm says, give me one good reason why I shouldn't call the police?

The handcuffed man tries to look as relaxed as possible in handcuffs. He says, Sometimes the police shouldn't be involved.

Maybe so, but that doesn't explain the handcuffs.

I'd rather not say.

Then I better call the police.

If you'll feel better about it, call them. But the reason for these cuffs has got nothing to do with them. It's more domestic.

I'm listening.

Cole's daddy was a snake handler and a preacher of the Gospel and of Jesus Christ the Savior, Our Lord. His daddy told Cole he was born from a God-blessed serpent. Cole shared his crib with snakes, he learned to walk with snakes, and the first word out of his mouth was *hiss.* These things made Cole's daddy proud. He took his son all over Texas to preach the faith and demonstrate with serpents that the Good Lord watched over the faithful. In a trance with a viper, Cole's daddy got bit in the mouth. His lips and tongue turned rotten and made speaking nearly impossible. He tried to preach with just his hands, but nobody listened. So he turned to drinking. And he turned to his boy.

Cole really did like snakes. They were mostly quiet and friendly, and if there was any evil in them, he couldn't find it. After his daddy got bit, Cole tried his best to keep the faith. He learned some sign language and tried to teach it to his father. His father just shook his fists and Cole got the message.

When the money ran out, Cole's daddy figured he could use his son's natural snake abilities to earn them a living. He believed God owed him that, at least. There were a lot of tourists and nonbelievers who would be impressed if they saw his boy crawl out of a sleeping bag filled with rattlers and moccasins and such. With the little money he had saved, Cole's daddy made flyers that said SEE THE SNAKECHILD ESCAPE FROM A SLEEPING BAG FULL OF POISON SNAKES! The performance didn't draw a big crowd, but it brought in enough money to travel and to get Cole's daddy cross-eyed drunk.

Cole found it tricky to crawl out of the sleeping bag filled with snakes because the snakes were packed so tightly together that they became irritated. He had to wait until they calmed down and then very carefully pull himself out to the crowd of anxious people and the applause. Each time he had to move a different way to keep from rolling over a snake's head. Once, after years of crawling out of the sleeping bag, during a snake roundup, just as Cole had pulled his head and shoulders out of the bag, a drunk said, Bullshit, those snakes aren't poisonous, and he threw his bottle. It wasn't a good throw and when it shattered in front of Cole a thin shard of glass struck the boy in the eye. The snakes hissed and snapped at one another as the crowd tried to decide what to do. The drunk thought he might have made a mistake. Everybody waited. Cole breathed lightly as his eye bled and the snakes settled. Finally, he crawled the rest of the way out.

The hospital couldn't save Cole's eye so they made him a glass one. Police went around arresting people for disorderly conduct and child neglect. Cole was sent to a foster home and Cole's daddy found refuge in the church, where he tried his best to apologize through cheap religious cards on which he wrote, *Son, I'm so sorry, I'm really proud of you, God loves you and I do, too!* in sloppy cursive.

Cole finished growing up quietly. He made few friends and had trouble looking people in the eye. His closest relationship was with God. After Cole understood that he wasn't born from a serpent, he tried to figure out who his mother was. Through hospital records, and with reluctant help from his daddy, Cole learned his mother lived in Florida and worked for a theme park there. Cole turned eighteen, took a bus to central Florida, and paid for a ticket. Information directed him to the Hop Along Trail! His mother was a costumed, pink-furred rabbit who sang a happy song and hopped from foot to foot. Cole watched her in the thin crowd and munched on a candy apple. She was good at her job; a group of children clapped and danced to the song. The tune was catchy. Cole hummed along with the children. Nearby, a tall young couple with a video camera glanced over disapprovingly. Cole realized he was out of place, all grown-up with candy apple on his mouth trying to have a moment with his mother in a sea of children. He blew a kiss and left.

An ad in the paper mentioned big bucks for capturing venomous snakes and selling them to pharmacies in order to make antivenom. Cole became a hunter and aged. On good days, he'd gather a dozen serpents. Once in a while the law gave him trouble for trespassing while he was wrangling snakes on private property. He bought a trailer out in the country and tried to mind his own business. He had girlfriends here and there. He attended a Methodist church. His daddy passed away Godless and broken. On the television, Cole learned about the missing boy and made a mental note to keep an eye out for him.

Out of the corner of his eye, Jakob caught sight of a frog at the waterline. It was a white frog. Jakob couldn't believe it. He had never seen a white frog and as far as he knew, they didn't exist. But here one was. Setting the gun aside, Jakob crept closer to the frog and dove for it. He missed, slid half into the water, getting his pant leg soaked, and leaned against the mound to wait for the frog to reappear. It popped up on the other side. Jakob stalked it more carefully and when he got close enough, he wiggled one hand out as a

distraction and plunged his other hand in after the frog. This time
Jakob was successful. He pulled it from the water by a long white
leg and clutched it to his body. His heart pounded and he tried to
catch his breath. A white frog. Tommy wasn't going to believe this.
Jakob had to keep the frog to show Tommy tomorrow after school.
The frog was slippery and he nearly dropped it as he climbed over
the mounds and away from the pond. He'd leave the pellet gun
there for now, find an old soda can or something to put it in, and
show it off tomorrow. Then he'd set it free. It wasn't dinnertime
yet; the sun still had some life in it. All he had to do was find a con-
tainer.

I've been seeing this woman named Samantha for a while, and the
other day she says she wants to spice up our lovemaking, Cole says
to Therm after a considerable pause in their conversation.

The rain turns to a wet mist. Cole leans his shoulder against the
side of the house. Therm sets the ax between his legs.

Of course, I don't know what this means, Cole continues. She
says the ways we've been doing it is how she's always done it and she
wants to try bondage.

Bondage? Therm asks.

That's what I said. I don't know about you, but I'm not exactly
the most experienced rooster in the coop.

Therm nods. Maddy never mentioned bondage.

So, I go over to her place around noon to see what she has in
mind.

She had handcuffs planned, huh?

Yes, and a blindfold. She cuffed me and called me a filthy bastard.
I thought she meant it, but she explained this was role-playing and
told me to wait in the dungeon while she freshened up. The dungeon was the bedroom, but I was supposed to use my imagination. I
waited a long damned time sitting there on her bed. When you
can't see and you don't know what's coming to you your mind
starts thinking awful things.

It does, Therm says, it sure does.

I tried to get out of the handcuffs but couldn't. I wondered
where she got the handcuffs and where she put the key. Hell, I even
started thinking that she was going to chop me up like you read
about in papers. Lovers get chopped up for one reason or another.

True, Therm agrees.

Then I heard some shouting out in the front yard. There was another man's voice. This made me nervous, as you can imagine. I didn't know if she was going to bring some guy into this bondage experience or what.

So what did you do?

I put my face into the bed and rubbed that blindfold off. Out the front window I saw Samantha arguing with this big guy, bigger than you, about something. Come to find out, it's her husband.

She's married? Therm asks.

Cole blows a low whistle.

That's awful.

I thought so, too. I looked for the handcuff key, but it wasn't in the bedroom. About the time that big boy comes busting in the front door, I manage to get out the back door and run for my life. I had to leave my car there. I imagine he had it impounded.

Therm rubs his fingers on the ax handle. After a moment he says, You shouldn't have run.

He probably would have given me a good whupping.

Maybe you deserved it.

Not in handcuffs.

How long have you been cheating with her?

Oh, I don't know, a month.

And you never thought to ask her if she was married?

It never came up.

Couldn't you tell a man lived with her? Men's shaving cream in the bathroom, shoes under the bed, trophies? Therm shifts the ax from hand to hand.

Most of the time she came to my place. She didn't wear a ring.

Of course she wouldn't wear her ring. Cheaters know better than that, Therm says.

Well, whatever. I just hate being caught up in this mess. I'd like to go back and sort it out with this guy. He's probably rational enough. I'll apologize. Is that what you think I should do?

It won't be enough, but it will be a start. The major damage is done. Don't even think about seeing her again, though. How would you feel if your wife was bonding with some other man?

I've never been married.

Yeah, well.

But I didn't know she was married.

Now you do.

I'll talk to him.

Therm sucks on his teeth.

I'll go right now. I just wish I didn't have these damned handcuffs on.

At approximately 3:15 P.M., Officer Ferris noted, a man in a blue
Chevy Nova, 1986 or so, drove by with a busted taillight. Ferris had
been instructed to stop any vehicles that drew suspicion and might
possibly be carrying the missing boy. A busted taillight suggests a
struggle; the boy could be in the trunk, tied down and helpless.
Ferris flipped his lights on and pursued the blue Chevy Nova.

The afternoon was calm with heavy, low clouds above harbor-
ing rain. Since the boy disappeared, the weather had been somber. Ferris had tried to stay objective about the disappearance; he
didn't want to rule out all the possibilities. The boy could have run
off or fallen into a sinkhole or just gotten himself really lost. But
Ferris had dismissed these considerations after combing the woods
with the boy's mother a few nights ago. Ferris had been assigned
to survey the woods with the mother while other officers worked
deeper in the woods and the surrounding neighborhoods. After
nightfall, the mother and Ferris followed their erratic flashlights
around the soft sounds of crickets and distant shufflings. The first
time the mother cried her son's name, Ferris had flinched. The
immediate loudness of her pain-filled voice frightened him. The
more she called out, the more serious the situation seemed. Ferris
eventually yelled for the boy, too, as much to hear his own voice responding to hers as to hope for a feeble reply from the woods. By
sunrise, Ferris was spent and hoarse and convinced the boy had
been nabbed. The mother's doomsday worry had seeped into Ferris throughout the night. A mother knows, she said, and Ferris
knew better than to disagree.

The team of officers uncovered a pellet gun by the pond, and a
dead frog in a paper bag near the old elementary school. Footprints were either trampled by the team or erased by the drizzle
and mist. Now, though, with the weather keeping the ground soft,
if the kidnapper made a move, there was a good chance they would
find prints or tire tracks or something that spelled foul play.

The blue Chevy Nova signaled and pulled to the shoulder of the road: 3:18 P.M., Officer Ferris noted, and it's showtime. He exited his squad car, adjusted his belt, keeping his hand near his side-piece, and approached the car. The perpetrator rolled his window down, stuck his head out, and said, Is there a problem, officer?

The perpetrator had stringy hair, sun-darkened skin, and a long chin. His eyes, Ferris determined, were shifty and cold.

License and registration, Ferris demanded, keeping his eyes on the perpetrator's hands.

The man dug into his glove compartment. A Bible fell out, which seemed odd to Ferris. Why would a man keep one in his glove box? It didn't make sense. You a man of the cloth? Ferris questioned.

No, sir, I'm not. There are some passages I like to read before I go to work.

The man handed Ferris the documents. The perpetrator's name was Cole Bateman, born on December 16, 1979. He had vision impairment and lived in a remote trailer park just over the county line. This Cole Bateman fit the profile of a child molester, Ferris knew: late twenties, white, scrawny, a loner, overly religious, dirt under the fingernails; all typical. As Ferris returned the license, he heard a faint thud in the trunk.

Out of the car, Ferris said, withdrawing his gun and pointing it in Cole's face.

What? Cole asked, recoiling.

Out, now. Ferris flung the door open and Cole cautiously stepped onto the road.

Hands on the hood.

Cole put his hands on the hood. Ferris yanked the perpetrator's arms behind his back and cuffed him.

Stay put, Ferris said.

What did I do?

Ferris glared at the handcuffed man. I'm going to find out just what you did.

It took Ferris a few moments to locate the trunk-release latch, and his adrenaline made his hands fumble and his heart jump. He heard movement in the trunk again, no mistake about it. The trunk popped.

The perpetrator said, I caught those on public property, and Ferris raised his gun again. He told Cole to shut up, pervert.

In the trunk was a large potato sack thrashing from side to side.

Ferris holstered his gun and pulled the sack to the edge of the trunk. It was lighter than a boy should be. He was probably starving, poor thing. Ferris loosened the knot at the neck of the sack and opened it. A cottonmouth struck his wrist, released its fangs, and struck his hand in an instant. A pygmy rattler attached itself to a finger on his other hand. Ferris flung the sack back into the trunk and shook the pygmy rattler from his finger. He screamed some oaths, drew his gun, and shot at the sack of snakes.

Cole ran.

Ferris lifted his gun and fired at the retreating perpetrator. His shot missed badly. The man scurried off into the forest. There was only a moment of hesitation, and then Ferris was in pursuit. A copperhead escaped, slid across the asphalt, and buried itself in a pile of woody pulp.

Jakob wandered around the woods looking for litter. He found a battered trash bag and broken glass, but nothing he could keep the frog in. His old elementary school was not far from here, maybe a half mile. The school had burned down after a fire started in the boiler room. The police said nobody was hurt, but the students believed the janitor had been trapped down in the basement and died. Tommy Tucker said that the teachers and parents didn't want the kids to know because the janitor's corpse had been burned so badly it would give everyone nightmares to think about. Everyone thought about it anyway.

In a trash can on the playground Jakob found a paper bag that could hold the white frog. The school was nothing more than a pile of rubble with a few scorched half walls tugging out of the ground. Firefighters had cleaned up the site and there were plans to reconstruct it in a few years.

The playground was undamaged. Jakob poked a few holes in the bag for the frog to breathe, set it near the jungle gym, and ran over to the merry-go-round. Jakob couldn't resist the merry-go-round. He grabbed the rusty green bars and grunted as he pushed it around, kicking up dirt. The merry-go-round squealed in protest, but as Jakob persisted and it gathered momentum, the noise stopped and with a final shove, he leaped up on it.

Jakob stood in the middle and tried to keep his balance without holding on to the bars. He loved the sensation of being dizzy; it was as if he were in a different world when he was spinning, a slower, dreamy world. He went around and around. Overhead, the high afternoon sky threw his shadow to the graveled ground. Jakob watched the image in front of him grow from kid-size to adult-size to giant-size. At its peak, Jakob raised his arms so that the shadow's fingers stretched nearly to the woods. And in an instant, as the merry-go-round rotated and he turned to face the sun, his shadow diminished to regular size and smaller until it disappeared altogether.

Blinded, Jakob could not see the shadow that had been pacing him rise up and out of the ruins of the school.

I'd help you, but I'm no good at picking locks, Therm says, considering the handcuffs. Besides, if you go to the husband restrained, you'll score sympathy points.

Yeah, or he'll see what Samantha had in mind. He'll be forced to think of she and me getting it on in bondage. Cole thrusts his hips. Probably won't paint a pretty picture.

Good point, Therm agrees.

No, I think it would be best if I went to him with open arms. Also, if you free me, I can look at that wound on your hand. If a snake bit you, we should do something about it.

I told you it wasn't a snake, and I told you I don't pick locks.

Well, I don't either. Do you know any locksmiths?

No, I'm new around here.

Maybe we could clip it with something from your woodshed?

I use that for the lawn mower and not much else.

What about the ax?

Therm lifts the ax and raises his eyebrows.

I'll bet you could bust the chains in three swings, big boy like yourself.

What if I miss?

I don't know, try not to. Take good aim. I'd do just about anything to have these off. You ever been handcuffed?

When they were children Therm and his brother used to play Cowboys and Indians. Therm always ended up the restrained Indian, but he didn't mind. Those were toy handcuffs made from plastic and when Therm pulled hard they'd open enough to slide free. When Therm tried to run away, his brother shot him up with cap guns.

Sure, Therm says to Cole, I've been cuffed before.

You know, then, the Good Lord never intended to keep a man locked like this, Cole says, shaking his arms. How am I supposed to pray with my arms behind my back?

Therm doesn't pray, but he thinks about it sometimes.

I've learned my lesson, Cole says. My wrists feel like they've been rubbed over with sandpaper.

They're red.

I'll go kneel by that stump, stretch the chain back as far as it will go, and let you have a whack at it. Then I'll go apologize and take myself out of Samantha and her husband's relationship for good. Maybe they can get counseling and patch things up.

Counseling could work if they're both willing to try, Therm agrees. It isn't a bad idea.

3:53 P.M., Ferris notes, and he is in trouble. The snakebite at his wrist has quickly pumped poison into his bloodstream. According to the police handbook, which Ferris knows by memory, you aren't supposed to try and suck the poison out of a snakebite, but he tries anyway. With a piece of his shirt, he makes a tourniquet around his arm. He fears this is too late. He has gotten himself lost in the woods and regrets his hasty decision to pursue the perpetrator. The handbook never mentioned chasing a suspected child molester into the woods after you've been bit repeatedly by deadly snakes. The handbook mentioned backup. So, Ferris rationalizes, I've made a mistake. His right hand looks like an eggplant and the damaged finger on his left hand is paralyzed and swollen. Breathing is difficult. It had rained around 3:45 P.M. and then it stopped; now there is mist. Ferris is pretty sure he has passed that pepper tree three times.

In a small clearing, Ferris notices footprints that are smaller than his own. They lead around a bramble bush and farther into the forest. Unsteadily, Ferris follows.

4:10 P.M., and Ferris is on his hands and knees, gasping for breath and crawling from one footprint to the next. He can no longer feel the right side of his body and his vision has blurred. Still, he struggles forward, not yet ready to die.

The footprints stop. Ferris props himself on his elbows where the woods end and the grass of someone's backyard begins. In the yard, a man lifts an ax and hesitates. Ferris only sees the back of a small person kneeling, arms behind him, before the executioner. He thinks of the missing boy. With his left hand, Ferris draws his gun, a last surge of energy carries his shaking arm up, and he fires. The ax falls.

Therm feels a burning in his chest as he heaves forward and drives the ax hard into the handcuffed man's wrist. He falls to his knees beside Cole and tries to find some explanation in the man's face.

The bite of steel in Cole's wrist doesn't hurt at first. He can't believe the idiot missed. He was so close to freedom. But the pain comes when he tries to move his hand and feels that it is mostly detached from his arm. The warm flow of his blood down his backside drains him quicker than he thinks it should, and Cole finds he cannot stand up or stop the bleeding.

Ferris congratulates himself for doing the right thing. The police handbook clearly says, in chapter three: at all costs protect the victim. He rests his face in the grass. He thinks he should check his watch to note the time of rescue. He doesn't have the energy to lift his poisoned arm.

Therm fingers the hole in his chest and recalls Cowboys and Indians. The wound is perfectly circular and seems fake peeking out from his torn shirt. He figures he'll play dead for a while as he falls forward and hides his face in the lawn.

Cole collapses, chin first. He tugs at the handcuffs weakly, but his hand won't snap off. There's still enough bone to keep him locked.

The men take in the scent of the earth. Each locates a memory from when he was a child playing in the freshly cut grass, invincible and alive. They remember how easy it was to be a boy.

RIDLEY PEARSON

Queeny

FROM *Death Do Us Part*

I LAST SAW HER at breakfast.

I work alone, in a room above the garage where a carpenter once told me the wood in the floor dated back pre–American Revolution. He could tell by the tightness of the grain, and the history of the building. People know that stuff. A friend of mine makes guitars. He once saw an instrument at a trade show and knew it had been made out of the same piece of African mahogany that he'd built a guitar out of. He exchanged stories with the luthier responsible, and sure enough he was right: same wood. People know weird stuff.

She'd mentioned it in passing, when I was furiously cooking pancakes for one of our daughters and scrambling eggs for the other; cooking oatmeal for my wife and me. It's the one real spoil I give our daughters: any breakfast you want, anything you name. But I'm a stickler with them in every other way. We get along well because the boundaries are set. There's respect and love now, not testing and challenges. There's harmony, real harmony, and that's a cherished commodity in a family.

"Some guy turned around running at Queeny Park and caught up to me, and ran with me."

"Seriously?"

"Yeah."

I think she told me to impress me, to remind me nine years into our marriage that other men still look. It wasn't news to me — I knew they looked — but I sensed that this was one of those moments in a marriage when you don't want to say the stupid thing. But she wasn't asking me if I liked her haircut.

"He say anything?" I ask.

"Yeah, we talked. He asked questions like how often I run. Stuff like that."

"You talked to him." I try not to make it sound accusatory, but my concern gets the better of me, and I blow it.

"I can't talk to a guy?" She goes back to the dishes. I have a pancake I'm burning. I flip it. The color of shoe leather.

She soaps up, runs the water a little louder than necessary.

"It isn't like that," I say, when I get a chance.

"No, it isn't," she replies.

"I mean . . . I'm not trying to tell you what you can and can't do. But it's a park, sweetie. You're a single woman, or at least a woman running alone, as far as he's concerned."

"You write too many of those books."

She often blames my occupation on my tendency to see criminal behavior in everyone. She's right, of course. She knows she'll always win this one, and she does.

A day passes. Two. It's breakfast again. It's crepes this time, and soft-boiled eggs for the youngest, a dish we call Fishies in the Brook — why, I have no idea. Soft-boiled eggs on pieces of torn bread in a bowl. No brook. No fishes. But the girls love it and eat it down to a yellow smear on the walls of the bowl.

"He was there again. Yesterday. He was running in my direction this time. Caught up to me and . . . and we ran together."

"I wish I could say something positive." But I can't. It's not that I care about the contact, the attention. Lord knows we can all use it. I get it too, the flattering comments out on book tour, the looks that go beyond a normal look. I don't act on them, and neither will she. That's not my worry at all. And if she does act on it, then that's dealt with then. But there's not a grain of jealousy spilling out of my shaker. This is straight concern, and I try to disguise it just enough so that I don't scare her. I'm good at scaring people. I've scared millions of readers for a very long time. I know the effect I can have, even when I don't mean to. I work hard not to scare my family, the kids especially.

"It's a dark park is all," I continue. "Long stretches in the woods. A long way from anywhere. Some guy pulls up to you out on Adams and runs along with you, you can at least scream. You scream in Queeny Park and you'll be lucky to scare off a few birds."

There's a hidden message here I'm not sure she gets. She stopped running for about five months — over a year ago now — because a car stalked her at five in the morning. It scared the pee out of her, literally. Slowed down and cruised alongside her before the sun was up, before the neighbors were up. When she hid behind a tree, the guy from the passenger window threw a can of soda at her and nearly hit her. We called the cops. I had the opening of *Mystic River* running through my head. She had laundry to do. The cop was pleasant and genuinely concerned. He took it around the block to the Bread Company, no doubt, and warmed up his cup and went on with his day. Bottom line: She stopped running. For five months.

Now she's back at it, and this time the guy's on foot and she doesn't see the parallels.

"If he was in a car 'running' alongside of you, how would you feel?"

"It's not the same thing," she says.

"What's his name?"

"I don't know."

"Where's he live?"

"I don't know."

"What's he drive?"

She goes back to the dishes because she can hear me say: "It *is* the same thing."

"How much does he know about you?" I ask.

She shakes her head. I sense she's blown it out on the trail and knows it, and doesn't have an answer.

We've been watching a movie on PBS where the husband is a jealous, controlling freak — it's Trollope — and I use that as my reference. "I'm not trying to be the guy in the movie. You know that, right? You want to run? Run. You want to talk? Talk. But maybe run with a friend so it's two against one. Maybe choose a park that isn't so completely isolated and dark. Queeny Park is so wrong for a woman running alone. It's totally wrong. You can see that, right?"

She shrugs.

I know that shrug. I've come to hate that shrug. It's the blow-off shrug. We're done here, and it's on her terms, and that burns me.

Another day or two. Three, maybe. She comes home that afternoon for lunch and lists the friends she ran with this morning. She doesn't do it in a way to sting me. She could, but she doesn't, and I love her for it.

"Thanks," I say between bites.

A couple days later it's the same: Laurel and Tracy, four-mile loop at Queeny, Starbucks afterward and a good talk. No mention of Him.

So today when the call comes from school, my first reaction is to be pissed off. Our eldest, at all of seven, wasn't picked up. Missed the bus and wasn't picked up. Missed the bus because her mother told her not to take it. Makes sense because it's Thursday and that's ballet. I'm on the way there when the BlackBerry rings and it's the private school. The youngest wasn't picked up.

Now, for the first time, the tick goes off in my brain. It's like a Tourette's misfire of a synapse: a burst of cursing aloud followed by near blindness and the inability to keep any one part of my body still. My seven-year-old is freaking out in the back seat. She's come out of the shoulder strap, and that really frosts me because she's been doing this *a lot* lately, and it isn't safe, and she knows it. So I brake to a stop rather dangerously, and get a bunch of car horns as my prize.

"Put your strap back on, young lady!" She's the nearest target and she gets both barrels. My mind is racing now and I'm wondering how much of this is me the writer and how much the husband. I can see it all in my mind's eye, and I erase it just as quickly. *Do not go there!* I tell myself. *Steady keel.*

It has been six days. There's no such thing as adjustment. I jump every time the phone rings. I hear cars on the street and am convinced she's pulling into the drive. But her car is down with the police. They found it at Queeny Park. Locked. Parked where she always parks, according to Laurel and Tracy. They never saw the guy. She'd never mentioned him to them. Embarrassed, maybe. Or private. Or a little bit of both.

No evidence. Dogs. Crime scene guys. Nothing. The TV shows are all liars. When they're gone, there's nothing left. They're just gone. No hairs and fibers. Not even a scent.

Day ten and a crew of five guys and one woman enters my office above the garage with a search warrant. Their arrival hits me like a fist in my chest. They confiscate my computer, all my bills, my BlackBerry, my car.

I can't focus on the questions they fire at me. Mainly because it's *at* me. The tone is adversarial. There's no mistaking it. Accusatory. I'm dumbfounded. And I'm pissed, the way they're dealing with my gear. I'm a freak about my gear. I treat it like most people treat their pets. They're dragging the server downstairs, wires trailing. I'm burning mad about everything. Just the *thought* that they would dare do this to me . . . I've written books about it; I've interviewed cops who are twice the cop of these guys about it: when all else fails, look pretty hard at the husband.

And now it's me squarely in the sights.

Day ten and a half. My attorney, a woman with a brain bigger than Texas. I've known her five minutes, but she comes as the choice of my New York entertainment lawyer, also a woman, and so well connected that I know this is the right one even before we meet. But now we've met and I even like her as well.

There's four of us in the small room. The cop looks tired, but it feels like an act. I've written better characters than this guy will ever be. He's Kmart to my Bergdorf. But I don't, I won't, challenge him. I won't out-cop him. I'm just alive enough somewhere in my brain to know not to do this. I tell myself to listen. Let the attorney do the talking.

I say, "What's this all about?" Wondering how my mouth can be so disconnected from my brain.

The attorney's head swivels like an owl's. She could have me for breakfast right now.

"When was the last time you visited Queeny Park?" the cop asks.

I look to the attorney. She nods.

"With you guys," I answer.

"Before that," he says. "The last time before that?"

I know where this is going. I'm mortified. I nod. "Okay," I say. "Okay, I see where this is going."

"Just answer the question, please."

I lean in to my attorney. She smells nice. I whisper my explanation.

She looks the cop in the eye and says, "Next question."

The cop's brow furrows. He's pissed. I don't blame him.

My car must have been seen by someone. It was *one morning*. Only

one. I went out there to see if I could see the guy, see the car he
climbed into, get something more on what she'd been telling me.
Shouldn't have done it. Never saw a thing. But there it is. And
I never mentioned it to them because I thought how stupid it
sounded. How *bad* it sounded. And now it does. It goes unan-
swered.

"Can you tell me about Magic Movies?" he asks.

I feel my face go red. A home movie website. Voyeurs. All adult
stuff. Amateur videos. Soft stuff for the most part. Some of it
graphic. They'll use it to imply a dissatisfaction with our sex life —
not true. They'll use it to suggest something troubled underneath
the surface — not true. They'll spin it into violent acts, and not
one of them showed any such thing. They're building a case. It's
their job. Kmart is having a sale, a banner day. Blue Light Special.

Day ninety-five. A jury of my peers. I don't think so. Their case is all
oblong shapes made to fit a square box. The twelve morons in the
real box are nodding and looking at me like I'm Manson. I'm
still in grief, still can't sleep or wrap my mind around her doing
the dishes and me cooking crepes and never bothering to get
one stitch of factual information. My one act of covert surveil-
lance meant to protect her is used against me, and used effectively.
What's amazing are the looks from Laurel and Tracy. Their trust in
me is gone. Shot. They've bought the story. And if they've bought
it, then what about the twelve morons? I tell my attorney it's a
twofer: he got her and he got me all in the same act. He's out there
ready to do it again. I'm going down as his surrogate. Mainly because I write this stuff. People know weird stuff; I'm one of the
weirdest. Their case keeps heading back there, looping around.
Who knows how to pull something like this off better than someone like me? If I decided to do this, would they expect to find much
physical evidence? Of course not. Who better than me to make up
a story about some guy? It's all me — but they don't know me.

They convict.

It's all me.

Down for the count.

Day six hundred and ninety-seven. Cell block C. My girls are nine
and seven. I've seen them once a month for the past two years.

They look at me like they want to love me but can't figure out how to do it.

They found the body. Sixty-three miles out of town, buried alongside an interstate. Two others within fifty yards of it. There's semen in the remains. DNA. Day eight hundred and seventy-four and a hearing, and I'm given my walking papers — DNA wasn't mine. I tried to tell them that. They say they're giving me my life back. Not true.

Two girls who don't want to be with me. They're living with Grandma. I'm told the transition will be difficult. No shit.

I go home and sit down and write.

It's all I know how to do.

The next Saturday I'm making crepes and Fishies in the Brook. They're looking at me with empty plates. Empty eyes. I catch myself holding my breath. I laugh. But they just stare.

I think I scare them.

JOHN SANDFORD

Lucy Had a List

FROM *Murder in the Rough*

THIS WAS THE WAY you won the Open.
This was the way you won a million dollars.
This is what you *did*.
    Lucy had a list, and she was sticking to it.
    Every morning, in the back bedroom, braced on the tinny, oil-canning floor, looking into a full-length mirror she'd bought at the Wal-Mart, Lucy did a hundred grips and a hundred turns. She'd grip the club and check alignment, start the turn and check her intermediate position in the mirror. When she was satisfied, she'd continue, let her wrists cock, hold at the top and check the final position. Then she'd start over.
    She was on the eighty-fourth turn when the screaming started. The screaming didn't affect the drill. Strange sounds came off a golf course, and besides, she'd do a hundred reps if the trailer burned down around her. At ninety-nine she hadn't even paused to look out the blinds.
    On her hundredth turn, she checked her form in the mirror, nodded at herself and relaxed. She was a middle-sized girl, lean from walking and working out, deeply tanned, dishwater blond with a pixie cut. She was sweating a little, and wiped the side of her nose on her shirtsleeve. She was dressed in a navy blue golf shirt and khaki shorts, with a Ping golf hat. Her blond ponytail was threaded through the back of the hat.
    She put the weighted club in the corner of the bedroom and walked down the central hall to the kitchen. Her mom was digging in a toaster with a fork, talking to it around a lit Marlboro, letting it know: "You piece of shit-ass junk, you let that outta there."

By some mistake, the television was turned off, so the screaming outside sounded even louder than it had in the back. Mom, still talking sticky-lipped around the cigarette, glanced sideways at the screen door and said, "Goddamned golfers," and turned the toaster upside down and banged it on the counter.

Lucy looked out through the screen, across the six-foot strip of grass that served as the front yard, past the corner of the Tobins' double-wide and over the fence, across the end of the driving range and the east corner of the machine shed, and judged the screams as coming from the first fairway. "Don't sound like drunks," she said. She corrected herself. "Doesn't."

"Yeah, well, fuck 'em anyway," Mom said. Lucy's mother knew about golfers, having had a number of hasty relationships with them over the years, including one with Lucy's father. Lucy knew little about him except that he was a 6-handicap and, under pressure, had a tendency to flip his hands at the beginning of his downswing.

"Duck-hooked me right into the county maternity ward," her mother told her. "Not that I didn't love you every minute, sweetheart."

Lucy would have liked to know more, but never would. She had two photographs of him, taken with a small camera, reds and greens in the photos starting to bleed: her mom and dad in their golf clothes, standing near the ball machine on the driving range, squinting at the camera, sunlight harsh on their faces. Her father had been murdered by a man named Willis Franklin, who at that very moment was probably sitting on a barstool at the Rattlesnake Golf Club, not five hundred yards away, having gotten away with it.

"How did this happen?" her mother asked, peering into the toaster. "That son of a bitch is *welded* in there."

"I told you, you *cannot* put frozen flapjacks in a toaster; it don't work," Lucy said. "When they thaw out they get sticky and they sink down and grab ahold of them little wires at the bottom . . . Ah, shit." She was tired of hearing herself talk about it; and a little tired of correcting her own grammar. She did it anyway: "*Doesn't* work," she said. "*Those* little wires."

Her mom looked up: "You been pretty goddamn prickly lately."

"I'm headin' out; see what's going on," Lucy said. She rattled through the golf bags stacked in the corner and pulled out her putter.

"Dinner at five thirty," Mom said.

"Yeah." Like it made any difference what time they fired up the microwave. "I'll be back before then, probably for lunch. I got a couple of lessons; then I gotta run into town."

Lucy took her putter, which she called the Lizard, and stuck five balls in the pocket of the golf vest she'd designed herself and produced on Mom's pedal-driven Singer — a sports-activity vest that sooner or later would be stolen by those sons of bitches at Nike, she didn't doubt, and somebody would make a million bucks, but it wouldn't be her. She went out the door, the Lizard over her shoulder, the new Titleists clicking in her vest pocket. On the step, she automatically touched her pocket again, didn't feel the book. "Shoot."

She went back inside: "Forgot my list," she said.

"Heaven forbid," Mom said. She'd given up on the toaster and was looking through the litter in the kitchen for her Marlboros. "Got to clean this place up," she muttered.

Lucy went back to the bedroom, got the little black book from the dresser, and headed out again, out the door, past the Tobins' place, through a hole in the fence and past the machine shed, where Donnie Dell was poking around the mower blades on an aging orange Kubota tractor. He called, "Hiya, Luce," and she raised the putter and called back, "What's all the hollerin' about?"

He shook his head: "I don't know. Too early to be drunks." She kept going and he called after her, "You gonna be around?"

"Maybe tonight," she called back. "Right now, I got a lesson with Rick Waite and his wife."

"Okay. Maybe, uh, I'll stop by. Later."

She smiled and kept moving. Donnie Dell was taking some kind of ag course over at UW–River Falls; a college boy. She knew exactly what he wanted; he'd been coming around for a month, ever since he got hired. What he didn't know, but that she did, was that he *was* going to get some, but not for a week. That's when he came up on her list, and she'd hold to it.

But tonight, tomorrow, the next day — uh-uh. She was busy.

She was passing the end of the machine shed, heading toward the putting green, when she saw one of the Prtussin brothers trotting down the first fairway. The sight stopped her. Dale Prtussin was forty-five years old and weighed upwards of 250 pounds. None of it was muscle, and seeing him run was like watching a swimming pool full of Jell-O in an earthquake. He'd once eaten one of his own salads and come down with food poisoning. The major symptom was projectile vomiting and she'd seen him *walk* to the john in midspasm.

Up the fairway, at the top of the hill, just shy of the 185-yard marker, a half-dozen golfers were gathered around the sand trap that guarded the inside elbow of the dogleg. They were all looking into the trap. Lucy went that way, twirling the putter like a baton.

One of the golfers, an older guy named Clark who always pretended to be taking an avuncular interest while he peered down her blouse, frowned when he saw her coming, held out a hand, and said, "This isn't for you, young lady."

"Don't make me hurt ya," Lucy said, pointing the putter handle at his gut. Harley Prtussin said, "Howya, Luce?" as she came up and looked in the sand trap. The first thing she saw was the ball that somebody had driven into the lip of the bunker; then she saw the nose in the divot.

"Holy shit," she said. She was gawking. "What's that?"

"Stevie," Prtussin said.

"Stevie? Is he dead?" All right, that was stupid. "How'd he get in there? Who found him?"

"Somebody must've put him in," the avuncular golfer said.

A golfer named Joe said, "I found him. Swung at my ball and felt the club hang up; I guess, Jesus . . . I guess it was his nose."

She looked again at the ball in the lip of the bunker. "What'd you use, a seven-iron?"

"Yeah." They all looked down toward the green.

"Never gonna clear that lip from there with a seven-iron, not with your ball flight," Lucy said.

"I played it a little forward in my stance," Joe said.

"Good thing," Prtussin said. "If you'd dug in hard with a wedge, you'da really fucked up his face."

They all looked back in the hole where Stevie's nose stuck up, like a picture of the Great Pyramid taken from Skylab. One of the golfers shook his head and said, "Boy," and another one said, "Not something you see every day."

Prtussin said to Joe, "After you're done here, come on back to the clubhouse and I'll give you a rain check."

"You closing the course?"

"No, no . . ." Couldn't do *that*.

"Well, I'll just go on . . ."

"I think the cops are gonna want to talk to you, Joe."

Joe scratched his head and looked down toward the first green. Nothing but blue sky and light puffy clouds and maybe a one-mile-an-hour wind. The fairway was freshly mowed and smelled like spring golf. "Ah, heck. You think?"

They all stood around looking at the nose, and then a cop car turned in the drive, stopped for a minute at the end of the parking lot, so the driver could talk to Dale Prtussin, who'd just come out of the clubhouse. Dale got in the back seat and the car bucked over the curb and headed up the hill through the rough.

The nose sticking out of the sand looked *austere*, Lucy thought, plucking a word from her presleep vocab list. White and semi-plastic. Like a priest's nose when the priest is pissed off at you. The cop car rolled up and Jamie Forester got out of the car, hatless, re-membered Dale in the back, popped the back door, and they both got out and Jamie said, "Everybody move back."

Everybody took a step back and he looked in the trap, nodded, said, "Everybody stay back." He had his hands on his hips, looked at the nose for another five seconds, then shook his head and said, "Man oh man," walked back to the car, and called in.

Mitchell Drury arrived five minutes later. Drury was a member of the club and the lead investigator for the St. Croix County sheriff's office. Half the people around the bunker said, "Hey, Mitch," when he got out of his brown Dodge. He looked around, then said to Forester, "Everybody who wasn't here when he was found, get them out of here." To Dale Prtussin, "You and Harley better stay." He caught Lucy's eye, showed a half inch of grin and said, "Heard about the Ladies'. Congratulations."

Lucy nodded, and Drury turned back to the sand trap, all busi-ness again. Forester shooed them all away from the trap and back down the fairway to the first tee. At the bottom of the hill, Wade McDonnell, a retired mailman who worked as a ranger, was waving people off the tee. When Lucy went past, he asked, "They take him out yet?"

"Nope. Can't see nothing but the nose." She corrected herself. "*Anything* but the nose." *The Businesswoman's One-Minute Guide to English Grammar and Usage.*

"You taking off?" McDonnell asked.

"Got the Waites."

McDonnell looked sympathetic. "Good luck."

"That ain't gonna help," Lucy said. Corrected herself: "*Isn't* going to help. Rick's got the reflexes of a fuckin' clam." Thought about deleting the "fuckin'," but decided to let it be; that was just golf talk.

The Waites were unloading their fly yellow Mustang when Lucy came up, and wanted to know what was going on; and then both of them had to walk up to the first tee to look up the hill and bitch at McDonnell about not being able to go on up to the bunker to look at the nose.

"It's a free goddamned country," Rick Waite argued.

"Tell that to Mitchell Drury," McDonnell said.

"Fuck a bunch of Mitchell Drurys," Waite said.

"Tell *that* to Mitchell Drury," McDonnell answered.

More cops arrived and drove up the rough to the trap; then a panel van from the St. Croix County medical examiner's office. Everybody from the bar was milling around the first tee by that time; and as players came off the ninth green and eighteenth, they joined the crowd.

Then nothing happened for a long time, the crowd waiting in the sunshine and the vanishing morning dew — always a few of them bleeding off to the bar, returning with beers and rum Cokes. Lucy wandered off to the practice green, pushed a white tee into the ground three feet from one edge, and began practicing lag putts across the width of the green. Sixteen of twenty had to stop past the hole, but not farther than seventeen inches past. Twenty minutes later, Rick Waite came over, his wife trailing, and said, "Might as well do that lesson," and Sharon Waite said, "Dale told us you shot a sixty-eight up at Midland Hills in the Minnesota Ladies'."

Lucy said, "It shoulda been a sixty-seven, but I lost discipline on number eight and three-putted."

"That happens to everybody," Sharon Waite said.

"Fuckin' shouldn't," Lucy said.

"But you won going away," Waite persisted.

"The Ladies' isn't the Tour," Lucy said. "They don't give you that stroke on the Tour." She turned away, and behind her back, Sharon Waite looked at her husband and shook her head.

Halfway through the lesson, Lucy told Rick Waite that "Your biggest problem, you're sliding your hips. Every time you go to swing, you slide your hips to the right. Then you got to slide them back to the left, for the club to come down at the same place that it started. That's too hard. You gotta rotate your hips instead of slidin' 'em. Like you're standin' in a barrel."

She demonstrated, but Waite shook his head. "I can't *feel* that," he said. "I gotta *feel* that before I remember it. Gimme a tip that'll make me *feel* it."

Lucy looked at him for a minute; behind him, his wife — who was a better natural golfer than her husband, but didn't much care for the game — shook her head.

"I'll give you a tip," Lucy said. "When you set up, your dick is pointing at the ball. Keep it pointing at the ball. If you rotate, it'll point at the ball. If you slide, it'll point at your right shoe. Think you can feel *that?*"

Behind him, Waite's wife was biting the inside of her cheeks to keep from laughing. Waite looked at his shoe and said, "Shit, honey, my dick is usually pointing at my left kneecap." His wife made a rude noise.

From the range, they could see up the hill to the crowd around the sand trap. People — cops — were crawling around the trap, and then a couple of guys hauled a black bag out of it. "Body bag," Rick Waite said.

"Poor old Stevie," Sharon Waite said. "Must've put it in the wrong place one time too many." Her eyes cut to Lucy: "Don't mind my mouth, honey."

"No big deal to me," Lucy said. "Stevie and me didn't get along all that well." She caught herself: "Stevie and *I*," she said.

The medical examiner's van went by a minute later, but the cops stayed up on the hill. Lucy finished the lesson, got the twenty bucks from the Waites, and walked back to the trailer, twirling the Lizard.

Her mom was around to the side in a lawn chair with a reflector under her chin and a damp dishcloth over her eyes. "I'm taking the truck," Lucy said. "Back in an hour."

"Get some oranges at County Market," Mom said. "Them real tart ones."

"I'll put it on my list," Lucy said. She took the notepad out of her vest pocket, clicked the small ballpoint, and added "Oranges" to her list for Tuesday.

Shamrock Real Estate was located on First Street in the town of Hudson, along the St. Croix River, in a flat cinder-block building that had been painted brown. Lucy parked in front and went in through the front door, the screen slapping behind her. The reception area smelled like nicotine, and held a desk, chair, computer, and a beat-up faux-leather couch that might have been stolen from an airport lounge; there was nobody at the reception desk, and never was, because there'd never been a receptionist. Two small offices opened off the reception area. One was dark because nobody worked out of it. A light shone in the second, and Michael Crandon, who'd been reading a free paper with his feet up on his desk, leaned forward to see who'd come in.

"Me," Lucy said, leaning in the office doorway.

"How you feeling?" Crandon asked. He dropped his feet to the floor. He was too old for it, but his brown hair was highlighted with peroxide and gelled up.

"You got it?" Lucy asked.

"You got the cash?"

She dug it out of her shorts pocket, a fold of bills: "Two hundred dollars." She dropped it on the desk, as though she were buying chips in Vegas.

He handed her two amber pill bottles and a slip of paper. "Pills are numbered," he said. "Take the big one the first day, the small one the second day. Read the instructions."

"Better be good, for two hundred dollars," Lucy said.

"They're good."

"Be back if they aren't," she said.

"Have I ever sold you any bad shit?"

Lucy shook her head: "You don't want there to be a first time," she said, her mouth shifting down to a grim line.

Crandon gave her his square-chinned grin, but he wasn't laughing.

When she left the real estate office, she put the pill containers in the truck's glove compartment and headed back up to Second Street and then out onto I-94, across the St. Croix Bridge into Minnesota, off at the first exit and south to the Lakeland library, which was in a strip shopping center a mile south of the exit. She parked in front of the post office, got a clipboard off the truck seat, and carried it down to the library.

The library had a couple of small computers tucked away in the back. She brought one up, typed for a few minutes, and printed out the paragraph. Then she took out a couple of rubber Finger Tips, the kind used by accountants and bank tellers, fitted them on her thumb and index finger, pulled the envelope out of the clipboard, printed that, wiped the screen, and shut the computer down. Handling both the paper and the envelope with the Finger Tips, she slipped them back in the clipboard and carried them out to the car.

The town of River Falls was back across the St. Croix and another fifteen minutes south of Hudson. She drove on down, elbow out the window, the wind scrubbing the fine hair on her left forearm, past all the golf courses and cornfields and dairy farms and yuppie houses. She went straight to the post office, sealed the envelope using a corner of her shirt dampened with Chippewa spring water, stamped it with a self-sticking stamp, and dropped it in the mailbox.

Looked in her book, at her list.

Good. Right on schedule.

Back home, Lucy put the oranges in the refrigerator; Mom yelled from the back of the trailer, "Lucy? That you?"

"Yeah."

Mom came out of the back, her face wet, as though she'd been splashing water on it. "Why didn't you tell me about Steve?"

"I figured you'd find out soon enough," Lucy said. "Didn't want to make you unhappy."

"Jesus Christ, Lucy, I needed to know." Her voice was coarse; she'd been crying.

"So you know," Lucy said. "I got the oranges."

"Jesus Christ, Luce . . ."

Lucy brushed past Mom and went into the bathroom, closed the door, and looked at the two yellow pill bottles and the piece of paper. The paper carried handwritten instructions, which looked as though they'd been Xeroxed about a hundred times. She read the instructions, then read them again, then opened one of the bottles, took out the pill, looked at it, bent over the sink, slurped some water from the faucet, then leaned back and popped the pill.

Everything would be better now. She flushed the toilet and went back out into the hall, could hear her mother in the bedroom; she might have been sobbing. "I'm taking my clubs," Lucy called out.

Mom blubbered something and Lucy picked up her clubs, then put them back down and went to the bedroom door and spoke at it.

"Can I come in?"

More blubbering, and she pushed the door open.

"I thought . . . I'm sorry, Mom, but I thought you were all done with that man."

"Well, I *was* all done," Mom said; her eyes had red circles around them. "Mostly. But I wouldn't want that to come to him. Being killed like that."

"Is there anything I can do about this? For you?"

"Naw, I'm just gonna sit around and cry for a couple of days. You go on."

"I mean, you aren't . . . pregnant or anything."

Now a tiny smile: "I ain't that stupid, honey. He never was a good bet."

"All right." Lucy nodded. "I'll be back for dinner."

The first fairway was empty, except for some yellow tape around the bunker. Lucy swerved away from the course and the practice green and crossed the driveway to the clubhouse. She dropped her bag in the office and looked out into the restaurant area. Jerry Wilhelm was sitting alone at the bar, smoking a cigarette and staring at a glass of beer; Perry, the bartender, was standing in the corner looking up at the TV, trying to tune it with a remote. Lucy drew herself a Diet Coke, then went around and slid up on a stool next to Wilhelm.

"You talk to the cops yet?" she asked.

"Waitin' right now," he said. "Mitch is downstairs with Carl Wallace." He looked at the stairs that went down to the basement party room. "Jesus, Luce, you shoulda seen him when they took him out of that sand trap. Stevie. Like to blew my guts. He was all . . . gray."

"Glad I didn't see it," she said, and tipped back the glass of Diet Coke.

"Rick Waite told me about your dick-pointing tip. You get that from Stevie?"

"Shoot, no; the only way Stevie's dick ever pointed was straight out."

"How would you know about that?" Wilhelm asked.

"He used to tell me about it," Lucy said. "Though I didn't believe but half of what he said."

"Shoulda believed about a quarter of it."

"About old Satin Shorts? Guess you'd know about that."

"Mary? Really? No, I didn't hear that one."

"Shoot, Jimmy, it was all over the club," Lucy said. "Give me some of those peanuts, will ya?"

As Wilhelm pushed the bowl of complementary peanuts at her, he said, "I thought him and your ma . . ."

"That was over two months ago." Christ, they couldn't think Mom did it? Of course they could, she thought — Mom and Stevie . . . "Two months ago . . . Where you been, boy?"

Wilhelm shrugged. "Working, I guess. Heard about your scholarship. You're going to Florida?"

"Yup. I'll give it two years anyway."

"Well, good luck to ya. You're the only person ever come out of this club might make it as a pro," he said.

"I'm gonna try," she said.

"It's on your list?" Her lists were famous.

She finished the Diet Coke and touched her vest pocket. "Yup. It's on my list," she said. She pushed away and touched his shoulder. "Good luck with the cops; Mitch is a pretty good guy."

"Thanks," he said. She could feel his eyes on her ass as she walked away. Nothing to that, though. That was just normal. And the mission had been definitely accomplished.

If Lucy let it all out, held nothing back at all, and was hitting on a flat surface without wind, she could drive one of her Titleists three hundred yards, and maybe a yard or two more — not to say that she knew exactly where it would go under those conditions. Backing off a little, she could average 272 yards and keep the ball in the fairway.

Good enough for the Tour.

But the Tour didn't pay for long drives; the Tour paid for low scores. So though she hit her three buckets of balls each morning and evening, she'd devoted most of her practice in the last year to the short game — and specifically, the game within thirty to sixty yards of the pin. Anytime you were standing in that gap, one of two things happened: you screwed up, or you were a little off, or a little short, on your second shot to a par 5.

So the next shot would either make par, if you'd screwed up, and therefore keep you in the game, or give you a birdie on the par 5. Both of those things were critical if you wanted to win on the Tour, and in the calendar in the back of her list book, she'd blocked out two months of thirty-six practice, two-and-a-half-hour sessions on Rattlesnake's par 3, twice a day. Get up and down every time from thirty to sixty, she thought, and you rule the Tour.

As she walked out to the par 3, she let her mind drift to the coach at the University of Florida. He'd come up to see her, and they'd played a couple of rounds at Bear Path, over in the Cities. At the end of the second round, he'd given her a notebook and said, "Write this down."

"A list?"

"A list," he said. He was a tough-looking nut, brown from the sun with pale blue eyes and an eye-matching blue Izod golf shirt buttoned to the top. "This is what I want you to do."

Over a Leinenkugel for him and a Diet Coke for her, and cheeseburgers with strips of bacon, he'd given her thirty putting drills and thirty more short-game drills.

"How long?"

"At least two hours a day," he said.

"I do six now," she said.

He looked at her, saw she was serious, and said, "Then don't quit, if you can stand it."

"If it'd put me on the Tour, I'd do ten," she said.

"We're gonna get along just fine, Lucy," he said through a mouthful of cheeseburger. "You do two hours a day, I'll put you on the

Tour. You do six hours and I'll put you on the leader board in the
Open. Whether you win or not . . . that depends on what you were
born with."

She looked flat back at him: "I been playing" — she didn't say *for
money,* but rubbed her thumb against her fingers in the money sign
— "since I was twelve," she said. "You give me a six-foot putt for two
hundred dollars with forty-three dollars in the bank, and I'll make
it every time."

He leaned back in his chair and smiled at her: "You're giving me
wet panties," he said.

She'd decided on this day to work on the ninth green on the par 3.
The ninth was slightly raised all around, a platform, with steep
banks climbing six feet up to the green. The pin was near the back,
and she walked around behind the green so she'd be coming in
from the short side; and she'd use nothing but the 7-, 8- and 9-
irons, punching short shots into the bank, letting the bank and the
rough slow the ball down, so it'd trickle over the top and down to
the pin. This was not a common approach. Most people would try
to flop the ball up to the pin, as she would, most of the time. But
sometimes you couldn't do that — like if there was a tree nearby —
and then you needed something different.

She was hard at it, punching an 8-iron into a spot two and a half
feet down from the top of the platform, trying to control the ball
hop, when she realized somebody was coming up behind her. She
turned and saw Mitchell Drury.

Mitchell. He must've been forty, she thought. But you sort of
thought about him anyway, looked him over, even if you were seventeen. That weathered cowboy thing, with the shoulders and the
small butt.

"Lucy," he said. His face was serious; usually he'd do a movie-star
grin when he was talking to her — he knew women liked him. Not
this time. "Gotta talk to you."

"Sure thing. About Stevie?" She sat back on the bank next to the
green and he plopped down beside her.

"Yeah . . . um. You know, I mean, everybody knows, he was seeing
your mom."

"C'mon, Mitch. That was over two months ago."

"Over for your mom?" His eyebrows went up.

"Yeah, *over.* It ain't the first time she's had a romance out here — Christ, she's only thirty-eight. I'm surprised *you* ain't been knocking on the door."

"Hmm," Mitch said, his eyes cutting away.

Lucy thought, *Holy cow.* "Mitchell," she said.

"Don't ask," he said. "But besides *that* . . . you're sure. About Stevie."

"I'm real sure," she said. "That motherfucker dropped her like a hot rock and she cried for four straight days. She's crying right now. But she never would have done anything about it." She looked up the hill toward the bunker. "Nothing like that."

"All right . . . She been out playing lately?"

Lucy shook her head. "Not much. Didn't want to run into Stevie, I think. Take the chance."

"All right," he said. He stood up. "I gotta talk to her, though."

"How was . . . um, I mean, was he shot? Stabbed? What?"

He shrugged. "I'll tell you, it's gonna be in the paper anyway . . . but I'd be a little happier if you didn't pass it around."

"Sure."

He looked both ways, as though somebody might be sneaking up on them, then said, "His skull was crushed."

"*Crushed?*" She shook her head. "Like with a car crusher? Like squashed?"

"No, no. Like somebody hit him in the temple with a driver."

She sat back. "Oh."

"What, '*Oh*'?"

"Nothing. I was just trying to think who I'd seen him playing with. But when I think about it, I ain't seen him playing with nobody, much. Mary Dietz a couple times, John Wilson last week."

"He have something going with Mary?"

Lucy shrugged: "I don't know. Might of just been playing lessons."

"Somebody else mentioned . . . I thought Mary was seeing Willie Franklin."

"Don't know about that, either," Lucy said. "Tell you the truth, Mitchell, I been a little out of it, ever since that letter come in from Florida. Gettin' ready."

Drury nodded. "Good luck on that, Luce," he said. Now he gave her the grin. "You're the best to ever come out of here. I think you'll go the whole way."

"That kinda talk'll get you a free lesson," Lucy said, grinning back.

Drury laughed and said, "May take you up on that."

Lucy stood up, brushed the grass off the seat of her pants and said, "Mom didn't have nothin' to do with it, Mitchell. Not a fuckin' thing. She's too kindhearted. I think you probably know that."

He might have blushed and he said, "Well, yeah, that's sorta what I think. See you later, Luce. Don't worry too much about your mom."

Lucy went back to hitting balls at the embankment. The first four or five hit too hard and trickled past, and she observed herself for a moment. Adrenaline. She had *this* feeling, *this* much adrenaline. Had to remember it: *this much* would get you nine feet past the pin . . .

Her mind drifted away from golf, just for a second or two. She'd made a lot of grammatical and usage errors when she spoke to Mitchell.

And that was good.

She thought about going back home. Mom probably could use some diversion. But she tarried at the putting green, trying again to make a hundred six-foot putts in a row. The drill was simple enough — you putted all the balls from the same spot, and after five or six, you could see a little pathway developing in the turf. If you could keep the balls in the pathway, you had a chance. But as the number went up, the stress built . . .

After two false starts, she made forty-eight, and missed on the forty-ninth when she saw Dale Prtussin hurrying toward her. "Howya, Luce? Did I make you miss?"

"Nah. Lost my focus."

"How far did you get?"

"Forty-eight in a row. Forty short of my record."

"I'm sorry . . . Listen. I hate to talk business like this, with Stevie not even in the ground, but do you think you could take over for him? For the rest of the summer, until you get to school? I mean, you aren't that experienced, so I couldn't pay you everything I gave him —"

"How much?"

"Six hundred a week, salary. You'd have to run the cash register in the mornings, starting at six o'clock, seven days a week. And you know, all the group lessons and supervise the school tournaments, but shit, it's not nothing you haven't done."

She nodded: "Start tomorrow?"

"That'd be good. I'll have Alice put you on the regular payroll, and you got a group lesson tomorrow at four in the afternoon. The ladies from 3M."

She poked her putter handle at his gut: "You got it, Dale. And thanks. It'll help me out at Florida, having a little bankroll of my own."

"Glad to do it," he said. But his tiny eyes were worried: "This is a bad day at Rattlesnake, Luce. Old Stevie was sorta an asshole sometimes, but nobody ought to go like that."

"Who's the hot name in the suspect pool?"

He shook his head. "Isn't any pool . . . yet. But, uh . . . never mind."

She raised her eyebrows. "Come on, you got somebody in mind?"

He looked both ways, like Mitch had earlier, and said in a hushed voice, "I'd like to know where Willie Franklin was Saturday night."

She looked away. "Didn't see him — and I wouldn't even want to say anything about that. You know, my daddy."

"I know; but I say the son of a bitch did it once, and if he can do it once, he can do it twice."

That night, Lucy did her vocab list, then lay in bed and thought about Willis Franklin, the man who'd shot her daddy. A group of men from Rattlesnake had been deer hunting, the weekend before Thanksgiving, up in Sawyer County. Out of tree stands. Franklin came running into the hunting shack, late in the day, and said he'd just found Lucy's dad dead on the ground, under his tree stand. Shot in the heart.

The body was taken into the coroner's office, and when it was examined by some state medical people, it was found to have a broken neck and small debris punched into the skin of the face — he'd been knocked right out of the stand.

Unusual. You'd have to be shooting *up* to hit him.

Then, blind luck, they'd found the remnants of a bullet in the tree, and metallurgical tests matched it to the fragments of metal found in the dead man's sternum. There was just enough of the slug left to match rifling marks made by Willis Franklin's gun. Franklin had denied shooting the rifle at all during the afternoon, but then admitted it, saying he was afraid of what he might've done. Said he wasn't even sure he'd done it — he'd been driving deer toward the stand, had one jump up close by, a buck with a big rack, and snapped an uphill shot at it . . . missed . . . and found Lucy's dad five minutes later.

That was all fine, except that Franklin had been after Lucy's mom like a bloodhound, until her dad stepped in and took her away. And Willis was a man known to have a foul temper and was not a man to forget. There was a trial, but nothing came of it: just not enough evidence, and the jury cut him loose. A tragedy in the woods, a few people said. A few more said, darkly, *murder* . . . And that was how Lucy learned the story.

Lucy thought about it all — her dad, Willis Franklin, and Stevie — and allowed herself to snuffle over it for a few minutes. She tried to switch her mind over to the Tour, as she usually did, but it didn't work: she just kept seeing the dark shape of her father falling out of a tree stand, a bullet in his heart.

She'd never known him. By the time she first heard the murder story, she was seven years old, and her daddy had been moldering in the ground for seven and a half years.

Lucy did the early morning cash register, and when Dale Prtussin came in at ten o'clock, walked back to the trailer, found her mom reading the paper. "Gotta do my grips," she said, and went on back to the bedroom. The grips and turns took a half hour, and then she was back in the kitchen. "You're still going to the Pin-Hi's this afternoon, aren't you?" she asked.

Her mom nodded. "Yeah. No point in hanging around here." The Pin-Hi's were a group of women golfers who played a circuit of eight courses during the summer. "Half the girls will have known Stevie — a couple of them in the biblical sense — and that'll be all the talk." She tried a smile again. "I got to protect my back."

"Did you talk to Mitchell?"

Mom nodded: "We had a good little heart-to-heart. Stevie was fooling with somebody, but it wasn't me. I'd heard maybe Satin Shorts —"

"That's what I heard. Mary."

Mom frowned. "And I heard a couple of weeks ago that Willie Franklin . . . Ah, shit, I'm not even going to *think* about that." She forced a bright smile. "So what are you doing, dear? With your new job?"

Lucy shrugged: "Usual stuff. Pretty much run the place in the early mornings, until the Prtussins show up. Stevie's job."

"So that's something you can cross off your list," Mom said.

"What?"

"Getting a bankroll together for Florida. A month ago, you were talking about getting a night job with UPS."

"Yeah, well. Stevie wouldn't mind, I guess. If he'd known it had to be this way."

Mom snorted, poured two tablespoons of sugar into a new cup of coffee. "Bullshit. I'll tell you something about Steve, honey — knowing that you were going to the pros was eating him up. He had a half year on the Tits Tour and that was the best he'd ever do. No way he'd ever make it on the regular Tour, make it through Q school. He hated every move he saw you make. He hated you out there practicing every day."

"C'mon. He was always helping . . ."

"Baby, I've known a lot more men that you have, and I knew Steve for fifteen years," Mom said. "That man would have run you over with his car if he thought nobody would catch him. Some god-damn *chick* stealing *his* glory at Rattlesnake? I don't think so."

"Then how come you were . . . seeing him?" Actually, Stevie'd come over and bang Mom's brains out on the other side of a six-teenth inch of aluminum wall.

Mom shrugged. "Company. He was a good-looking man, and he could make me laugh. I don't got that many years left, with men coming around."

Lucy fished the Lizard out of the bag in the corner. "Maybe you ought to look for somebody steadier. Somebody who doesn't play golf."

Mom snorted again. "Like that might happen."

Lucy did the group lesson at noon, then two private lessons, and then went back in and pushed Dale Prtussin out of the cash register station, even though she didn't have to. At three o'clock, she walked home. Mom was gone, and she went back to her bedroom, found the second pill case, blanked her mind, and went into the bathroom, looked at the second pill, took a breath, bent over to suck water from the faucet, looked at the pill, and popped it.

At four o'clock, she had the 3M women. They liked her, but they were all talking about Stevie. At five, she went into the bar, got a salad out of the refrigerator, ate it, and then walked back home, twirling the Lizard.

At the trailer, she lay down, waiting for the pill to work; fetched Dan Jenkins's *Dead Solid Perfect* from her rack of golf books and giggled through the best parts, though Jenkins sometimes cut a little close to home — a little too close to the way she and Mom lived in their little trailer off Rattlesnake.

She was waiting for the pill when she heard a ruckus out by the fence line, and then somebody started banging on the door, the whole trailer trembling with the impact. She climbed out of bed and went to look. Donnie Dell, the boy from the machine shed, the college student she was going to sleep with in a week, stood at the bottom of the steps. His straw-colored hair was sticking out wildly from beneath his ball cap, like the Scarecrow's in *The Wizard of Oz*.

"What?"

"You hear?" he croaked.

"Hear what?"

"The cops arrested Willie Franklin."

Lucy stepped out the door. "You're shittin' me."

"I'm not shittin' you," Donnie said. His eyes glowed with the excitement of it. "They found blood in the trunk of his car. And a hair, is what people are saying. Jim Doolittle got it straight from the cops."

"How would Doolittle know?"

"Works up with the hospital . . . I'm tellin' you, he *knows*. Jim's over in the bar right now. The cops found blood in Willie's trunk, and they matched it. He's absolutely fuckin' toast."

That was a moment that Lucy knew she'd remember forever.

She might someday be an old lady with a mantel full of Open trophies, and maybe a big scroll from the Hall of Fame, and maybe five kids and twenty grandkids — but she'd always remember standing outside the trailer door with somebody playing a Stones record off at the other end of the park, and a car accelerating away from the club, and the crickets in the cinder-block foundations, and the smell of cut grass and gasoline coming off the course, the best smell in the world. The moment she'd heard.

"Thanks for coming, Donnie," she said.

"You coming over to the bar?"

"I'd like to, but I'm feeling not so good. I ate one of them fuckin' salads . . ."

"Aw, Jesus," he said. "You know better than that."

"I know, I know, but I was hungry . . . So . . . see you next week?" She touched his shoulder.

"Maybe catch a movie," he said.

"That'd be cool, Donnie," she said.

She went back to the bed, but ten minutes later, a car pulled into their parking space, the lights sweeping over her window. Too early for Mom, unless something happened.

"*Goddamn it,*" she said. She pushed herself up, went to the door. Mitchell Drury.

"Mitch?"

"Hi, Luce. Is your mom home?"

"No, she's got the Pin-Hi's over at the Hollow tonight. Donnie Dell was just here, said you arrested Willie."

He nodded: "I was coming to tell her. 'Cause it's so much like what happened with your dad."

"How'd you catch him?" Lucy asked, crossing her arms and leaning on the door frame.

"Got a note from somebody at the club — said they saw him running off the course with his bag the night Stevie disappeared. Looked like he was panicked . . ."

"A note? From who?"

"We're trying to figure that out," Mitchell said. "Anonymous. Kind of think it might be one of the schoolteachers. One of the profession guys. The language was . . . high level."

"No shit," Lucy said.

"Had access to a computer and a laser printer. We'll find him, one way or another."

"What's Willie say?"

"Same thing he did with your dad — that he didn't have anything to do with it. Now he's got an attorney, and he's not saying anything."

"Well, fuck him," Lucy said fiercely. "Two people? Fuck him."

"That's sort of what I think. I was talking to . . ." Drury paused and took a half-step back. "You feel okay?"

"Ah, I got an upset stomach from one of the Prtussins' fuckin' salads," Lucy said.

"Well, uh, you got . . ."

He looked down, and Lucy looked down and saw the dark spot near her crotch. "Oh, Jesus." Her hands flew to her face. "Oh, God, I'm so embarrassed, Mitch. My period, I, God, it's early, God . . ."

"That's all right," he said hastily. "You go take care of it, honey. Tell your mom to call me at home whenever she gets in. I'll be up till midnight or later."

"Aw, jeez, Mitch . . ."

He was still backing away. "Take care of it, honey . . ."

She shut the door and got a Kotex from the box under her bed, strapped it on, pulled on a fresh pair of pants, then squirted ERA all over her stained underpants and shorts and threw them in the washer. She grinned at the thought of Drury's face: men would generally cut off their arms rather than have to deal with something like that, she thought.

Men.

Like that goddamned Stevie. Fuckin' Mom all night, then coming on to little Lucy in the shop. Holding her hips during the lessons, when he was showing her how to turn; hands on her rib cage, standing her up straight. Hands all over her. And more than his hands, down there in the basement room of the club, after he'd closed it down. He called her *tasty*, like she was some kind of fuckin' bun. Nobody knew because Lucy had to deal with stealing her mother's boyfriend; and Stevie had to deal with the problem of statutory rape, which he knew all about.

Then last week, when she told him she'd missed her period, out there on the fairway, he'd laughed at her: "So much for the fuckin' Tour," he said, and he turned away, laughing. If there'd been anybody else out there in the semidark, they'd have heard him, laughing, laughing, laughing.

The driver had been right there, poking out of her bag. She'd had it out in an instant, a lifelong familiar. Stevie'd started to turn when the club head caught him in the temple, and he'd gone down like a shot bird.

She'd buried him in the bunker, because it was convenient, and she had a lot of thinking to do; lists to make. She was back in the house before she noticed the blood on the club. She went out to wipe it on the grass when she noticed the taillights blinking in the club parking lot, and down on the far end, where it always was, the hulk of Willie Franklin's Tahoe. He never locked the back doors . . .

Mom was home by eleven and knocked on the bedroom door. "Okay in there?"

"Yeah. Gotta get up at five," Lucy called back.

Mom opened the door: "You heard about Willie Franklin?"

"Yeah. Oh — you're supposed to call Mitchell if you get in before midnight. He wants to talk to you about it."

"I'll call him," Mom said. "See you in the morning."

Lucy listened to her footsteps down the hall, then got up and looked at the latest Kotex. It was fairly bloody, but the flow seemed to be slowing. That's what the instructions had said: the onset would take a couple of hours, then the flow would be heavy for a couple of more, and after that, it would be more or less like a regular period. She switched pads and crawled back in bed.

This was what it took to go on the Tour, she thought. A fierce *determination:* nothing would stand in the way. A fierce *organization:* determination was nothing without focus.

And talent. She had all of that, Lucy did.

And her lists.

Her lists. Better do something about those. She reached across the familiar darkness, found her vest, and took out the small book. She had matches on her bed stand, to light the evergreen-scented candle. She lit it, and in the candlelight, found the pages and carefully ripped them out.

One note said, *RU-486.* Ripped and burned.

Another said, *New job.* Ripped and burned, the paper flaring in the near dark.

A third one said, *Frame Willie.* Ripped and burned.

She looked at the last note for a while, the only note not written with a golf pencil. It had been written the week before, in pale blue ink. Girlie ink, she thought now.

It said, *Marry Stevie?*

No fuckin' way. Not at this stage of her career, she thought. A pro went it alone, until the money got big. Then she'd have her pick.

Marry Stevie?

A tear trickled down her cheek. Ripped and burned, the smoke smelling of damp pulp paper and evergreens.

But it was gone in a moment, and everything was back on track.

Lucy lay in the bed she'd made, and dreamed of lists.

BRENT SPENCER

The True History

FROM *Prairie Schooner*

Teudilli sent a message to Moctezuma in Mexico describing everything he
had seen and heard, and asking for gold to give the captain of the strangers,
who had asked him whether Moctezuma had any gold, and Teudilli had
answered yes. So Cortés said: "Send me some of it, because I and my
companions suffer from a disease of the heart which can be cured only with
gold."
> — From *Narratives of the Coronado Expedition 1540–1542*, edited by George P.
> Hammond and Agapito Rey (Albuquerque: University of New Mexico Press, 1940)

LET IT BE SAID here and now that a Texian has no taste for discipline. This I freely admit. But when a man of parts hears the call to
arms, when his mind's eye imagines the sweep of his country's swift
sword of destiny, there can be little choice but to heed the call. And
so, as a servant of God and the state, being twenty years of age,
bold, fearless, and believing the Mexicans to be a feeble, mongrel,
priest-ridden race, I took it upon myself to enlist in Sam Houston's
Army of the Republic. There was also, I admit, some talk of treasure. But then, there's always talk of treasure, the soldier's goad.

I had made a hash of farming, or so my good wife ceaselessly insisted. My name is Ellet Mayfield, and even this she turned against
me with "May-Not-Field," her constant joke to the ladies of her circle. Not content to stay at home and play the fool for her amusement, and desperate to establish some other way of life before next
planting season, my enlistment was, I admit as well, an effort to re-
assert the manhood that God bestowed upon me. I yearned for the
crisp uniform, the polished boot, the sound of the charge arousing
noble hearts. These fine features, I was soon to learn, were not

part of Mr. Houston's army, which was so poorly supplied that we looked more like a band of brigands than a well-sorted-out brigade of soldiers. Still, it was well known that the towns along the lower Río Grande were groaning with the weight of treasure heretofore beyond calculation. The stores of silver alone would make each of us a rich man. But there was more, as any faithful reader of the *Telegraph* and *Texas Register* well knew. Mountains of gold and the landscape a moving black mass of livestock as far as the eye can see. How such a backward race had been able to amass such riches was a question that did not much trouble us.

Our little company of thirty-four volunteers was bivouacked for the night on our way to San Antonio. Not two days before, General Santa Anna had taken the city, but reports of late had him already leaving. Was it cowardice or deep strategy from the Napoleon of the West? For us, it was the first of many confusions. Why did we make haste to San Antonio if he was already halfway to the river? Houston would never give the order to follow. He believed a war on Texas soil was winnable but not on Mexican soil. And yet he had surprised us before this sudden about-face, now sounding the call to arms where before he played the coward's part.

Our lieutenant joined a few of us at our campfire, where we enlivened ourselves with liquor. We talked as if we'd been soldiers for many years, when in fact, we were veterans of a day. He was a fair-featured man whose brown hair, even in the field, was oiled and combed smartly to the side. Indeed, some said he dressed his hair with so much pomade it was proof against any musket ball. And though his jaw was fringed with a trace of beard, there was something womanish about his face, a softness that I took for good breeding. He had the eyes of a poet, focused distantly on other worlds. He did not impress as a man of action. But then, right few of us did.

"Lieutenant," I said, trying to draw out our commander, "how did you busy yourself before enlistment?"

"I had a business concern in Virginia." He seemed about to go on but, instead, stirred the fire with a piece of kindling. Joe let fly a low chuckle, for it was widely known that the lieutenant's "business concern" was a shop for ladies' garments.

The lieutenant seemed a man unsuited to the company of men. It was as if he had started the conversation because it seemed the right thing to do, and now, once into it, he wasn't for certain how to handle himself.

"Mr. McKendrick?" he said, turning the topic to another at our fire.

McKendrick was the constant companion and "business partner" of Joe Sprague, who had made something of a companion of me from the first moment of enlistment. But the business he, McKendrick, and a third man named Blaine conducted was beyond the limits of all honesty. They were partners in cattle rustling. They had prospered by raiding only Mexican herds, which the law was loath to prosecute. In the eyes of some, Joe and his freebooters were contributors to the cause of freedom.

McKendrick was a tall, taciturn man who sat beside Joe like a shadow and whose deep-set eyes went untouched by firelight. He wore mismatched boots and woolen trousers that were too short. His shirt was a former feed sack that gave him cause to scratch, often his only contribution to conversation.

At the lieutenant's question, he turned to face him but without the slightest hint that he would speak. It was a discomfiting gesture. After a moment, the lieutenant turned to me.

"And you, Mr. Mayfield? What was your profession?"

"I was a farmer," I said, "though it was never a life I cared for."

"I should say not!" said Joe Sprague, whose bottle we passed. "Farming's nothing but a fool's game." In contrast to his partners, Joe dressed in plain buckskin and a heavy cotton shirt of indeterminate color. He was a man whose face you forgot the second after seeing it, the round, self-satisfied cheeks, the darting eyes always alert for the main chance. I liked him for a quick-spoken saucebox and someone to help pass the time. War, I was finding, could be powerful boring.

"And you, Joe," I said, "what were you before enlistment?"

Joe looked at me with scornful eyes over the bottle he raised to his mouth. When he finished drinking, he said. "Same as I am now — a young man in search of oppterunity."

Joe passed the lieutenant the bottle, who swirled the brown liquor and held the bottle high to look through it in the moonlight. "And what 'oppterunity' is that?" he said.

"Never you mind what all I done in life. More than you, I'll tell you what. But right now? Right now, I'm fixing to put ole Santy

Anny to the knife." He flashed a hunting knife that glinted awfully
in the firelight. "Mexico's nothing but a nigger republic. I'll take
my knife to the lot of them. And if Sam Houston isn't careful, he'll
feel the nick of my blade, too."

Your knife is your sure stopper of conversation, but the young
lieutenant was unflummoxed. "Is it everyone you're after killing?"
came his mild reproof.

"Them what needs killing will get killing. That's all I'll say."

The lieutenant fell into a dark study of his drinking companions.
"And does that include your superior officers?"

At these words, Blaine, the fifth and last of our party, entered the
clearing with an armload of firewood. He was a small, rough man
of misshapen features, accented by his habit of cutting his own hair
with a hunting knife. Hearing the lieutenant's words, he dashed
the firewood to the ground and, with fearsome aspect, said, "There
ain't no superior officers in the Texian army." He dropped heavily
to the ground beside me and clawed at the air for the bottle.

I plucked at the front of my shirt. Emboldened by drink, I said,
"There's no superior anything in the Texian army."

After a long drink from the bottle, Blaine said, "That's the God's
honest truth of it."

He himself wore an odd assortment of clothing — buckskin trousers with a frilly French shirt whose cuffs he'd tied closed, making it
impossible for him ever to take the shirt off without tearing it from
his back.

Eyeing me with a mixture of suspicion and pride, he said, "Mr.
Sam Houston hisself never had so fine a shirt as this here'n."

"Sir," I said, "you must be wondrously dextrous of hand to tie
such knots in your own sleeve ends."

He brushed the side of his nose with a finger and in a hushed
tone said, "Nor I but the feller what . . . dedicated . . . this here shirt
to me."

To the lieutenant, whose wife had fashioned a personal uniform
for him, complete with a bit of modest brocade at the shoulder, I
said, "I ask you, sir, how we are to feel like proper soldiers wearing
nothing but our own soiled homespun? A soldier's not a soldier
without a proper uniform." At the very least I wanted to smell of
blood and bravery, but the smell of the stable was still overmuch
about me. And my spirits were not kindled by our inglorious mode

of transportation — three buckboards that had also been "dedicated" to the cause. I was beginning to feel badly humbugged by the "grand campaign."

The lieutenant said, "These are hard times, but there will be better days ahead."

Joe stuck his knife in the ground between his legs. "Better times indeed! I hear tell border towns are chock-a-block with silver and gold. I expect we'll soon have ourselves some *fine* uniforms and then some!"

"How is it," I wondered aloud, "that a nation so phlegmatic has been able to store up such riches?"

Joe's eyes narrowed, suspecting betrayal. "All I know is there's gold and glory and more beeves than you can eat in any number of lifetimes. And that's not to mention the headright land we'll get once our services are no longer needed. Boys, there's no way we can lose!"

"You'll follow orders," the lieutenant said as he lowered the bottle. I could see that he had stoppered the mouth of the bottle with his thumb. He wasn't really drinking with us, only making a show of it to help maintain decorum. "Do you hear me, Mr. Sprague?" he said, stiffening. "You'll follow orders. And orders will never be given to sack the Mexican towns of the border."

Joe looked at him long and hard. "Maybe not," he said finally. "But there are orders and then there are orders. And him what gives them today may not give them tomorrow."

The lieutenant launched himself to his feet. "Is that a threat?"

Casually, as if his only aim were to amuse himself by the fireside, Joe pulled the knife out of the ground and flipped it, catching it first by the hilt, then by the blade, then by the hilt again. I have seen carnival performers who have not half his ease with a blade. At last, he looked up at the lieutenant and said, "Only the guilty man would see that as a threat."

The lieutenant, with a grievous tone, said, "What of patriotism?"

"What of it?" Joe replied. "Patriotism is not high on my list. And soon as I make the thing pay, I'll light out for parts unknown."

The lieutenant, stepping forward, said, "You'll follow orders. You hear?"

Just then Joe flung his blade hard at the ground before the lieutenant's feet, where it buried itself to the hilt in the soft dirt.

The lieutenant could not help darting backward, dropping the bottle as he did so. His first step made the next step all the easier, and then the next. Soon the darkness took him to its bosom. He had all the courage of a ten-years' child.

Joe retrieved the bottle, calling after him, "Your Mexican is the boon companion of the bloody Comanch, a feaster on infants. Tell me anything we do to him would be unseemly in the eyes of God or even Sam Damn Houston!"

McKendrick sat stonelike before the fire, but Blaine did not miss the opportunity to catch me by the buttonhole and, raising his close-set eyes to mine, say, "Ain't he the original daredevil? Ellet Mayfield, have we not seen a true man at last?"

From that moment on, the lieutenant kept pretty much to himself, his commands taking the character of suggestions. The whole affair made Joe, whose cohorts gave him a battlefield promotion to general, feel powerful important.

The closer we came to San Antonio, where we would join up with General Somervell's army, the more our spirits grew. At last, Sam Houston had put his cards on the table. The glory of Texas would amass on the frontier and run the alien marauders to ground. With each town, more and more of our brave lads answered the call. They fell in behind our wagons, they clung to the sides of our wagons. They came on their own mounts, some of them plough horses. In one town a judge dismissed murder charges against a woman so he, the lawyers, and the jury could join our great march to glory. We were near about one hundred strong, though we still looked as ragtag as any band of gyps. But the president himself was reported to be moving among his foundling troops, predicting the stern rebuke with which we would confront Santa Anna.

And so it was that we came to the crest of a hill covered with mesquite and prickly pear, within sight of our goal, San Antonio. My first thought on seeing the white stone walls of the city was of the New Jerusalem. It was the largest and most glorious city I had ever laid eyes on. It was not so much a city as it was a brilliant whiteness in an otherwise empty place. But as we made our way down the hill toward town, our eyes revealed Nature's cunning deception. The city was a ruin, its fair white walls peppered with grapeshot and musket balls, its streets strewn with Comanche arrows, its residents too fearful even to find hope in our advance. Like a ghost ship adrift on the desert, San Antonio's five thousand residents had been reduced to a frightened few hundred, and not a white face among them. Even the Alamo itself seemed less like the site of that heroic battle and more a glorified sod house. What was here, I asked myself, that was worth defending?

We made camp with many other volunteers in a pecan grove just south of town, near an abandoned mission one of the townsmen called Concepçion. Our immediate task was to procure supplies — wood, food, whatever we could lay hands on. Joe himself turned up with the copper baptismal font from the mission, which was used to cook soup for the company. For we were a company now, ill fed, ill shod, and lacking in even the very rudiments of military training, but still a company of free men bound to free the Republic from barbarous hands.

While we waited for orders, most of the men kept to camp, either sleeping or consulting the book of prophecies (of which there are fifty-two one-page chapters). Orders were given but few were obeyed. In truth it seemed as though we had been forgotten by Washington-on-the Brazos. Rumor told of some men slipping away into the night, having no stomach for such waiting.

I and some others spent our days gathering pecans from the groves and selling them in town. I scoured the streets for ammunition, communicating my needs quickly to prospective sellers by holding up a musket ball between the thumb and finger of one hand and a coin between the thumb and finger of another. Even the meager pecan profits were more than I could spend. There seemed to be very little powder and lead to be had in the town, and some of the balls I bought were so misshapen that I feared they would fly no faster or truer than a toad, but I was determined to be as well equipped as possible.

In this way, I came to know the people somewhat. I learned a few words of their language and took the odd meal with them now and again, finding them a warm, outgoing people. Now and again I visited a *rancho*, where I was a quick study of Mexican farming practices. Black cattle were the stock of choice in all the places I visited. The need for water — something that had vexed my own efforts at farming — was satisfied with a system by which a hoodwinked mule was made to turn a shaft that connected ingeniously to a configuration of drum and buckets, bringing a constant supply of fresh water from underground to a reservoir on the surface. The mule, being blindfolded, loses all of its mulishness and turns the shaft until another is hitched in its place. In this way, one man may tend a small herd. I must say they were so skilled at disguising their savagery that the Mexicans seemed as civilized as the best of us. In short, I began to suspect they did not deserve the lot they had drawn.

There came a day, after two months, when my hunger was so great that I could not bear to part with the pecans I had collected, not even if it meant I would forgo the purchase of the musket ball that would save my life. There was almost no meat to be had, fresh or jerked. Some men set snares for jacks, but I could not bring myself to eat the stringy-looking creature. Eventually, the men were hard put to find even a jack and subsisted on naught but pecans and acorns. So when General Somervell ordered us to move farther west, to a place where game was more plentiful, not a man grumbled but made the move and gladly.

We ate well for the first time in two months — deer, mostly. And we were grateful for the chance to ease them of their jackets, with which we made breeches that helped us endure the unseasonable cold. There were so many skins lying about that our camp resembled a tanyard. Yet full bellies could not chase the thought each man feared to put into words — that our brave campaign for glory and treasure was now no more than a distant memory. To the naked eye, we were little more than a straggling band of idlers.

At last General Somervell gave the order to march on Laredo. Once on the main road, we were ordered to make a left oblique into the chaparral in order to confuse Santa Anna's spies. But it was we who found ourselves confused, losing our way in the heavy rains and losing whatever good spirits remained to us. We foundered in a place called Atascosa, a post-oak bog and very like hell. The ground was solid enough under a man's tread, but a beast could not move forward by ten feet without sinking to the haunches in the morass. We pulled the animals out of one bog hole — three to five men per beast — only to mire it in another. We found that the muck was so deep that at times we had to roll the animals through it until they could find purchase on drier ground. Men carried the burdens mules once bore. Our progress was measured in feet per hour. After a time some of the animals refused to be moved and had to be shot where they stood, the muck so thick that they could not fall down but stood there in a grisly parody of life, blood streaming down their lowered heads.

Hip-deep in oozing mud, we slaughtered the last of the beeves we had taken from the residents of San Antonio, thinking that it would be easier to carry the meat derived than to drive the beasts through the bog. But soon it was clear that we had merely traded one horror for another.

And yet, despite the horror, I felt strangely content. Atascosa, ludicrous beyond all power of description, was no more than we deserved. I would have been happy without measure at the sight of Joe, his cohorts, and I myself sinking forever into the brutal bog. I had to settle for the sight of their booty dislodged and made worthless, like so many of our supplies, when it was ground into the mud under flailing, desperate hooves.

At length we found more secure footing that allowed for better progress, and we shifted our thoughts to other matters than mud. Hunger, for one. There was little to eat but a small portion of meat, a bit of jerky, and some panola, cornmeal that we would moisten and mold into balls, eating them like apples. Mexican musket balls, we called them. Somehow, there seemed never enough to serve Joe and his cohorts. They were reduced to eating tubers they'd dig up from the roadside, producing so powerful a tumult in their stomachs that, once, Blaine prayed every man who looked in his direction to blow his head off and put him out of his misery.

In another few days, we reached the Nueces, the border to Mexico and a peaceable stream during good weather. The rains, however, had turned it into a torrent so broad that it prompted some men to think we had marched all the way to the Gulf. Somehow our advanced guard had constructed a passable bridge and we were able to cross. There was talk of Mexican soldiers to the west. Owing to our ordeal in Atascosa and the certainty of impending battle, General Somervell authorized a two-day rest, after which we would at last have our try for glory.

Joe Sprague, resourceful to a fault, brought a freshly killed three-hundred-pound bear back to camp, causing shouts of joy to spring from the men. But Joe made plain that he would share not of his bounty, except with his friends, whom I was surprised to find he counted me among. For the rest, dark looks were the fare of the day.

With the help of McKendrick and Blaine, Joe dragged the carcass a little way from our camp and dug a pit in which to cook it. I took part, so as not to offend him, and at the insistence of my hunger, but I feared for my reputation among my comrades.

"Do you not think, Joe," I said, "that we might share our bounty with our fellow soldiers?"

"General Sprague chooses not to share his vittles with no man!" His pick fell viciously to earth. After some time, we finished the pit and dressed out the bear, and soon the smell of roasting meat carried over the camp. Men gathered, but at a distance, like frightened animals around a clearing. With no way to change his mind, I fell to the bear meat at the end of my stick and ate with gusto. Before long our appetites ran aground, our bellies full, our faces raised to the sky.

It was then that we heard the shots, first one, then two more. "Indians!" came a distant cry. And then another musket report split the air. A search party was assembled and it seemed like the grossest injustice that we of the bear feast had to take part. In the general tumult I lost track of Joe, busying myself with the hunt under every bit of brush and in every cat hole. I began to suspect something when I realized my comrades gave all manner of commands but did precious little searching themselves. I returned to camp only to find that Joe had never left. He stood guard over his bear, a smoking musket in his hand. Nearby, a man sat on the ground glowering up at him and clutching a bloody arm. Joe had shot him in the act of stealing our meat. It turned out that the entire alarm was a sham inspired by the taste for bear. Joe had single-handedly turned us into a band of conniving chancers. But later on, when one of our comrades shot another bear, enough to feed the rest of the men, tempers cooled considerable.

On the third morning, having oiled our muskets and made ready to meet the enemy as best we could, we set off in a most cutting north wind toward the town of Laredo. I was now grateful for the foresight that led me to collect upon my own hook upward of fifty musket balls and powder to add to the meager ration we were given. We marched for all the world like a real army. So many men were clad in deerskin breeches that we even seemed to be in uniform. My blood drummed with war fever, and I steadied my nerves by reading the bloody mottoes on my fellow soldiers' caps — Liberty or Death, *Patriae Infelici Fidealis,* No Quarter. For one mad moment I thought of trading some of my ammunition for one of the caps, they made my heart swell so, but sanity prevailed and I kept my mind on the march.

Before long we found ourselves on the outskirts of Laredo, the war storm raging in our blood. The town presented a fair prospect, though not so grand as San Antonio. At the center was a square flanked by the *palacio* and other important buildings surrounded by modest *adoby* houses, some with arched doorways of cunningly fitted stones. As we came closer to the square, we could see people shopping and visiting with each other. Near the center of the square was what looked at first like a wrought-iron throne, but then it became clear to me that it was a shoeshine stand. On one of the two perches sat an elderly gentleman reading the paper and smoking a cigar. Every few moments he'd say a word or two to the man shining his boots, who returned a comment of his own. I had never, for all the world, seen a sight so civilized under the blue sky. I longed to be in the empty seat next to his, trading pleasantries, discussing independence, discussing anything.

It was not until a group of townspeople including the *alcalde* came forward that I realized what was missing from the town. Soldiers. There were no soldiers to greet us, no volleys of musket fire or grape to lay our ears back, no mounted men charging us in the narrow streets. I listened for the rattle of cavalry gear, but heard only bird song. Instead of soldiers, a delegation of townspeople greeted us with cakes and cries of *"Buenos hombres! Buenos Americanos!"* It was as if we were arriving at a party where we were the guests of honor. They gave us the run of town, promising to bring to our camp all the supplies on the long list presented to them.

In consideration of civility, we withdrew to a position outside town, where we made camp and waited for the supplies, but the wait was in vain. After many hours, the *alcalde,* which I understood to be the mayor, brought only a dozen mangy beeves, a few dirty hats, and blankets not thick enough to warm a gnat.

General Joe's fury knew no limit. He paraded up and down the camp, rousing his fellow soldiers to bloody deeds. "Is this what we come all this way for?" Joe cried, his knife flashing. "For a few skinny beeves and a sack of mite-infested flour? The pumpkin-colored heathen has proved hisself a coward and a liar! His inkwitty knows no bounds!"

"It's true, Joe," I reasoned. "These are poor people. I know. I have been inside their homes." More than once, of an evening, I was a guest at the tables of various San Antonio families. And later, the amiable ladies of the house would beguile the heavy hours by singing and playing upon the guitar. And sometimes there was dancing. I am not much for the step-and-hitch, but I could not resist the lightsome ladies, who taught me the mysteries of their quadrilles and contradances, their waltzes and gallopades being too much for my unsophisticated toes.

Joe looked at me as though I had admitted to having the smallpox. He addressed the men and me at once. "Little Ellet among the greasers! What's next? Will you forgo suspenders and tie up your pantaloons with a red bandanna?"

Men laughed, casting me scornful looks.

"I only meant these poor people have —"

"These *poor* people gone and betrayed us with a *show* of kindness, hoping to take the heart out of our blood lust. But we will teach them *and* their friends a thing or two about Texas." A cheer went up among the men, and, fearful of the fire in their eyes, I cried out, "Do, men, for God's sake, remember yourselves!"

But the men had eyes and ears only for Joe's windy gasconnade. "And now they act like they ain't sitting on King Midas's gold, going so far as to wear these ragged clothes and live in these mud huts, all to throw us off the scent! My nose tells me there's gold here, boys! And I for one aim to take my share! We were not put afoot the earth to suffer such indiggities. Are you with me?"

Men cheered, desperate men, and began to gather around Joe. Somehow they had found reason in his words, or a mirror for their desperation. They followed him into town. I followed, if only to talk sense into Joe. I should have known better. There was talk of treasure, of gold doubloons. Even a sudden shower of rain could not dampen their enthusiasm. When we came to town, the men split off into small gangs. Soon I could hear the sound of breaking glass and frightful laughter.

This time, of course, the streets were empty and the houses were closed up tight against us. No doubt the townsfolk had had enough of armies. The only living thing we saw was an old burro, the fur gone white around his eyes, giving him a look of permanent surprise.

"Look at that," Joe said, his face streaming rain. "Too stupid to get in out of the rain."

"Joe," I said, gesturing at our sorry band, which was comprised of McKendrick, Blaine, and myself, "the same might be said of us."

He whipped the steaming rain away from his face. "Watch how a real man takes destiny by the reins!" He stalked through the flooding street to the nearest house of mud-stained *adoby* and banged on the heavy plank door. Receiving no satisfaction, he banged again, louder.

Words of encouragement came from soldiers passing in the street. "Go to it, General Joe!"

Before we knew it, the frenzy was upon Joe and he began charging the door, using his shoulder as a battering ram. Soldiers watching, approving his brave display, battered their way into other homes. The sounds of destruction filled the streets. Joe's two friends gave him a hand, as if housebreaking were a talent they shared, and soon the door was torn from its hinges, and we stood in the dark interior of what appeared to be an uninhabited house.

The whitewashed walls contained prominent niches filled with carved figures in various postures of holy rapture.

"Ho!" said Blaine, taking up a dark-skinned figurine, "a nigger doll for priests!" He began to dance it around the room, upending small tables. When the joke was cold, he dashed the relic to the floor, then took it upon himself to knock all the relics out of their niches, including the one they called The Lady, whose golden halo was the only gold to be found among these poor people.

Joe peeled off his soaked shirt and headed for the cook room at the back of the house, intent on a real meal. When Blaine tired of destruction, he and McKendrick began to collect all objects of value. They found beaded necklaces, a tin of tobacco, a dress in mid-repair, and a cross embedded with small silver medallions.

"Sacrilege," Blaine said of the medallions, using a corner of the cross to knock the glass out of a silver frame.

"Do we not make fine soldiers, men, fine sons of the Republic?" I said, trying to josh them out of their appetite for looting, but my words only seemed to spur them on. Their arms were full of the goods of the house, and I soon realized I had been a fool to think all they wanted was a dry roof over their heads, a fool to think anything I said or did ought matter to them.

Joe came back into the room nearly knocking his head on the low arch of the doorway. He held a coffeepot in his hand. "Feel that," he said, pressing the pot to the side of Blaine's face.

"Ye gods!" Blaine yelled.

"There, see?" Joe said. "It's not true what they say, that you're as dumb as a cowpie!"

"Why'd you want to go and do that for?" said Blaine, rubbing his burned cheek.

Joe turned to McKendrick, addressing him with his honorary title. "Captain? Would you care to educate him?"

McKendrick, true to form, just stood there staring blankly back at him.

"Hot coffee," Joe said, "means people. People who had no time to clear out when we came a-calling." He tossed the pot over his shoulder, its contents crashing to the floor, and began to search the rooms with alacrity. McKendrick and Blaine fell in.

"To what end, Joe?" I said, following from room to room. But the house was small and the search soon ended. My relief knew no bounds. I did not know what Joe was planning, but I knew it could not be for the benefit of those whose house we had upended.

Then Joe's eyes fell on the carpet at the center of the room. It lay askew, as if hastily twitched into place. With the toe of his boot, he drew it aside, revealing a door set flush in the floor. Joe's eyes lit as he held a finger to his lips and leaned down to the inlaid handle, jerking it with sudden force to reveal, in the shadowy interior as narrow as a grave, a woman lying stiffly, her eyes closed tight, the only sign of life being the fact that she was all atremble with fear. Joe grabbed her harshly by the waist. She made no sound as he hauled her up into the room and dropped her to the floor.

She rolled over quickly onto her stomach and curled into a ball, her eyes still clenched tight, but not tight enough to prevent tears from dampening her cheeks.

"Look at them hams," McKendrick said quietly, the only words I had ever heard him say.

"She's Mex," Blaine added.

"She's mine," said Joe, quickly undoing his buckle and dropping his trousers.

"Joe!" I cried, but the beastly fire was strong in him, and my appeal had no effect. He began to paw at the woman's white cotton dress, tearing at it. I laid hands on him but was pulled back by McKendrick or Blaine. I shook free and flew at Joe again, this time falling on him and on the woman, who still made no sound. She might have been a piece of furniture. Joe rolled me off and hauled me to my feet by the collar, his knife in his hand. In a flash, the tip of his blade was inside the bone of my jaw. When it slid inside my skin, I could not keep from shivering.

"My friend," he said, "you shall wait your turn like a good boy."

"Don't do this, Joe," said I through clenched teeth. And though it exacerbated my wound to do so, I could not help but speak again. "We have not marched these long miles and endured such privations to be reduced to this."

"You may not, my good little Ellet, but this is exactly what I come for."

Joe gave the knife a quarter turn, and I felt a warm finger of blood move down my neck. "But are we not men of honor?"

At this, McKendrick and Blaine laughed heartily. I tried to pull my jaw free of Joe's blade, but his cohorts had me by the hair.

"And if you interfere," Joe went on calmly, "I shall cut her from groin to gullet, and you to follow."

At that, McKendrick and Blaine threw me toward the door. I righted myself and prepared for another assault, but Joe tossed his knife to Blaine and turned to the woman, making himself ready like a beast in rut. He turned her and roughly pulled apart her legs, instructing McKendrick and Blaine to plant a boot on each ankle. They took to the task as if they had apprenticed in evil.

I moved toward them, but McKendrick pointed the knife at her and then at me.

"Think, men," I said, my voice filled with tears. "Think of the fires of hell!"

Joe turned to me. His face was not a face. "I already been," he said and then dropped to his knees to perform the devil's work.

I could not stay. I could not go. I could not watch. I cried out for help, but the woman's hands covered her face, and she could not know what help I meant to bring. I threw myself into the rainy street, intent on finding a sheriff, an officer, someone. But there was no one in the street save more marauders and the stunned burro. I ran from house to house shaking the latches, rattling the windows, and pounding on the planks, but no one would answer me. In the distance, I heard the muffled sound of musket fire. I stopped a soldier who came careening out of a shop, a sack of tobacco held in his arms like a baby. Words would not give shape to what I had seen.

"Terrible!" I cried. "A terrible thing!"

"Yeah," the soldier said, eyes glinting with long withheld joy. "I guess we seen the elephant now!"

I stood in the driving rain, the dumbest of brutes. At length, the woman's tormentors came out into the street, their arms loaded with the goods of the house. I ran to them and pushed past them roughly, as if any show of violence now could undo the horror within. Inside, the woman lay on her side again. Her eyes were open and she did not tremble, but merely stared at the floor before her face. I knelt to give what comfort I could.

"No," she said in a dull voice, a voice beyond pain, "No mas."

I recoiled, as if the point of Joe's blade had come to my throat again, and staggered out into the driving rain. My cohorts had made their way a little down the street in the direction of camp but turned when I came out.

"You get you some after all?" Blaine called.

Then Joe added, "Sure hope we left a little bloom on the rose!"

The three men laughed and headed down the road, bearing the proceeds of their iniquity, looking for all the world like refugees being driven from their homes. I followed at some distance, sick at heart, eyes burning, the wound in my neck swollen and stinging. I felt every bit as guilty as they should have felt.

Back at camp, it was clear that Joe and his friends were not alone in their misdeeds. What they did, many had done. Men staggered painfully into camp, their backs heaped high with loot — coats, trousers, blankets, nightclothes, ladies' dresses and undergarments, even baby clothes. They drove mules stacked high with saddles, furniture, cookpots, and embroidered pillows. So overburdened were the mules that they could barely set one foot in front of the other. Mountains of loot stood everywhere, a thieves' market. To whom could I report their behavior? There was no law, and the eyes of God were closed to this infamy.

Joe and his cohorts went straight to their hidden cache of bear meat, pulling off the clever covering of mesquite branches and brush. Not clever enough, it seemed. They uncovered charred hunks of glistening, dripping meat. It seems the men who stayed in camp had found Joe's private store and unburdened their bladders upon it, every man contributing his share like a pack of amiable hounds.

Joe cried out and stamped the ground and kicked at his pile of booty while his henchmen stared fiercely at their former comrades. The men stared back with mild amusement, but already the joke was stale and they were ready to move on to some new enormity. Joe paced back and forth in front of them, filling every ear with the story of his suffering and lamenting the lack of honor among his fellow soldiers.

"A man sacrifices for his country, and for what? I hereby take my bloody vow never to follow another order and to stay in Damn Houston's army only long enough to get my share of treasure."

While he ranted, McKendrick and Blaine stood by his side, nodding sagely. But I could listen no longer, my mind in other ways intent.

The lieutenant, passing, caught my eye. "Leave them to heaven," he said.

Without a word, I took myself some distance apart and stood in the driving rain as I watched their shameful tableau. I felt dreadful small. I had shaken the yoke of the plough, only to take on the yoke of a burden I could never shake. While shameful men did shameful deeds, I stood by. And now the eyes of heaven would be forever turned away from me.

That night, under cover of midnight darkness, I smote them with my Barlow knife. I slew them, first one then the other, as each man lay sleeping, delivering a sharp blow to their throats to prevent any cries of alarm. I do not know whether I did the right thing or merely made myself a part of the bad. When it was finished, I made my escape through the chaparral and prickly pear with naught but the North Star to guide me.

Pinwheel

FROM *Murder at the Racetrack*

EVERY NIGHT THAT JUNE, from my cell window at Orofino, I watched the fireworks color-burn the midnight sky over the Indian reservation across the road. The colors lit up fields and sometimes the sparks would drift to earth and the old horses the Indians kept would scatter, faster than you would think they were capable of. Speed left from races they never ran, I told myself. I knew horses when I was a kid near Saratoga, in upstate New York. Whole worlds had happened since then. Those horses and fireworks were my only friends at the beginning of that summer.

I wasn't in the race to win anymore. I'd fallen on some hard times in eastern Washington and a gang that was a branch of the Posse made a deal with me. They'd pay me to finish off another man's time in Idaho. I don't know how they rigged it up, who they paid off. But one day they brought me into a hospital room in Spokane and the deputies that shackled me and took me to Orofino called me by a different name. I was inside under a new name and eight years stood between me and the door.

The Idaho State Correctional Facility at Orofino was an old brick campus, housing twice as many men as it was built for. It was a mixed classification facility, which is the worst, because the killers are in with the guys who forgot a child support payment. The guys doing a decade don't look very kindly on the guy who gets to go home in three months. I was a maximum classification at that time, because the guy I was pretending to be had a record that began in the womb.

The guards came for me early one morning and cuffed me and shackled me for transport. I knew it couldn't be good. Someone had filed a writ with the Federal Circuit Court and the federal judge had ordered that I be brought to his temporary chambers, in Boise. They were being forced to produce me, except I wasn't anyone — I wasn't the man they wanted incarcerated and I certainly wasn't going to tell anyone I was working for the Posse. In my own mind, they may as well have been driving a mute to Boise. We passed south through the beautiful Idaho mountains and trees and blue sky. The deputies driving me didn't say a word, just stopped once for coffee and then drove on. We drove into the streets and city of Boise. I slept on a bench overnight in a holding cell and they brought me upstairs into chambers in the morning.

The judge was in robes and seated behind a large desk, with an older woman stenographer in front of the desk. My brother and an Asian man, both impeccably dressed in gray suits, stood in the back of the room. The judge addressed me.

"The court has been made aware of some unusual circumstances surrounding your case." He pointed at my brother and the Asian man. I nodded and the judge continued. "We're convinced . . . the court has been convinced . . ." He paused. "The court is convinced that a sealed record and immediate release is the only way you'll be alive at the end of the week. The state of Idaho didn't seem inclined to let you go — so the appeal was passed up to me."

I didn't say anything. The court bailiff came over and unlocked my cuffs and shackles. I rubbed my wrists.

The judge stood. "I'm instructing one of my marshals to escort you to the Nevada border so we don't have a problem. I can't help you if you reenter this state. And you're on your own with other problems — but we won't hold you here as a stationary target." He handed me some paperwork. "You're free to go, as long as you're leaving the state."

I looked at my brother, who spoke to the judge. "He'll ride with us to Nevada, Your Honor."

"Keep your head down," the judge said. He looked directly at me. "And watch behind you."

My brother shook hands with me, but we didn't say anything, not a word. He drove the new sedan behind the marshal's car, with Mr. Osaka in the back and me in the passenger's seat. It was a long ride, but finally we saw a sign for the Nevada state line. We crossed it and the marshal pulled a U-turn and headed north, back into Idaho.

Mr. Osaka mumbled something and my brother spoke to me.

"I'm sorry we couldn't warn you, but we had a heck of a time finding you. You got yourself in pretty deep."

"What's going on?" I asked.

My brother nodded as he drove. "We'd been looking for you, to come help with Mr. Osaka's operation. In looking for you, we found out that the man you went as, the real man, just got arrested in Montana. It was only a matter of time before the Posse tried to get to you on the inside."

Mr. Osaka mumbled to my brother.

"What'd he say?" I said.

"Mr. Osaka doesn't speak," my brother said. "He understands English perfectly well and he probably speaks it, although I've never heard him. I speak for him. Always, for the past five years. He talks in a kind of yakuza dialect — he and I speak it to each other and that's it. Nobody else."

"Handy," I said. I hadn't seen my brother much at the beginning of the last decade and not at all in the past five years, but years didn't come between us. I just figured he had his own job going on, somewhere, and when my plans started to fail, I didn't want to bring him down with me. He was a couple years younger than me and maybe I felt responsible. He'd gotten bigger since I'd seen him last.

"Do you want to work for Mr. Osaka?" my brother asked.

"What are we doing?" I said.

"Watching whales," my brother said. And as we drove, he detailed the operation to me. In the end, I agreed.

Whales are a select group of Japanese businessmen, probably only two hundred worldwide, who come to the United States to gamble. They're called whales because they bet huge — they're up seven million, they're down thirty million. If one of these guys walks into a small casino on a good night, he can bankrupt the place, or lose enough to let the casino build another club and a hotel.

Whales like bets that other gamblers can't get their hands on and sometimes it can be exotic — betting on street fights, illegal car racing. But the yakuza control the horse racing and that means that the yakuza can sometimes control the whales.

Mr. Osaka bought seven hundred acres of land outside Reno, flattened it all out, put in a private horseracing track and was getting set to lay in a private airfield when some of his contractors thought they'd muscle him for more money. Those contractors are gone and now my brother and I are in charge of the operation.

A private racetrack, with all the barns and stables. The whales own stuff all over the world and pretty soon, the private jets are coming in, with the stallions and racehorses the whales have accumulated. A horseman's field of dreams. We've got the compound gated off and the whales pull up, with their limos and their drivers and their party girls. Every morning the races start at eleven and they walk around, drinking, looking at the horses.

Mr. Osaka has only two betting windows open, run by Asian men the same as him. Tattoos on their hands, one guy with a Japanese character right on his throat. These are the honest men, bound to count the money, to take the verbal bets and always pay. No slips, no tickets. These guys are taking bets in the hundreds of thousands and never sweating.

Mr. Osaka walks the compound with us and mumbles to my brother as we pass the honest men by the bet windows.

"As children, they are not taught about wanting. Then, when they learn about money, they are taught it is filthy. The combination makes them honest," my brother translates.

The favorite bet for the whales is the pinwheel. The pinwheel lets the whale run his horse on Mr. Osaka's track, but bet against other horses running at other tracks that come in by satellite feed. Your horse can finish second here but if you've matched it up against the right combo, say from Saratoga, or Pimlico, or Yonkers, you can double or triple your take. Or you can throw your money in a bigger hole. Money is green paper, to these people. They give more money to the party girls to keep them quiet than I've ever earned in my life. But that ended, too, once I got on Mr. Osaka's payroll.

The horses thundered around the track every day, a different group. Sired by names you'd recognize. The track stayed hard for the rest of the summer and there were winners — Jack Rabbit Fast, Sun Comet, the Last Laugh. Some of the names didn't translate into English.

One morning, my brother and I had to take pistols out to the building where the stable hands slept and escort someone to the gate. We came back by the track and Mr. Osaka stood at the rail, watching the horses take their morning exercise. He mumbled and my brother spoke.

"Do you know the secret of a fast horse?" my brother translated.

"No," I said.

Mr. Osaka mumbled at length and my brother fed me bits and pieces.

"When horses run fast, all four feet leave the ground. They fly. They like to fly. It's their fantasy. But they have to push themselves back down to the ground, so their hooves can touch the track again. So when you look at a horse, or watch him in a race, see the look on his face and the jockey's. If they like to fly, that is no good. They must like to push themselves back to ground, to run."

"Do you bet?" I asked.

Mr. Osaka mumbled. My brother spoke.

"I swore a vow in the beginning never to bet on horses and I have kept that vow. Once, a horse had to be shot in front of me and my father told me, You can see someone's life in the pattern of their death blood. The horse's blood stopped at my feet and it was a sign to me that I should not bet on horses."

I nodded. Mr. Osaka moved his lips and my brother continued.

"If you were shot right now, and we saw your death blood, where would it go?"

I looked at the ground, which sloped slightly onto the track, and Mr. Osaka followed my gaze.

My brother finished. "Stay close to horses then, maybe that is your life."

We watched Mr. Osaka walk back to the white clubhouse and he disappeared inside.

They slammed out of the starting gates all summer and soon my brother and I had to make a bank trip to Reno. We didn't go to a bank. It was just a house on the outskirts of the city; it looked like a regular white and blue ranch-style. We put the money in the suitcase on the kitchen table and left, as we'd been told to do by Mr. Osaka. I think I saw the blue sedan following us that day, but I'm not sure. We went to the house later in the week, twice, and the second time, I'm sure I saw it. My brother saw it, too.

We had dropped the money off an hour before and were a mile away from the racetrack when the blue sedan pulled in front of us and cut us off. I knew as soon as they got out of the car they were cops. Two cops, undercover. My brother opened the passenger-side door and ran up over the bank, as they pulled their guns. I slammed them both out of the way with my car and took off. There were shots behind me, and as I looked in the rearview mirror, my brother was getting into the blue sedan, following me.

You've never seen so many people in such a hurry from anything. Mexican stable boys running into the desert, limos pulling around with half-dressed women, and the whales, sunglasses falling off, waving for them to hurry. Planes taking off. My brother watched the gate. Running an illegal racetrack, illegal gambling operation, weapons, now shot cops. We needed to leave.

A fire started near the horse barn. I was still looking for Mr. Osaka, but he was nowhere. There was a bulldozer next to the airfield, left from the contractors. I started it, bulldozed the fence down, got off the rig and opened the stall doors as the flames licked the wood. The horses took off across the field, into the heat. I watched them, shining, maybe three hundred million dollars of property on hooves, running like they wanted to. The owners wouldn't be happy, but I had done it. My brother and I climbed into a new truck and cut the corner of Idaho, before slipping into Montana and up into Canada. We took our pay with us, nothing more — maybe we hoped that honorable thing would calm Mr. Osaka. The yakuza were like an ocean, deep and violent, and I knew and my brother knew we would live small lives from now on. If we wanted to live life at all.

It was Saratoga that finally called us back. We were there in August on a Sunday, walked down Main Street, bought a racing paper, and then made our way over to the track. Years had passed, we had different names, and we'd just done a big deal in Manhattan. One stop at the track before returning to north of the border. We settled in, examined the sheet with golf pencils and went to the window.

In the third race, we were by the clubhouse rail. There was a tremendous field coming around; the crowd was cheering. It was close. The brown blur of the pack slammed past us to the finish.

A young Asian boy stood in front of us. He'd come out of the crowd; I hadn't seen him till now. He mumbled to my brother and I almost felt bullets piercing my back. Nothing happened. My brother spoke.

"Mr. Osaka says we did the right thing and that we should look for a particular horse in the next race."

The boy bowed and walked into the clubhouse crowd. Sweat ran down my ribs. My brother held up the racing sheet and I looked at it.

It was the maiden race for Komodo Dragon, blinders on, Lasix, and we checked the tote board. Leading off at 85–1. None of the other names could be it. We went to the window and put it all, over seven thousand dollars — that was the lucky limit we'd agreed to bet — on Komodo Dragon. On the nose.

They brought the horses into the starting gate and *bang, ring,* they're off. Komodo Dragon is at the back of the pack and as they come around the first turn, it can't be. Komodo Dragon is dead last and drifting to the outside. Then it starts. Komodo Dragon passes one, passes two, passes Two-Time Loser, passes Long Johnny. Now it's Komodo Dragon on the outside and the horse starts to fly, to push itself back to the ground, to fly, to push, passing as though the other horses are standing still. You can feel it in the ground and now they're headed for the final turn, it's Komodo Dragon and Rummy, the favorite, Komodo Dragon, Rummy, and the final stretch, Komodo Dragon is flying and pushing and the whip gets him back down on the ground, Komodo Dragon is ahead and farther, by a length, Komodo Dragon.

We're walking up to the window with the ticket and we're not saying anything. But it's there in my head and as soon as we're in the car, safe, moving, back in our own race, we'll talk about it. Beautiful houses in Vancouver and the chance to start over again, a little safer. To run under another name, in a different city, with better chances, another day.

Contributors' Notes
Other Distinguished Mystery Stories
of 2006

Contributors' Notes

Chris Adrian is a pediatrician and divinity student in Boston. *McSweeney's* published his second novel, *The Children's Hospital*, last year, and Farrar Straus & Giroux will bring out a collection of stories called *Why Antichrist?* in May of 2008.

▪ I wrote this story back in 1996, not very long after my brother died, and at the same time that I was working on a rather goofy master's thesis about conjoined twins. As part of the research for the thesis I read interviews with some survivors of separation surgeries in which one twin had died. It was not surprising to read that the survivors all missed their siblings, even though they had been separated as toddlers or infants and did not remember them very clearly. And one person in particular described his life as being shaped more than anything by the subsequent absence of his twin.

At about the same time I had a terrible nightmare in which I was Karen Black being chased around by that little fetish doll from *Trilogy of Terror* (except it had scraggly blond hair instead of scraggly black hair, and was wearing a fancy dress). And somehow the bad dream and the sad testimony became the inspiration for an odd story.

Robert Andrews is a former Green Beret and CIA officer whose first four novels dealt with the spy business. His last three novels, however (Marian Wood, G.P. Putnam's Sons), feature homicide detective Frank Kearney and José Phelps. Andrews and his wife BJ live in Washington, D.C.

▪ I was noodling around, thinking about a plot for a fifth spy novel, when Chuck and I had lunch. Chuck was one of the *Washington Post's* best investigative reporters. An acolyte of Bob Woodward, Chuck specialized in prying the tops off well-guarded cans of worms Washington's political elite hoped to hide from their constituents.

"Story on the wire," Chuck tells me one day at Stoney's. "Hit-run kills a Catholic priest in Boston. He's got eighty thousand bucks . . . cash . . . in shoeboxes in his closet."

Chuck smiled. "They trace it to a Brinks holdup."

The Soviet Union had gone belly-up almost ten years before. And terrorists hadn't yet driven into the Trade Center. BJ and I had just moved into D.C. from a quiet Arlington, Virginia, neighborhood. That year, the district earned the honor of becoming the nation's murder capital.

And so my first crime novel, *A Murder of Honor:* A drive-by shooting, and Father Robert J. O'Brien sprawls dead on Pennsylvania Avenue. The more detectives Kearney and Phelps work the case, the more fingers point to the good priest's involvement in a nasty drug operation. At the same time, more comes out that paints O'Brien as a man of honor.

Martha Mitchell, wife of Nixon's attorney general, described Washington as "too small to be a state, too big to be an insane asylum." In writing *A Murder of Honor* and its sequels, I realized that Washington's swamp-fever looniness offered more permutations for intrigue and mischief than did international espionage.

And so Kearney and Phelps show up in the draft of the fourth D.C. cop novel: On the same morning that an advertising executive kills himself in the upper-class Northwest, a student in ragged Anacostia murders a beloved high-school teacher. And there's a connection . . . some three hundred pages from now.

Back to "Solomon's Alley": Kearney and Phelps have cameos. But the protagonist is Solomon, who tends to his Georgetown alley and argues with his Voices.

Peter Blauner is the author of six novels, including *Slow Motion Riot,* which won the 1992 Edgar Award for best first novel of the year, and *The Intruder,* a *New York Times* bestseller as well as an international bestseller. His most recent novel is *Slipping into Darkness.* He lives in Brooklyn, New York, with his wife, author Peg Tyre, and their two children.

▪ I have only one firm rule about writing: Don't do it about the kids. Any so-called grownups I run into are fair game; I tell them I'm a writer and they take their chances when they talk to me. Children don't have that choice. Still, "Going, Going, Gone" might be an indirect tribute to the fact that they sometimes understand the world around them better than the adults who are supposed to be looking after them. The story was also intended as an homage to Morris Engel's wonderful 1953 film, *Little Fugitive* — a seminal influence on New Wave directors like François Truffaut and John Cassavetes. Not that many people have seen it, though it used to pop up occasionally on the late, late movie back in the sixties and seventies. It's about a little kid who runs away to Coney Island after he thinks he's killed his older brother. Though my story obviously goes in a different direction, it's a debt I've been meaning to make good on. So I'm glad for the opportunity to settle up here.

Lawrence Block is a devout New Yorker and enthusiastic world traveler. He has won Life Achievement awards from writers' organizations here and abroad, and characterizes them as "a way for your colleagues to tell you that your future lies largely in the past." Like Keller, he's a passionate philatelist; unlike any of his heroes, he's an apparently deranged participant in marathons and ultramarathons.

• Keller first saw the light of day in a short story, and the three books about him (*Hit Man, Hit List,* and *Hit Parade*) are either short-story collections or episodic novels, as you prefer. The guy seems to be a true guilty pleasure for readers, who tell me they don't want to like him, but they can't help themselves. This particular story came about because an editor wanted something for a collection of basketball stories; I told him I couldn't think of anything, and then, curiously, I thought of something.

John Bond is a raconteur living in Dania Beach, Florida. A licensed pilot and boat captain, he has been a lawyer, realtor, adjunct professor of journalism and creative writing, tour group leader, scuba instructor, columnist, newspaper editor, political campaign manager, lobbyist, developer, and more. He is the coauthor (with Roy Cooke) of six books about poker, including 2007's *Home Poker Handbook.* His day job is to love his wife, Jeannie, who is too good for him.

• I'm still trying to explain to both my wife and mother why I gave up practicing law to write and play poker. And that poker really isn't gambling. Some fifteen years later they remain skeptical.

I am a true newbie in the short-story world. "T-bird," from the anthology *Miami Noir,* is not only my first published fiction, it is the first short story I have ever submitted anywhere. I have some 5,000 pages of unfinished novels, failed screenplays, character sketches, and plot notes. But no short stories.

I got lucky when I quit lawyering that Florida International University's Creative Writing Program was just a few miles from my home. It's a small program counting among its alumni the likes of Dennis Lehane and Barbara Packer, and lesser-known but stellar writers like Vicki Hendricks, Sandra Rodriguez Barron, and Christine Kling. Thanks eternally to the FIU faculty: Les Sandiford (*Miami Noir* editor), John Dufresne (also represented in this anthology), Lynne Barrett (Edgar winner), Campbell McGrath (Guggenheim genius grant winner), and Jim Hall (kick-ass thriller writer) for molding me into something of a writer. To the extent my work has any merit I owe it to them; to the extent I suck that's my own damn fault.

Writing a short story, especially one with defined themes (Miami and Noir) is something like writing a sonnet. Form can dictate content, force you to be creative in ways you would not normally have considered. When I think Noir, I think night, I think betrayal, I think lust trampling over reason. My femme fatale Rebel is surnamed O'Shaunessy, a tip of the hat to Hammett's *Maltese Falcon*, which for me epitomizes Noir. And then there's the delightful irony of setting darkness amid the palms and banyans in the sun-dappled tropical paradise, perfected by the editor of this collection, Carl Hiaasen. The form indeed dictated much of the story.

I used to run a game like McKool's — the statute of limitations has run, so I can admit it. I loved how the day and night worlds collided there, the incredible variety of people one meets at the poker table. It seemed a suitable place to set something dark. It was there I met a girl who ran a scam not unlike that described in the story, though rather than die at the end she hit pay dirt.

My FIU mentors say I should take another shot at the short story. As their advice so far has been nothing but dead-on right, I may just do that.

James Lee Burke was born in 1936 in Houston, Texas, and grew up on the Louisiana-Texas coast. He attended Southwestern Louisiana Institute (now called the University of Louisiana at Lafayette) and later the University of Missouri at Columbia, where he received a B.A. and an M.A. in English literature.

Over the years he has published twenty-five novels and one collection of short stories. The stories have appeared in the *Atlantic Monthly, The Best American Short Stories, New Stories from the South,* the *Southern Review, Antioch Review,* and *Kenyon Review.* His novels *Heaven's Prisoners* and *Two for Texas* were adapted as motion pictures.

Burke's work has received two Edgar Awards for best crime novel of the year. He is also a Breadloaf fellow and a Guggenheim fellow and has been a recipient of an NEA grant. He and his wife of forty-six years, Pearl Burke, have four children and divide their time between Missoula, Montana, and New Iberia, Louisiana.

▪ "A Season of Regret" was my literary attempt to show that a good man remains in conflict with the world regardless of the era in which he lives. The story is naturalistic in theme and indicates that criminals, political and otherwise, usually find banners and uniforms to hide behind. Albert Hollister carries a stone bruise in the soul, one that was visited upon him because of his humanity. Ultimately he is set free from the past, but in ways he will never be able to share with others.

His tragedy becomes ours. The wisdom he acquires cannot be passed on. This may seem a dismal thought, but I suspect that's just the way it is.

John Dufresne is the author of three novels, two collections of stories, a book on fiction writing, and the forthcoming novel *Requiem, Mass.* He lives in South Florida.

▪ I decided to write about the direst crime I could imagine. A man kills his children. His wife and children. My job, then, was to try to figure out how and why a person would or could commit such an unspeakable act. I didn't want to spend all my time in the murderer's head, so I invented my hero, a man with the same interest in the crime as I had. And then the murderer killed his parents. What now? I was in St. Petersburg, Russia, while I was writing the story. My friend David Beaty was also in St. Petersburg and was also writing a story for the same anthology, *Miami Noir.* We wrote separately during the day, got together at night over vodka and shashlyk, or vodka and blinis, or vodka and vodka, and read our stories to each other. We walked in the steps of Raskolnikov, along the Gribodeva canal through Sennaya Ploschad, up to his apartment, and on to the unfortunate moneylenders' apartment. We wrote some more. We read some more. And in this entertaining way, we helped each other tell the stories of some disturbed people possessed by demons. As it were.

Louise Erdrich, the critically acclaimed Native American writer, has written such best-selling novels as *The Antelope Wife, Love Medicine, The Beet Queen,* and *The Bingo Palace.* She also collaborated on *The Crown of Columbus* with Michael Dorris, her late husband.

▪ Gleason's description matches a former boyfriend of one of my teenage daughters. I imagined that he was just the sort of person whose meek and soulful demeanor masks his dark tendencies. Fictionalizing him helped give a shape to my paranoia, but as far as I know he went on to be a decent citizen.

Jim Fusilli is the author of four novels, including *Hard, Hard City,* which was named Best Novel of 2004 by *Mystery Ink* magazine. A journalist and critic, Jim writes about rock and pop music for the *Wall Street Journal,* and his reviews and essays have appeared in the *New York Times Magazine,* the *Los Angeles Times,* the *Boston Globe,* and on National Public Radio's *All Things Considered.* His *Pet Sounds,* a highly personal look at Brian Wilson and the classic Beach Boys album, was published in 2005.

▪ My private-eye novels are written in the first person, set largely in the present New York City, and revolve around contemporary social issues. "Chellini's Solution" is one of several short stories I wrote recently to open my fiction writing style. It's set in 1953 in a small town in New Jersey, and it's a third-person narrative. The protagonist isn't a robust private investigator out to right wrongs. He's quiet and deeply felt, an immigrant seemingly out of step here, and he's driven to take action in defense of his family.

In the end, "Chellini's Solution" wasn't a radical deviation from what I had been doing — I can't seem to write about anything but families on the verge of collapse — but it did allow me to see a new way to tell my stories. It was anchored in my experiences: I was born in Hoboken, New Jersey, in 1953, and Chellini is based on my grandfather, a barger who had a one-eyed bulldog named Mickey. Thinking of him infused the story with the sentimentality it needed. I love to write dialogue in that sort of hyperventilated half-English, half-Italian dialect I used to hear as a kid. Those voices, and Chellini's walk, reconnected me to my childhood, and that's where I found that unadorned purposefulness that's at the heart of Chellini's character.

William Gay's most recent novel, *Twilight*, was published in the fall of 2006. He is the author of two other novels and a collection of stories. He lives in rural Tennessee, where he is at work on a novel.

▪ A friend of mine who'd lost someone was talking to me about the difficulty he was having dealing with loss. This got me thinking about the depth and nature of grief. Around the same time I saw a documentary about crystal meth. These two elements fused into The Jeepster's adventures in the drug trade.

Robert Knightly was born in Greenpoint, Brooklyn, in 1940. He's never resided outside New York City except for two years in the army. He was institutionalized at an early age: Catholic schools, the army, then the New York City Police Department in 1967. He worked in Brooklyn and Manhattan precincts as patrol officer and sergeant for most of the next twenty years. Having earned a law degree from Fordham University Law School at night, he joined the Legal Aid Society of New York in 1989 as a criminal defense lawyer, where he remains. In 2002, Aaron Spelling-TV Productions bought his script for an NBC pilot. He published his first short story in *Brooklyn Noir* in 2004 and is editor of *Queens Noir*, due from Akashic Books in 2007.

▪ "Take the Man's Pay" came from my twenty years of watching NYPD detectives ply their trade. Every partner I had made detective eventually. (Me? I was not ruthless or pushy enough, I guess. They gave me lieutenant instead.) There are no better interrogators than NYPD detectives (not even Jack Bauer's torturers on *24*). I've verified this fact with my clients/defendants. No matter how hardened the "perp," how often incarcerated, invariably he spills his guts. If I ask why, my client will often reply, "They said if I told them what really happened, I could go home." The interrogator plays on the fears of the arrestee, who may be held incommunicado in a precinct squad room for several days (unlike TV, no lawyers or visitors allowed). I call him "arrestee" rather than "suspect" to underscore the fact that once in, he's not walking out. It's quite unnecessary (and problematic) to subject the arrestee to the old "third degree." Lies, half-truths, a physical manhandling no more severe than Detective Vera Katakura's slapping the face of Hoshi Taiku work just fine. Once extracted by the detective, a confession is as fragile as an objet d'art. Never to be examined too roughly by a judge at a future suppression hearing into its legality or voluntariness. No servant of the System — cop, prosecutor, judge — wants to mess with a fait accompli.

Detective Morrie Goldstein's interrogation of Hoshi Taiku, on the other hand, is about as legally correct as any arrestee will ever encounter. The character of Hoshi is based partially on my long-ago reading of Edwin O. Reischauer's scholarly work *The Japanese*. But mostly on my childhood viewing of World War II movies like *The Purple Heart* (1944). Dana Andrews, a downed bomber pilot, and his crew, despite torture, have refused to confess to war crimes at their Tokyo show trial. And as they march in step from the courtroom to the strains of the U.S. Air Force song — "Off we go into the wild blue yonder,/Climbing high into the sun . . ." — the Jap general keels over at the prosecution table, having committed hara-kiri in expiation for his failure as an interrogator. Ergo, Hoshi, although the shoe here is on the other foot.

This is **Laura Lippman**'s third appearance in *The Best American Mystery Stories*. A former newspaper reporter, she is the author of nine novels in the award-winning Tess Monaghan series and three standalone crime novels. She lives in Baltimore.

• The character in "One True Love" began rattling around in my brain in 2001; I remember the date because it was only two months after 9/11 and I was at a conference in Washington, D.C., where I kept trying to explain the concept to anyone who would listen. "Wouldn't prostitution, under certain conditions, be a great job for a single mother? Wouldn't it be funny if a prostitute lived in a pricey suburb and turned out to be its most principled resident?" Everyone thought I was crazy. Then *Desperate Housewives* showed up on ABC, and people thought I was merely derivative. It was only when Harlan Coben invited me to write a story for *Death Do Us Part* that I saw how melancholy the story would have to be. But I don't think I'm done with Heloise, not by a long shot.

David Means's stories have appeared in *The New Yorker*, *Harper's*, and *Zoetrope*, and in numerous anthologies, including *The Best American Short Stories*, *The Best American Mystery Stories*, and *The O. Henry Prize Stories*. He is the author of three short story collections, including the award-winning *Assorted Fire Events* (just published in a new edition by Harper/Perennial) and *The Secret Goldfish*. He teaches at Vassar College.

▪ It's hard — for me at least — to tweeze apart a story and to find exact links to specific points of inspiration, but I can say that on the way through Cleveland — at least once a year for the past few years — I've stayed at the Holiday Inn along the shore of Lake Erie, not far from the Rock & Roll Hall of Fame. Out in front of the hotel, near the entrance to the parking lot, is a plaque commemorating the first water intake pipe — not far offshore — for the Cleveland water supply. Each year, I stood and looked out at the lake and thought to myself: when the time's right, I'll make use of this spot in some kind of story. Something struck me about the idea — more than the actual, physical reality — of a large pipe, not far from shore, sucking in the water supply for an entire city. That image sat in my mind and fermented until, one day, after I read a devastating essay by Peter Landesman (in *Best American Crime Writing 2005*) on sex trafficking, my imagination took over, and, drawing from a long personal history in the Midwest, I began writing a story that is, in part, about a young woman caught in a different kind of torrential flow, one of unforgiving, raging violence.

Kent Meyers is the author of four books. *The River Warren* and *Light in the Crossing* were New York Times Notable Books, and *The Work of Wolves* won a Mountain and Plains Booksellers Association Award. Meyers is a writer-in-residence at Black Hills State University in Spearfish, South Dakota.

▪ Shane Valen began as a minor character in *The Work of Wolves,* whose sole role was to move a particular piece of plot along. During the third draft of the book, I had him driving his pickup across a hay field toward a major character, Carson Fieldling, when I became interested in Shane himself. I gave in to my interest and to the rhythms of language and suddenly had seven or eight pages describing Shane's family background, his poaching, his father's trip to Minneapolis, the shooting of the wind-vane rooster, and even Sarah's life after she abandoned Shane and Rodney. None of this made it into the final draft of *The Works of Wolves,* but I decided to try to salvage it as a short story. Several versions of this story are told from Sarah's point of view and are focused on her relationship with her father instead of her husband and son. In fact, the story was originally titled "The Patron Saint of Travelers," in reference to duplicate St. Christopher medals Sarah and her father kept in their cars. The story never quite worked, however, until I decided to make it part of a novel-in-stories and tell it in Greggy Longwell's voice. Greggy quotes one of Shane's letters referring to the murder of a girl. This murder — of Hayley Jo Zimmerman

— ties the various stories in the collection together. I suspect it was the overall mood of the collection — and of course Greggy's voice — that brought out the qualities of "mystery" in the story: the attempts to understand events and the feeling that the real mystery lies not in the events themselves but in the paradoxes of the human heart and mind.

Joyce Carol Oates is the author most recently of *The Museum of Dr. Moses,* a gathering of mystery-suspense stories, and the novel *The Gravedigger's Daughter.* She is the 2005 recipient of the Prix Famina for her novel *The Falls* and the 2006 recipient of the Chicago Tribune Lifetime Achievement Award for Literary Achievement.

• Like most of my fiction, "Meadowlands" springs from both personal experience and invention. My idea of setting a story at the famed Meadowlands racetrack springs from an intense, almost unbearably suspenseful visit to the track in the late 1980s, when my husband and I watched a beautiful Standardbred mare (Impish Lobell — so named for the Lobell Horse Farm in New Jersey), whom we part owned, win her first race. My writing is nearly always generated by a powerful sense of place, and so the Meadowlands stables, the track, the prerace suspense among the horse owners and spectators, provided the impetus for a story that came to be written only years later, with characters who both are, but are not, "real"; a story of missed love, winning and losing, heartbreak.

Jason Ockert has won several National Fiction Awards and is the author of the short-story collection *Rabbit Punches.* His stories have appeared in many journals, including *Oxford American, Mid-American Review, Indiana Review, Alaska Quarterly Review,* and *McSweeney's.* He teaches at Coastal Carolina University.

• The very first idea I had for this story was to create two men (one in handcuffs) who were telling lies to each other. Eventually, I wanted the reader to understand that the cuffed man was the victim while the free man was the villain. But as I began to investigate these characters I quickly realized that my initial concept was too reductive. After spending more and more time with Therm and Cole, I started to hammer out their sensibilities and concerns. The intangibles of these characters led me to Jakob's story and that sense of menace we often overlook when we romanticize childhood as a time of uncomplicated innocence. Perhaps the hardest part of writing this story was letting Jakob disappear.

Ridley Pearson is the author of twenty-three crime/suspense novels, and the coauthor, with Dave Barry, of a trilogy of award-winning books for young readers exploring the origins of Peter Pan: *Peter and the Starcatchers.*

He presently divides his time writing both crime and young adult novels. In 1991, Ridley was the first American awarded the Raymond Chandler Fulbright Fellowship in Detective Fiction Writing at Wadham College in Oxford, England.

• When Harlan Coben wrote me, asking if I would contribute to a short-story anthology, I agreed without hesitation. You don't say no to Harlan. My wife had had an edgy experience while running in a park near where we live — the same male runner appeared by her side several days in a row — and I used this experience to leapfrog into writing "Queeny." I've been basing my novels on extensive research for years, but this took it up a notch, as the threat to my wife felt palpable. There's a voice at work in "Queeny" that is the most comfortable one in which I've ever written. I've spoken with my adult novel editor, Dan Conaway, about exploring this voice in a larger work. That's still on hold, but it's something I look forward to. In all the books I've written (over some twenty-five years now), I've never had a new voice just fall on the page as it did in "Queeny." It was a gift, I think, that resulted from a total lack of pressure — I was doing Harlan a favor. And now, as it turns out, he did me one. Way of the world.

John Sandford is the pen name of John Camp, a former journalist who is the author of twenty-three best-selling thriller novels and two nonfiction books, one on art and the other on plastic surgery. He is a winner of the Pulitzer Prize in journalism. Long interested in history and archaeology, he is the primary backer of the Tel Rehov archaeological dig in Israel (rehov.org) and is a member of the board of directors of the Albright Institute of Archaeological Research in Jerusalem. He lives near St. Paul, Minnesota.

• In the writing of thrillers, there are two opposing worldviews: one that sees crime as the result of conspiratorial thinking, in which the hero destroys a clockwork process set up by the forces of evil; and one that sees a world of chaos, greed, lust, mistake, prejudice, stupidity, and impulse, in which the hero struggles to restore order and some sense of justice. I belong to the latter school, the product of having grown up covering crime in large metropolitan areas. Evil is in the small stuff: somebody tries to steal $50, or somebody wants somebody else's spouse, and somebody gets killed; and that event sets off a chain reaction. I also tend to see cops as workaday guys who hustle on a murder eight hours a day, and then punch out and go home, eat a cheeseburger, watch the game on TV, chase the old lady around the bedroom, and don't get all angst-up about the job. But that's just me.

Brent Spencer is the author of a novel, *The Lost Son*, and a collection of short stories, *Are We Not Men?*, chosen by the editors of the *Village Voice Lit-*

erary Supplement as one of the twenty-five best books of the year. His short fiction has appeared in the *Atlantic Monthly,* the *American Literary Review, Epoch,* the *Missouri Review, GQ,* and elsewhere. He teaches creative writing at Creighton University and is at work on a new novel.

▪ I had spent several weeks along the U.S.-Mexico border, trying to unravel the mystery of my father's life and death, when I came upon one of the sites of the ill-fated Somervell and Mier expeditions, among the most notorious incidents of the Texas Revolution. Maybe it was frustration over my own expedition that drew me to the subject. The more I looked into it, the more I wanted to know. The story contained everything — from political intrigue to bravery to foolhardiness and racism. In the end I decided to write a short story that I hoped would embody the whole complex of ideas and incidents by focusing on the life of one unwilling foot soldier whose life is changed forever by what he witnesses and by his attempt to put it right. The story I wrote was so unlike anything else I had ever written that I couldn't tell if it was good or bad. All I knew was that it was a story I had to tell.

Scott Wolven is the author of *Controlled Burn* (Scribner). Six years in a row, Wolven's stories have been selected to appear in *The Best American Mystery Stories* series.

▪ "Pinwheel" started as a conversation with Otto Penzler — "What do you know about horseracing?" Otto said. My brother is a terrific artist and showed me a painting he had done of two Japanese carp with the words STAY TRUE written in shaded graphics between the two fish; his painting provided a lot of fuel for this story. The yakuza, the honorable outlaws, added a huge moving shadow. Maybe that's part of the job of fiction — to arrest those various shadows for the reader.

It's an honor to have my story appear in this volume. Special thanks to Cort McMeel and Mug Shot Press; Nick Mullendore and the very gracious Loretta Barrett of Loretta Barrett Books. Anthony Neil Smith, Victor Gischler, and Charlie Stella — Crimedogs never fail. Go Chelsea FC. Very special thanks to DW for Rummy, M, T&K, WSBW, and a big HBK thank-you to best brother Will.

Other Distinguished Mystery Stories of 2006

ABBOTT, JEFF
Tender Mercies. *Damn Near Dead*, ed. Duane Swierczynski (Busted Flush)

BEATY, DAVID
The Last of Lord Jitters. *Miami Noir*, ed. Les Standiford (Akashic)

CHENEY, MATTHEW
Blood. *One Story*, September
CHILD, LEE
James Penney's New Identity. *Thriller*, ed. James Patterson (Mira)
COAKE, CHISTOPHER
His Mission. *Murder in the Rough*, ed. Otto Penzler (Mysterious Press)
COLLINS, STEPHEN
Water Hazard. *Murder in the Rough*, ed. Otto Penzler (Mysterious Press)
COOK, THOMAS H.
Rain. *Manhattan Noir*, ed. Lawrence Block (Akashic)

DOOLITTLE, SEAN
The Necklace. *Damn Near Dead*, ed. Duane Swierczynski (Busted Flush)

ESTLEMAN, LOREN D.
The Devil and Sherlock Holmes. *Ghosts in Baker Street*, ed. Martin H.
Greenberg, Jon Lellenberg, and Daniel Stashower (Carroll & Graf)

GARSTANG, CLIFFORD
Heading for Home. *Baltimore Review*, winter/spring
GRADY, JAMES
The Bottom Line. *D.C. Noir*, ed. George Pelecanos (Akashic)

HALL, JAMES W.
  Ride Along. *Miami Noir,* ed. Les Standiford (Akashic)
HERDER, MARK
  King Cotton. *Antimuse,* January
HILL, BONNIE HEARN
  Part Light, Part Memory. *Death Do Us Part,* ed. Harlan Coben (Back Bay)
HOUSEWRIGHT, DAVID
  Mai-Nu's Window. *Twin Cities Noir,* ed. Julie Schaper and Steven Horwitz
  (Akashic)

KARDOS, MICHAEL P.
  One Last Good Time. *Gulf Coast,* summer/fall
KUHLMAN, EVAN
  End Times. *Notre Dame Review,* summer

MCMAHAN, RICK
  The Cold Hard Truth. *Death Do Us Part,* ed. Harlan Coben (Back Bay)
MAES, AGUSTIN
  Beauty and Virtue. *Ontario Review,* spring
MONTEITH, DONOVAN ARCH
  Capacity to Kill. *Thuglit,* March/April
MORROW, BRADFORD
  The Hoarder. *Murder in the Rough,* ed. Otto Penzler (Mysterious Press)

PELECANOS, GEORGE
  String Music. *Murder at the Foul Line,* ed. Otto Penzler (Mysterious Press)

RANDISI, ROBERT J.
  The Bocce Ball King of Farragut Road. *Hard Boiled Brooklyn,* ed. Reed Farrel
  Coleman (Bleak House)

SPIEGELMAN, PETER
  Location, Location, Location. *Hard Boiled Brooklyn,* ed. Reed Farrel Coleman
  (Bleak House)
STELLA, CHARLIE
  Writing for Gallo. *Hard Boiled Brooklyn,* ed. Reed Farrel Coleman (Bleak
  House)

TOMLINSON, JIM
  The Accomplished Son. *Potomac Review,* winter 2007
TREADWAY, JESSICA
  The Nurse and the Black Lagoon. *Five Points,* vol. 9, no. 3

WARD, ROBERT
  Fat Chance. *Baltimore Noir,* ed. Laura Lippman (Akashic)

THE B·E·S·T AMERICAN SERIES®

THE BEST AMERICAN SHORT STORIES® 2007. STEPHEN KING, editor, HEIDI PITLOR, series editor. This year's most beloved short fiction anthology is edited by Stephen King, author of sixty books, including *Misery, The Green Mile, Cell,* and *Lisey's Story,* as well as about four hundred short stories, including "The Man in the Black Suit," which won the O. Henry Prize in 1996. The collection features stories by Richard Russo, Alice Munro, William Gay, T. C. Boyle, Ann Beattie, and others.

> ISBN-13: 978-0-618-71347-9 • ISBN-10: 0-618-71347-6 $28.00 CL
> ISBN-13: 978-0-618-71348-6 • ISBN-10: 0-618-71348-4 $14.00 PA

THE BEST AMERICAN NONREQUIRED READING™ 2007. DAVE EGGERS, editor, introduction by SUFJAN STEVENS. This collection boasts the best in fiction, nonfiction, alternative comics, screenplays, blogs, and "anything else that defies categorization" (*USA Today*). With an introduction by singer-songwriter Sufjan Stevens, this volume features writing from Alison Bechdel, Scott Carrier, Miranda July, Lee Klein, Matthew Klam, and others.

> ISBN-13: 978-0-618-90276-7 • ISBN-10: 0-618-90276-7 $28.00 CL
> ISBN-13: 978-0-618-90281-1 • ISBN-10: 0-618-90281-3 $14.00 PA

THE BEST AMERICAN COMICS™ 2007. CHRIS WARE, editor, ANNE ELIZA-BETH MOORE, series editor. The newest addition to the Best American series — "A genuine salute to comics" (*Houston Chronicle*) — returns with a set of both established and up-and-coming contributors. Edited by Chris Ware, author of *Jimmy Corrigan: The Smartest Kid on Earth,* this volume features pieces by Lynda Barry, R. and Aline Crumb, David Heatley, Gilbert Hernandez, Adrian Tomine, Lauren Weinstein, and others.

> ISBN-13: 978-0-618-71876-4 • ISBN-10: 0-618-71876-1 $22.00 CL

THE BEST AMERICAN ESSAYS® 2007. DAVID FOSTER WALLACE, editor, ROBERT ATWAN, series editor. Since 1986, *The Best American Essays* has gathered outstanding nonfiction writing, establishing itself as the premier anthology of its kind. Edited by the acclaimed writer David Foster Wallace, this year's collection brings together "witty, diverse" (*San Antonio Express-News*) essays from such contributors as Jo Ann Beard, Malcolm Gladwell, Louis Menand, and Molly Peacock.

> ISBN-13: 978-0-618-70926-7 • ISBN-10: 0-618-70926-6 $28.00 CL
> ISBN-13: 978-0-618-70927-4 • ISBN-10: 0-618-70927-4 $14.00 PA

THE BEST AMERICAN MYSTERY STORIES™ 2007. CARL HIAASEN, editor, OTTO PENZLER, series editor. This perennially popular anthology is sure to appeal to mystery fans of every variety. The 2007 volume, edited by best-selling novelist Carl Hiaasen, features both mystery veterans and new talents. Contributors include Lawrence Block, James Lee Burke, Louise Erdrich, David Means, and John Sandford.

> ISBN-13: 978-0-618-81263-9 • ISBN-10: 0-618-81263-6 $28.00 CL
> ISBN-13: 978-0-618-81265-3 • ISBN-10: 0-618-81265-2 $14.00 PA

THE B·E·S·T AMERICAN SERIES®

THE BEST AMERICAN SPORTS WRITING™ 2007. DAVID MARANISS, editor, GLENN STOUT, series editor. "An ongoing centerpiece for all sports collections" (*Booklist*), this series stands in high regard for its extraordinary sports writing and topnotch editors. This year David Maraniss, author of the critically acclaimed biography *Clemente*, brings together pieces by, among others, Michael Lewis, Ian Frazier, Bill Buford, Daniel Coyle, and Mimi Swartz.

ISBN-13: 978-0-618-75115-0 • ISBN-10: 0-618-75115-7 $28.00 CL
ISBN-13: 978-0-618-75116-7 • ISBN-10: 0-618-75116-5 $14.00 PA

THE BEST AMERICAN TRAVEL WRITING™ 2007. SUSAN ORLEAN, editor, JASON WILSON, series editor. Edited by Susan Orlean, staff writer for *The New Yorker* and author of *The Orchid Thief*, this year's collection, like its predecessors, is "a perfect mix of exotic locale and elegant prose" (*Publishers Weekly*) and includes pieces by Elizabeth Gilbert, Ann Patchett, David Halberstam, Peter Hessler, and others.

ISBN-13: 978-0-618-58217-4 • ISBN-10: 0-618-58217-7 $28.00 CL
ISBN-13: 978-0-618-58218-1 • ISBN-10: 0-618-58218-5 $14.00 PA

THE BEST AMERICAN SCIENCE AND NATURE WRITING™ 2007. RICHARD PRESTON, editor, TIM FOLGER, series editor. This year's collection of the finest science and nature writing is edited by Richard Preston, a leading science writer and author of *The Hot Zone* and *The Wild Trees*. The 2007 edition features a mix of new voices and prize-winning writers, including James Gleick, Neil deGrasse Tyson, John Horgan, William Langewiesche, Heather Pringle, and others.

ISBN-13: 978-0-618-72224-2 • ISBN-10: 0-618-72224-6 $28.00 CL
ISBN-13: 978-0-618-72231-0 • ISBN-10: 0-618-72231-9 $14.00 PA

THE BEST AMERICAN SPIRITUAL WRITING™ 2007. PHILIP ZALESKI, editor, introduction by HARVEY COX. Featuring an introduction by Harvey Cox, author of the groundbreaking *Secular City*, this year's edition of this "excellent annual" (*America*) contains selections that gracefully probe the role of faith in modern life. Contributors include Robert Bly, Adam Gopnik, George Packer, Marilynne Robinson, John Updike, and others.

ISBN-13: 978-0-618-83333-7 • ISBN-10: 0-618-83333-1 $28.00 CL
ISBN-13: 978-0-618-83346-7 • ISBN-10: 0-618-83346-3 $14.00 PA

HOUGHTON MIFFLIN COMPANY www.houghtonmifflinbooks.com